THE RED MOTH

Sam Eastland lives in the US and the UK. He is the grandson of a London police detective.

Praise for the 'Inspector Pekkala' series:

'An intriguing blend of curious fact and fiction.' *The Times*

'There are a lot of twists on the way . . . The fast-moving narrative kept me reading, as did the author's feeling for Russia, the descriptions of life in the Siberian outback and the nightmare conditions of Stalin's prisons.' *Independent*

'Particularly satisfying . . . Pekkala is a likeable and believable protagonist.' *Mail on Sunday*

'Eastland has a keen eye for the sensual, brutish elemental details of the time and place.' *Independent on Sunday*

'A vivid picture of a country still in a state of flux as the storm clouds gather . . . A page-turner of a book with enough neatly resolved twists and turns to keep any thriller fan happy.' *Shots*

Also by Sam Eastland

Eye of the Red Tsar
The Red Coffin
Siberian Red

The Red Moth

SAM EASTLAND

FABER & FABER

First published in 2013
by Faber and Faber Limited
Bloomsbury House, 74–77 Great Russell Street,
London WC1B 3DA
This paperback edition first published in 2014

Typeset by Faber and Faber Ltd
Printed and bound in England by CPI Group (UK) Ltd, Croydon, CR0 4YY

A CIP record for this book
is available from the British Library

ISBN 978-0-571-27848-0

2 4 6 8 10 9 7 5 3

Russia

August 1941

A thousand feet above the Russian front, a German scout plane weaved among the clouds, searching for a place to land. The aircraft was a Fiesler 156, whose broad wings and spindly looking wheel struts had earned it the nickname of 'Stork'. The pilot, Hanno Kosch, was a captain in the Luftwaffe. Beside him, nervously clutching a briefcase, sat a lieutenant of the Waffen SS named Karl Hagen.

One hour before, the Stork had taken off from a forward operations base of Army Group North, just outside the town of Luga, bound for a grass strip runway near the village of Vyrista, a short distance by air to the north-east.

Kosch tilted the plane and squinted down at the ground below, searching for some contour of the earth which corresponded to the flight-plan chart clipped to a map board on his knee. 'I don't see it,' he said.

'Maybe we should turn back,' replied Hagen, shouting to make his voice heard over the engine.

'It's too late,' replied the pilot. 'I gave you that chance half an hour ago and you refused. Now we don't have enough fuel to return to Luga. If we can't find the runway at Vyrista, our only chance is to set down in a field and start walking.'

The Stork shuddered as it passed through a pocket of turbulence, causing Hagen to grip the briefcase even more tightly.

'What's in there, anyway?' asked Kosch.

'Something I have to deliver.'

'Yes, but what?'

'If you must know, it's a painting.'

'You mean some priceless work of art like a Rembrandt or something?'

'Priceless yes. Rembrandt no.'

'Can I see it?'

'I don't think I can do that.'

'Oh, come on!' Kosch persisted. 'Just so I can know why I've been risking my life for the past hour.'

Hagen considered this for a moment. 'Well, I suppose it wouldn't hurt to look.' He unfastened the brass latch of the briefcase, removed a canvas in a small wooden frame and held it up for Kosch to see.

'I'll be damned,' said Kosch. 'What is it? A butterfly?'

'Actually,' replied Hagen, 'I believe it's a moth.'

'It doesn't look that special.' Kosch shrugged. 'But I guess I'm no lover of art.'

'I don't like it any more than you do,' Hagen told him as he slipped the painting back inside the briefcase and re-fastened the latch. 'All I want is to be rid of this thing and then I hope I never have to get inside an aeroplane again. I'm not like you. I hate flying. I didn't sign up to be a bird.'

'You won't be a bird for much longer,' Kosch told him, 'and neither will I, with fuel enough for five more minutes in the air.'

'How can we possibly have missed the airfield?' demanded Hagen.

'In these clouds, we could have missed the whole city of Berlin!' Kosch growled with frustration. 'It's no use, Lieutenant.

I have to start looking for a place to set us down.' With those words, he began a gradual descent through the clouds. Raindrops speckled the Perspex canopy. Below them, the thatched roofs of a Russian village slid by, the whitewashed walls of the houses glowing warmly in the summer evening light. Spreading out from the village in all directions lay neatly planted fields of wheat, barley and rye, separated by reddish-brown dirt roads. There was no sign of people. It was the same with the other villages over which they had flown in this past hour. The entire population appeared to have vanished into thin air.

'What is that?' Hagen called out. 'Down there! Look!'

Following Hagen's gaze, Kosch glimpsed a wide expanse of manicured grass, cut through with ornate pathways. At the head of this park stood a huge building, painted blue and white, with what must have been hundreds of windows, set into gilded frames which gleamed blindingly out of the vivid green below. Another huge building, this one less ornate, stood off to one side. Other, smaller structures lay about the grounds, along with several large ponds. Kosch's momentary fascination with the beauty of the architecture was followed by the burning of adrenalin in his guts as he realised how far they had strayed from their original course.

'It's beautiful,' admitted Hagen, somewhat reluctantly. 'I didn't know such things existed in Russia any more. It almost looks like a palace.'

'It *is* a palace!' replied Kosch. 'It is the old village of Tsarskoye Selo, which the Soviets now call Pushkin. All that down there was once the summer estate of Tsar Nicholas II. There is the Catherine Palace, the Alexander Palace, the Lamskie Pond and the Chinese Theatre. I learned about them in an architecture class I took at university.'

'Now that we know where we are,' said Hagen, 'how close are we to where we ought to be?'

Kosch glanced down at his chart. 'According to this map, we're almost thirty kilometres behind the Russian lines.'

'Thirty kilometres!' Hagen exploded. 'You don't understand, Captain, this painting—'

Kosch didn't let him finish. 'If we come around on a north-by-north-west heading, we might be able to reach our own lines before we run out of fuel.' Banking sharply, Kosch turned the little scout plane towards the west, on a course which took him directly over the vast rooftop of the Catherine Palace.

'It looks deserted,' said Hagen, his forehead pressed against the heavy Perspex of the side window. 'Where did they all go?'

Suddenly the plane lurched as if it had flown into an invisible wall. This jolt was accompanied by a sound which reminded Hagen of the pebbles he used to throw by the handful at a corrugated-iron shed at the bottom of his grandfather's garden. 'What happened?' he shouted. 'What's going on?'

Kosch did not reply. He was too busy struggling to keep the plane steady.

Bright yellow tracers, like a shower of meteors, flickered past the wings. Bullets clattered through the fuselage. In the next instant, a white stream of vaporising coolant poured from the cowling.

The firing died away as they cleared the palace grounds.

'We must be out of range,' Hagen said hopefully.

'It's too late,' Kosch told him. 'The damage has already been done.'

'What do you mean? We're still flying, aren't we?'

'We have to land now,' replied Kosch, 'before the engine catches fire. Look for a field, or a road not bordered by telegraph wires.'

'We're behind the lines!'

'On the ground, we stand a chance. If we stay up here any longer, we have none.'

Seconds passed. The Stork's engine began to sputter as the temperature gauge climbed into the red.

'What about that?' asked Hagen, pointing just beyond the starboard wing. 'Is that a runway?'

Kosch peered through the blur of the glycol-smeared windscreen. 'I think it is! It's pretty crude, but I think I can get us down all right.'

'Thank God,' murmured Hagen.

Kosch laughed. 'I thought you SS types didn't believe in God.'

'I'll believe in anything that puts me safely on the ground.'

The Stork circled the airfield. At the far end of the runway stood a hangar, its roof painted dull olive green and overlaid with black amoeba-like shapes to camouflage it from above.

Kosch levelled the plane for a final approach, lowered the flaps to drop air speed, throttled back and came in for a landing.

The plane bounced once on its stilt-like legs, then settled on the ground. Silver threads of water sprayed up between the grass and tyres.

The pilot cut the engine and the Fiesler rolled to a stop with little room to spare on the short runway. As the blurred disc of the propeller stuttered to a halt. Kosch pressed his hand against the silver metal disc on his chest which connected the four seat straps, turned it to the left and then released the clips.

Hagen was still struggling with his straps, one of which had become tangled underneath the leather holster of the SS officer's P38 pistol.

Kosch reached across and unfastened Hagen's seat belt.

Folding back the canopy, Kosch climbed out of the plane and jumped down to the ground, followed closely by Hagen.

The two men began to look around them. The doors of the hangar were closed, but fresh vehicle tracks showed that the place had been visited recently. The rain was still falling softly.

'If we move quickly,' said Kosch, 'we should run into our own lines within a few hours. The Russians must have seen us go down but, with luck, they'll be so busy retreating that they won't have time to worry about us.'

A sound of creaking metal made them jump. Both men turned to see the doors of the hangar sliding open. A face appeared from the darkness and then a man stepped into the light. He was a Red Army officer. There was no mistaking the rotten-apple green of his *gymnastiorka* tunic, the enamelled red star on his cap and the Tokarev automatic he clutched in his right hand. Strapped across his waist was a thick brown leather belt, which carried the holster for his gun.

Now two other men appeared from the darkness. They wore helmets and carried Mosin-Nagant rifles, on which long, cruciform bayonets glinted in the brassy evening sun.

Hagen dropped the briefcase and drew the P38 from its holster.

'Are you mad?' hissed Kosch, raising his hands in the air.

'There are three of them, and probably more inside that hangar. We can't get back now. We have no choice but to surrender.'

Seeing that one of the Germans had drawn his weapon, the Russian officer came to a sudden stop. He raised his gun and barked out a command. The two men behind him took aim with their rifles.

'You were right,' whispered Hagen.

Kosch turned to him, his eyes wide with fear. 'About what?'

'I don't believe in God.' With those words, Hagen set the gun against the side of Kosch's head and pulled the trigger.

Kosch went down so fast it was as if the ground had swallowed him up.

Then, as the Russians looked on in amazement, Hagen placed the barrel of the P38 against his front teeth, closed his eyes and fired.

It was late at night.

Pekkala lay on the floor of his tiny apartment in Moscow, still wearing his clothes and boots. Against the far wall, neatly made, and with an extra blanket folded at the end, stood his bed. He never slept in it, preferring the floorboards instead. Neither did he wear pyjamas, since they reminded him too much of the clothes, known as *rubashka*, which he'd been made to wear in prison. A coat rolled up beneath his head for a pillow was his only concession to comfort.

He was a tall, broad-shouldered man, with a straight nose and strong, white teeth. His eyes were greenish-brown, the irises marked by a strange silvery quality, which people noticed only when he was looking directly at them. Streaks of grey ran through his short, dark hair and his cheekbones were burnished by years of exposure to the wind and sun.

He stared at the ceiling, as if searching for something in the dull white paint. But his thoughts were far away. In his mind, at that precise moment, he was charting a rail journey from the city of Kiev across the entire length of Russia to Vladivostok on the Pacific coast. He made a mental note of every stop along the way, the places where he would need to change trains and the times of each connection. Pekkala had no intention of actually making the trip, but he had taken to memorising rail timetables in order to help himself fall asleep at night. Having acquired the entire twenty-four-volume set of timetables for the Soviet State Railway System, which he kept on the shelf in his office, Pekkala now knew the departure and arrival times of almost every train in Russia.

He had just stepped out on to the platform in the city of Perm and now had fifteen minutes to wait for the connecting train to Omsk, when the buzzer rang beside the door, indicating that someone in the street below was waiting to be let into the building.

Pekkala sat up suddenly, the journey evaporating from his mind.

Grumbling, he picked up the revolver placed beside his head. The weapon was an English Webley .455, and had been a gift from Tsar Nicholas himself. As Pekkala made his way down five flights of stairs to the street, he set the gun back in the holster which he kept strapped across his chest. The holster was designed so that the revolver lay almost horizontally across that place where the two sides of his rib cage joined to form an inverted letter V. The rig had been made according to Pekkala's own specifications by the master armourer Emilio Sagredi, gunsmith to Nicholas II. The angle at which the gun was carried required a perfect fit inside its holster. To achieve this, Sagredi had soaked the leather in saltwater, placed the weapon in the holster and then allowed the leather to dry around the gun. The result was a fit so perfect that neither a flap nor a retaining strap was required to hold the weapon in place. The unusual angle at which the gun was carried allowed Pekkala to draw, aim and fire the weapon in a single fluid movement. It had saved his life on more than one occasion. One final modification, made on the suggestion of Sagredi himself, was a pin-sized hole drilled into the top of the barrel just behind the front blade sight. The large .455 round employed by the Webley meant that the gun would buck significantly when fired. This required the user to steady and re-aim the weapon each time he pulled the trigger. Sagredi's adjustment permitted a small amount of pressure to be released vertically through the pinhole when the gun was fired, with the result that the barrel would be forced down with each shot, at the precise moment when the force of the escaping bullet caused the barrel to rise upwards. The two opposing forces allowed Pekkala to hold the gun more steadily, and thereby to aim the next round more quickly and accurately than he could otherwise have done.

At the time of Pekkala's arrest one freezing winter's night in 1917 on the Russo-Finnish border, both gun and holster were confiscated by the Bolshevik militiamen who dragged him off the train. Once Pekkala's identity had been confirmed, he was transported directly to a prison in Petrograd. There, Pekkala underwent weeks of torture before being shipped to the gulag of Borodok, in the Valley of Krasnagolyana.

Unknown to Pekkala, Stalin had ordered the Webley delivered to him personally. He had heard about the weapon, whose solid brass grips had been added by King George V, when the English monarch had originally made a gift of it to his cousin the Tsar. The size, weight and power of the gun had proved to be, in the words of the Tsarina, too 'sauvage' for the more delicate sensibilities of the Tsar, and so he had presented it to Pekkala. Stalin had been anxious to see this weapon and considered holding on to it for his own use.

Reluctantly, the Webley, together with its holster, was surrendered by the militiaman who'd claimed it at the time of Pekkala's arrest. Upon receiving the gun, Stalin retired to his quarters and secretly tried on the holster. But this new pairing of man and weapon did not prove successful. Stalin had always maintained an aversion to heavy clothing, or any garment that restricted his movements. This was particularly true of his boots, which he had custom-made from fine kid leather normally reserved for gloves. Although ill-suited for walking the streets of Moscow, Stalin rarely went out on foot and did not need to worry about freezing his feet in the middle of a Russian winter. After only a few minutes, the weight of the gun and the constriction of its holster caused Stalin to abandon the idea of keeping them for himself.

Rather than dispose of the Webley, however, Stalin placed it in storage. The reason for this safeguarding was that even as Stalin sent Pekkala away to what should have been a certain death in the notorious gulag, he was by no means convinced that Siberia could kill the man. One thing Stalin did know for sure, however, was that the skills of the Tsar's personal investigator would prove profoundly useful to him, if Pekkala could ever be persuaded to employ them in the service of the Revolution.

It was nine years before the opportunity finally presented itself, when the newly promoted Lieutenant Kirov arrived at Borodok, bearing the offer that would release Pekkala from the forest which had been his prison. Kirov, who had since become Pekkala's assistant at the Bureau of Special Operations, returned to him not only the Webley and its holster but the badge which had been Pekkala's mark of service to the Tsar.

The badge was fashioned from a disc of solid gold, as wide

across as the length of his little finger. Across the centre was a stripe of white enamel inlay, which began at a point, widened until it took up half the disc and narrowed again to a point on the other side. Embedded in the middle of the white enamel was a large, round emerald. Together, the white enamel, the gold and the emerald formed the unmistakable shape of an eye. As the Tsar's investigator, Pekkala had been granted absolute authority. Even the Tsar's own secret service, the Okhrana, could not question him. In his years of service to the Romanovs, Pekkala had become known to all as the one man who could never be bribed or bought or threatened. It did not matter who you were, how wealthy or connected. No one stood above the Emerald Eye, not even the Tsar himself.

Since Pekkala's release from the gulag, he had formed an uneasy alliance with the ruler of the Soviet Union.

Stalin, for his part, had always known that Pekkala was too valuable to be liquidated, as millions of others had been.

Outside Pekkala's apartment, shoulders hunched in the rain, stood Major Kirov. He was tall and thin, with high cheekbones that gave him an expression of perpetual surprise.

Their car, a 1939 model Emka, waited at the kerb, its engine running and windscreen wipers twitching like the antennae of some nervous insect.

'Your belt is upside down,' said Pekkala, as he walked out of the building.

Kirov glanced down at the brass buckle, whose cut-out pattern of a five-pointed star emblazoned with a hammer and sickle was indeed facing the wrong way. 'I'm still half asleep,' he muttered under his breath as he undid the belt and strapped it back on the right way.

'Is it the Kremlin?' asked Pekkala.

'This time of night,' replied Kirov, 'it is always the Kremlin.'

'When does Stalin expect us to sleep?' grumbled Pekkala.

'Inspector, you lie on the floor in your clothes, occasionally lapsing into unconsciousness, and in between you memorise railway timetables. That does not count as sleep. Where was it this time? Minsk? Tbilisi? Were all the trains running on time?'

'Vladivostok,' replied Pekkala as he walked towards the Emka, buttoning his heavy wool coat against the chill of that damp night. 'Change at Ryazan and Omsk. And my trains are always on time.'

Kirov shook his head. 'I can't decide if it's genius or madness.'

'Then don't.'

'Don't what?'

'Decide,' replied Pekkala as he climbed into the passenger seat and shut the door. Once inside the Emka he breathed the musty smell of the leather seats, mixed in with the reek of Kirov's pipe tobacco.

Kirov slipped behind the wheel, put the car in gear and they set off through the unlit streets.

'What does he want?' asked Pekkala.

'Poskrebychev said something about a butterfly.'

Poskrebychev, Stalin's personal secretary, was a small, slope-shouldered man, bald on top and with a band of thinning hair worn like the leafy garland of a Roman emperor. Poskrebychev, who wore round glasses almost flush against his eyeballs, was rarely seen without his dull brownish green uniform, the short mandarin collar buttoned tight against his throat as if it was the only thing to stop his head from falling off. Unremarkable as he was in his appearance, Poskrebychev's position as assistant to the Supreme Leader of the Soviet Union had placed him in a position of extraordinary power. Anyone who wanted to see Stalin had to deal first with Poskrebychev. Over the years, this influence had earned him countless enemies, but none who were prepared to act on it, and risk losing an audience with Stalin.

'A butterfly?' whispered Pekkala.

'Whatever it is, Inspector, it must be important. He has asked to meet with you alone.'

For a while, neither of them spoke. The headlights of the Emka carved a pale tunnel through the night, the sifting rain like veils of silk billowing past them in the darkness.

'I heard on the radio that Narva fell to the Germans today,' remarked Kirov, anxious to break the silence.

'That's the third city in less than a week.'

In the distance, over the slate rooftops, gleaming like fish scales under the blue-black sky, Pekkala could see the domes of St Basil's Cathedral and the Kremlin. All across the city, the skeleton claws of searchlights raked the sky for German bombers.

Earlier that day, the surviving members of the 5th Anti-Aircraft Section of the Red Army's 35th Rifle Division had been ordered to take up defensive positions on the grounds of Tsarskoye Selo. After two months of fighting, the section had been reduced to four men, one Maxim machine gun and a single 25-mm anti-aircraft piece which was towed by a ZiS-5 army truck.

For weeks, they had travelled across a landscape which the war had laid open like a medical cadaver. Death was everywhere, lying crumpled in the ditches of Osmino, floating lazily and bloated in the lake by Kikerino and pecked by ravens in the barley fields of Gatchina. Along this route, most of their vehicles had either broken down or were reduced to smouldering heaps by the strafing runs of Messerschmitts.

In charge of the section was Commissar Sirko, a career officer with small, hostile eyes, a shaved head and two rolls of fat where his neck joined the back of his skull.

Second in command was Sergeant Ragozin, whose deep and reassuring voice did not belong with the bony, pinch-faced man who owned it. Lacking any military bearing, Ragozin fitted like a scarecrow into the baggy riding breeches and flared-waist tunic which made up his military uniform. Ragozin had been a radio announcer in his other life and ran a Sunday evening music show on Moscow Radio. During the 1930s, as the list of approved songs shrank, grew and shrank again without any pattern Ragozin could understand, he resorted to playing the same handful of tunes over and over until finally, in 1938, the authorities ran him off the air. Convinced that he would soon be denounced for anti-Soviet sentiments, he did the only patriotic thing he could think of and enlisted in the Russian Army just as the war broke out.

Gun loader Corporal Barkat, a strawberry farmer from the Ukraine, was a slope-shouldered man with a bulging Adam's apple, nervous, effeminate hands and a hacking laugh which made him sound as if he were trying to cough up a fish bone.

The last and lowest-ranking member of the squad was Rifleman Stefanov. His tasks were to maintain the weapons, drive the truck and monitor the radio, which left very little for the others to do except complain and eat their rations.

Stefanov was a heavy-set man, whose shoulder blades hung like the yoke of an ox across his back. His hair, which normally grew thick and curly, had been shaved in the manner of all Red Army soldiers. This baldness made his large, round eyes seem big as saucers, and gave him the indignant expression of a baby owl which had been pushed out of its nest. Like Ragozin and Barkat, Stefanov was not a career soldier. He had been called up in the first week of the war. Since then, it had occurred to Stefanov that even if this wasn't his first job, it would most likely be his last. The gentle, quiet Rifleman had little to say for himself, so little in fact that the other members of the section wondered if he was mentally impaired. Stefanov knew exactly what they thought of him, and he let them go on thinking it rather than explain the complicated past which had forced him to take up this silence as a barricade against their curiosity.

Instead, he had embraced the strange companionship that men often have with machines, most particularly the ZiS-5 truck, with its wooden slatted sides and headlights which goggled from their wheel cowlings, giving the vehicle a haughty, academic look. The twenty-five side vents on its hood, which resembled a line of dominoes forever falling backwards but never collapsing completely, were so familiar to him now that they seemed to have been scored into his flesh.

No sooner had the men taken up their assigned position on the grounds of Tsarskoye Selo than they heard the whine of a small aircraft engine.

'There it is!' shouted a voice. A moment later, Barkat came loping across the ground and skidded to a stop in front of Stefanov. He pointed to the sky above the Catherine Palace. 'It's some kind of reconnaissance plane. Just a little thing buzzing about.'

Now Stefanov caught sight of the machine. It was a Stork. He had only seen pictures of them before. The plane banked sharply, and seemed to be lining up to fly directly over the palace and across the grounds of the Alexander Park. If Stefanov's guess was right, the Stork would pass directly over their gun position. He turned to Barkat. 'Ready the weapon!' he shouted.

Barkat ran to the 25-mm, whipped off the oil-stained canvas tarp which had been laid over it for camouflage, and flipped up the large circular gunsight.

While Barkat checked the ranging mechanism, Stefanov sprinted to the foxhole of Sergeant Ragozin, who was sleeping under his rain cape. 'Sergeant, you must get up!'

'Is it supper time?' asked Ragozin, as he pulled aside the cape and rose blearily to his feet. The ground had left a crackled imprint on his skin, like the glaze on an earthenware pot.

'We've spotted a German reconnaissance plane,' Stefanov told him.

'My God! At last a target we can hit!' Ragozin staggered over to the gun and took his place beside the spare ammunition, ready to reload the 25-mm the second it ran out of ammunition. Still half asleep, he opened a waterproof storage can and lifted up a belt of ammunition. The heavy brass cartridges hung across his forearms like the carcass of a snake.

'Where is Commissar Sirko?' asked Ragozin.

'He went to find something to drink!' Barkat shouted in reply.

Although Stefanov had fired the weapon many times, he had never managed to actually shoot down a plane. The months he had spent training on that gun, which travelled on a small four-wheeled platform, had proved to be useless. His private fantasy of painting one white band after another down the barrel, each one indicating a downed enemy plane, had begun to seem ludicrously far-fetched. There was only one thing at which he had become an expert and that was digging foxholes.

But now, as he watched the Stork begin its run over the palace grounds, Stefanov realised that this might be his chance to alter that record of failure. In a matter of seconds, just as he had predicted, the plane would pass directly overhead. With his heart thundering in his chest, he chambered a round into the breech and squinted through the spider web of the gunsight.

'Range six hundred metres,' said Barkat, down on one knee

beside him and adjusting the elevation of the gun. 'Six hundred and closing.'

Sweat slicked Stefanov's forehead. He wiped his torn and dirty sleeve across his face. 'Set at two hundred.'

'That's too close!' replied Barkat.

The plane had cleared the roof of the Catherine Palace and was now flying across the Alexander Park. Gracefully, it dipped its wings from side to side as its occupants gazed down upon the grounds.

'Set it anyway!'

'Setting at two hundred,' confirmed Barkat.

Behind him, Stefanov heard the soft, metallic rustle of Ragozin adjusting his grip on the belt of spare ammunition.

The plane dipped into the loop of the gunsight. For a second, Stefanov was struck by how much it looked like one of those gangly, long-legged insects which used to stray into the webs of spiders in the woodshed by his house. He pulled the trigger.

Stefanov's body shook at the first clanking bang of the 25-mm. Tracer bullets, one for every five live rounds, arced into the sky. Out of the corner of his eye, Stefanov saw the long, spent cartridges spitting in flickers of brass from the ejection port. On the other side of the barrel, the belt of ammunition slithered into the gun.

'Hit!' shouted Barkat. 'Hit! Hit!'

'Shut up!' bellowed Stefanov, although he could barely hear himself over the roaring of the gun.

At that moment, the plane appeared overhead, as if out of nowhere. The shadow of its wings raced past them. Stefanov leaned back until he almost tipped over, catching a glimpse of the black crosses on the undersides of its wings before the machine continued on towards the north.

Only now did Stefanov let go of the trigger.

Ragozin was busy reloading the gun, trying not to burn his fingers on the hot metal of the breech.

Stefanov turned to Barkat. 'Did I really hit it?'

'Yes!' Barkat replied excitedly. 'Right in the engine. The wing, too, I think.'

As the two men spoke, a strange odour filtered down from above. To Stefanov, it smelled like burnt sugar.

Ragozin stopped what he was doing. 'That's glycol,' he said. 'Engine coolant. He won't get far now.'

'I said you hit it in the engine!' Barkat slapped Stefanov on the arm.

Stefanov stood up from the crouch of his firing position. His hands were trembling. Then, without another word, he turned and started running through the woods, heading in the direction of the plane.

Barkat and Ragozin were too startled even to speak. They just watched him go, his stocky legs pumping, until he had vanished among the trees.

'What was that about?' asked Ragozin.

'I think,' replied Barkat, 'he has gone to finish the job.'

Ragozin did not reply to this. Something had caught his attention. He stepped out into the open expanse of the Alexander Park and stood with his hands on his hips, gazing into the distance.

'What is it?' asked Barkat.

Ragozin turned around, a look of astonishment on his face.

'I knew he hit the plane a couple of times, but I wondered where the rest of those bullets were going.'

'What are you saying?' demanded Barkat.

'Stefanov just shot the windows out of the Catherine Palace!'

Barkat walked out and stood by Ragozin. At the far end of the park, he could see the gaps of shattered windows. Jagged shards remaining in the frames winked at him as they caught the sun. 'Well,' said Barkat, 'he didn't break *all* of them, anyway.'

At a flat-out run, Stefanov cleared the grounds of the estate. A few soldiers from the battery, concealed in their leafy, camouflaged hideouts, had seen the plane take fire as it flew over the park, but had been unable to join in the attack due to the positioning of their guns. Now, as they watched him sprinting by, the soldiers made no move to stop him, knowing that a man moving at that pace must be bound upon some vital task.

But Rifleman Stefanov did not even know where he was going. The only clear thought in the shambles of his brain was to find the plane he'd just shot down. He wasn't even certain that he had shot it down. Perhaps it had only been damaged and would still be able to return to the German lines. Could a plane continue flying without engine coolant? Stefanov had no idea.

After leaving the grounds of the estate, Stefanov continued down the long road leading north. He was no longer sprinting now, but still moving as quickly as he could, searching the fields which stretched out on either side of the road for any sign of a forced landing. At the same time, he scanned the horizon for any telltale signs of smoke, in the event that the plane had crashed and burned.

It was twenty minutes later that Stefanov spotted the Stork, pulled up beside a small hangar at the edge of a grass strip runway.

Gasping for breath, he stepped off the road, clambered through a ditch choked with wildflowers, and stumbled out on to the runway.

Several soldiers were gathered in a circle.

Stefanov walked straight towards them. For the first time, he wondered what had become of the pilot and suddenly imagined himself meeting the man, perhaps even shaking his hand and introducing himself as the one who had brought him down. No, Stefanov reconsidered. He couldn't shake the hand of a Fascist. The commissar might hear about that.

Stefanov walked past the Stork, which stood between him and the cluster of men. He was impressed that the pilot had managed to land it safely. Bare metal showed along the cowling where rounds had hit their target. Stefanov counted only three holes and felt momentarily ashamed at such a small number, considering that he had fired off a belt of 120 bullets. It does not matter, he consoled himself. One hit or a hundred hits is all the same, as long as the plane is brought down.

The soldiers, noticing Stefanov's approach, all turned to stare at him.

It was only now that Stefanov caught his first glimpse of two bodies stretched out on the ground.

The breath caught in his throat.

'Where did you come from?' asked one of the soldiers.

Stefanov did not reply. He pushed his way through until he was standing right over the dead men. Both had been shot in the head. Their faces were disfigured in a way that reminded

Stefanov of two broken earthenware pots. He stared at the uniforms of the two men, the grey-blue tunic of the Luftwaffe officer and the field-grey tunic of the man who, by the silver lightning bolts at his collar, Stefanov recognised as SS. Lying on the chest of the SS man was a leather briefcase, spattered with blood. 'Why did you do it?' asked Stefanov. He looked at the men who stood around him. 'Did they refuse to surrender?'

'We didn't kill them,' said one. 'That SS officer took one look at us and then he shot the pilot of his plane.'

'He did what?' The sweat was starting to cool on Stefanov's back. He felt numb and dazed, as if he had been sleepwalking and had woken up in an unfamiliar place. 'Why would he do such a thing?'

'That's what we'd like to know,' replied the soldier, 'especially since, right afterwards, he blew his own brains out. Our officer thinks it has something to do with whatever's in that briefcase. He's gone to find a commissar who can take charge of it.'

The mention of the commissar seemed to snap Stefanov out of his trance.

'Who are you, anyway?' asked the soldier.

'Nobody,' replied Stefanov. 'I'm nobody.' He walked out of the circle of men and back across the airfield. After clambering back over the ditch, he reached the road and started retracing his steps towards the Catherine Palace. At first he only walked, but after a minute, Stefanov began to run again.

The Emka rolled beneath the archway of the Kremlin's Spassky Gate, with its ornamental battlements and gold and black clock tower looming from the misty night. Arriving at a dead end on the far side of Ivanovsky Square, Kirov parked the car and turned to Pekkala.

'I'll wait here for you, Inspector.'

'Get some sleep,' replied Pekkala as he climbed out of the Emka. He made his way to an unmarked door, which was guarded by a soldier. As Pekkala approached, the soldier slammed his heels together with a sound that echoed around the high brick walls and gave the traditional greeting of 'Good health to you, Comrade Pekkala!'

This was not only a greeting, but also a sign that he had been recognised by the soldier and did not need to present his identity book.

Unlike the glittering emerald which had guaranteed Pekkala's authority during the time of the Tsar, his ranking in the Soviet State consisted of a single piece of paper contained within his pass book. This book was the size of a man's outstretched hand, dull red in colour, with an outer cover made from fabric-covered cardboard in the manner of an old school text book. The Soviet State seal, cradled in its two bound sheaves of wheat, had been emblazoned on the front. Inside, in the top left-hand corner, a photograph of Pekkala had been attached with a heat seal, cracking the emulsion of the photograph. Beneath that, in pale bluish-green letters, were the letters NKVD and a second stamp indicating that Pekkala was on Special Assignment for the government. The particulars of his birth, his blood group and his State identification number filled up the right-hand page.

Most government pass books contained only those two pages, but in Pekkala's, a third page had been inserted. Printed on canary-yellow paper with a red border around the edge, were the following words:

THE PERSON IDENTIFIED IN THIS DOCUMENT IS ACTING UNDER THE DIRECT ORDERS OF COMRADE STALIN.

DO NOT QUESTION OR DETAIN HIM.

HE IS AUTHORISED TO WEAR CIVILIAN CLOTHES, TO CARRY WEAPONS, TO TRANSPORT PROHIBITED ITEMS, IN-CLUDING POISON, EXPLOSIVES AND FOREIGN CURRENCY. HE MAY PASS INTO RESTRICTED AREAS AND MAY REQUI-SITION EQUIPMENT OF ALL TYPES, INCLUDING WEAPONS AND VEHICLES.

IF HE IS KILLED OR INJURED, IMMEDIATELY NOTIFY THE BUREAU OF SPECIAL OPERATIONS.

Although this special insert was known officially as a Classified Operations Permit, it was more commonly referred to as a Shadow Pass. With it, a man could appear and disappear at will within the wilderness of regulations that controlled the State. Fewer than a dozen of these Shadow Passes were known to exist. Even within the ranks of the NKVD, most people had never seen one.

After passing through the unmarked door, he climbed a set of narrow stairs up to the second floor, emerging on to a long, wide corridor with tall ceilings. The floors were covered with a brownish-red carpeting, so that his footsteps made no sound. Tall doors lined the walls of this corridor on either side. By day, these doors would all be open and the hallway filled with people coming and going. But at this hour of the night, all the doors were closed as Pekkala walked towards a set of large double doors at the far end, beyond which lay Stalin's reception room. It was a huge space, with eggshell-white walls and wooden slatted floors. In the centre of the room stood three desks. Only one was occupied, by a man wearing a collarless olive-green tunic in the same style as that worn by Stalin himself. The man stood as they entered. 'Inspector.'

'Poskrebychev.'

Advancing across the room to Stalin's office, Poskrebychev knocked once and did not wait for a reply. He swung the door open, nodded for Pekkala to enter. As soon as Pekkala had walked into the room, Poskrebychev shut the door behind him.

Pekkala found himself in a large room with red velvet curtains and a red carpet which lined only the outer third of the floor. The centre was the same mosaic of wood as in the waiting room. The walls had been papered dark red, with caramel-coloured wooden dividers separating each panel. Hanging on these walls were portraits of Marx, Engels and Lenin, each one the same size and apparently done by the same artist.

Close to one wall stood Stalin's desk, which had eight legs, two at each corner. On the desk lay several manila files, each one lying perfectly beside the other, as well as a leather briefcase which Pekkala had never seen before. Stalin's chair had a wide back, padded with burgundy-coloured leather brass-tacked against the frame.

Apart from Stalin's desk, and a table covered with a green cloth, the space was sparsely furnished. With the exception of a large eighteenth-century grandfather clock, made by the English clockmaker John Ellicott, which had been allowed to wind down and was silent now, the full yellow moon of its pendulum at rest behind the rippled glass window of its case.

The red curtains were drawn and the light in the room came from a three-bulbed fixture fitted to the ceiling. A thread of smoke rose from a cigarette which Stalin had recently stubbed out in a brass ashtray on his desk.

Stalin himself stood in the centre of the room, his back to Pekkala, staring at the wall.

It took Pekkala a moment to realise what Stalin was looking at.

Between the portraits of Lenin and Engels hung another painting, much smaller than the ones on either side of it.

'Perhaps it would look better over there, Comrade Stalin.'

Stalin turned and squinted at Pekkala, his eyes red-rimmed with fatigue. 'What did you say?'

'Over there,' repeated Pekkala, gesturing towards the blank wall behind Stalin's desk.

'Do you know what this is?' demanded Stalin, aiming a finger at the painting.

Pekkala stepped forward and peered at the painting. 'A cecropia moth.'

Stalin shook his head in amazement. 'How is it, Inspector,'

he began, 'that you can neither feed nor barely dress yourself except in clothing so long out of fashion that people regularly mistake you for a ghost, and yet you can tell me the name of that insect?'

'I used to see them around the house where I grew up,' explained Pekkala. He remembered the long path through the woods to the place where his father, an undertaker in the town of Lappeenranta in eastern Finland, had built a crematory oven. Pekkala's mother had once given him a sandwich and a thermos of hot milk to take to his father, who was working all night at the oven. Four bodies were to be cremated that night, which meant eight hours of tending the fire. Carrying a lantern, Pekkala had set out along the path, staring straight ahead, convinced that the pine trees on either side were closing in on him. Arriving at the oven, he found his father stripped to the waist and sitting on the stump of a log. At first, Pekkala had thought the man was reading a book, but then he realised that his father was just staring at his hands. Behind him, the crematory oven roared like distant thunder. The iron door to the oven was so hot it had begun to glow a poppy-red. Reaching up into the darkness, the tall chimney belched black smoke, which spread across the sky as if the smoke itself had spawned the night. Fluttering around his father's head, Pekkala saw three moths, each one larger than a man's palm. His father took no notice of them, even when one landed on his naked shoulder, which glistened with sweat from the heat of the oven. At last his father looked up from studying the wrinkles in his palm.

'I see you're not alone,' said Pekkala.

His father smiled. Gently he slid his fingers beneath the moth which had landed on his shoulder and lifted it into the air. Then he blew on the insect, as if blowing out the flame on a candle, and set the insect fluttering once more about his head. '*Hyalophora cecropia*,' he told Pekkala. 'They are an ancient breed, unchanged for thousands of years.'

'Why have they not changed?' asked Pekkala.

'Because they are already perfectly adapted to the world in which they live. These moths keep me company out here, and remind me of the many imperfections of the human race.'

Although it had been many years since then, Pekkala had never forgotten the distinctive pattern on their wings; the two eyes at each wing tip and the four reddish-white splashes and the scalloped line which trailed along the edges, its colours fading from reddish-brown to white like ink which had bled through soft paper. The painting was not an exact representation. The artist appeared to have taken liberties with colours and the symmetry of the design, but there was no mistaking the cecropia.

'If you have brought me here to admire your painting, Comrade Stalin,' said Pekkala, 'I think you could have chosen someone better qualified.'

Stalin glared at him. 'If all you had to offer me was your love of the finer things in life, I would have left you to rot in Siberia.'

'Then why am I here, Comrade Stalin?'

'You are here,' Stalin explained, 'because I believe that the value of this painting does not lie in its artistic merits. Two days ago a German scout plane got lost in the clouds and landed at an airfield behind our lines. Of the two men aboard, one was a Luftwaffe pilot and the other an officer in the SS. The SS man was carrying a briefcase that contained this painting. If he had been transporting money, or jewellery or gold, I wouldn't have thought twice about it. But why would that officer be flying around with this painting in his briefcase?'

'Did anybody ask them?'

'They never had the chance. The SS man murdered the pilot and then took his own life. Given what he had just witnessed, the Red Army officer on the scene realised that the painting must be of some importance, so he handed it over to NKVD. They considered it worthless, but filed a report all the same. When news of this painting reached my office I ordered it to be sent here right away. There's something about it, Pekkala. Something that troubles me. I just can't figure out why. For that, I am relying on you.' Stalin walked over to the painting, removed it from the wall and replaced it in the German officer's briefcase in which the painting had been delivered to Stalin. He handed the briefcase to Pekkala. 'Bring me some answers, Inspector.'

By the time Pekkala and Kirov departed from the Kremlin, it was growing light.

Pekkala studied the painting, which rested on his lap. His attention was drawn to the tree in which the moth was resting. The leafless branches looked gnarled and crooked, like those of a magnolia in winter. He didn't know enough about moths to be certain whether they would be out in the winter, but he doubted it.

Turning the painting over, he noticed something written in pencil on the untreated back of the canvas.

'What does it say?' asked Kirov, glancing over as he manoeuvred the Emka out of the Kremlin gates.

'Ost-u-baf-engel,' replied Pekkala, carefully deciphering the unfamiliar syllables. 'I assume it is German, although I've never seen the word before. "Ost" means "east". "Engel" is the word for "angel". The whole middle section makes no sense to me.' Turning the painting over again, Pekkala brought his face close to the canvas, as if the delicate creature might whisper to him the meaning of its existence.

'Where do we even begin?' Kirov wondered aloud.

'The Lubyanka,' replied Pekkala.

'The prison? Why would we be going there?'

'To speak with a man who can tell us if this painting is worth anything at all.'

'And if it isn't?'

'Then he will tell us why.'

'What's a man like this doing in prison?'

'Paying the price for his genius.'

'Look, Inspector,' Kirov tried to reason with him. 'What about the Museum of the Kremlin? The director is Fabian Golyakovsky, the most famous art curator in the whole country. Perhaps we should speak with him instead.'

For a moment, Pekkala considered Kirov's suggestion. 'Very well!' he announced. 'Turn us around, Kirov. The museum will be our first stop.'

'But the museum isn't open yet,' protested Kirov. 'I don't know what the hours are now that Moscow is on alert for air raids. We might have to make a special appointment . . .'

'We'll find a way in,' Pekkala told him. 'I already know what I need in that museum. I don't need an expert to tell me where it is. Now take us back to the Kremlin.'

'Yes, Inspector,' sighed Kirov. Then he jammed on the brakes and performed a sharp U-turn, tyres squealing as he cornered.

Although the Museum of the Kremlin was indeed closed at that hour, Fabian Golyakovsky himself came to see who was pounding on the doors.

Golyakovsky was a tall, stooped man with an unkempt mop of curly reddish hair. He wore a dark blue suit and a cream-coloured shirt with a rumpled collar and no tie.

'Who on earth are you?' demanded Golyakovsky. 'Do you have any idea what time it is?'

Pekkala held up his Shadow Pass. 'We need a few minutes of your time.'

Golyakovsky glanced at the text, his lips moving as he silently pronounced the words. 'Very well,' he replied suspiciously. 'Anything to oblige the Bureau of Special Operations, whom I had not realised until this moment were lovers of great art.'

'Why are you here so early?' asked Kirov.

'I've been here all night,' explained Golyakovsky as he stood back to let them enter, 'cataloguing items which may soon have to be evacuated from the museum and transported to safety further east.'

Followed by a nervous Golyakovsky, Pekkala and Kirov strolled through the cold and musty-smelling halls and soon found themselves in a room whose walls were festooned with Russian icons.

With his hands clasped behind his back, Pekkala walked past the icons, studying each one intently.

'Inspector, what does this moth painting have to do with ancient icons?' Kirov asked in a low voice.

'Nothing, as far as I know,' replied Pekkala.

'Then what are you looking for, Inspector?'

'I will know it when I see it. Ah!' Pekkala halted sharply in front of a small wooden panel on which had been painted the head and shoulders of a bearded, long-haired and angry-looking man. His skin was a greenish-yellow, as if illuminated by the light of a candle. The white background had been chipped in many places. 'This one!' he whispered, and proceeded to remove the icon from its hanging place.

'Inspector!' hissed Kirov. 'You're not supposed to touch them!'

'Stop!' shouted Golyakovsky, his voice echoing through the museum. 'Are you out of your mind?' He advanced upon Pekkala, waving his arms. 'Have you no respect for the treasures of this country?'

It was Kirov who answered the question. 'Believe me, Comrade Golyakovsky, he does not.'

By now, Golyakovsky had reached the place where the two men were standing. 'Please.' Golyakovsky reached out towards Pekkala, using a tone of voice reserved normally for people about to leap to their deaths from the tops of tall buildings or bridges. Gently, he removed the icon from Pekkala's grasp. Golyakovsky cradled the panel in his arms, as if Pekkala had somehow awoken the man in the painting and now he meant to lull the angry Saviour back into his sleep of centuries. 'Do you have any idea what this is?'

'No,' admitted Pekkala.

'It is a priceless fourteenth-century icon from the Balkans, originally located in the Cathedral of the Assumption. It is known as *The Saviour of the Fiery Eye*. What could you possibly want with this?'

'Major Kirov may be right about my regard for the treasures of Russia,' replied Pekkala, 'but I have seen what he has not, namely what becomes of those who covet them. I will soon require the help of someone whose knowledge of these works of art is matched only by his hatred of this country. I must persuade this man that there is still something sacred left in the world –' Pekkala pointed at the icon – 'and the face of that man may convince him.'

'Couldn't you just bring him here to see the icon?' pleaded Golyakovsky. 'I will give him a personal tour!'

'I'm certain that he would like nothing more,' replied Pekkala, 'but the laws of Lubyanka don't allow it.'

'Lubyanka?' whispered Golyakovsky.

'No harm will come to it,' Pekkala assured him. 'In his hands, your icon will be safer than in any of the vaults of your museum.'

'Who is this man, Inspector?' asked Kirov, as they stepped out of the building a few minutes later, the icon wrapped in three layers of brown archival paper and safely tucked under Pekkala's arm.

'His name is Valery Semykin and he is an expert at identifying works of art and, in particular, whether a piece is genuine or a forgery. Before you see him, Kirov, we have one more stop to make. This is not a man you'll want to deal with on an empty stomach, and neither are the isolation cells of Lubyanka.'

'I suppose this means we're going to the Café Tilsit?' asked Kirov in a long-suffering voice.

Noting Kirov's tone, Pekkala glanced at him out of the corner of his eye. 'I don't know what you have against that place.'

'It's not a café,' he replied indignantly. 'It is a feeding trough.'

'Nevertheless,' Pekkala told him, 'they make the kind of art I can appreciate.'

Years ago, when Pekkala first started coming to the Café Tilsit, it was mainly for the reason that the place never closed and he ate when he was hungry, without regard to mealtimes, which sometimes meant in the middle of the night. Before the war, its customers had been mostly taxi drivers or night watchmen or insomniacs who could not find their way into the catacombs of sleep. Now, almost all the men were in the military, forming a mottled brown-green horde that smelled of boot grease, *machorka* tobacco and the particular earthy mustiness of Soviet Army wool. The women, too, wore uniforms of one kind of another. Some were military, with black berets and dark blue skirts beneath their tunics. Others wore the khaki overalls of factory workers, their heads bundled in blue scarves, under which the hair, for those employed in munitions factories, had turned a rancid yellow.

In spite of the way things had changed, Pekkala still found himself drawn to the condensation-misted windows and the long, bare wood tables where strangers sat elbow to elbow. It was the strange communion of being alone and not being alone which suited him.

Pekkala had found a seat at the back, facing the door. Kirov sat across from Pekkala. Between them, on the table, lay the leather briefcase, which now contained both the painting of the moth and *The Saviour of the Fiery Eye*.

Valentina, the woman who ran the Café Tilsit after her husband had been gunned down in the street two years before, approached them with a wooden mug of kvass, a half-fermented drink which looked like dirty dishwater and tasted like burned toast. Valentina was slender and narrow-shouldered, with thick, blonde hair combed straight back on her head and tied with a length of blue yarn. Her feet were buried up to the knees in a worn-out pair of felt boots called *valenki*, in which she shuffled silently between the rows of customers.

Valentina set the mug down before Pekkala. 'There you go, my handsome Finn.'

'What about me?' asked Kirov.

Valentina stared at him, narrowing her eyes 'You are handsome, too, but in a different way.'

'That's not what I mean,' replied Kirov. 'I mean, I would like some, too. And I wouldn't mind breakfast, as well.'

'Well, what do you want?'

Kirov gestured at Pekkala. 'I'll have whatever he's having.'

'Good,' she turned to leave, 'because there is no menu, only what I choose to serve.'

'She thinks I'm handsome,' whispered Pekkala, as he watched Valentina heading back into the kitchen.

'Well, don't let it go to your head,' grumbled Kirov.

Pekkala sipped at his drink. 'You are handsome, but "in a different way".'

'What does that even mean?'

Pekkala shrugged. 'You should ask her when she comes back.'

'I think I won't.'

Pekkala nodded in agreement. 'Always better not to know exactly what they're thinking.' He opened his mouth as if to say more, but then thought better of it and stayed silent. His gaze became distant and sad.

'You still think about her, don't you?' asked Kirov.

'Valentina?'

'No. The other one.'

'Of course,' admitted Pekkala.

'It was so many years ago, Inspector. If she saw you now, she'd probably think you were a ghost.'

'We are all ghosts in this country,' he muttered.

'When was the last time you saw her?'

'At the railway station in Petrograd, the night before Red Guards overran the city. The whole place was in chaos. I could not leave without the Tsar's permission and I was afraid that if she delayed any longer, we might both be trapped. She agreed to go on ahead. We had arranged to meet in Paris. But I never made it. When the Tsar finally released me from my duties to him, I caught a train heading north into Finland. I was travelling under a forged passport, but the Red Guards arrested me anyway. After that,' he shrugged helplessly, 'prisons, interrogation and finally they put me on another train, but this one was heading to Siberia.'

'And that's where I found you nine years later,' said Kirov, 'living like an animal in the forest of Krasnagolyana.'

By then, Pekkala no longer even had a name. He was known only as prisoner 4745-P of the Borodok labour camp. Immediately upon his arrival, the director of the camp, fearing that other inmates might learn Pekkala's true identity, had sent him into the wilderness, with the task of marking trees for logging crews who came to cut the timber in that forest.

The average life of a tree-marker in the forest of Krasnagoly-ana was six months. Working alone, with no chance of escape and far from any human contact, these men died from exposure, starvation and loneliness. Those who became lost, or who fell and broke a leg, were usually eaten by wolves. Tree-marking was the only assignment at Borodok said to be worse than a death sentence.

The commandant assumed he would be dead within the year, but by the time Kirov was sent to bring him back, Pekkala had already begun his ninth year of a thirty-year sentence for crimes against the State. Prisoner 4745-P had lasted longer than any other marker in the entire gulag system.

Provisions were left for him at the end of a logging road. Kerosene. Cans of meat. Nails. For the rest, he had to fend for himself. Only rarely was he seen by the logging crews. What they observed was a creature barely recognisable as a man. With the crust of red paint that covered his prison clothes and the long hair maned about his face, he resembled a beast stripped of its flesh and left to die which had somehow managed to survive. Wild rumours surrounded him – that he was an eater of human flesh, that he wore a breastplate made from the bones of those who had disappeared in the forest, that he wore scalps laced together as a cap.

He strode through the forest with the help of a large stick, whose gnarled root head bristled with square-topped horse-shoe nails. The only other thing he carried was a bucket of red paint to mark the trees. Instead of using a brush, because he had no turpentine to wash the bristles, Pekkala stirred his fingers in the scarlet paint and daubed his print upon the trunks. These marks were, for most of the other convicts, the only trace of him they ever saw.

They called him the man with bloody hands. No one except the commandant of Borodok knew where this prisoner had come from or who he had been before he arrived. Those same men who feared to cross his path had no idea this was Pekkala, whose name they'd once invoked just as their ancestors had called upon the gods.

At the time of their first meeting, Kirov had been a newly minted lieutenant in the Bureau of Special Operations. He had been transferred to the field of Internal State Security from the Leningrad Culinary Institute, where he had hoped to begin his career as a chef. The entire institute was closed down one day without prior warning. The students, Kirov included, showed up after a long weekend break to find the building where they worked completely empty. The stoves and cutting tables where they once practised their art had been removed, along with the sinks and desks and chairs. The faculty had vanished and, in spite of several attempts to contact the Master Chefs who served as his professors, Kirov never heard from any of them again. By the time he had arrived back at the flat which he rented with another student from the Institute, transfer orders for both of them had already arrived in the mail.

Numbly, Kirov had surveyed the document. Until that moment, he had never even heard of the Bureau of Special Operations.

Kirov's roommate, a stout and pink-faced boy named Beldugov, sat on his bed and wept quietly, dabbing the sleeve of his white chef's tunic against his cheeks.

'What did they do with you?' asked Kirov.

'I appear to have joined the Navy,' replied Beldugov, 'but I cannot swim. I cannot even float!'

The next morning, the two men, each carrying a small suitcase, shook hands outside the apartment building. In a futile gesture of defiance, Beldugov still wore his white chef's tunic as they went their separate ways.

By the end of that day, Kirov had begun his studies as a commissar of the Red Army. Although, as Pekkala's assistant, Kirov had prospered in the Bureau of Special Operations, rising to the rank of major, he had never forgotten his dream to be a chef.

Proof of Kirov's refusal to abandon his dreams was that their tiny office, on the fifth floor of a dilapidated building near the Dorogomilovsky market, had been transformed into a menagerie of herbs, vegetables and exotic fruits, which grew in earthenware pots on every surface in the room except Pekkala's desk. That was where Pekkala had drawn the line, but the truth was his desk was so heaped with files, pencils, pencil sharpeners, ink pots and loose rounds for the Webley revolver, that there was no room for foliage.

It had become a tradition that, on Friday afternoons, Kirov would prepare a meal for them, using a small stove he had set up in the office. He cooked chicken braised in butter and served with chestnut stuffing, or salmon poached in Madeira wine with shrimp and lemon sauce, or Siberian *pelmeny* beef turnovers, with wild mushroom and scallion filling. The herbs he used in his recipes had been carefully trimmed from the plants upon the window sill. This food was not only the best meal of the week for Pekkala. It was, collectively, the best food he'd ever eaten. This was why Pekkala tolerated the irregularity of these sweet and musky plants, knowing that Kirov was one of the only people he had ever encountered who could put up with his own eccentricities.

Without Kirov, and without the Café Tilsit, Pekkala might have starved to death.

Valentina came with bowls of *gribnoi* soup, made with potatoes, onions and morel mushrooms, which she grew under beds of alder leaves in window boxes at the back of the café. She set the bowls down on the table, then from her flower-patterned apron, she fished two pewter spoons made in the Russian style, with the handle as long and thin as a pencil and the bowl round and shallow. Gathering a handful of her apron, she wiped the spoons. Oblivious to the look of disdain on Kirov's face, she handed one to each of the men. As Valentina turned to leave, in a gesture so slight that it almost seemed accidental, she rested her hand on Pekkala's shoulder. Valentina did not look at him or speak. And then she was gone, shuffling back towards the kitchen.

Where Valentina's hand had touched him, Pekkala felt a slow and heavy warmth settling into his blood, as if, for that fraction of a second, their bodies had become entwined.

Kirov saw none of this, having been momentarily distracted by the mushrooms in the soup, whose spiced and earthy fragrance wafted straight into his brain. 'One woman or another. There are plenty of fish in the sea,' he commented as he ladled a spoonful of soup into his mouth. 'That's my philosophy.'

'And yet you have remained single all these years,' remarked Pekkala. 'So what is the difference between us?'

'I have remained single on purpose,' Kirov wagged his spoon at Pekkala. 'That is, until now.'

Pekkala glanced up from his soup. 'What do you mean?'

'I have found someone.'

Pekkala stared at him blankly.

'And you are . . .' Kirov turned his spoon in a slow circle, encouraging Pekkala to complete the sentence.

Pekkala blinked.

'Happy,' prompted Kirov.

'Happy!' Pekkala echoed, coming to his senses. 'I am happy for you, Kirov.' He dropped his spoon into his bowl, splashing his chest with soup although he did not seem to notice. Then he sat back heavily. 'This is good news.'

'You don't look like you think it's good news.'

'Well, how am I supposed to look?'

'Would you like to know her name?'

'Yes! Of course I would.'

'Her name is Elizaveta Kapanina. She works in the records office at NKVD headquarters.'

'And where did you find this woman?'

'At the records office!' Kirov raised his hands and let them fall heavily on to the table. 'Where do you think I found her?' He shook his head. 'I knew you wouldn't handle this well.'

'I'm handling it just fine,' Pekkala replied testily. 'I just didn't think . . .'

'What? That I'd ever find anybody?'

'That's not what I meant. I just didn't think you were looking for anyone to be with.'

'I wasn't,' said Kirov. 'It simply happened.'

'Well, congratulations. When do I get to meet her?'

'The answer is soon, and you'd better be nice.'

'Of course I'll be nice. I'll be my usual self.'

'No you won't, Inspector! Your usual self is exactly what I am afraid of.'

'I'll be nice,' muttered Pekkala, retrieving his spoon from the bowl. 'Now can I finish my soup?'

After their meal, Kirov and Pekkala drove across town and soon reached the gates of Lubyanka. In tsarist times the building had been one of the grand hotels of Moscow, but during the Revolution, its suites were converted into cells and its broom closets into punishment cells known as chimneys, where prisoners were forced to stand hunched over for days on end, their foreheads leaning against metals grilles behind which burned powerful light bulbs which were never turned off.

The guard, recognising Pekkala's Emka, swung the gates open to let them pass.

Kirov parked inside the high-walled courtyard, whose pale yellow walls reflected the morning sun.

As he strode towards the entrance, Pekkala paused to look up at the window openings, which had once offered some of the finest views in Moscow. The windows themselves were long gone, replaced by long metal awnings which drooped like sleepy eyelids, cutting out all but the faintest of daylight seeping in from the world outside.

Inside, Pekkala and Kirov signed their names in the vast entry book, on which all other spaces but the ones in which they wrote their names were concealed by a heavy metal plate.

The guard behind the desk was new, his expression fierce and focused. He had not yet acquired the slightly dazed look of the other Lubyanka guards who, like the prisoners they oversaw, passed their days in such stifling routine that their senses grew dull to everything but pain.

Pekkala opened his identity book and, in the regulation manner, held it up beside his face.

The guard barely glanced at it. 'What is the purpose of your visit?' he snapped.

'I am here to question a prisoner.'

'The name?'

'Semykin, Valery.'

'Wait,' replied the guard. After consulting a book in which the locations of all prisoners were listed, he picked up the heavy black telephone receiver on his desk. 'Bring Semykin, Block 4, Cell 6.'

'Leave Semykin where he is,' interrupted Pekkala. 'I will go to him.'

'Prisoners cannot be visited. They must be brought to one of the holding cells. No exceptions!'

'I understand,' said Pekkala, as he slid his pass book across the counter.

The guard snatched up the book and peered inside. It took a moment for the man to realise he was looking at a Shadow Pass. His lips twitched. 'My apologies, Inspector.' Carefully, the guard closed the book and returned it to Pekkala.

Another call was made, another guard summoned, who led them directly to Semykin's cell.

The boots of those guards operating within those parts of the Lubyanka occupied by prisoners had special felt soles, enabling the guards to move silently along the corridors, which were padded with grey industrial carpeting. The walls were also grey, as were the dozens of cell doors which lined each corridor inside this labyrinth.

After his arrest on the Finnish border, Pekkala himself had been prisoner here, before being transferred to the Butyrka prison and from there to Siberia. Even more than the silence of this prison, which seemed to suck the air out of his lungs, it was the smell – of bleach and new paint and the particular sour and metallic reek of sweat from terrified men – which hurled Pekkala back into the waking nightmare of his days inside this place. As Pekkala walked behind the guard, eyes fixed upon the back of his shaved head just visible beneath his cap, he recalled the orders of these men each time they escorted him from his cell. 'Do not look to the left. Do not look to the right. Fail to obey and you will be shot.' It was spoken so often that the words seemed to flow together and become meaningless, adding to the feeling of this prison, that all of them, guards and prisoners alike, were trapped in a dream from which they were unable to wake.

With his heartbeat thumping in his temples, Pekkala prayed their stay would not last long, since he knew it was only a matter of time before the memories of his own confinement in this prison overwhelmed him.

At cell 6 of block 4, the guard halted and slid back the bolt. Before he opened the door, he turned to Pekkala. 'It's no use, Inspector. You won't get anything out of him. Valery Semykin is the most stubborn old fool we've ever locked up in this place.'

'Nevertheless,' said Pekkala.

The guard swung the door wide. A waft of stale air brushed past them, tinged with the sour ammoniac reek of an unwashed body.

'Not again!' exclaimed the guard.

There was a scuttling inside the little room, whose walls were glossy brown up to waist height and cream white from there to the ceiling. Covering almost an entire wall was a network of hundreds of fingernail-sized speckles, which ranged in colour from black to red. At first, Pekkala couldn't understand what he was looking at. He could find no pattern in the markings. They appeared to have been applied completely at random. But as he continued to stare, his eyes refocused and he realised he was looking at a painting of several half-dressed people lounging on a river bank, and others standing in the water. One boy had his hands raised to his mouth, as if taking a drink. In the distance, a few small sailing boats scudded about on the river and smoke rose from the chimney of a factory. In that same moment, he grasped that each of those hundreds of spots was made by a fingertip covered in blood.

On the other side of the room, standing with his face against the wall was a burly, thick-necked man. He wore a set of standard prison pyjamas, made from thin beige cotton, the bottoms of which had no drawstring, forcing the man to constantly hold them up with one hand.

Pekkala could see that the man's fingertips were a mass of unhealed wounds, some of them still bleeding.

'I warned you not to do this again,' said the guard. 'When I come back, you'll have to clean this up and then I'm going to put you on half rations for a week.'

The man did not reply. He remained motionless, forehead pressed against the wall.

'Hello, Valery,' said Pekkala.

Still there was no reply.

'Why does he not speak?' asked Kirov.

'New regulation,' replied the guard. 'Prisoners in solitary must face the wall when in the presence of a visitor and may not speak without permission from a member of the Lubyanka staff.'

'Then would you give him permission?'

The guard scowled. 'And listen to him curse us black and blue? Because that's what he'll do, you know, no matter what we throw at him.'

Pekkala waited in silence for the guard to finish his tirade.

'Suit yourself,' replied the guard. 'The prisoner may speak!'

Semykin sighed. His body seemed to slump.

'Let me know when you're finished wasting your time on this old fool.' The guard's felt-soled boots swished over the carpeting as he made his way down to the end of the corridor.

Slowly, Semykin turned. His face was framed by dark eyebrows, fleshy lips and three days' growth of stubble. Before entering the Lubyanka, he had been portly, but the sudden loss of weight caused his skin to hang loosely on his frame. His face had the look of a bloodhound stripped of its fur.

'Pekkala!' Semykin's expression showed a mixture of surprise and hostility. 'What does the great Emerald Eye want with me? And why have you brought this commissar, unless it is to taunt me with something else I might regret, apart from finding myself locked up in here.'

Instead of answering the question, Kirov turned to the mass of bloody speckles on the wall. 'Seurat?' he said.

Semykin gave a murmur of grudging approval. 'It is called *Une Baignade*, as well as I can remember it, anyway, since I am allowed no books or pictures. Given the lack of materials, I find the pointillist style most approachable. In here, beauty is worth its weight in blood,' Semykin held up his shredded fingers, like the paws of a lion whose claws had been torn out, 'but there is only so much of it one man can spare.'

'The guard thinks you have gone mad,' said Pekkala, 'and it is easy to see why.'

'But a man who knows he has gone mad is still sane enough to know the difference between madness and a normal mind. So when I agree with that felt-booted philistine, you may take it as proof that I'm still sane.'

'It doesn't look that way to me,' said Kirov.

Semykin folded his arms. Blood continued to drip from his fingertips. 'Do you even know why I'm in here, Comrade Major?'

'Not exactly, no,' admitted Kirov.

'Tell him, Valery,' said Pekkala. 'It is important that he hears it from you.'

'Very well,' said Semykin. 'I was approached, several months ago, by a certain People's Commissar of the State Railways named Viktor Bakhturin.'

'Bakhturin!' exclaimed Kirov. 'You certainly know how to pick your enemies.'

'As I have discovered.' Semykin glanced around the confines of his cell.

Several times in the past few years, Pekkala and Kirov had crossed paths with Viktor Bakhturin. He was a proud, vindictive, petty man, whose name had come up in connection with several murders. Each case presented a clear triangulation between the victim, the killer and Bakhturin, but there was never enough proof to convict him of actual involvement in the crime. He had also been tied to political denunciations of government officials, which had ended either with the execution of these men, or else their deportation to Siberia.

The previous People's Commissar of the State Railways had been turned over to NKVD by his own wife for travelling on a rail carriage set aside for transportation of officials on government business in order to travel back and forth from Moscow to his holiday dacha on the Black Sea. Although the practice was widespread and usually ignored by NKVD, the fact that the commissar's own wife had denounced him caused an embarrassment which could not be overlooked. The commissar received a twelve-year sentence in a gulag on the border of Mongolia.

The reason the commissar's wife had turned in her own husband was that she suspected him of having an affair. The source of this rumour, which turned out to be false, was believed to be Viktor Bakhturin. At the time, Bakhturin had been a junior commissar of State Railways, but he quickly rose to take the place of the man now in Siberia.

There were other examples. A bank manager, threatened with exposure for offering to loan money to Bakhturin at an interest rate below that set by the government, arrived for work with flowers for his secretary, then locked himself in his office and blew his brains out. An investigation revealed that the manager had initially refused Bakhturin's application for a loan, on the grounds that he wanted to pay no interest at all. When the manager suggested a compromise between no interest and that which had been established by the government, Bakhturin turned him in for corruption. Convicting Bakhturin of complicity in this crime proved to be impossible because no documentation of the crime could be found and the only witness, the bank manager's secretary, refused to testify against Bakhturin.

Although Viktor Bakhturin had consistently eluded prosecution, his brother, Serge, who was also an official in the State Railways, had not proved to be as lucky. It was well known that Serge's position in the State Railways had been arranged for him by his brother and, no matter how incompetent and corrupt Serge had proved himself to be, all attempts by officials of the State Railways to dislodge him from his position had been unsuccessful due to Viktor's influence with the minister of Transport.

It was Pekkala who finally brought down Serge Bakhturin.

He had been working on a case which involved the deliberate duplication of bills of lading, which allowed railcars loaded with black-market goods from China, Poland and Turkey to be transported into and then across the Soviet Union. The railcars used in this scheme were special heated wagons known as *teplushki* which, once sealed, could not be opened until they reached their final destination, in order to maintain temperature control.

Pekkala's investigation traced the issuing of the duplicated bills of lading to Serge's office, and interviews with railway personnel who were also convicted in the scheme confirmed what Pekkala had suspected from the start, which was that Serge himself made sure that the wagons carrying these black-market goods were diverted, before they reached their destinations, to railyards whose workers were complicit in the scheme. There, the wagons were unloaded and promptly reassigned to other transport jobs. Meanwhile, when the original train convoys arrived at their end-points, the number of wagons and their contents matched all bills of lading.

It was a lucrative business, but also complicated to maintain, since it involved the disappearance of dozens of wagons at any one time and even though this disappearance was temporary, the discovery of even one wagon, loaded with silk, opium or alcohol, would likely have unravelled the entire operation.

The fact that Serge had been issuing false bills of lading for over three years by the time he was caught led Pekkala to believe that greater minds than Serge's were behind the scheme. Although Pekkala had suspected Viktor's involvement from the start, he was never able to prove anything.

The charges against Serge were very serious, and it was only by thanks to Viktor's intervention that he did not find himself transported to Siberia, or even executed. Instead, Serge received the very mild sentence of two years without hard labour, to be served at the Tulkino Prison in Kotlas. Tulkino was a place known for the leniency that could be purchased by its wealthier inmates, and Viktor wasted no time procuring better treatment for his incarcerated brother.

Although Pekkala's investigation put a stop to the black-market wagons, at least temporarily, he had made a permanent enemy of the People's Commissar of State Railways, who would not soon forget the sight of his brother behind bars.

'How exactly did you get on the wrong side of this man?' asked Kirov.

'Bakhturin had a painting,' explained Semykin, 'which he had personally removed from the house of a railway official in Poland after the invasion of 1939. It was a painting by the Polish artist Stanislaw Wyspianski. He showed me a photograph of it and asked if I would sell it for him. I agreed, on condition that he obtained papers which legalised his ownership of the painting. While these were being drawn up by the Department of Cultural Affairs, I contacted someone I thought would be interested, a government minister named Osipov. Osipov was so taken with the picture I showed him that we agreed on a price before the painting had even touched our hands. When I told Bakhturin what I thought I could get for the painting, he was very pleased. But when the painting arrived . . .' His voice trailed off.

'What?' demanded Kirov. 'What happened? Was it a fake?'

'Technically, it was a copy. Not a fake.'

'What's the difference?'

'Wyspianski always signed his work, but he had the eccentricity of signing the back, not the front. So when I looked at the photo and saw that the work was not signed, that did not trouble me, because I assumed that the work had been signed on the back.'

'But it wasn't signed?' asked Kirov.

Semykin shook his head. 'Someone had simply made a copy of a Wyspianski painting. He often made several paintings based on the same subject matter and I had assumed this was simply part of a series. Whoever this artist was, he or she wasn't trying to fool anybody. If they had been creating a forgery, they would have put Wyspianski's name on the back.'

'If they had done that, would you still have known it was a fake?'

'Of course!' Semykin replied indignantly. 'To tell which art is real and which is not, that's what I have been put on earth to do.'

'That much the Inspector did tell me,' said Kirov.

Semykin gave a snort of satisfaction. 'Why else would you be here? And why else would I be here if not because I informed Bakhturin that his painting was a copy and that I would have to renegotiate with Osipov?'

'And did you renegotiate?'

'Before I had the chance an old colleague of mine, Professor Urbaniak, summoned me to the Catherine Palace. The poor man had been given the impossible task of packing away the hundreds of art works on display there before the Germans arrived. He knew it couldn't be done in the time he had been given, so he asked me to help him prioritise which treasures should be transported first. The rest, we knew, might have to be left behind. It was a grim task, I assure you, like being forced to choose which of your friends should live and which of them should die.'

'And when you returned from the palace,' asked Kirov, 'what happened with the Wyspianski painting?'

'I had been hoping that Bakhturin might decide to forget the whole thing, but the commissar had other ideas. He ordered me to keep my mouth shut about the Wyspianski being a copy. He told me to sell it to Osipov as authentic, even to fake Wyspianski's signature on the back if I thought that would bring in the money.'

'And you refused?'

'Naturally. And then Bakhturin had me arrested.'

'On what charge?' demanded Kirov.

'Trying to sell forged works of art.'

'But you were trying *not* to sell it!'

'A subtlety which was lost upon the court, their minds no doubt swayed by the fact that the man who brought charges against me was a Senior People's Commissar.'

'You are lucky to be alive,' said Kirov. 'How long will you be here?'

'My sentence is five years. In my business, you must often ask yourself – what is the price of integrity? And now I know. Five years in solitary confinement. Which brings me back to my original question. What are you doing here and what do you want with me?'

This time, it was Pekkala who answered. 'I need you to look at something and tell me what you think.'

'And why should I help you –' he flipped his hand with irritation, spattering Kirov's tunic with blood – 'or anyone else out there?'

'I had anticipated that your country's gratitude might not be enough to win you over.'

58

'Which I accept as proof of your own sanity!' blustered Semykin.

Pekkala held up the paper-wrapped parcel, which he had removed from the briefcase before entering the cell. 'In recompense for your help, I have brought you this. To examine. For two minutes.'

Semykin eyed the package suspiciously. 'Well, what is it?'

'First, you will help, then I'll show you what is underneath this paper.'

'For a Finn, you bargain a lot like a Russian.'

'Your people have taught me a few things.'

It became very still in the room.

Semykin gave a low growl. 'Very well,' he whispered. 'What do you need me to do?'

Kirov handed him the leather briefcase.

Semykin sat down on the bench and carefully wiped his bloody fingers on the knees of his prison pyjamas. After opening the brass latch, he slid out the painting of the moth. The first thing he did was to study the back of the canvas. 'Ostubafengel,' he said, reading out the word which had been written on the reverse. He began to work his thumbs along the wooden stretcher as if searching for some hidden defect in the wood. Afterwards, with equal care, Semykin slowly raked his nails across the canvas, eyes closed with concentration while he listened to the sound they made. Only then did he turn the painting over and examine the picture itself. 'It is curious,' he said. 'The canvas was made in haste, but the painting itself shows considerable precision. The pattern on the wings was made with a brush containing only a few strands of hair. The painter would have had to use a large magnifying glass, like the kind employed by those who tie flies for trout fishing. It is not a forgery, if that is what you've come to ask me, or if it is, then I have never seen or heard of the original, but if you're here to ask me what it's worth, I'm afraid this briefcase is more valuable than its contents.'

'What about the artist?' asked Kirov. 'Have you ever heard of anyone named Ostubafengel?'

Semykin shook his head. 'But that doesn't mean he or she isn't out there somewhere. Sounds like one of those complicated Habsburg names to me. Hungarian perhaps. Where did it come from?'

Pekkala told him the story.

'Then it is obviously worth something,' said Semykin, 'but its value does not lie in the painting itself. That much I can tell you for certain.'

'Do you think there may be a message hidden inside the frame?' asked Kirov.

Semykin shrugged. 'Possibly. Or else there might be something underneath the paint. An X-ray might reveal it, or ultraviolet light perhaps.' He tilted the painting on its side and squinted along the flat surface of the canvas, like a man taking aim down a gunsight. 'But I doubt you will find anything. The paint is very thin, and I don't believe there is anything beneath it. The trouble is, once you start ripping it apart, the painting itself will be destroyed. Is that a risk you are prepared to take?'

'Not yet,' replied Pekkala.

'Two men died to protect this painting,' protested Kirov. 'They obviously thought it was valuable.'

'They did not die protecting the painting,' countered Semykin. 'The reason they died was to protect its secret.

Whatever that secret is lies beyond my expertise. I've told you everything I can.'

'And if an X-ray turns up nothing,' said Kirov, 'we will be right back where we started.'

'There is someone else you could take this to,' suggested Semykin.

'And who is that?' asked Pekkala.

'Her name is Churikova. Polina Churikova. Until the war broke out, she was a student at the Moscow State Institute of Art. She spent the summer of 1940 as my assistant. Her speciality was forensics.'

'But specialising in forensics makes her a student of crime, not of art,' said Pekkala.

'Actually,' Semykin told him, 'it made her a student of both. The business of art forgery is extremely lucrative. It is also more widespread than most people can imagine. It's possible, for example, that up to a third of the paintings in the world's great art museums could be fakes. By making a chemical analysis of a painting, using microscopic portions of the paint, the wood, the canvas and so on, those trained in forensics can determine whether an art work is authentic. But Polina Churikova was not only my student. She was also my friend. She was the only person who came to visit me before I began serving my sentence here at Lubyanka.'

'When was that?'

'Only a few weeks ago.'

'And do you know where we can find her now?'

Semykin shrugged. 'Ask the Red Army. When Churikova came to see me, she was in uniform, like everybody else. At the time, she said she was stationed in Moscow, but where she might be now is anybody's guess. She told me she had joined the Army Signals Branch in late June, right after the Germans attacked, and subsequently became a cryptographer. Apparently, she has already made a name for herself by breaking something called the Ferdinand Cipher, which the Fascists were using to communicate between Berlin and their front-line headquarters.'

'How does someone who studies forensics end up as a cryptographer?' asked Kirov.

'The two fields are quite similar,' explained Semykin. 'Forensics taught her to uncover things that lay hidden in works of art in order to determine whether they were originals or fakes. The forger will always leave traces, sometimes by accident, sometimes on purpose. Now, instead of paintings or sculptures, she finds what has been hidden in the labyrinth of words and numbers.'

'What makes you think she can help us?' asked Kirov.

'I make no guarantee that she can, only that when two people look at a work of art, they rarely see the same thing. That is what makes it art.'

'This is all very well,' grumbled Kirov, 'except her location is as much of a mystery as this painting!'

'Solve one,' Semykin told him, 'and you may solve the other. For that, you must rely on your own art, Comrade Commissar.'

'Thank you, Semykin,' said Pekkala, as he handed over the first paper-wrapped package. 'We appreciate your assistance.'

Then he and Kirov waited while Semykin carefully untied the string. After folding back the layers of archival tissue, he gasped, as the face of the fiery-eyed saviour came into view. 'Now this . . .' murmured Semykin, '*this* is authentic.' As carefully as if it was a newborn infant, Semykin lifted the icon from its cradle of brown paper. Touching only the outermost edges of the frame, he held it up and sighed with admiration. 'Is it Balkan?'

'So I'm told,' said Pekkala.

'Late thirteenth century? Early fourteenth?'

'Somewhere around there.'

'Tempera on wood. Notice the asymmetrical nose and mouth, the deep furrows on his brow and the way this white lead backing brings to life the greenish ochre of his skin. The tension! The expressivity!' Suddenly a look of consternation swept across Semykin's face. 'Wait,' he said slowly. 'I've seen this before somewhere.' Sharply, he raised his head and stared questioningly at Pekkala. 'Haven't I?'

'Yes,' admitted Pekkala. 'You have seen it hanging on the wall of the Museum of the Kremlin, and you will find it there again when you get out of here, Valery.'

Semykin's eyes bulged. 'You *took* this from the Kremlin Museum?'

'Borrowed it,' Pekkala corrected him.

'Then see that it finds its way home,' said Semykin as he carefully rewrapped the icon, 'before Fabian Golyakovsky has a heart attack.'

'It may be too late for that,' muttered Kirov.

'I may have lost faith in the country that owns this work of art,' Semykin told them, 'but the art itself is sacred, and will remain so, long after you and I and the butchers of Lubyanka have turned to dust.'

As they walked across the courtyard to their car, a van arrived at the Lubyanka. These vehicles, which shuttled inmates to and from the prison, were camouflaged to look like delivery trucks. Painted on their sides were advertisements for non-existent bakeries, cigarette companies and distillers of vodka. Inside, in spaces barely big enough to hold a human being, the inmates were packed in side by side, bent double, shackled by the wrists to bars fixed at floor level against the walls of the truck so that the prisoners had to ride with their heads forced over to the level of their knees.

Only the most oblivious of Muscovites believed that these vans actually contained what their cheerful logos promised. By seeking to hide their real cargoes as they careened through the streets of Moscow, the illusion they created became even more sinister than the truth.

'Are you all right, Inspector?' asked Kirov, as they climbed into the car.

'What do you mean?' asked Pekkala.

'You don't look well. You're sweating.'

With a swipe of his palm, Pekkala smeared the moisture from his forehead. 'I can't stand it in there.'

'Is there any way to get Semykin released, Inspector?'

'Probably, but as miserable as Semykin might be inside that

cell, he is still safer there than out walking the streets of this city.'

'I don't understand.'

'As you yourself mentioned, Semykin has a talent for choosing his enemies. Bakhturin is one of the worst. Our visit to Semykin will not have gone unnoticed by the commissar. As soon as word gets out to him, you can be sure Bakhturin will pay us a visit. And as for Semykin, he wouldn't last a week outside that prison cell, as long as Bakhturin is watching. And if we successfully petitioned for Semykin's release, how long do you think it would take for Bakhturin to conjure up another reason to have him arrested?'

'I did not think of that,' whispered Kirov.

'And here is something else you did not think about,' continued Pekkala. 'Bakhturin would see to it that Semykin did not go back to prison. At best, he would find himself on a train bound for the east. At worst, the Lubyanka guards would drag him down into the basement, and you and I both know what happens there. There are worse things than sitting in prison. Five years might seem like a very long time to Semykin, but it is one of the shortest sentences given out to convicts at the Lubyanka. You know as well as I do that there are men who've been behind those walls for ten or fifteen years or even longer.'

A long silence followed, in which each man retreated into his thoughts.

For Pekkala, the sight of Semykin, soaked in his own blood inside that windowless cell, had brought back memories whose vividness had failed to dull with time. Nor could he find a way to frame within the scaffolding of words what his own time in prison had done to him. The truth was that he did not know the answer. Although he could remember every detail of his life in the service of the Tsar, in those memories he no longer recognised himself. It was like looking at the anonymous photographs he saw heaped upon tables in the Sukharevka market, along with the chipped plates and mismatched cutlery which were all that remained of those who had been swept away by the Revolution.

It was Kirov who broke the silence. 'Do you think you would have survived,' he asked, 'if Stalin had forced you to serve out your full sentence?'

Pekkala shuddered as an image returned to him, of a man he had known in the forest. His name was Tatischev, and he had once been a sergeant in the Tsar's Zaporozhian Cossacks. After his escape from a nearby camp, which was known as Mamlin-Three, search parties had combed the forest looking for him. But they had never found Tatischev, for the simple reason that he had hidden where they were least likely to search – within sight of the Mamlin-Three camp. Here, he had remained, scratching out an existence even more spartan than Pekkala's.

Pekkala and Tatischev met twice a year in a clearing on the border of the Borodok and Mamlin territorial boundaries. Tatischev was a cautious man, and judged it too dangerous to meet more often than that.

It was from Tatischev that Pekkala discovered exactly what was happening at Mamlin. He learned that the camp had been set aside as a research centre on human subjects. Low-pressure experiments were carried out in order to determine the effects on human tissue of high-altitude exposure. Men were submerged in ice water, revived and then submerged again to determine how long a downed pilot might survive after ditching in the arctic seas above Murmansk. Some prisoners had antifreeze injected into their hearts. Others woke up on operating tables to find their limbs had been removed. It was a place of horrors, said Tatischev, where the human race had sunk to its ultimate depths.

To Pekkala, the old Cossack Tatischev had seemed indestructible, but on the third year of their meetings, Pekkala showed up at the clearing to find Tatischev's marrowless and chamfered bones scattered about the clearing, and metal grommets from his boots among the droppings of the wolves who had devoured him.

'Maybe I could have survived after living that long in the forest,' said Pekkala, 'but I doubt I would have wanted to.'

Exhausted from his run, Rifleman Stefanov arrived back at the Alexander Park. Until this moment, he had been so numbed by the relentless and deadly ritual of retreating, digging a foxhole, grabbing a few hours of sleep beneath his rain cape and then repeating the process again the following day that he'd barely had the energy to feel more than a vague sense of bewilderment at finding himself at Tsarskoye Selo, or Detskoye Selo, or Pushkin Village or whatever they were calling it these days. Only now was the focus returning to his mind, and as he stared across the untended grounds, the grass so deep it stood knee high in places, Stefanov was at last confronted with the past he had worked so hard to keep secret from everyone around him.

He had spent the first ten years of his life here, within sight of the Catherine and Alexander Palaces, as the son of the head gardener, Agripin Dobrushinovich Stefanov, whose family had worked on this estate for generations. Since the Revolution, he had lived in terror that this mere association with the Romanovs, however innocent, might, in the eyes of his comrades or, even worse, the Battalion Commissar, somehow constitute a crime against the State. This was why, when Sergeant Ragozin misread the map he had been given, insisting they were in the Alexander Park rather than the Catherine, Stefanov did not offer to help. Neither, when Ragozin pointed out the building which he referred to as the Japanese Pagoda, did Stefanov offer the correction that it was, in fact, known as the Chinese Theatre, having recognised it immediately from its bullet-shaped windows and gabled rooftops tweaked up like moustaches on old tsarist generals. It was only now, as he stumbled through the huge gates of the North Entrance, that Stefanov was awed to see again the huge oaks and elms which grew beside the Lamskie Pond, at the mildewed walls of the neglected Pensioners' Stable and at the little cottage, with its buttery yellow walls and blue shutters, where the Emerald Eye himself had lived until vanishing into the snow one winter's night in 1917, never to return.

Stefanov's own departure had not been far behind. His father had continued to work at Tsarskoye Selo, even after the arrest of the Tsar and the incarceration of the royal family within the boundaries of their estate, until finally the Bolshevik guards who patrolled the grounds had warned him to leave, and take his family as well, if he valued their lives.

That same night, Stefanov's father led one of the Tsar's prize horses from the stable, harnessed it to a wagon and set off with his family to the house of his brother, a butcher in the distant town of Borovichi.

The last glimpse Stefanov had of Tsarskoye Selo was of the Catherine Palace, its rooftop gleaming like fish scales in the moonlight.

He never thought he would see the place again, let alone race along the Podkaprizovaya Doroga in a noisy army truck, with orders to defend the place from air attack.

It was just as well that Stefanov's father had died years ago. The old man had spent years raking leaves from the riding paths so that they would not stick to the hooves of the Tsar's horse as he cantered by, or composting the asparagus, potatoes and carrots which the Romanovs left from their meals, or pruning the juniper hedges so that the Tsarina, who liked to walk past them with her hand held out, flat as a knife blade, skimming along just above the deep green needles, could marvel at the precision of his blade. To see the grass this deep, the hedges wild and overgrown, would probably have broken the old man's heart.

The place where they had chosen to deploy the 25-mm anti-aircraft gun stood at the edge of the Alexander Park, close by the Krasnoselskie Gates. Here, the wide expanse of open ground offered a good field of fire for any planes swooping low over the Pushkin Estate. The wheels of the gun carriage had been cranked off the ground, allowing the weapon to be placed on four outrigger posts, which provided a stable base for firing.

The blast shield had been painted with mud and dead leaves. This had to be done from scratch every time they set up the weapon. He could not rely on old, dried mud to do the trick. The colour of mud differed every time they stopped and the type of leaves might also give away a gun's position if they were not properly matched to the environment. If the weapon was spotted and came under air attack, there was little they could do except grimly blaze away at the diving plane in a duel which rarely ended well for the crews of 25-mm guns, the smallest in the arsenal of Red Army anti-aircraft weapons.

When Stefanov returned to the shelter of the trees, the other members of the gun team, in an unusual display of tact, refrained from asking what he had just witnessed. The expression on his face told them all they needed to know. Taking up the shovel which served his three-man section as both foxhole and latrine digger, Stefanov began to hollow out a shelter for himself.

He worked quickly, and softly chanted the two-word prayer he had invented for himself when digging holes. No stones. No stones. No stones. To be effective, the hole had to be knee deep and large enough to accommodate his body when curled into a foetal position. Lined with a few strips of cardboard from a carton of *tushonka* meat rations and covered with his *plasch-palatka* rain cape, a properly dug hole would provide him not only with protection but a place to grab a few hours' sleep before the order came to rig the gun for transport once again.

When the foxhole had been completed, Stefanov swept his arm back and forth around the edges, scattering the dark earth which might give away his location from the air. As he performed this ritual, his sleeve caught on something which tore into the fabric and jabbed him in the wrist. At first he mistook it for a twig but, lifting his arm, he realised it was a toy soldier. The soldier was frozen in a marching posture. Propped on his shoulder was a rifle, whose tiny bayonet had cut through Stefanov's shirt.

Carefully, Stefanov removed the soldier from his sleeve, spat on it and rubbed away the dirt which had accumulated on the metal. He could still see the colours on the tunic: dark green with red piping, which, Stefanov seemed to recall, was the uniform of the Tsar's Chevalier Guard.

He immediately recognised this little solider as having once belonged to the Tsarevich Alexei. Stefanov recalled the day he had been helping his father to push a wheelbarrow full of rotten apples destined for the compost heap, and the two of them had come across the Tsarevich playing a game with what had seemed to Stefanov to be hundreds of these soldiers, ranks of them lined up along the path. There were foot soldiers and soldiers on horseback and soldiers with bugles and others with flags and cannons and one tall man on a fine, white stallion who, by his gold-trimmed uniform, Stefanov supposed to be the Tsar himself. Beside that figure rode another, smaller but wearing an identical uniform. It was a moment before Stefanov grasped that this must be the Tsarevich. To be in the game, marvelled Stefanov, and not even have to pretend.

The soldiers had been brought outside in wooden boxes, in which special velvet-lined trays had been fitted to accommodate each piece. Sitting on the knee-high stack of boxes and smoking a short-stemmed pipe was the Tsarevich's bodyguard, a sailor named Nagorny. He had high cheekbones and a long, sharp nose. His ears bent slightly outwards at the top, giving the sailor a slightly mischievous expression. Alexei had two bodyguards. The other man was a giant named Derevenko. Both men were sailors and often carried the Tsarevich when the boy's haemophilia prevented him from walking on his own.

When the Revolution began, the giant Derevenko had turned upon Alexei, ordering the boy to run errands, just as the boy had once commanded him to do. But Nagorny had stood by the Romanovs, accompanying them in their exile to Siberia. He was shot, Stefanov had heard, for trying to prevent the Bolshevik guards from taking a gold chain that belonged to the Tsarevich.

The Tsarevich, on his knees in the middle of his toy army, looked up as Stefanov and his father moved past, leaving in their wake a trail of rotten apple juice which leaked through the wooden boards of the wheelbarrow.

Finding himself in the presence of the Tsarevich, Stefanov's father removed his cap and bowed, then snatched the cap from his son's head as well.

The Tsarevich blinked at them and did not speak. There was no sign of anger or impatience. He simply waited for them to pass by, as a person might wait for the passing of a cloud which had obscured the sun.

As soon as they were out of earshot, Stefanov's father turned to him. 'What were you thinking, boy?' he snapped. 'You know you should remove your cap in the presence of a Romanov!'

The answer to his father's question, which Stefanov was wise enough not to say out loud, was that he had not been thinking about anything except the sight of that army of toy soldiers. He would have given anything for the chance to join that game, to set up his own army in that yellow dust.

Setting off again with their burden of rotten apples, they eventually reached the compost pile, which was hidden from view by tall hedges made of dense holly and barred by a wooden gate, held fast by a length of rusty chain.

Stefanov's father would come to this heap of rotting vegetation whenever he wanted to be alone, because the reek of the compost guaranteed his solitude. He called it his thinking place, although what the old man thought about, if anything, remained a mystery to his son.

The compost pile was a black mound of leaves, potato peels, turnip tops, to which Stefanov now added his wheelbarrow full of apples. Although the smell was strong, it was not entirely unpleasant, since the compost contained only vegetation and no bones or scraps of meat. The father never seemed to notice it, but that odour filled the young Stefanov's senses in a way he found quite overwhelming. It was heavy, sharp and seemed to spark along the branches of his nerves as if it was somehow alive.

Stefanov's father sat down upon an empty barrel which had once held a shipment of slivovitz, the plum brandy so favoured by the Tsar that he had bought an orchard in the Balkans specifically for the purpose of keeping him supplied. 'You can rest for a minute,' he murmured to his son.

'Did you see?' asked Stefanov. 'One of those soldiers was painted to look just like the Tsarevich himself!'

Stefanov's father grunted, unimpressed, as he was unimpressed by most things which served no practical purpose. 'Last year,' he said, 'the Tsarevich was given the opportunity to command a group of real soldiers. And do you know what he did? He marched them into the sea.'

'And did they do what they were told?'

'Of course! It was their duty to obey.'

Stefanov pressed his hands together, feeling the burn in his palms from holding the wheelbarrow handles. 'I would like to march some men into the sea. They must have looked silly, standing out there in the waves.'

The father leaned across and cuffed him on the back of his head. 'There is nothing to be proud of in ridiculing men who have sworn to give up their lives in order to protect you!'

Stefanov's father always seemed to be losing his temper, and the young Stefanov never knew when the moment would come. He lived in constant fear of crossing the invisible limits of his father's patience. 'But the Tsarevich is only a boy,' he remarked hesitantly.

'That is like saying that the Tsar is only a man!' barked the father.

Their conversation was interrupted by a quiet rustle on the gravel path which ran beside the hedge.

The father's head snapped up. 'It's him,' he whispered.

Stefanov's heart slammed into his chest. 'Who?' he whispered back.

Rising from his barrel seat, his father peered through the hedge.

'Who is it?' Stefanov asked again, still afraid to raise his voice above a whisper.

The father beckoned to him, teeth bared with urgency.

It was hard for Stefanov to see anything through the screen of holly leaves, whose needly points jabbed at his forehead as he attempted to follow his father's gaze.

A dark shape moved past on the other side of the hedge.

Stefanov held his breath. An inexplicable sensation of dread washed through his mind.

When the strange figure had gone, the father turned to his son. 'That was him,' he whispered. 'That was the Emerald Eye.'

Stefanov had heard of Inspector Pekkala. Everyone on the estate knew of his existence, although few had ever seen him in the flesh. Many times, in the company of his father, he had walked past the little cottage where the Emerald Eye was said to live. Both had searched for any sign of the famous investigator, but no one ever seemed to come or go from that lonely little building. There were rumours among his friends at school that the Emerald Eye did not really exist, but was, in fact, just a figment of the Tsar's imagination. Lately, Stefanov had begun to wonder if those rumours might be true.

Overcome with curiosity, Stefanov stepped over to the gate which separated the compost yard from the path which lay beyond it. With his feet on the lowest rung of the gate, he leaned out beyond the hedge, hoping to catch a glimpse of the Inspector.

What he saw was a tall figure in a dark coat, gloved hands clasped behind his back. The man walked with an unusually straight back and each of his steps seemed deliberate, like that of someone who was counting out his paces.

A moment later, Stefanov's father appeared beside him. 'See the way he moves? Like a phantom. He's not even human, you know.'

'Then what is he?' demanded Stefanov.

'A demon or an angel. Who can say except the Tsar who summoned him?'

Even at that age, Stefanov knew that he and his father did not live in the same world. They might breathe the same air, and clean the same dirt off their shoes at the end of every day, but for Stefanov's father, nothing was as it appeared. Each gust of wind, or rumble of thunder in the distance, or the body of a dead bird lying on the path, to be removed before the Tsar or any of his family could glimpse its crumpled form, represented a sign of what was to come. The Tsarskoye Selo estate, whose earth and stones and trees the man had tended for so long that he knew the grounds better than their owners ever could have done, was only a shadow to Stefanov's father. Only the portents it contained were real, and deciphering them was his father's only defence against the terrible randomness of life and death which he witnessed in the world around him.

The young Stefanov had already learned to see with different eyes. For him, sometimes thunder was just thunder, the wind only the wind, and the body of a bird no more than the trophy of a cat.

'Summoned him from where?' demanded Stefanov, in a tone that almost taunted the old man, knowing full well that such a challenge might cause his father's patience to snap yet again, and that he would then be hauled from the fence and dragged behind the compost heap for punishment. But Stefanov was past caring about the half-hearted drubbings his father administered, slapping the young boy as if trying to beat the dust out of a carpet.

'I'll tell you where he came from.' The father raised his hand, jabbing a dirt-rimmed fingernail towards the Catherine Palace. 'From there. From that room!'

Stefanov gazed in bewilderment at the hundreds of windows, each one of which blankly returned his stare, hiding the dozens of rooms which lay behind them.

Sensing his son's confusion, the father continued. 'The room whose walls are made of fire.'

Stefanov had never heard of such a room, nor did he believe that one existed. It belonged, he felt sure, in that world of half-realities with which his father made sense of the universe. His father had never set foot inside the Catherine or Alexander Palaces. For a groundskeeper, their polished marble floors lay beyond the dimensions of his work. The closest he, or Stefanov, had ever come was the back door of the Alexander Palace kitchen, where he collected the midday meal to which he was entitled.

Suddenly Pekkala stopped in his tracks. The only movement was a wisp of dust, which swirled around his polished boots.

'He's turning around!' hissed the father. 'He's coming back!'

Stefanov and his father scuttled back behind the hedge and waited. Stefanov placed his hand over his chest, as if to muffle the sound of his heart.

The dark figure passed by, half hidden by the bushes, but only an arm's length away.

At that instant, Stefanov heard a voice which seemed to come from inside his own head.

'Good day,' said Inspector Pekkala.

And then he was gone.

At his first glance of Pekkala, Stefanov had wondered if, perhaps, there was nothing so magical about the great inspector as an extraordinary man doing his best to lead an ordinary life, out for a stroll at the end of a hard day's work. But now that Pekkala had spoken, Stefanov wasn't so sure. There was something about the Emerald Eye which did not seem fastened to the world of flesh and bone.

As the memory evaporated from his mind, Stefanov found himself once again in the filthy cocoon of his foxhole. Realising that the toy soldier was still in his hand, Stefanov stood the tiny warrior upright in the dirt, then settled back, arms folded across his chest, and studied the figure, as if, at any moment, he might march away to battles of his own.

The door to Pekkala's office burst open.

Pekkala was stooped over his desk studying a sketch he had made of the red moth painting before Kirov had taken it away to have the canvas X-rayed, along with the icon, which he planned to return to the museum. At first, Pekkala thought the major had returned, hopefully with news not only of the painting's significance but also, perhaps, on the whereabouts of Polina Churikova. But his eyes narrowed with hostility when he saw who'd just stormed in.

It was a tall man with a black moustache and a pale, sweating forehead, who was dressed in the uniform of a high-ranking government official.

'Bakhturin,' muttered Pekkala.

'People's Commissar of the State Railways Bakhturin!' He shook his fist at Pekkala. 'Put some respect into your voice!'

'I am not required to respect you,' replied Pekkala, 'and even if I was, I doubt you would find me convincing. Have you come about my visit to Semykin?'

'As a matter of fact, yes, and to ask what you thought you were doing, speaking with a man whose sentence requires him to be kept in solitary confinement for the duration of his time in Lubyanka. That means no visitors. Not even you, Inspector!'

'I was sorry to hear that the Wyspianski painting turned out to be a fake.'

'Not a fake!' snapped Bakhturin. 'It was done in the style of Wyspianski, that is all.'

'And was Wyspianski's signature also done in the style of Wyspianski?' asked Pekkala.

Bakhturin made a faint choking sound. 'I spent a great deal of time and energy bringing that painting back from Poland and I brought it to Semykin because I'd heard he was the most reputable art dealer in Moscow. Is that so hard for you to understand?'

'No,' replied Pekkala, 'but why is it so difficult for you to comprehend, Comrade Bakhturin, that the reason Semykin has such a good reputation is because he does not engage in the sale of paintings which are not authentic?'

Bakhturin began to pace back and forth, like a cat locked in a cage. 'He could have kept his mouth shut. Instead of that, he practically announced in public that I was trying to cheat Minister Osipov.'

'You mean you weren't?'

'I'm the one who was cheated! I didn't know the painting wasn't right.'

'And when Semykin explained that to you . . .'

'By then it was too late! I had already borrowed money to pay for a dacha north of the city. I had to forfeit the contract. I lost a great deal of money thanks to that pompous art dealer.'

'So you put him in prison.'

'I could have done worse!' bellowed Bakhturin. Then he paused for a moment, and when he spoke again, a sinister calm had entered his voice. 'I did not come here to explain myself to you, Pekkala, only to advise you to keep your distance from Semykin. Remember what you saw in that prison cell today.'

Pekkala would never forget. More than the blood-dappled walls, or the ragged stumps of Semykin's fingertips, or the choking sensation of confinement in that cell, it had been the look in Semykin's eyes which bore witness to the full measure of Bakhturin's cruelty. But Bakhturin had been wrong when he'd said that he could have done worse. For a man like Semykin, accustomed to spending his days surrounded by art, five years staring at the blank walls of a prison cell was worse than the deaths which Bakhturin's other victims had suffered.

On his way out of the office, Bakhturin turned and aimed a finger at Pekkala. 'You know what it means to be shut away in Lubyanka and you know it can happen to anyone. Anyone at all, Inspector.'

Pekkala managed to contain his irritation until Bakhturin had descended to the bottom of the stairs, before muttering a seemingly endless string of Finnish obscenities.

It was after dark when Kirov returned to the office.

By then, Pekkala had been staring at the drawing for so long that when he closed his eyes, the outline of the moth's wings remained imprinted on his sight as if he had been staring at the sun. Blearily, he focused on the major. 'Any luck?'

Kirov removed his gun belt and hung it on the coat hook by the door. 'NVKD believes that the painting may have been delivered to the German Embassy in Stockholm in a diplomatic pouch originating from the Swedish consulate in Turkey. Given its size the painting could easily have been smuggled through our borders. Agents of ours at the German Embassy in Stockholm report that something roughly the size of the painting arrived by diplomatic pouch about a week before the plane went down over our lines, although they were not able to view the contents and did not realise at the time that it was of any significance, since diplomatic pouches arrive there every day from all over the world.'

'But what about the painting itself?' asked Pekkala. 'Have you determined whether anything was concealed inside the frame?'

'I had the painting X-rayed at the Moscow Central Hospital, but there was nothing in the frame except the wood used to construct it. Then I brought it over to the School of Agriculture and exposed the canvas to the ultraviolet lights they use on some of their tropical plants.'

'Nothing there either?'

Kirov shook his head. 'It's just a painting, Inspector, and if Comrade Stalin himself called right now and asked me what I thought, I'd tell him we were wasting our time.'

Pekkala took the sketch he had made and held it up to the light. For a moment, in the glow of the bulb through the paper, it looked as if the moth had come to life. 'One thing I've learned about Stalin,' he said, 'is that his instincts are usually right, even if he doesn't know why. Our job is to give him the answer, which, in this case,' he crumpled up the sheet and threw it into the corner of the room, 'may turn out to be impossible.'

'Especially without the help of Polina Churikova.'

'You couldn't find her?'

'NKVD are searching now,' Kirov replied. 'If anyone can locate her . . .'

At that moment, the phone rang. The loud clattering of the bell startled both men.

Kirov picked up the receiver. 'Yes, this is Major Kirov. You have?' There was a long pause as he listened to the voice at the other end. 'Where? When? I see. Never mind, then.' He replaced the receiver in its cradle.

'More bad news?'

'I'm afraid so, Inspector. One hour ago, Lieutenant Polina Churikova boarded a train at the Ostankinsky District railyard, bound for the front, along with the rest of her signals battalion. We'll never catch up with her now.'

'You say she has boarded the train?'

'That's what they just told me, yes.'

'But did they tell you that the train has actually departed?'

'Well, no, but . . .'

'It takes them forever to load those transports,' interrupted Pekkala. 'Call the Ostankinsky station. Tell them who we're looking for and order them to hold the train until we have arrived.'

For a moment, Kirov remained frozen, as if still searching for the words to reason with Pekkala.

'Now!' shouted Pekkala. 'And as soon as you've done that, get down to the car as quickly as you can!'

The sound of Pekkala's voice jolted Kirov into action. He snatched up the phone and dialled for the operator.

Pekkala, meanwhile, grabbed the keys for the Emka and tramped down the stairs. Before he disappeared into the street, one final command echoed up the battered staircase. 'And bring that blasted painting with you!'

The Emka skidded into the Ostankinsky railyard just as the last carriage of the troop transport clattered away into the dark.

'Damn!' Kirov mashed his fist on the steering wheel.

'Did you call them?' asked Pekkala.

'Of course I did, Inspector. I spoke to the stationmaster. He asked who I was looking for and I told him. Then I asked him to delay the departure of the train.'

'And what did he reply?'

'That he'd do the best he could.'

Both men fell silent as they watched the red light of the caboose growing smaller and smaller until finally it vanished in the black.

Kirov cut the engine.

Then they both climbed out and looked around the deserted platform, on which the only trace of the hundreds of soldiers who had crowded on to the wagons just a few minutes before were a few cigarette butts, smouldering on the concrete. The light of an oil lamp flickered in the station house – a long, squat building fashioned out of heavy logs and roofed with tar-paper shingles.

'Maybe we can find out where the train's next stop is going to be,' Pekkala wondered aloud. 'Perhaps we can get there before it arrives.'

'The movement of military trains is classified,' Kirov reminded him, 'even for NKVD. By the time we've pulled enough strings to find out, the train will be at the front. We might as well face the fact, Inspector. We've lost her. But perhaps we can still get by without her help.'

Wind rustled through the pine trees on the far side of the tracks.

At that moment, the door to the station house burst open and a soldier strode out on to the muddy railyard. Bundled in a greatcoat against the chill of the night, the figure advanced upon the two men.

Only when the soldier had come to a stop in front of them did Pekkala notice it was a woman. She was tall, with long hair which stuck out from under her brimless *pilotka* cap, but more than this Pekkala could not tell, as her face remained cloaked in the shadows.

'The stationmaster ordered me off the train,' she growled, 'and told me to wait here for someone named Kirov.'

'That would be me,' admitted the Major.

'Well, there had better be a good reason for this!' She pointed down the tracks. 'My whole battalion's just departed for the front. I have a job to do. I am needed where they're going. And I didn't even have time to get my rucksack off the train!'

'You are needed here as well,' Kirov informed her, 'by the Bureau of Special Operations.'

'Special Operations! You men are NKVD?' The indignation vanished from her voice.

'I am,' said Major Kirov.

'What do you want with me?' she asked, suddenly sounding afraid.

It was Pekkala who explained. 'We have come into possession of a painting, which we believe might be significant. Valery Semykin advised us to ask your opinion about it.'

'Valery Semykin is in prison.'

'That is where we found him,' confirmed Pekkala, 'and he sends you his regards.'

'Well, if Valery couldn't tell you whether it's important, believe me, nobody can.'

'The importance might not lie in its artistic value,' Pekkala told her. 'That's why he said you might help us.'

'Now you are speaking in riddles.'

'It is a riddle we are asking you to solve.'

'We have the painting here.' Kirov lifted the briefcase. 'If you could just take a look at it and tell us what you think.'

'I might as well.' She nodded at the empty tracks. 'It looks as if I'm not going anywhere for a while.'

They walked to the station house and stepped inside, stamping the mud from their boots on a rough hemp mat spread out on the floor of the little room which served as a conduit between the interior of the station house and the outside air. Both ends of this narrow passageway were blocked off by a door. During the winter, patrons would make sure that one of the doors was kept closed while the other was open, in order to keep out the cold. Now, since it was summer, the windows had been opened and the inner door was propped wide by an old army boot. Even with the added ventilation, the air was still thick and stale and smelled bitterly of Russian army tobacco.

It was only now, by the soft light of paraffin lanterns which hung from iron hooks along the walls, that Pekkala got his first look at Churikova's high cheekbones and eyes the same dark blue as in Delft pottery. As he studied the woman his face grew suddenly pale.

'Inspector Pekkala, is something the matter?' asked Kirov.

'Pekkala?' echoed Churikova. 'The Emerald Eye?'

'Yes.' Pekkala turned over the lapel of his coat. The jewel winked in its iris of solid gold. 'That's what they used to call me.'

'Then this must be very important.' As Churikova spoke, she removed her bulky greatcoat, which was standard issue for both men and women in the Red Army. The coats were made of thick olive-brown wool and fastened with black metal buttons, each one emblazoned with a hammer and sickle set inside the outline of a star.

'It might be important,' Pekkala told her. 'And it might mean nothing at all. We are relying on you to tell us.'

The two men sat down opposite Lieutenant Churikova at a rickety table on which a red and white checked table cloth had been laid out, its pattern blotched with stains and cigarette ash.

Kirov removed the painting from the leather briefcase and handed it to her.

'Where did you get this?' she asked, as her eyes fanned across the canvas.

Over the next few minutes, Kirov told her everything they knew.

When he had finished explaining, Churikova sat back slowly in her chair. 'What did Semykin have to say about it?'

'That the painting was basically worthless,' said Kirov.

A faint smile passed across her lips. 'Semykin was right. Partly, anyway.'

'What do you mean?' asked Pekkala.

'It is worthless as a painting,' she replied, 'because it is, in fact, a map.'

'A map?' the two men chorused.

'You must be mistaken,' said Kirov. 'I had the canvas X-rayed and even ran it under ultraviolet light in case special inks had been used. We found nothing that looked like a map, Comrade Churikova.'

'I did not say that it contains a map,' explained Churikova. 'The painting itself *is* the map. This is known as a Baden-Powell diagram. It was named after the British officer Robert Baden-Powell, who sometimes operated as a spy while posing as an eccentric butterfly collector, complete with a pith helmet, butterfly net and sketchbook. He even spied on our own fortress at Krasnoe Selo back in 1886, and escaped with details of our observation balloons and a new type of flare which had just been issued for the Russian military. He often employed the drawings of these butterflies as a way of encoding his information, contained within the wing structure of the butterfly. In the case of Krasnoe Selo, the speckles on its wings denoted where guns had been positioned, while the lines created the shape of the fortress walls. The next time you see a mad Englishman with a net and a sketchbook full of butterflies, take my advice and arrest him, Inspector.'

'A map,' whispered Pekkala, as he began to think it through. 'But who made it? And why? Were the men in that plane picking it up or delivering it?'

'And why,' Kirov wondered aloud, 'in an age of electronic messages, would someone resort to a technique as outdated as this?'

'Sometimes the simplest techniques are the most difficult

to crack,' Churikova tapped her fingernail upon the crude wooden frame of the painting, 'and, unfortunately for you, this one is virtually impossible to break. Even if you could decipher the matrix of symbols, you have no way of knowing what those symbols refer to, or where the object is or the scale of the map. It could be the size of something you keep in your pocket or it could be the size of Moscow. Without some pre-existing codex, which would have been agreed upon by the two people sharing the map, there is no way to determine what is hidden in this painting.' Churikova rose slowly to her feet. 'Perhaps you can take consolation in the fact that, at the rate the Germans are advancing, the location detailed in this map, wherever it was, is probably behind their lines by now.'

They walked out into the railyard. The Milky Way arched across the sky, like the vapour trail of a plane bound for another galaxy.

'We can drive you back to your barracks in Moscow,' offered Kirov.

'There's no one there,' replied Churikova. 'My whole battalion was aboard that train. I'd rather stay here and wait for the next one.'

A few minutes later, as the Emka pulled out on to the road, Pekkala glanced back at the station. In the darkness, he could just make out the silhouette of Churikova. She stood alone in the middle of the deserted railyard, staring up at the stars as if to decipher the meaning of their placement in the universe.

Rifleman Stefanov breathed in sharply and sat up, pushing aside the olive-brown rain cape he had been using as a blanket. His back ached sharply from lying in the foxhole. Barkat's voice had woken him.

On the other side of the clearing, the gun-loader was moaning about the lost love of a woman named Ekaterina, whom he confessed was actually one of his cousins. 'I was going to marry her!' he announced.

'You can't do that!' shouted Ragozin, who had left behind a wife and three children when he enlisted. He always seemed to be on the verge of hysterics, when he was not actually hysterical.

'Can't do what?' asked Barkat. He was frying bread in a blackened mess kit full of bacon grease, which he had collected over several weeks.

'Marry your cousin is what! You'll end up with maniacs for children.'

'I don't think the correct word is "maniac",' said Stefanov.

'Well, forgive me, Professor!' Ragozin rolled his hand in mock obeisance.

'I can think of better uses for the word maniac,' replied Stefanov.

'I'm not going to marry her now,' said Barkat. With the

point of a bayonet, he poked the bread around the pan, chasing the bubbles of boiling bacon grease. 'I've changed my mind.'

'I used to worry that my wife couldn't manage without me.' Ragozin sighed and rubbed his face. 'Now I worry that she can. They're all long gone,' he muttered. 'Yours. Mine.' He wagged a finger in Barkat's direction. 'His sister or whoever she is. Every day that goes by is one step away from being able to pick up where we left off. Eventually, we'll all reach a point where we can never pick things up. We'll have to start again from scratch.'

At that moment, they heard a rumble of thunder in the distance.

'Oh, no, not rain,' groaned Ragozin. 'We'll drown in these foxholes if it pours.'

'It can't be rain,' Stefanov countered. 'The sky is clear.'

'He's right,' said Barkat.

The three men looked around in confusion.

'There!' Stefanov pointed towards the north, where a wild, flickering light danced along the horizon.

'They're bombing Leningrad,' Ragozin muttered sadly. 'That poor city. They used to love my radio broadcasts.'

On the ride back to Moscow, Pekkala remained silent. Ahead of them, the converging headlights of the Emka seemed to burrow the dirt road from the black cliff face of the night.

'Inspector,' asked Kirov, 'why did you seem so nervous back there?'

'The last time I saw eyes that colour was at the train station in Petrograd, back in 1917.'

'Your fiancée.'

Pekkala nodded.

Kirov was in no mood to commiserate. 'I don't understand you, Inspector. For nine years, you lived like a savage! Nine years of Siberian winters! By every law of nature, you should be dead by now. Sometimes I think the reason Stalin gives you the worst assignments is not only because no one else can solve them, but because nobody else could survive them. And, in spite of all you have endured, it is the eyes of a woman that defeat you.'

To this, Pekkala only shrugged and looked the other way.

They were back inside the city limits now, racing along the unlit streets.

'Shall I drop you at your apartment, Inspector? We could both use some sleep, you know.'

'No. We must keep working.'

'But you heard what the lieutenant said. Without the codex, deciphering the map becomes impossible.'

'*Virtually* impossible. That is what she said.'

With a sigh, Kirov turned down a potholed street which ran beside the Dorogomilovsky market and began the familiar bumpy ride towards their office.

It was after midnight. The market stalls were empty. A few tattered awnings flapped in the cold, damp breeze. In the distance, the pale sabres of searchlights from anti-aircraft batteries stationed in the Kuskovo Park scratched restlessly against the night sky.

Minutes later, they were trudging up the stairs to the fifth floor, the soles of their boots rasping against the worn wooden steps.

Once inside the office, Kirov turned on the light switch but nothing happened.

Pekkala waited in the hallway, the painting tucked under his arm, listening to the metronomic click as Kirov flipped the switch impatiently back and forth. 'Must be our turn for a black-out,' he grumbled.

There had been several of these in the past weeks, mostly at night, rolling like waves of darkness across the city. Initially, the Moscow authorities denied the existence of any black-outs. These denials only led to speculation that these electricity failures were the work of German spies. Since then, the official line had been changed to assure the people of Moscow that all black-outs were deliberate, but nobody believed that, either.

While Kirov lit an oil lamp, Pekkala cleared away every scrap of paper on the large notice board which covered one wall of their office, leaving behind a constellation of drawing pins in the cork backing.

Then Pekkala cleared everything off his desk except for the painting, the oil lamp and a roll of waxy baker's parchment which Kirov sometimes used for baking *piroshky*.

Kirov lit a fire in the old iron stove in the corner of their office and lit the samovar to boil water for tea. For a while, the only sound was of the kindling, spitting as it burned inside the stove.

Hunched over his desk, Pekkala laid a piece of parchment paper over the canvas. Then, using a pencil, he traced every line on the painting, including the tree branches in the background and the flecks of colour which had been daubed across the wings of the moth. He handed the tracing to Kirov. 'Pin this on the wall,' he said.

After that, Pekkala made a tracing only of the background, leaving the double-heart shape of the moth as a blank in the centre of the picture. This, too, went up on the wall.

Next, Pekkala traced only the lines within the wings of the moth. 'Pin this.'

Then he traced only the flecks and followed it with a sketch containing just the horizontal lines, and another with only verticals. All of these, he pinned up on the wall. Finally, when Pekkala could think of no other way of breaking down the framework of the picture, he stood back and surveyed the now-crowded cork board. The strange, skeletal images seemed to flutter through the air, brought to life by the motion of the oil lamp's flame.

'Do any of those look like a map to you?' he asked Kirov,

who had retreated to the chair behind his desk and now sat with his heels up on the blotter.

'Honestly? No.'

Behind him, faint breaths of steam seeped from the brass samovar's spout, as if it too were considering the situation.

Pekkala went over to the bookcase, from which he retrieved a folded map of the entire country. 'Is this the only one we've got?'

'We'd have room for more if you would get rid of those railway timetables,' replied Kirov.

It was true, the twenty-four volumes did take up half the shelf, but Pekkala chose to ignore the comment. He spent a minute unravelling the map which, like some complicated piece of origami, at first resisted all attempts at being unfolded. Having finally completed the task, Pekkala laid the chart on the floor and stood in the middle of it like a giant, one foot in the Ukraine and the other in Siberia, peering down at the arteries of rivers – the Volga, the Dnieper, the Yenisei – and at the dense muscularity of the Ural and Stanovoy mountains. 'Somewhere,' he muttered, 'the lines on that wall overlap with the contours on this map.'

'If what's hidden is even in Russia. And even if it is, you'll never find it, because the lines in that painting might represent a single street in a village so small it isn't even listed.' With that pronouncement, Kirov got up from his chair and headed over to the samovar, whose steady jet of steam had travelled to the window, painting it with beads of condensation. Then he set about preparing tea. From the window sill, between two kumquat trees whose orange fruit stood out against the blackness of the night beyond the windowpane like meteors hurtling to earth, Kirov fetched out an old tin, containing his precious supply of tea, from which he selected a pinch of black crumbs and sprinkled them into the samovar. 'Not much left,' he muttered, peering at the dwindled contents of the tin.

The dealers in the market had taken to shrugging their shoulders when Kirov chanted out the names of teas – Mudan, Jin Zan, Karavan – whose abundance he'd once taken for granted.

While the tea brewed, both men stood before the wall of sketches.

'The Germans already have maps of our country,' remarked Kirov. 'Maybe, instead of trying to figure out where this map is supposed to be, we should be asking ourselves what they need a map of that they don't already possess.'

Kirov's words snagged like a fish hook, trolling through Pekkala's brain. 'So what this is,' he began, advancing to the wall and touching his fingertips first against one tracing and then another, 'is of a place for which there was no map before.'

'Or else a place that has been changed,' suggested Kirov.

'The layout of a fortress, perhaps, just like the one drawn by the British spy.'

'Perhaps,' agreed Kirov, 'but what fortresses exist in the path of the German advance?'

'None,' admitted Pekkala.

The two men sighed as their train of thought ground to a halt.

The tea had brewed by now. From the drawer of his desk, Kirov brought out two tea glasses, each one nestled in a brass holder. He poured a small amount of tea into each one and added some boiling water to dilute the strong mixture, which would otherwise have been too bitter to drink.

Reaching across the map, he handed one glass to Pekkala.

'No sugar?' asked Pekkala.

'We have run out of that, as well,' Kirov replied gloomily.

As Pekkala breathed in the smell of the tea, its smoky odour reminded him of his cabin in Siberia, where, in the winter, he sometimes returned from hunting so frozen that he would curl up in his fireplace and warm himself by lying in the embers.

When the sun came up three hours later, splashing like molten copper across the slate rooftops of Moscow, Kirov and Pekkala were still staring at the wall, as helpless as they'd been when they first set eyes upon the painting.

'There must be some way of looking at them which we haven't tried yet,' said Pekkala.

Kirov tilted his head to the side and blinked at the wall.

'I doubt you have found the solution,' said Pekkala.

'I wasn't looking for one,' replied Kirov. 'I am simply too tired to hold my head up straight.'

Equally exhausted, Pekkala let his eyes droop shut for a moment. All the maps he'd ever seen crowded into view inside his skull. The lines of streets, the paths of rivers and the thumb-print contours of mountains flickered behind his eyes like a pack of shuffled playing cards. 'Go home, Kirov,' he said. 'Get some sleep.'

Kirov was too tired to argue. 'Very well, Inspector. But what about you?'

'I'm not tired,' lied Pekkala.

'I'll be back in a few hours.'

Pekkala listened to the heavy tread of Kirov's boots as he

made his way downstairs. Then came the bang of the heavy door at the front of the building and finally the rumble of the Emka as its engine sprang to life.

For a moment, Pekkala stared longingly at a chair in the corner. Two years before, Pekkala had salvaged the chair off the street after spotting it lying in the snow outside the Hotel Metropol. Before the Great War, the hotel had been famous as a meeting place for gamblers, spies and black market millionaires. Pekkala himself had often met there with the former Moscow Bureau Chief of the Okhrana, a fleshy man named Zubatov. Although Zubatov had been forced out of his position in 1903 by Interior Minister Vyachyslav von Plehve, he continued to work for the Okhrana as a field agent. He often smuggled himself into neighbouring countries with the help of a shadowy branch of the Okhrana, known as the Myednikov Section, who specialised in infiltrating foreign Intelligence networks. Using a variety of disguises and forged identities, Zubatov would hunt down any plots which might endanger the life of the Tsar. Rarely did he return without news of some conspiracy. His paranoia proved infectious, and it wasn't long before he had convinced the Tsarina to order the construction of hidden passageways within the Catherine and Alexander Palaces. These tunnels emerged in groves of trees outside the buildings themselves or even beyond the grounds of the estate. But it did not stop there. At Zubatov's urging, secret hiding places were built in all the residences at Tsarskoye Selo. Behind invisible doors, staircases carved out of the bedrock led to rooms deep beneath the ground. In these tomb-like chambers, members of the Romanov family, and anyone who worked for them, could vanish from the guns and knives of those who might come to do them harm.

Pekkala returned to the estate one evening to find the Tsar's horse tied to a fence post outside his cottage and the Tsar himself emerging from the front door.

'Pekkala! I have left you a present inside.'

'That is very kind of you, Majesty.'

The Tsar smiled. 'You might not think so when you see where I have left it.'

'It's not in the cottage?'

'It's underneath the cottage,' replied the Tsar, untying the horse and climbing into the saddle, 'in your own private sanctuary from the madmen of this world.'

Pekkala did not reply.

'I know how you feel about confined spaces,' the Tsar told him, 'and that you have no intention of going down into that hiding place if you can help it.'

'That would be correct,' replied Pekkala.

'So, as a reward, or call it a challenge if you like, I have gone down there myself and left you a bottle of my finest slivovitz plum brandy. All you have to do is go and get it.'

The construction of these hideaways did little to quell Zubatov's fears.

Although many of Zubatov's contemporaries believed him to be paranoid, the Okhrana had learned that it was better to err on the side of caution, in case the failure to report a legitimate threat would recoil upon their heads.

Inevitably, word would reach the Tsar.

Then the Tsar would summon Pekkala.

'Go to Moscow,' he would say. 'See what Zubatov has dreamed up this time.'

Zubatov insisted that all his meetings take place face to face, since he did not trust the phone system. As head of the Okhrana, Zubatov had tapped every phone exchange in the country, so there was good reason for his lack of faith.

'Will I find him at the Metropol?' asked Pekkala, his eyes glazing at the thought of another long train ride from St Petersburg.

'Of course,' replied the Tsar. 'That's the only place where he feels safe, although I'm damned if I know why.'

'It's because the anarchists also meet there, Excellency. They like the food too much to blow it up and Zubatov is convinced they are planning to turn it into their headquarters some day.'

The Tsar laughed. 'I know what you think of Zubatov, Pekkala, but please don't judge him too harshly. After all, he's only trying to save my life.'

But Pekkala knew this wasn't quite true. Zubatov's greatest fear was not the death of the Tsar, but rather the removal of the Tsar from power. In Zubatov's cold thinking, the Tsar himself could be replaced. But if the Tsar stepped down from power, Zubatov knew exactly who would seize control in the name of Revolution. Most of these men and women he knew by name, having spent his career trying to kill them.

In 1917, when the Tsar abdicated the throne, Zubatov's nightmare came true. After dinner with his family, Zubatov excused himself from the table and went out onto the balcony of their Moscow apartment to smoke a cigar. When the cigar was finished, instead of returning inside, he leapt to his death into the street below.

Although the chair's tapestry upholstering was faded and torn, Pekkala had immediately recognised the ornate wood-work on its arms as being the same type which once graced the lobby of the Metropol.

True to their word, the Bolshevik Central Committee had taken the hotel over as their headquarters during the 1920s, during which time most of its original furnishing, including the crystal chandeliers, polished brass and navy-blue carpeting, had lapsed into disrepair. Now that it had been converted once again into a grand hotel, frequented by foreign diplomats, journalists and actors, the original, dilapidated furniture often found its way out into the street.

Driving past the hotel one dreary winter's day, Pekkala had spotted the chair, covered with snow and left out for the sanitation department to remove, or for someone to smash to pieces, and use the wood for kindling.

'Stop!' Pekkala had ordered.

Kirov skidded to a halt. 'What is it, Inspector?'

Without a word of explanation, Pekkala left the car and picked up the chair. After carrying it to the Emka, he man-handled it into the boot.

In spite of Kirov's initial groan of disapproval, Pekkala had often since returned from meetings to find Kirov sitting fast asleep in the chair, arms folded on his stomach and heels resting on the edge of his desk.

Pekkala couldn't help wondering if he himself might once have sat in this same chair, head bowed towards Zubatov, while the man spelled out his fears.

Now Pekkala settled his body on to the battered upholstery, feeling the horsehair stuffing rustle as it took his weight. He had not slept for so long that his brain was grinding to a halt. His consciousness was fading away. The last things he saw as his eyes drooped shut were the drawings on the wall. They seemed to slide back and forth, one over the other, as if the puzzle of the red moth was trying to piece itself together.

While these images replayed in Pekkala's mind, something caught his attention.

Slowly, his eyes reopened.

Rising to his feet, Pekkala went to the wall and removed the tracing he had made of the background in the picture, which left the moth itself as an empty space in the drawing. Then he pulled down the drawing he had made which traced only the diagonal lines within the framework of the moth.

Carefully, he placed one drawing over the other.

Then he stood back, fingertips pressed expectantly together, and examined the combination of lines.

What Pekkala had noticed was that some of the lines of the background, which were made to look like branches, corresponded to some of the lines which had been drawn as patterns on the wings of the moth.

Now Pekkala made a third sketch, using only the lines which matched up.

With a grunt of anticipation, as if afraid the lines might at any moment rearrange themselves into obscurity, Pekkala lunged for the bookshelf and began hauling out the volumes of railway tables. In the twenty-four volumes of the Soviet railway system each district was given a letter. Within that district lay a numbered grid, which broke the district down into smaller sections. The front page of each volume contained a map of that grid, the remainder of the volume listed all trains either arriving in or departing from locations within it. Pekkala flipped through one and, not finding what he wanted, let it fall to the floor. Thirteen volumes later, he finally came across the chart which had flashed behind his eyelids, as if he had been staring at the sun.

The volume Pekkala had chosen contained the layout of the Leningrad district.

Returning to his desk, Pekkala laid the grid page next to the painting. For a moment, his eyes raced over the two images. Then his back straightened suddenly. 'There!' he shouted, momentarily startled by the sound of his own voice.

It wasn't the railway lines which had caught his attention. Instead, it was two crooked paths, at their widest in the top left-hand corner of the picture, and narrowing until they almost touched as they dropped down to the right. What Pekkala had noticed was that the course of these two lines, transforming from a tree branch into the pattern on the wings of the moth, corresponded exactly to the outline of the Gulf of Finland as it narrowed into the Neva River, which turned sharply to the right before trailing down to the bottom of the image, where it once again metamorphosed into the background of the picture, but he could see it now, like glimpsing the bones beneath the skin of a translucent deep-sea fish.

He could clearly make out the island of Kronstadt, depicted as a fleck of colour on the moth's wing. And there was the promontory where the fortress of Oranienbaum stood. His finger tapped nervously against the wide stretch of ground that marked the location of Peterhof.

By now, Pekkala was dizzy from concentrating, but he could not tear his eyes from the diagram. So many other lines and speckles criss-crossed the painting that he wondered if what he had found was nothing more than a coincidence, or else perhaps these other lines had just been placed there in order to camouflage the outline of the city.

He lost track of time.

Pekkala had no idea how long he had been staring at the painting when another idea began to take shape in his head. What if, he thought, the diagram contains not one map but two.

Within an hour, he had isolated everything which corresponded to the outlines of Leningrad. This left him with a strange, segmented shape which at first glance resembled an oblong piece of honeycomb, divided by a line down the middle. The segments were not symmetrical, however, nor were they all the same size.

This second map appeared to be a narrow street, with houses marked on opposite sides. It was obviously a built-up area, judging from the proximity of the buildings to each other.

Where before his mind had stalled out in the maze of dots and lines, now his brain seethed to the point of overload as layers of meaning appeared like mirages from the once indecipherable blur.

The next thing he knew, a bell was ringing in his ear.

Pekkala sat up with a snort. He had fallen asleep on the floor. Exhaustion had finally overtaken him. He had no memory of deciding to rest. He wondered for a moment if he had fainted as he sat there at his desk. A piece of wax paper was stuck to his forehead. He peeled it away and blinked as he tried to clear his blurry vision.

The bell rang again.

Kirov must have forgotten his key and is buzzing me from downstairs, Pekkala thought to himself as he got up and headed for the door.

The sky was glowing in the east. Soon the sun would rise above the rooftops of Moscow.

The bell rang a third time and he realised it wasn't the door buzzer. It was the telephone.

Pekkala spun around, walked to the far end of the room and grabbed the black receiver from its cradle.

'Have you figured it out?' asked a curt and hostile voice.

Pekkala didn't need to ask who it was. Only Poskrebychev, Stalin's perversely efficient secretary, would call this early in the morning and only Poskrebychev would begin a conversation without bothering to identify himself.

'We're close,' replied Pekkala.

'How close?' demanded Poskrebychev. 'Stalin wants to know precisely where you are with this.'

'It's a map,' explained Pekkala.

'What is?' Poskrebychev's voice rose in confusion. 'I was asking about the painting, the one with the butterfly or moth or whatever it is.'

'The painting is a map,' Pekkala told him. 'Actually, it appears to be two maps, one overlapping the other.'

'A map?' Poskrebychev repeated. 'Are you sure?'

'Yes! It is somewhere in the district of Leningrad. I hope to have it narrowed down within the next few hours.'

'It's a good thing you didn't need that woman's help after all. What was her name? Churikova?'

'But she did help. Lieutenant Churikova helped a great deal.'

'Impossible. The woman is dead!'

Pekkala felt a jolt, as if a door had been slammed inside his chest. 'What are you talking about, Poskrebychev?'

'Her train was bombed last night. Blown to pieces. I heard they found one of the engine's wheels more than half a kilometre away.'

As Pekkala struggled to absorb the information, Churikova's blue eyes seemed to radiate inside his skull, like lights shining up from deep water.

'The whole cryptographic section was wiped out,' continued Poskrebychev. 'It is a shame. We could have—'

'Wait a minute!' Pekkala cut him off. 'Churikova wasn't with the cryptographic section. She was ordered off the transport after we put in a call to the station. She missed that train, Poskrebychev!'

'Then she owes you her life, Pekkala. If it hadn't been for you she'd be scattered across the Russian countryside by now.'

'And where is she now?' asked Pekkala.

'I'm damned if I know. Either she's on a different train or else she's still sitting there at Ostankinsky station.'

'I'm on my way there now. Tell Comrade Stalin we will have an answer for him as soon as we can.'

'Soon might not be soon enough, Pekkala. The Wehrmacht are almost at the gates of Leningrad.'

'When are they expected to enter the city?'

'They aren't,' said Poskrebychev. 'It appears that the Germans have something else in mind for Leningrad.'

'What do you mean?' asked Pekkala.

'Intelligence reports indicate that they are encircling the city. They are laying siege, Pekkala. If what you need to find is inside Leningrad you had better get in there and get yourself back out again before the Germans complete the encirclement. By Christmas, the people of Leningrad will be eating rats. If it lasts any longer than that, they're going to start eating each other.' With those words, Poskrebychev ended the call.

Pekkala replaced the receiver, hearing the distinctive click as the cradle took its weight, the sound like a child clicking its teeth together.

Moments later, Kirov returned to the office. 'You didn't sleep, did you?' he asked as he removed his gun belt and hung it on a coat peg by the door. 'I had a little bet with myself that you wouldn't even close your eyes . . .'

'It's Leningrad.'

Kirov stopped in his tracks. 'You figured it out?'

Pekkala showed him the railway map, then the overlapping maps he had traced off the painting.

'I see that your memorising of those timetables wasn't complete madness after all.'

'We must speak to Churikova again,' said Pekkala. 'She might be able to help us pinpoint the exact street more quickly than if we were working on our own. Call the station. Ask if she's still there.'

'Inspector, that's virtually impossible. You saw how anxious she was to catch up with her section and these days there must be half a dozen troop trains passing through Ostankinsky every night. She would have just hopped on the next one headed west.'

'The Germans bombed the train she was supposed to have been on. Her entire section was wiped out. They probably destroyed the tracks as well. She might still be at the station.'

'Very well, Inspector. I guess it's worth a try.'

Minutes later, they were on the road.

This time, Pekkala sat behind the wheel. As always, he drove fast and recklessly. Each time they were forced to stop, he waited until the last moment before slamming on the brakes. Then he floored the accelerator to get the Emka rolling again.

Kirov, meanwhile, was studying the painting so intently that he barely seemed to notice as he lurched back and forth in his seat. Scattered in the seat well at his feet were the numerous sketches Pekkala had made. Reaching down, Kirov snatched one up and held it beside the red moth. With one eye closed and the other squinting as if he were aiming down the barrel of a gun, Kirov compared the painting to the sketch which formed the branches of the tree. 'I see the Neva!' he exclaimed. 'I see the Gulf of Finland!'

'But what about the pattern on the wings?' asked Pekkala. 'What street is it depicting? There can't be too many places in Leningrad where the houses are bunched so closely together.'

Kirov fished around in the seat well until he came up with

the sketch he wanted. 'Inspector,' he said, 'I don't think this is a street map.'

'What? It has to be! Those little squares and rectangles are houses.'

'No.' Kirov shook his head. 'There are two layers of these shapes on either side of what you are calling a street.'

'Then those must be gardens behind the houses.'

'Inspector, houses this densely packed in the city of Leningrad would not have gardens.'

'But what else could it possibly be?'

By now, they had put central Moscow behind them and were travelling through an area of warehouses and factories, some of which were only half finished and whose construction had been abandoned at the outset of the war. Gaps left for windows in the brickwork assumed the hollowness of eye sockets in skulls.

'It's an apartment building,' said Kirov. 'It has to be. This thing you call a street is actually some kind of hallway, with rooms leading off it on either side. At least . . .' Kirov's doubts began to overtake him. Frowning, he turned the first one way and then the other.

'They're the wrong shape. Where are all the entran—?' And even as Pekkala spoke, the words froze upon his lips.

He slammed on the brakes.

The Emka skidded until it was almost sideways, finally halting in the middle of the road.

'Why have we stopped?' shouted Kirov. 'You haven't spotted another one of those hotel chairs, have you?'

'Give me the painting,' said Pekkala.

Kirov handed it over.

A car approached them, headed in the opposite direction. The driver slowed as he passed, eyeing them suspiciously, and did not stop.

'Look, Inspector,' began Kirov, 'maybe you're right. I don't know Leningrad that well. They could be gardens, I suppose.'

'They aren't,' murmured Pekkala. 'They're rooms.'

'Rooms? What kind of apartment building has so many rooms laid out in rows like that?'

'A palace,' replied Pekkala.

'But there are many palaces in Leningrad. There's the Winter Palace, the Stroganov, the Menshikov, the Taurida . . .'

'This is the layout of the Catherine Palace. I'm sure of it. There,' he said, aiming with the tip of his finger at the honeycomb of cells. 'The Arabesque Hall, the Blue Drawing Room, the Stasov Staircase. The sizes all match. The spaces you thought were gardens are the rooms up on the second floor.' While he spoke, Pekkala's eyes darted back and forth over the canvas. It was as if the insect had disintegrated, and from the blur of colours, the skeletal frame of the palace had risen to take its place.

At first, the uniformity of each tiny blue and red and green paint fleck, mirrored in both of the wings, seemed to rule out any correlation between the colours and the rooms. But then he spotted a mistake. One of the cells on the right wing had been painted orange, whereas the same marking on the left wing was red. 'There,' he told Kirov, pointing out the tiny dabs of paint. 'These are the only two which don't match. There is red elsewhere in the design but this is the only place where the painter has used orange.'

'What room is that?' asked Kirov.

Pekkala closed his eyes, concentrating as he drifted like a ghost through each room along that corridor. 'The White Dining Room. The Crimson Dining Room. The Green Dining Room. The Portrait Gallery.' And then he paused. His eyes flicked open. 'The Amber Room,' he said.

As moonlight glinted off the shattered windows of the Catherine Palace, Stefanov surveyed the damage he had done. It was not only windows he had broken while blazing away with the anti-aircraft gun. The walls and doors and railings also bore the scars of bullet strikes. He had expected Commissar Sirko to say something about it, but all the commissar had done was to place the building off limits. The man seemed much more concerned about the plane Stefanov had brought down, and had even scrounged up a small pot of paint and a brush for Stefanov to paint a white band on the barrel of his gun, signifying their first kill.

Wrapped in the oil-stained blanket of his rain cape, Stefanov climbed out of his foxhole. Out in the darkness, he could see the little cooking fires of the other gun crews, and the glow of burning cigarettes. The rough smell of *machorka* tobacco reached him on the still night air.

He walked over to the tiny crater Barkat had dug for himself. 'Barkat,' whispered Stefanov.

'What is it?'

'I was thinking we might take a look around the palace.'

'What? Now?'

'Why not?'

'You mean walk around the outside?'

'We could maybe take a look inside as well.'

Now Ragozin appeared from his foxhole where, also unable to sleep, he had been eavesdropping on the conversation. 'What's this? You can't go inside the palace. Commissar Sirko has forbidden it.'

Barkat sighed irritably. 'Were you like this as a child, Ragozin? Did you tell on people in the school yard?'

'Commissar Sirko—' Ragozin began.

Barkat didn't let him finish. 'Is not here! He's wandered off somewhere and found himself a bed in which to sleep. Now are you coming to look around the palace or aren't you?' he demanded, as if it had been his idea all along.

'There might be food,' added Stefanov, removing from his mess kit a piece of Russian army bread which had been steeped in grease and allowed to congeal, forming it into a waxy brick. Contemptuously, he tossed it into Ragozin's lap. 'Better than this stuff.'

'Food,' Barkat egged on Ragozin. 'I bet they've got everything in there.' Thoughtfully, he set a strand of grass between his teeth. It hung from his mouth like the tongue of a snake.

'Shut up,' Ragozin told him. 'You know I am starving to death.'

'The Romanovs could have anything they wanted,' Barkat assured him.

Ragozin huffed. 'They've been gone a long time.'

'But who knows what they left behind, eh?' Barkat broke in.

'Oh, fine!' Ragozin threw up his hands. 'You realise we'll all probably end up in a penal battalion because of this. Still, it would be worth it as long as we can scrounge up something better than the canned pig skin I've been living off ever since I joined the Red Army!'

Cloaked in the darkness, the three men set out across the park.

Kirov and Pekkala sat in the Emka, which was still in the middle of the road.

'You've been in the Amber Room, haven't you?' asked Kirov.

'Of course,' replied Pekkala. 'I met the Tsar there many times.'

'Then can you tell me why the Fascists would be so concerned with getting their hands on it?'

'If you had ever seen it for yourself,' Pekkala told him, 'you wouldn't need to ask the question. And if the sight of it wasn't enough to convince you, then consider that the amber in that room is worth ten times its weight in gold.'

'And how much amber is in the room?'

'Seven tons of it,' replied Pekkala.

'What are they planning to do?' asked Kirov. 'Tear the walls apart?'

'They wouldn't have to,' Pekkala informed him, 'because the amber is not actually embedded in the walls. It's fitted into panels, some about twice the height of a man and others which would come up to your waist. Once those had been removed, the room would be an empty shell.'

'I am beginning to understand,' said Kirov. 'We should go straight to the Kremlin. Now that you've figured out the purpose of the map, Comrade Stalin will want to know immediately.'

'Not before I have confirmation from Lieutenant Churikova that my assumptions are correct. There are still many questions which have yet to be answered. Like why those two men would have been transporting the map when it was already too late to get their hands on the amber.'

'Why is it too late?'

'The contents of the room, including the amber, were evacuated to safety, along with most of the other treasures in the palace. Everything has been boxed up and shipped east of the Ural mountains. The Amber Room is somewhere in Siberia by now. I heard about it on State radio over two weeks ago, but it's only been seventy-two hours since the two men who were carrying the painting went down over our lines.'

'Perhaps they didn't hear the broadcast,' suggested Kirov. 'I know I didn't.'

'The Germans monitor Russian State Radio, just as we monitor all of their radio stations. They would have known, for sure. And there's something else I can't figure out.'

'What's that, Inspector?'

'The location of the Amber Room is not a secret. It has been there for two hundred years. Why would someone go to the trouble of preparing an elaborately coded message to inform the Germans of something they could find out from any art history book?'

'A pity we don't have Comrade Ostubafengel to speak with,' said Kirov, remembering the word they had found scrawled on the back of the canvas. 'I'm sure he could have told us everything.'

'Let's hope Lieutenant Churikova has the answers,' Pekkala remarked as he put the car in gear and steered them back on course towards the train station.

On their previous visit to Ostankinsky, they had found the place almost deserted. Now hundreds of soldiers crammed the railyard. Some lay sleeping on the ground, using their rucksacks as pillows. Other sat in tight circles, playing cards or coaxing mess tins full of water to the boil over fires made from twigs.

Many looked up when they heard the growling of the Emka's engine, hoping that some other form of transport might have arrived at last. Seeing only one four-seater car, the optimism faded from their eyes.

'All the trains must be held up because of the bombing last night,' said Pekkala. 'She's probably still here.'

'But how are we going to find her in that crowd?' wondered Kirov.

Pekkala turned to him. 'I believe I have the solution.'

Five minutes later, Kirov was making his way along the spine of the steeply angled roof, his arms held out to the side and wobbling unsteadily, like a tightrope walker high above the big ring of a circus.

By now, every pair of eyes in the railyard was following his progress.

'Go on, Commissar!' shouted a soldier, who wore a filthy greatcoat so long that it trailed along the ground as he walked towards the station house. 'Jump! Jump!'

Arriving at the centre of the roof, Kirov came to a stop. Slowly, he turned to face the crowd and cupped his hands to his mouth. 'I am looking for a woman!'

At first, the soldiers simply stared at him in confusion.

Then, one by one, came the replies.

'Let me know when you find her!' shouted a soldier, rising slowly to his feet, a fan of playing cards clutched in his fist.

'I am also looking for a woman!' boomed another man, raising his rifle in the air. 'She must report to me at once!'

'Come down here, Comrade Commissar,' called a broad-faced man with piggy eyes, his head so closely shaved that his scalp gleamed in the sun. Unlike the others, this man did not smile as he hurled his insults at the figure on the roof. 'Come down here and . . .'

A shot rang out across the station yard.

Hundreds of men flinched simultaneously. The laughter ceased abruptly.

Kirov waited until the last sliver of smoke had escaped from the barrel of his Tokarev before replacing the weapon in its holster. 'Her name,' he called into the silence, 'is Lieutenant Churikova!'

There was a creaking sound, which seemed to come from directly beneath Kirov's feet. It crossed his mind that the roof might be collapsing under him.

But the sound was from the door of the station house, which now fell back with a clatter against its crooked frame.

A soldier walked down the three steps of the station house into the dust of the railyard, then stopped and turned. It was Churikova. She squinted up at Kirov, half blinded by the sun behind his back. 'I didn't think I'd seen the last of you,' she said.

On the ground once again, Kirov led Churikova to the Emka, where Pekkala handed her one sketch after another as he explained what they had learned about the map.

Churikova examined each one, carefully and in silence.

'Well?' Pekkala asked, unable to disguise his impatience. 'What do you think?'

It was a moment before she replied. 'I think you are correct,' she said at last, 'but even if you have deciphered this Baden-Powell diagram, the map contained within it has no purpose any more. You must have heard the broadcast on State Radio, reporting that the Amber Room has been removed from the Palace. What's more, even if the Kremlin hasn't admitted it yet, every soldier in that railyard knows that the Germans will soon be at the gates of Leningrad. The Catherine Palace lies directly in the path of their advance. Whatever information this map might have provided is useless now. You might as well throw it away.'

'Before I can do that,' replied Pekkala, 'there is someone who will want to hear the opinion of an expert. For that, I must bring you back to Moscow.'

'Who is this person?'

'You will know him when you see him.'

'But I have a train to catch,' protested Churikova. 'I must rejoin my battalion.'

Kirov and Pekkala exchanged glances, realising that the results of last night's bombing raid had either been suppressed by the authorities, or else had not yet reached the Ostankinsky railyard.

Pekkala opened the door of the Emka, gesturing for Churikova to take a seat. 'Please, Lieutenant,' he said gently.

Driving back to Moscow, Pekkala relayed the grim details about the train which had been hit.

Churikova struggled to absorb the information. 'Surely they weren't all killed, Inspector? There must have been survivors.'

Pekkala thought of what Poskrebychev had told him about the wheel which had been found over half a kilometre from the wreck. He imagined it, smouldering in the dirt like a meteor which had just collided with the earth. 'I am told that there were none.'

Having crossed the wide expanse of the Alexander Park, the three men stood at last before the entrance to the Catherine Palace.

Stefanov tried the doors but found them both locked.

'Well, what did you expect?' hissed Ragozin. 'We should go back at once!'

But Barkat had already climbed in through a broken window. A moment later, there was a rattling as he slid back the bolt. 'Your majesties,' he said, swinging wide the double doors, and bowing extravagantly as the other two walked past him into the palace.

In front of them, the grand staircase rose up into the darkness of the floor above. At the base of the stairs, balanced on a short white marble pillar, stood a huge porcelain vase, strangely out of place in the otherwise empty hallway.

The three men went over to the vase, drawn to it like boys towards a pie left on a window sill to cool. Barkat wrapped his arms around the vase. 'Maybe I can get this into the truck.'

'You shouldn't do that,' muttered Stefanov, but even as he spoke, he wished he had thought of it first.

Barkat grunted. 'I can't even lift it!'

'Let me try,' said Ragozin, pushing Barkat aside. He had no luck either. 'This thing is heavy!' he whispered.

Now it was Stefanov's turn. Folding his arms around the vase, he hugged the vase to his chest, braced his legs and lifted. The vase seemed to shift, as if it was a living thing determined to stay rooted to the spot. And then he understood why none of them could move it. The vase was filled with water.

'Why would they do that?' asked Ragozin.

'Maybe it had flowers in it,' suggested Barkat.

'No,' said Stefanov. 'It's so the vase won't shatter from the concussion of an exploding shell. My family used to live right by the railroad tracks. Sometimes those trains would make the whole house shake. If the vibration reached a certain pitch, it could shatter a window, or a glass inside a cabinet, or a vase. At home, my father used to fill our only flower vase with water, so that it could absorb the shock. Whoever did this,' Stefanov tapped a fingernail against the vase, 'thinks there's going to be a battle here. Come on. We have to hurry. It's this way.'

Although Ragozin had brought an army-issue torch, there was enough moonlight coming in from outside that they could make their way around without it.

Instead of climbing the stairs, the three men went through a doorway to the right and entered a space which had once been the picture hall. No paintings hung there now and the gaping frames that once contained them lay scattered on the floor amongst handfuls of straw and a pile of empty, musty-smelling suitcases.

Of the furniture that once decorated the hall, only a single sideboard cabinet remained, its drawers pulled out and missing, as if the place had already been looted. On top of the sideboard, looking strangely out of place, sat a broken American-made Sylvania radio, the guts of its wires hanging out the back.

Ragozin gently took the radio in both hands and lifted it so that the speaker pressed against his ear. 'They listened to me on this,' he whispered. 'My voice came out through here. I can feel it.'

Thick velvet curtains still hung in front of the windows, moonlight winking through tears in the fabric where Stefanov's gunfire had smashed through the window and strewn the floor with dagger-like shards of glass.

'Where is everything?' whispered Barkat. 'Where did they put it all?'

Stefanov said nothing. He had heard stories, assembled piece by rumoured piece, about what had become of the treasures of Tsarskoye Selo. In the years after the Revolution, the office of Internal State Security, known to men like Stefanov simply as the 'Organi', had taken over one wing of the Alexander Palace, for use as a rest home for their senior officers. In reality, it was just a place for them to bring their mistresses. Things soon began to disappear, not just from the Alexander Palace but from the Catherine Palace as well. In the beginning, they were only small items, like letter openers and fountain pens. Later, whole paintings went missing, along with icons, lamps and even life-size statues, only to reappear for sale in the auction houses of London, Paris and Rome.

They arrived at a closed door.

Stefanov took hold of the brass handle, but remained frozen, as if suddenly afraid to go on.

'What are you waiting for?' demanded Barkat.

Stefanov knew that beyond this door lay the Amber Room, which his father had once described to him as the place where the walls were on fire.

At first, Stefanov had dismissed the old man's description as another figment of his primitive and superstitious mind. But then, one summer evening, when many of the palace windows had been opened to let out the heat of the day, Stefanov had caught a glimpse of what at first he took to be flames, leaping from the walls inside.

The next day, in school, it was his teacher, Madame Simonova, rumoured to be the fiancée of Inspector Pekkala, who had provided the explanation. The thousands of pieces of amber, each one worked into huge panels, reflected the light in such a way that they sometimes appeared to glow like embers.

Stefanov longed to see the Amber Room, but the palace was off limits to all but specially appointed staff, of which his father, the gardener, was not one. And if the chances of Stefanov's father getting in were zero, his own seemed even less. In spite of this, he couldn't let it rest. Thoughts of the amber consumed him and it was not long before he had devised a scheme to catch a glimpse inside the room.

The following week, he casually mentioned to his father that the ornamental hedges which lined the base of the Catherine Palace looked as if they needed trimming. Being well aware that this job required the use of ladders, and that his father did not like to climb on ladders, it came as no surprise to him when, a few days later, his father assigned him the task of trimming the hedges.

By ten o'clock the next morning, when Stefanov arrived for work, he had already planned it all out. He would have been there sooner, except it was not allowed to begin work anywhere on the estate before that time, in case the Tsarina was still asleep and might be woken by the noise.

The Amber Room lay nearly in the middle of the palace, on the ground floor, between the Hall of Pictures and the Portrait Gallery. For Stefanov, the simplest course of action would have been to begin working on the hedge directly beneath the windows of the Amber Room, but he reasoned that this would soon alert any bystanders to his real motive. Instead, beginning outside the choir anteroom on the left-hand side of the building, Stefanov worked his way across the front of the palace. It was difficult balancing on the rickety, paint-spattered ladder and the repetitive motion of cutting with the shears soon caused the muscles of his forearms to cramp. His only consolation was the fact that the hedge didn't need trimming as badly as he had conveyed to his father, and the old man had taken his son's word for it, rather than wait and risk having to do the job himself.

Finally, the young Stefanov arrived beneath the large double windows of the Amber Room, the bases of which stood about twice the height of a man above the level of the ground. Sweat pasted his shirt to his back. His head was reeling in the still, close heat of that July afternoon. He set up the ladder, careful to position it in such a way that he would, if he looked up from his cutting, be able to see directly into the room.

Slowly, Stefanov climbed the ladder and began his work, blinking sweat from his eyes as he snipped away at those individual branches of the hedge which had dared to grow beyond the level of the rest. The noise of the shears filled his brain, its sound like a clashing of daggers. At first he did not dare look up, petrified that someone might be watching.

Finally, Stefanov judged that the moment was right. At this point, he still had his back to the window. Glancing from beneath the brim of his cap, he scanned the grounds, in case anyone else might be watching. He had been planning this moment for so long that his mind had begun to play tricks on him. The act of simply peering into the room had, in Stefanov's mind, taken on the magnitude of a great crime, the punishment for which lay beyond his comprehension.

The grounds were empty. Anyone with any sense was sleeping in the shade. Heat haze weaved and shimmered off the crushed stone of the riding path, as if ghostly horses were galloping by.

He began to turn, his movements practised and precise. The great glass panes slid into view. At first all he could see was his own reflection: a damp, dishevelled figure, unrecognisable even to himself. Slowly, however, like someone staring at the ripples on a pond, his eyes began to make out the interior of the room. He saw a desk, a chair, and a table on which he could make out the figures of a chess set. The walls looked dirty and mottled, as if they were covered with a layer of soot. He bared his teeth in concentration, leaning towards the glass until his breath condensed upon its surface. Now he began to see the colours. The walls took on a deep brownish-orange tint, and he could not escape from the notion that they were, in fact, on fire, and that his father had been right all along. Now the colour changed, both lightening and deepening at the same time. The whole room appeared to be losing its shape, expanding into that strange and parallel dimension, of which his father had always been aware. The amber seemed to shudder, as if the light of the sun which streamed into the room had brought the ancient sap to life.

In that moment, Stefanov finally grasped why the delicate

amber was so valuable, and it did not surprise him that the Romanovs had learned to covet the substance whose origins were still a mystery to him. In fact, it seemed the perfect treasure for the Tsar and his family. Everything about the Romanovs had always seemed to Stefanov to exist in a separate dimension, whose glittering fragility could not endure the crude and rough-hewn world in which he lived.

Suddenly, a figure materialised inside the room. It advanced upon him, drifting across the floor, seemingly enveloped in white smoke. Another angel, his heat-dimmed mind announced, seeking vengeance for my crimes.

His legs began to shake. His left knee buckled. He did not fall exactly. It was more like a slow, clumsy, painfully controlled descent, bumping down the rungs on elbows, knees and chin until he came to rest upon the ground. High above him, the handles of the shears poked like the ears of a wooden rabbit from the top of the hedge.

There was a rattling noise and the double windows swung open. He saw two arms, swathed in the thin fabric of a white summer dress, and then a face. He gasped. It was the Princess Olga. Or was she a Grand Duchess? Suddenly, he could not remember. All of the Tsar's daughters looked somewhat similar to him. They usually wore the same clothes and had more or less the same hairstyles. There was little to tell them apart, as far as Stefanov was concerned, but Olga's face had always seemed to him the most distinctive. Her almond-shaped eyes and the steadiness of her gaze would have made her appearance too severe if it weren't for the fullness of her lips. He had fallen in and out of love with her several times already.

She stared down at him, her expression a mixture of amusement and concern. 'Are you hurt?' she asked.

Stefanov knew that the correct response when in the presence of a Romanov was to take off his cap and hold it in his hand and to look at the ground before answering any question. But his cap had fallen off and it seemed foolish to be staring at the earth when he was already lying upon it. So he stared at Olga, eyes wide in awe and fear. 'I'm not hurt,' he finally managed to say.

'What is your name?' asked the Princess.

'Stefanov. I am the son of the head gardener, Agripin Dobrushinovich Stefanov.'

'Well, Stefanov, son of the head gardener, you should be more careful in future.' She smiled at him, then closed the windows and from somewhere in the room came the sound of men and women laughing.

Too ashamed to feel his pain, Stefanov retrieved the shears, found his cap and, with sweat stinging in his eyes, carried the ladder back to the work shed, where the implements for gardening were stored.

Along the way, Stefanov pondered the repercussions he felt sure would follow soon. No doubt, he thought, the Princess would not hesitate to tell the story of him lying there in the dirt, and fumbling with his words as he identified himself. The Tsar himself would hear of it. Or worse. The Tsarina. Perhaps they already knew. Maybe it was their laughter he had heard after Olga closed the window. But now what? Would they punish him? Would they punish his father? And what would the punishment be? Would the Emerald Eye be summoned?

For days, Stefanov lived in terror of the moment when

Pekkala himself would come knocking on the door to his family's cottage.

But it never happened. Gradually Stefanov transformed from being certain of disaster to being only reasonably sure and from there he went to suspecting and finally, at the end of this strange journey, he arrived at a state of relieved confusion where he had been, more or less, ever since.

He would see the Princess Olga only once again, on a bitterly cold night in March of 1917.

Petrograd had fallen to the revolutionaries. Rumours reached Tsarskoye Selo that an 8,000-strong mob of soldiers, deserters from the army, was heading towards the estate with the intention of destroying the palaces and murdering anyone inside them.

With the Tsar still en route by train from the military headquarters at Mogilev, the Tsarina Alexandra summoned all troops still loyal to the Romanovs, including the Garde Equipage, the military escort of the royal yacht, to take up defensive positions around the Alexander Palace, which was the residence of the Tsar and his family when they were staying at Tsarskoye Selo. In all, these soldiers numbered some 1,500 men, including Stefanov's father, who had brought along his son to offer their assistance.

Confronted with the old gardener and his son, who was too awestruck by the ranks of uniforms and bayonet-fixed rifles even to speak, the soldiers turned them away. Hearing this, Stefanov's father threw himself at the mercy of the troops, pointing out to them that he had nowhere else to go and stood little chance of survival if thousands of armed hooligans came swarming across the estate.

After a brief consultation among the officers, Stefanov and his son were allowed to remain, provided they kept out of the way.

All day, with fingers on the triggers of their guns, the loyal soldiers waited for the revolutionaries to arrive. But the mob never materialised and, by that evening, the nerves of the men were frayed almost to breaking point.

Throughout that night, the soldiers kept their watch.

Although several of the Tsar's daughters had come down with measles, the Tsarina emerged several times from the Palace, drifting through the courtyard in her black fur cloak and pleading with the soldiers to remain vigilant. No fires were lit, in order to deny the enemy the advantage of illumination.

It was on one of these visits that the Tsarina, accompanied by her daughter Olga, chanced upon Stefanov and his father, who were sitting on the steps with only a piece of cardboard to insulate them from the stone. They were, by then, so frozen, that it was only with difficulty that the old man and his son were able to get to their feet.

'What are you doing here?' asked Olga, having recognised the gardener's son. In spite of the cold, her face was glistening with sweat brought on by sickness.

'Who is this?' demanded the Tsarina, before either of them could reply. Her face, framed by the fur of her hooded cloak, looked pale and haggard.

It was Olga who answered for them. 'It's the gardener, Agripin, and his boy.' In spite of her illness, Olga smiled at Stefanov.

'And what are you doing here?' the Tsarina asked. Her voice sounded harsh and impatient.

'Majesty,' explained Agripin, 'we came to help.'

The Tsarina's tone changed suddenly. 'But the soldiers are here. Your duties do not lie with them. There is nothing you can do.'

Agripin drew himself up to his full height, which was not considerable. 'There would be if I had a gun,' he said.

Overhearing this comment, some of the soldiers began to laugh.

'Perhaps you would do better with a shovel,' said one.

'Or a rake!' added another.

Seeing his father mocked by the soldiers, the young Stefanov felt ashamed. Helplessly, he looked down at his feet.

Agripin glared at the soldiers. Then he faced the Tsarina again. 'Majesty,' he said solemnly, 'I would rather help you now than spend the rest of my life knowing that I could have and didn't.'

For a moment, the Tsarina said nothing. Then she turned to the soldiers. 'Get this man a rifle,' she commanded.

Two weeks later, on the orders of the Tsar himself, Stefanov and his father loaded their belongings on to a cart and left the grounds of the estate, bound for the home of a relative. But they did not stay long. In the years that followed, Agripin and his son made their way from town to town, working in fields, repairing walls, doing any job that would guarantee a meal and a roof over their heads. Fearing reprisals from the revolutionary committees that maintained a choke-hold on every village in Russia, Agripin never mentioned his years of service to the Tsar and, likewise, his son remained silent.

Now, deep within the deserted hallways of the Catherine

Palace, Ragozin shoved Stefanov out of the way, opened the door, and the three men piled into the room.

Ragozin turned on his torch. The weak light played across a high ceiling and smooth, bare walls which were the same pale blue green as a duck's egg.

'But this is the Amber Room!' gasped Stefanov.

'You must have it wrong,' whispered Barkat. His footsteps echoed in the empty space

'This *is* the Amber Room,' insisted Stefanov. 'I'm sure of it.'

'Maybe it was,' quipped Ragozin. 'But it isn't any more.'

Then, from the main entrance, they heard a voice call out, 'Who's there?'

'That's Commissar Sirko!' Barkat hissed. 'If he catches us in here . . .'

The three men panicked. They ran to the window, opened it and jumped down into the garden. It was a hefty drop, but their falls were broken by the same ornamental hedge which Stefanov had trimmed that summer day, already lifetimes ago.

'Is anyone there?' Sirko called out.

Stefanov, Ragozin and Barkat sprinted across the Alexander Park, their long shadows, lapis blue in moonlight, pursuing them across the grounds. By the time they reached their gun emplacement, all three were out of breath. Looking back, they saw the blade of a torch splashing across the empty walls of the Portrait Hall, as Commissar Sirko continued his hunt for intruders.

Their moment of relief was cut short by a grinding, squeaking, metallic sound, like that of a huge machine whose moving parts required oil, which reached them on the night breeze from somewhere to the west.

'Tanks,' said Barkat.

'Can you tell if it's ours or theirs?' asked Stefanov.

It was Ragozin who replied. 'Whoever they belong to, they're headed straight towards us.'

While Pekkala made his report about the map to Stalin, Kirov and Churikova waited in the outer office.

'You should have told me we were coming here!' she whispered urgently to Kirov.

'Would it have made any difference if I had?'

'Perhaps she would have told you no,' remarked Poskrebychev, 'as perhaps she already has.' He had not only been eavesdropping on their conversation but had also been listening to them in the next room via the intercom that connected the inner and outer offices.

Kirov shot him a hostile glance. 'You are an irritating little man, Poskrebychev.'

'And you are not the first to tell me so.'

Behind the closed doors, Stalin sat in his red leather chair, a cigarette wedged between his fingers. Several piles of paperwork had been swept aside to make room for the canvas, which Stalin examined carefully as Pekkala, standing on the other side of the desk, explained where the maps lay buried in the picture. 'Remarkable,' muttered Stalin. Not taking his eyes from the picture, he fitted the cigarette between his lips. The tip glowed red, crackling faintly and Stalin drew the smoke into his lungs. 'Devious. Diabolical!'

'It may be all those things,' Pekkala told him, 'but it is also useless now, as Lieutenant Churikova will explain to you.' Pekkala gestured towards the door. 'If you will permit me to bring her in.'

'Before you bring in this expert, tell me what *you* think. Have we deciphered the full meaning of the map or haven't we?'

'Not all of my questions have been answered,' admitted Pekkala, 'such as who made it and who was its intended recipient, but I do think the map no longer serves the purpose for which it was intended. As you will recall from the broadcast on State Radio, the amber itself has been moved to a safe location in the Ural mountains, along with all the other treasures in the palace . . .'

'Ah.' Stalin leaned back in his chair, stroking his moustache with tobacco-yellowed fingertips. 'Then we may have a problem, after all.'

'What kind of problem, Comrade Stalin?'

'The removal of those treasures was not carried out as efficiently as the news broadcast implied.'

'You mean they didn't move the art works?'

'Oh, they moved some of them.' Stalin brushed his hand casually through the air, 'but there were too many objects and too little time. The curators ran out of packing materials. In the end, they resorted to using the Tsar's collection of luggage, which was itself extremely valuable, for transporting things out of Pushkin. Huge statues had to be protected. They couldn't be moved, so engineers blasted craters in the palace ground and buried them. It was a monumental task, but, in the end, dozens of paintings, priceless vases and entire rooms of furniture were left behind.'

'But what about the Amber Room, Comrade Stalin? Surely that would have been a top priority.'

'Indeed it was. The panels were to have been included in the first transport and, if everything had gone according to plan, they would, by now, be safe from the clutches of the Fascists. But when the curators attempted to remove the panels from the walls, they turned out to be too fragile. The curators quickly realised that the amber would never have survived the journey to Siberia.'

'So what did they do instead?' asked Pekkala.

'The curators decided that their only option was to leave the panels where they were, but to conceal them beneath layers of muslin cloth, which were then papered over in order to give the impression that the space had been transformed into an ordinary room.'

Pekkala tried to imagine the amber muffled behind wallpaper, but in his mind its honeyed light kept burning through, as if the whole palace was blazing.

'Afterwards,' continued Stalin, 'I approved an announcement on our national radio that the amber had been transported far from the palace. We knew that the Germans would be listening to the broadcast, and gambled that they might believe what they were hearing, especially when all they found was ordinary paper on the walls. Adding to the illusion, I also declared the Amber Room to be an irreplaceable State treasure, banking on the fact that the Germans would never believe I would do such a thing unless I knew the amber was safely out of their reach. If the gamble paid off, and the Amber Room was not discovered, then it would, in fact, be safer in its original location than if we were to try to move it the entire length of Russia.'

'So whoever made that painting,' said Pekkala, 'must have known that the radio reports were false. They were trying to warn the Germans that the amber was still at the Palace. It's fortunate that we intercepted the map before it could be delivered.'

Viciously, Stalin stubbed out his cigarette in the already overflowing ashtray on his desk. 'But it still means we have traitors among us!'

Their conversation was interrupted by loud voices coming from the outer office. A moment later, the door burst open and Churikova stepped into the room.

Close behind her was Poskrebychev. 'Comrade Stalin, I apologise! I tried to stop her!'

Stalin fixed his eyes on the woman. 'You must be the expert,' he said.

'Comrade Stalin,' Pekkala announced, 'this is Lieutenant Churikova of the Army's Cryptographic Section. She has assisted us in this investigation.'

'Ostubafengel,' Churikova blurted out. 'I've just figured out what it means!'

Stalin glanced towards Pekkala. 'What is she talking about?'

'The word on the back of the canvas. Ostubafengel.'

Frowning, Stalin picked up the painting, flipped it over and squinted at the letters. 'Well?' he asked.

'It represents a name,' explained Churikova. 'The person to whom it was supposed to be delivered is called Engel.'

'And the rest of it?'

'Ostubaf is the abbreviation for a rank in the German

military, specifically the SS. It means Obersturmbannführer. Ostubaf.'

'What rank is this man?' asked Stalin.

'The equivalent of a lieutenant colonel in our military,' replied Churikova. 'Since the war began, we've intercepted many such abbreviations, particularly from the SS, in which the system of ranking is not only different but abbreviated by the men who use it. For example, they use the word "Ustuf" for Untersturmführer, "Stubaf" for Sturmbannführer and so on. I had never come across Ostubaf before, but when the Inspector spoke the word aloud while we were driving here, I began to put the pieces together in my head. Forgive me for intruding, Comrade Stalin, but the meaning only just became clear to me, and I assumed you would want to know immediately.'

'I don't see how this helps,' he told her bluntly. 'Now we know there is some colonel in the SS who hasn't got his painting. What good does that do us?'

'It would do us no good at all, Comrade Stalin,' said Churikova, 'except I know this man.'

Stalin's expression froze. 'Go on,' he said quietly.

'Before I joined the army,' she explained, 'I was an art student at the Leningrad Institute. As part of my studies, I was sent to work with the authenticator, Valery Semykin, in order to learn about the detection of forgeries. He had many contacts in the art world, and was often brought in to appraise whole museum collections. One of these collections was the paintings of the Romanov family, located at the Catherine Palace.'

'Ah, yes.' Stalin nodded. 'I remember. That was in July of 1939, not long before we signed the Molotov-Ribbentrop Pact with Germany. As a gesture of good will, the Germans had offered to return several paintings which had been stolen from us in the last war. In return, their Ministry of Culture requested the opportunity to view the art collections of the Catherine and Alexander Palaces. We granted the request, as a way of greasing the wheels of the upcoming diplomatic talks.'

Churikova told the rest. 'The director of antiquities at Pushkin, Professor Urbaniak, was assigned the task of formally accepting those paintings from the Germans, which were to be presented at the time of their visit to the palaces. Semykin and I were brought in to examine the paintings as soon as they'd been handed over.'

'You mean in case they tried to pass off forgeries to you?' asked Pekkala.

'Yes, but, as it turned out, the paintings were genuine. All of them.'

'Only the treaty was fake,' grumbled Stalin. 'As we have now learned, the Molotov-Ribbentrop Pact, which was supposed to have guaranteed peace between our countries for the next ten years, wasn't worth the paper on which it was written.'

'Go on,' Pekkala urged the lieutenant. 'What happened when you arrived at the palace?'

'We got there before the presentation of the paintings had taken place. While we waited, Semykin asked Professor Urbaniak for permission to inspect the art works which were already part of the Catherine Palace collection. He gave us the go-ahead and it so happened that we were viewing the art works at the same time as the delegation from the German Ministry of Culture. Most of them just looked like graduate students to me, but one man was clearly in charge. He was older than the rest, and wore a heavy three-piece suit. Semykin and

I had taken the opportunity to view the palace collections for ourselves. That was when we ran into the man in charge of the German delegation. He introduced himself to us as Professor Gustav Engel, head curator of the Königsberg Castle Museum. He already seemed to know a great deal about the paintings in the Catherine Palace and he seemed particularly fascinated by the Amber Room.'

Stalin turned his head towards the door. 'Poskrebychev!' he boomed.

In the outer office, there was the sound of a chair scudding back across the floor. A moment later, the door opened and Poskrebychev stepped into the room. 'Comrade Stalin!' he shouted as he crashed his heels together in salute.

'See if we have a file on Gustav Engel, Head Curator of the museum at Königsberg Castle. If we have one, bring it to me now.'

'Yes, Comrade Stalin.' Moving with the confidence and gracefulness he had perfected during his many years as Stalin's secretary, Poskrebychev exited the room. But the second the door closed behind him, the secretary hurled himself into motion. He pushed past Kirov, who had wisely remained in the outer room when Churikova paid her unannounced visit to Stalin, and set off at a sprint towards the department of records. With his arms flailing and head thrown back, he propelled himself down the long hallway like a man pursued by wolves.

Behind the doors of Stalin's office, Churikova was still answering questions.

'When you ran into this man Engel,' continued Stalin, 'did Semykin already know him?'

'By reputation, I believe, although I don't think they had ever met.'

Stalin turned to Pekkala. 'Go to Semykin. See if he can tell you what a museum curator is doing in the SS.'

The thought of another visit to Lubyanka sent a jolt of dread crackling like static electricity across Pekkala's mind.

Moments later, Poskrebychev returned, red-faced and panting, a dull grey file clutched in his hand. The folder had a green stripe running vertically down the centre, indicating that it contained documents relating to a foreign national who was of interest to Internal State Security. He lifted his chin, breathed deeply, then opened the door and walked in. Advancing stiffly towards Stalin's desk, Poskrebychev placed the file before his master.

Without even a glance at Poskrebychev, Stalin opened the file. Hunched over his desk, his face only a hand's length from the print, he squinted at the documents. 'Where is the man's picture?' he asked.

'No picture was obtained,' replied Poskrebychev.

'Everyone who has a file must have a picture,' Stalin told him in a low voice. 'How are we supposed to find the man if we don't even know what he looks like?'

Nervously, Poskrebychev cleared his throat. 'No picture was—'

'It must have fallen out.'

'No, Comrade Stalin. It says quite clearly in the file that no picture—'

'I don't care what it says!' roared Stalin, bringing his fist down with a crash onto the desk. 'All files are to contain a photograph of the subject. Go and find it. Now, you fool!'

On the other side of the room, Churikova shuddered, as if the rage in Stalin's voice had struck her physically.

But Pekkala had been present at many such exchanges between Stalin and Poskrebychev. Now he stood by, his jaw clenched, silently waiting for Poskrebychev's customary subservient bow, followed by the man's swift return to the labyrinth of the Kremlin records office. But something was different this time. Poskrebychev remained frozen to the spot, his eyes fixed upon the Boss. An expression of disbelief spread across the face of Stalin's secretary, but for once the source of Poskrebychev's perpetual anxiety did not seem to be Stalin. Instead, it appeared to be coming from Poskrebychev himself, as if he were suddenly unsure whether he could control the secret thoughts which were parading through his skull.

'What is the matter with you?' demanded Stalin. 'Did you not hear what I said?'

Without a word Poskrebychev spun on his heel and left the room.

As Pekkala watched him go, he wondered how much of Stalin's bullying Poskrebychev could stand before he cracked. A man like that, moving almost unnoticed through the halls of power, could change in an instant from a harmless, grovelling servant into someone who could bring down an Empire.

'What is wrong with that man?' Stalin muttered to himself.

Pekkala felt a drop of sweat run down his cheek, wondering how close Stalin had just come to being murdered by a man whose blind loyalty he took for granted with a blindness even greater than his servant's.

Stalin returned to his inspection of the file. 'Medium height, regular features, dark hair. Approximately fifty-five years old.

Known to be employed at Königsberg Castle, where he has been curator of antiquities since 1937. Member of National Socialist Party since 1936. Applied for permission to visit Catherine and Alexander Palaces. Permission granted by Minister of Cultural Affairs. Arrived August 1939. Departed August 1939. Appeared to be fluent in Russian.' He stopped abruptly.

'What else does it say?' asked Pekkala.

'Nothing,' replied Stalin. 'The file was only opened on him when he came to visit the Catherine Palace. Before that, it's as if he didn't exist.'

'And after his visit?'

'He vanished back to Germany and that's the last we heard from him.'

'Until now.'

Stalin closed the file, pushed it away to the corner of his desk and turned his attention to Polina Churikova. 'That is if these two men are the same person, and I am beginning to think they are not. The man in this file is fifty-five years old, which makes him a little too old for someone with the rank of lieutenant colonel. Someone of this age would either have been promoted or would have retired by now. So you see, Comrade Churikova, it is clear you are mistaken.'

'But, Comrade Stalin . . .' she began, but then words seemed to fail her.

Stalin had made up his mind. Now he behaved as if Churikova was no longer in the room. He reached for his box of cigarettes and then began patting his pockets as he searched for his lighter.

Pekkala touched Churikova on the arm. 'It's time for us to go,' he said quietly.

'It *is* him,' Churikova insisted to Pekkala as they stepped into the narrow side street where Kirov had left his car waiting. 'It's Gustav Engel. *That* Gustav Engel, I'm telling you.'

'Even if it was,' said Kirov, 'what good would the knowledge do us now?' He opened the rear door of the Emka for Churikova, who climbed into the back seat. Then he opened the passenger side door for Pekkala.

'I must return to Lubyanka,' said Pekkala, 'for another conversation with Semykin.'

'That may prove difficult,' replied Kirov. 'It was hard enough getting him to talk on our first visit. You'll be lucky to get anything out of him at all this time.'

Pekkala nodded. 'It will be an uphill climb, for certain, but I think I might be able to persuade him. There's no need to drive me. I'll walk.'

'All the way to Lubyanka?'

'There is some business I must attend to first.'

Kirov realised from the tone of Pekkala's voice that it would be no use trying to persuade him otherwise. 'Very well, Inspector.'

Pekkala nodded towards Churikova. 'Where will you take her?'

'Back to the barracks, I expect,' replied Kirov. 'There must be someone who can reassign her to another cryptographic unit.'

Pekkala cast a glance at Churikova, his mind a confusion of pity and regret, then turned and walked away across Red Square.

'Oh, it's you again,' said Fabian Golyakovsky, curator of the Kremlin Museum, as he caught sight of Pekkala wandering amongst the icons.

Pekkala had stopped before *The Saviour of the Fiery Eye*, now safely re-hung upon the wall. 'I see that he found his way home.'

'Yes.' The curator laughed nervously and reached his hand out towards the icon, as if to trace his fingers down the long dark hair of the prophet. But just before he touched the work of art, his fingers curled in upon themselves. 'I must admit you had me worried, Inspector.'

'And I regret I am about to worry you again.'

'Oh,' he replied faintly.

'Do you know a man named Valery Semykin?'

'Of course! Everybody in the art world knows Semykin, and I can tell you with equal certainty that everybody hates him, too. He is the most pompous, arrogant, self-satisfied . . .' the curator gasped for breath, and would have continued with his tirade if Pekkala had not leaned towards the twitching Golyakovsky and, in a lowered voice, explained the reason for his visit.

The colour drained from Golyakovsky's face, as if someone

had pulled the plug on his heart. 'Oh, no, Inspector,' he gasped. 'Oh, please. I beg of you . . .'

'You will see to it then?'

For a moment, Golyakovsky looked as if he might refuse. His eyes began to bulge. His fists clenched at his sides. Then the futility of all resistance seemed to dawn on him. Golyakovsky's shoulders slumped and he sighed like a leaking balloon. 'I will see to it.' Then, with a final burst of indignation, he called out, 'But under protest!'

One hour later, the door to Semykin's Lubyanka cell slammed shut, leaving Pekkala locked in with the prisoner.

Semykin had been facing the wall, in keeping with prison regulations. Now, as he slowly turned around, his eyebrows arched with surprise when he saw who'd come to visit. 'Inspector! Back for another consultation?'

Pekkala noticed a fresh coating of blood daubed on the wall, which seemed to show two women, each accompanied by a child, standing in a sloping field of tall grass with a house among trees in the distance.

'It is Monet's *Les Coquelicots*,' explained Semykin. 'I have branched out into Impressionism. I don't have enough blood left in me to be a pointillist. So!' he clapped his butchered hands together. 'What brings you here this time, Pekkala?'

'Does the name Gustav Engel mean anything to you?'

'It might.'

Pekkala nodded slowly. 'Your sense of civic duty is unchanged.'

'Civic duty?' Semykin laughed angrily. 'My sense of duty is neither more nor less than it should be.'

'Have you considered what might happen to you if the Germans reach Moscow?'

'I have,' replied Semykin, 'and I suspect that anyone who was considered an enemy of the Soviet State is likely to be welcomed with open arms by the people who smashed it to bits. And the men who run this jail might find out for themselves what it feels like to be inmates. It has happened before, Pekkala, as you have witnessed for yourself. And if things are as bad as I think they are out there, there's little to stop it happening again.'

'That may be true, Valery, but you wouldn't live long enough to see it.'

Semykin frowned. 'What do you mean, Pekkala?'

'Before your jailers take to their heels, they'll kill every convict in this prison.' Seeing the look on Semykin's face, Pekkala knew he'd struck a nerve. 'You hadn't thought about that, had you?'

Semykin did not reply at first. He stared at his most recent work of art, as if, for a moment, he believed that he might walk through the wall and vanish into the crimson universe beyond. 'Gustav Engel,' he said, 'is the curator of the Königsberg Museum, and a world expert on amber.'

'Why would such an expert find himself in Königsberg?'

'That city is the ancient capital of the amber trade. For centuries, the Baltic coast has been one of the most reliable sources of amber, but the truth is it is difficult to find no matter where you are.'

'And why is that?'

'Because, unlike gold or silver, it does not tend to exist in large deposits. It is fossilised sap, after all, and because a good portion of it washes up on those windswept beaches, the location is determined by the motion of the waves, not where it originally formed into the amber. A mineralogist can look at a soil sample and calculate whether gold might be found in that place, but you cannot look out over the waves and know where the amber is lying beneath them.'

Pekkala thought of the long, windswept beaches of the Baltic coast, the scudding foam and greybeard rollers coughing up their treasure piece by piece.

'So!' exclaimed Semykin. 'Has the red moth yielded up its secrets?'

'Some,' he replied, 'but not all.' Pekkala went on to explain about the map they'd found embedded in its wings.

'Have you been to Spain?' Semykin asked suddenly.

'What?'

'Spain,' he repeated. 'Have you ever been there?'

'No. One day, perhaps, but . . .' Pekkala replied, confused at the abrupt change of topic.

'When you do go,' Semykin told him, 'you must visit the city of Granada.'

'What does this have to do with Gustav Engel, or the Amber Room?'

'Everything,' Semykin assured him. 'In the city of Granada, there is a palace called the Alhambra. It dates back to a time when the Moors controlled Spain and inside this palace is a mosque whose walls are so ornately carved that if you try to absorb them in a single glance, you will inevitably fail. You have no choice but to study the details instead. And so it is, the Moors believed, with the idea of God. You try to see him all at once, and you will not succeed. So you focus on the details, knowing that you cannot fathom the picture as a whole. It is the same with the Amber Room. You have seen it for yourself, have you not?'

'Of course,' replied Pekkala.

'Then you know that it is not possible to grasp the vast complexity of those thousands of fragments of amber. You might as well try to comprehend the very fabric of the universe. Once in a thousand years, we forget about butchering each other just long enough to create a work of art so much greater than ourselves that it becomes a symbol of achievement for the entire human race. The Amber Room is such a thing.'

Although Pekkala had visited it on many occasions during his time of service to the Tsar, and had seen the amber-laden panels for himself, he had never learned the history of the room. The Tsar had thousands of possessions, most of them priceless and all of them with elaborate tales of provenance. It had always frustrated the Tsar that Pekkala placed so little importance on these works of art, or even on the thousands of bars of gold he had kept hidden in a cell dug deep into the ground beneath the Alexander Palace.

The Tsar had alternately ridiculed and admired the simplicity of Pekkala's existence and had made a virtual hobby of trying to tempt Pekkala with ornate and expensive gifts as a way of luring him into the fascination held by so many for the lifestyle of the Romanovs.

The Tsar had always failed in this endeavour. In failing, however, he had come to realise that Pekkala was one of the only people on this earth whom he could really trust since those who were beguiled by wealth and exclusivity could never be counted upon when the time came to choose between what was right and what nourished the beast of their obsession.

'Where did the Amber Room come from?' asked Pekkala.

'It was commissioned by King Frederick of Prussia, back in 1701. The work was completed by artisans trained in the art of carving ivory, since there had never been a project like this one undertaken before using amber. Unfortunately, the king's son, Wilhelm, did not share his father's tastes and gave the room away to Tsar Peter I as a gift. According to legend, it was in exchange for a bodyguard of Russian giants. Not only did Peter have no particular fascination for amber, he had no idea how to assemble the room and quickly gave up trying. As a result, it wasn't until half a century later that the panels were installed in the Catherine Palace on the orders of Catherine the Great. It was her son, Peter the Great, who became obsessed with the room and its contents. In 1715, he toured the Baltic coast disguised as a regular army officer, buying up amber wherever he could find it. He later incorporated pieces from his own amber collection into the panels, including one containing the perfectly preserved body of a large moth, I suspect the same kind depicted in the painting.'

'How did it end up embedded in the amber?'

'In prehistoric times, the moth became trapped in the sap oozing out of a tree. The more it struggled, the more enveloped it became, until it was literally embalmed in sap. Over thousands of years, the sap was fossilised into amber, and the insect was preserved inside. Many such things have been discovered in pieces of amber – stones, pine needles, even fish scales.'

'Where did this piece of amber come from?'

'According to legend,' replied Semykin, 'it had been sold to a

Viking by an American Indian on the island of Newfoundland some seven hundred years before. The piece had found its way back to Norway and, in the year 1700, was sold to a merchant in Königsberg by a Norwegian sailor who needed the money to repair his ship, which had been damaged in a storm. And Königsberg is where Peter the Great tracked it down. He paid his weight in gold for that one fragment and had it installed in one of the panels, high up near the ceiling. You can't actually see the insect unless you get up on a ladder. Peter the Great considered it too precious to be viewed by those who did not value it as he did. Even among those who spent their whole lives working at the palace, most people didn't know the insect was there.'

'His weight in gold?' gasped Pekkala.

'He would have paid *ten* times his weight,' explained Semykin. 'That is the nature of the collector. He must possess what he covets, no matter what the cost. It is one of the great failures of our species. Like war. Like the cooking in this prison.'

'How large a piece of amber was it?' Pekkala imagined a vast yellow slab, the size of a motor car.

Semykin held up his mangled hand, as if to show the insect embedded in his flesh. 'No larger than this.' Until now, he had been smiling, amused at Pekkala's amazement. But suddenly his face grew serious.

'How is Engel involved in this?' asked Semykin.

'Apparently, the painting was on its way to him when the plane that was carrying it ran out of fuel over our lines. You were there at the Catherine Palace, weren't you,' asked Pekkala, 'when the curators were packing up the art work?'

'Yes. As I told you before, I helped to prioritise which works of art should be removed first, in case we didn't have time to transport them all to safety.'

'Then you know they had to leave the amber behind.'

Semykin nodded grimly. 'We were sworn to secrecy, but I guess none of that matters now. The panels were too fragile. We tried moving one of them, but the amber started coming loose from the panel. It was clattering down around us like hail. Sealing it beneath the wallpaper became our only option. That, and broadcasting on the radio that it had all been moved to safety.'

'So whoever sent this painting to Engel was trying to let him know the amber's real location.'

'Yes,' agreed Semykin. 'Only someone very familiar with the history of the Amber Room would know the significance of that moth. And believe me, Engel would know. But this doesn't change the fact that the panels still can't be moved without destroying them and even if Engel would love nothing more than to get his hands upon the amber, he can't just walk in under the noses of the German army and pilfer it like a boy robbing candy from a shop. He is a provincial museum director, not Herman Göring. Engel simply doesn't have the credentials to pull off that kind of stunt.'

'We believe he may have joined the military.'

'What? No, you must be mistaken, Pekkala. Engel is not young and he is certainly no soldier! The day may come when the Fascists are desperate enough to enlist men of that age into their army, but as far as I know, it hasn't happened yet.'

'We have reason to believe he has joined the SS,' said Pekkala, 'although we can't understand why he might have done so. Comrade Stalin is convinced that the man to whom the painting should have been delivered is not the same Gustav Engel at all, but a completely different man who just happens to have the same last name.'

A shadow seemed to pass behind Semykin's eyes. 'The SS, you say?'

'What is it, Semykin? What's troubling you?'

'It may be nothing.'

'Well, whatever it is, tell me now, before it's too late.'

'Long before the war,' began Semykin, 'Hitler spoke of his dream to build an art museum in the city of Linz. It was to be the largest of its kind in Europe, perhaps in the whole world. When I first heard about the project, which the Germans called *Sonderauftrag Linz*, I was glad. Many collections would be changing hands and there would be a need for authenticators like me. But then I heard a rumour that the Nazis had begun sending people all across Europe, posing as art students, but who were, in fact, members of a secret organisation whose mission was to catalogue the names and locations of artworks in every country which the Germans planned to occupy. Then I realised that, if that rumour was true, the Nazis would not be buying art. They would be stealing it. The task of this secret organisation would be to follow behind the German Army, seizing entire collections from private homes, galleries and ...'

'... and palaces. This organisation. Do you know what it was called?'

'It is known by the initials ERR, which stands for the Einsatzstab Reichsleiter Rosenberg. But its existence was only a rumour, and there were so many rumours going around, nobody knew what to believe. The whole thing seemed too diabolical to be real, but if you are telling me that Gustav Engel is working for the SS, I think it must be true. That new museum in Linz will soon require a curator. What better credential than delivering the Amber Room to Adolph Hitler could a man like Gustav Engel ever need?'

'You are forgetting that we intercepted the painting before he could see it for himself. There is still a chance that he will be fooled by the wallpaper and the radio announcement.'

'If there is anyone on earth who can see through that charade, it's Gustav Engel. He covets that amber, just as Peter the Great did before him, for the simple reason that amber exists in defiance of time, holding its beauty even as its owners crumble into dust. Each piece is unique and perpetual, qualities all men long to possess. That's why a Tsar will pay his weight in gold for a slab no larger than my hand. And that's why a man like Gustav Engel will not stop searching for that amber, until he has bound his name forever to the greatest treasure in the world.'

'Thank you, Semykin,' said Pekkala as he turned to leave. 'You have been most helpful.'

'Where shall I send the bill?' he asked sarcastically.

'The bill has already been paid,' replied Pekkala. 'Be patient Semykin. Your reward is on its way.'

Late that August afternoon, the members of the 5th Anti-Aircraft Section were sitting in their underwear beside their foxholes, running candle flames up and down the seams of their shirts and trousers to get rid of the lice with which they had become infested. The candle flames sputtered as lice eggs exploded in the heat, filling the air with a smell like burned hair.

The noise of tanks, which they had heard the night before, had ceased. Since no alerts had been sounded, the men assumed it must have been the sound of Russian vehicles.

Only Stefanov remained unconvinced. With gritted teeth, he scanned the trees which saw-toothed the horizon.

A fine rain had begun to fall. Fog drifted across the Alexander Park, gathering in the trees north of the Lamskoy Pavilion.

Commissar Sirko lay in the back of their truck, puffing on one cigarette after another. Smoke slithered from holes in the canvas roof. Now and then, he swatted at mosquitoes with a rolled-up newspaper from his home town of Pskov, which he had been carrying with him, reading and re-reading, since the invasion of Poland almost two years before. The paper was so frail by now that every time he struck an insect, fragments scattered into the air like seeds blown from a dandelion.

This moment of relative peace was interrupted by the

rumble of trucks heading east along the Parkovaya road, which ran along the southern edge of Tsarskoye Selo.

'What's happening?' asked Ragozin.

'Go and find out, Sergeant,' ordered Commissar Sirko.

Ragozin turned to Barkat. 'Go and find out,' he said.

'Yes, Comrade Sergeant.' Still in his underclothes, Barkat ran through the woods until he could see passing trucks. For a while he stood there, with his hands gripping the metal railings, watching the vehicles go by and breathing the exhaust-filled air.

Then he spun around and sprinted back to the cabin.

'All those vehicles are ours,' said Barkat. 'It looks as if the whole Division is retreating.'

'We should get going, too,' Stefanov told the group.

'Not so fast,' growled Sirko. 'No one has given us permission.'

'But who do you think they'll blame,' demanded Stefanov, 'if someone else forgot to give the order, and you have done nothing but lie there on your fat arse, without even calling to confirm?'

Barkat and Ragozin stared at Stefanov, slack-jawed with astonishment at the way he had just spoken to a commissar.

Sirko hesitated. 'Make the call,' he ordered.

Stefanov was already in motion. Climbing into the back of the truck, he switched on their Golub field radio, a heavy, clumsy thing whose black dials resembled the expressionless eyes of a fish. Stefanov kept one piece of the headphone set pressed against his ear as he tried to get in touch with headquarters. After several minutes of calling into the static, he put the headphones down and reported to Commissar Sirko. 'No one's there.'

'No answer at all?'

'None, Comrade Commissar.'

Ragozin began putting on his clothes, wincing as the candle-singed cloth burned his skin. 'That's it. I can't believe I'm saying this, but I agree with Stefanov. We should leave while we still can.'

'Do you have any idea what they will do to me if I let us roll out of here without permission?' asked Sirko.

'Look!' shouted Barkat. 'The others are going, as well.'

It was true. All across the park, gun crews were packing up their weapons. Truck engines roared to life.

'Perhaps you'd rather take your chances with the Germans,' Ragozin told Sirko.

The commissar required no further convincing. 'Load up!' he bellowed uselessly, since that was what the men were already doing.

Gunfire sounded from the woods north of the Alexander Park. A minute later, Russian soldiers appeared, having thrown away their weapons as they retreated. 'The Germans are right behind us!' shouted the men as they bolted past. 'They're killing everything that moves!'

Stefanov dragged the Maxim machine gun over to the tailgate of the truck. 'Can somebody help me?' he asked.

The Maxim, its stocky barrel slathered with layers of bamboo-green paint, was too heavy for one man to lift on his own due to its iron blast shield, designed to protect the person firing the weapon, and the three-wheeled carriage mounting, which allowed it to be towed across the battlefield.

'Just remove the recoil spring and leave the rest for the Germans!' ordered Ragozin, as he climbed into the back of the

ZiS-5. 'Let them break their backs trying to carry that thing around!'

Meanwhile, Barkat got behind the wheel. He pressed the ignition switch, but the engine would not start.

The sound of gunfire was growing louder.

The truck engine coughed.

'Oh, please!' Ragozin clasped his head in his hands.

Stefanov grabbed hold of the Maxim's towing bar and began dragging it back towards the foxhole.

'What are you doing?' barked Sirko. 'I told you to abandon it!'

'I know,' said Stefanov. He pulled the Maxim gun into the foxhole and aimed it in the direction of the German advance.

Ragozin gaped at him, struggling to comprehend. 'Stefanov, have you gone mad?'

'They're coming in too quickly,' he replied, nervously etching his thumb along the Maxim's barrel, where a line of bubbles, like varicose veins, had formed beneath the paint. 'Somebody's got to slow them down or you'll never get out of the park.'

A stray bullet struck the cowling of the ZiS-5, tearing a pale stripe into the metal.

The truck's engine coughed again. This time it started.

Barkat revved the motor. Thick black smoke poured out of the tail pipe.

They heard voices shouting in German, somewhere out among the dense thickets of trees.

'Stefanov!' In frustration, Barkat slammed the flat of his hand against the door, making a hollow boom which echoed among the trees. 'Let someone else slow them down.'

'There is no one else,' Stefanov said as he opened an

ammunition box and fitted a belt of bullets into the Maxim. 'Go. I'll find you.'

Commissar Sirko leaned out of the passenger side, glanced at Stefanov, then sat back inside the truck and shouted, 'Drive!'

For one more second Barkat hesitated. Then he floored the accelerator and the vehicle began to move, slewing around in the wet grass. In a few seconds, it had disappeared down a weed-choked trail that led to the southern entrance of the estate.

Ahead of Stefanov, among the trees, boots crackled on fallen twigs. He heard whispering and hunched down behind the gun. Stefanov was surprised to find that he was not afraid. Later, if there was a later, he knew the fear would come and, once it had, it might never leave, but for now he felt only a shuddering energy coursing through his body and his thoughts raced back and forth inside his skull, like a school of fish trapped in a net.

A few seconds later, he saw movement in the mist. There was no mistaking them – the grey-green uniforms, the sharply angled helmets. The German soldiers were bunched together in a line. They advanced at a walking pace, rifles held out in front of them as if they meant to sweep aside the mist using only the barrels of their guns.

Next to his boot, a garter snake slipped dryly through the leaves.

Stefanov's eyes filled with sweat. He tried to swallow but couldn't. One soldier was walking straight towards him. He seemed to materialise out of the fog.

Clearly now, Stefanov could see the man's unshaven face, the grey pebbled tunic buttons, the thick, greased leather belt, the creases in the leather around the ankles of the man's jack-boots, the blood-drained flesh beneath his dirty hands as they clenched a Mauser rifle.

The man kept walking.

A few more paces and he would have tumbled into Stefanov's foxhole.

Stefanov himself felt frozen, unable to comprehend why he hadn't yet been spotted.

Suddenly the soldier stumbled to a halt. For a moment, he just blinked at the figure hidden in the undergrowth. Then he opened his mouth to cry out.

The Maxim seemed to go off by itself. Everything ahead of Stefanov became a blur of smoke and flickering brass from the empty cartridges which spun into the air and rained back upon him, pinging off the barrel of the gun. Birch and pine branches cascaded down. All the while the cloth belt which had held the bullets spewed from the side of the gun like the shed skin of a snake. Stefanov's hands ached from the vibration of the gun. His lungs filled with cordite smoke. He had no idea if he was hitting anything.

Then the clanking bang of the Maxim suddenly quit. All Stefanov could hear were the last few empty cartridges ringing as they clattered to the ground.

Stefanov looked down at the ammunition crate. It was empty. The ground on which he knelt was a carpet of spent cartridges, tiny feathers of smoke still drifting from their opened mouths. The Maxim's barrel clicked and sighed as it began to cool.

In a daze, Stefanov stood up from behind the gun and stumbled out among the twisted dead. He counted twelve of them. Their bodies were horribly torn. More lay back among the bullet-gashed trees. He saw the shiny hobnails on their boots.

Then he saw that one of the soldiers had remained on his feet. The man's tunic was torn open. Beneath that, from a large wound ripped into his stomach, the soldier's entrails had unravelled to the ground. Slowly, he took off his helmet, its green paint smeared with a camouflage of mud. He got down on his knees, as if he meant to pray, then carefully gathered up his guts into the shell of the helmet. His lips moved but he made no sound. The man climbed to his feet and started walking back towards the German lines. He had only gone a few paces before he fell face-down on the pine needles.

Shouting echoed through the pines. More soldiers were advancing through the woods.

Stefanov turned and ran, dodging like a rabbit through the trees, and caught up with the truck at the southern end of the park, just as it was passing the Crimean War memorial. He tumbled into the back among the Golub radio, ammunition for the 25-mm and a terrified Sergeant Ragozin.

A few seconds later, they passed beneath the Orlov gates and out on to the main road.

The last Stefanov saw of Tsarskoye Selo was the roof of the Catherine Palace, its grey tiles shimmering through the mist, just as it had been when he fled with his father from the tidal wave of revolution.

Later that day, Pekkala reported back to Stalin. 'I spoke to Semykin. The person we're looking for does, in fact, appear to be the same Gustav Engel who is mentioned in your file.'

Stalin opened his mouth to speak.

'There's more, I'm afraid,' said Pekkala. 'A special task force has been created by the SS for the purpose of removing thousands of art works from the countries occupied by Germany.'

'I am already aware of that,' replied Stalin. 'Since we last spoke, I have learned from one of our agents in the Red Orchestra network, a woman who is based in Königsberg, that, two weeks ago, Gustav Engel gave the order for the Seckendorff Gallery, which is the largest gallery at the Castle, to be cleared and repainted in order to make room for the Amber Panels, which they plan to display there until such time as the museum in Linz has been completed. Engel spent the past two weeks at Königsberg, supervising the refurbishments and yesterday, according to our agent, departed from Königsberg in a truck which had been specially outfitted to transport the panels back to Königsberg. According to the agent, Engel is the lynchpin to Rosenberg's entire operation in the East and the Amber Room is their top priority.'

'The German army is already at the gates of Leningrad. We cannot stop them from reaching the Palace . . .'

'That is true,' agreed Stalin, 'but maybe we can put a stop to Gustav Engel.'

'How is that possible?'

'It is possible,' replied Stalin, 'because I am sending you to get him.'

At first, Pekkala was too stunned to reply. 'I am not an assassin,' he finally managed to say.

'I am not asking you to kill him, Pekkala. I want you to bring him back to Moscow.'

'And what would be the point of that? If we got rid of him, they would just appoint somebody else.'

'That is where you are wrong, Pekkala. The Nazis chose Engel precisely because nobody else knows what he knows. With Engel at their head, this organisation will systematically rob our country of its cultural heritage, after which, if we can't find a way to stop them, they'll destroy whatever is left. Engel compiled the list of what they'd steal, what they'd ignore and what they would destroy. I need to know what's on that list, Pekkala, along with the name of the traitor who's been helping him. Gustav Engel can provide that information, and he will, if you can bring him to me. We can't save everything, but we can at least deprive them of the treasures they have come to steal. Thanks to you and Major Kirov, we have identified the perpetrator of what may still become the greatest theft in history, unless you bring the criminal to justice.'

'And the fact that he's behind enemy lines . . .'

'That is merely an obstacle to be overcome, as you have overcome other obstacles in the past. You are the perfect choice for this task. After all, you know the layout of that palace and, according to your file,' Stalin lifted up a tattered grey envelope, 'you even speak German.'

'That was part of my training with the Okhrana, but, Comrade Stalin, even if it was possible to arrest Engel and to bring him back to Moscow, is there enough time to accomplish the mission?'

'Yes, if we move quickly. It will take Engel a week to travel from Königsberg to the Catherine Palace. When he discovers the wallpaper instead of the panels, he may be convinced that the amber has been removed. Then, again, he may not. In either case, Engel is likely to remain at Tsarskoye Selo until he has conducted a thorough search. This will give you time to apprehend him and then to smuggle him back across our lines.'

'I can find my way around the palace, Comrade Stalin, but whatever advantage that affords me is lost by the fact that I don't know what this man Engel looks like.'

'I have not forgotten this detail, and neither has Lieutenant Churikova. That is why she will be coming with you to the palace.'

'You cannot ask her to take on a mission like this!'

'I didn't have to,' replied Stalin. 'She volunteered.'

'When?'

'After you left to find Semykin, Kirov drove her back to the Kremlin.'

'Why would he do that?'

'She told him to. When they arrived at the barracks where Churikova's company had been quartered, in the hopes of finding someone, anyone, remaining from her signals unit, they found the place deserted. Everyone she had worked with died aboard that train when it was bombed. When Kirov asked

Churikova where she wanted to go, she asked to return to the Kremlin. She returned to this office and offered to help in any way she could. I admire this woman, Pekkala. Without her, the task becomes impossible. She knows this. That's why she volunteered, and why you should be grateful for her assistance.'

'Send me,' Pekkala told him. 'Send Kirov, if you have to, but . . .'

'But not Polina Churikova?' Leaning back in his chair, Stalin folded his hands across his stomach. 'I wonder if that's really who you're trying to save.'

'What do you mean, Comrade Stalin?'

'Is it her, or is it someone she reminds you of?'

Pekkala felt the breath catch in his throat.

'I have seen pictures of Comrade Simonova. The resemblance is uncanny, don't you think? How difficult it must have been to say goodbye to her, that night she boarded the train.'

'Leave her out of it.'

'I have, Pekkala. Have you?'

Pekkala stood there in silence. The room was spinning around him – the red curtains, the red carpet – like a whirlpool filled with blood. 'How on earth do you expect me to get through the German lines, with or without Churikova?'

'You will require help, of course. Unlike the rest of the population, I do not believe you can simply vanish into thin air and reappear at the location of your choice.'

'But you don't know who the traitor is,' replied Pekkala. 'It could be someone from the staff who packed up the treasures at the Catherine Palace. Or from NKVD. Even someone from inside the Kremlin. If word gets out about this mission, the Fascists will be waiting for us when we arrive.'

'I have considered that,' said Stalin, 'and I agree that we must choose someone unconnected with our current operations who can spirit you and the lieutenant through the lines.'

'But the only people who possess those kinds of talents are already working for NKVD.' He thought of Zubkov, the Tsar's old Moscow bureau chief for the Okhrana, who had slipped back and forth between countries, both during and after the last war, aided by the ghost-like figures of the Myednikov Special Section.

'I know what you're thinking, Pekkala. You're thinking that if the Bolshevik Secret Service hadn't hunted down and killed every member of Myednikov Section, including Myednikov himself, those men might have proved very useful at a time like this.'

Pekkala remembered the head of the Bolshevik Secret Service, a Polish assassin named Felix Dzerzhinsky. He was a thin, humourless man with a sharp face and permanently narrowed eyes, who had personally sent thousands of people to their deaths.

'The fact is,' said Stalin, 'Dzerzhinsky was not quite as efficient as he claimed to be.'

'I don't understand,' said Pekkala.

'Not all of Myednikov's men are dead. One of them survived, an old friend of yours called Shulepov.'

'You must be mistaken, Comrade Stalin, I know of no one by that name.'

Stalin smiled. 'Of course not. Shulepov is the name he has used since the Revolution. You might know him better as Valeri Nikolayevich Kovalevsky.'

Pekkala blinked, as if a handful of dust had been thrown into his eyes. 'That can't be true. Valeri Kovalevsky has been gone for years.'

As Pekkala spoke the dead man's name, the face of his old friend loomed into the forefront of his mind.

In the Tsar's Secret Service, Pekkala and Kovalevsky had both trained under the guidance of Chief Inspector Vassileyev.

But within days of completing their course of instruction, Kovalevsky disappeared. One day he was there, in the stuffy, stone-walled basement of Okhrana headquarters where Vassileyev conducted his lessons, and the next he was gone, without a word of farewell or forwarding address.

'What has happened to him?' asked Pekkala, staring at Kovalevsky's empty desk.

'He has been chosen for Myednikov's Special Section,' replied Vassileyev.

'I've never heard of it.'

'Most people haven't,' said Vassileyev, and he went on to explain.

The Myednikov section trained men for duties so secret that their very existence was denied. They lived in the twilight of Russian society, without recognition, without family contact, without even their own names to track the passing of their lives.

'What are these men? Assassins?'

'Certainly,' replied Vassileyev. 'They are killers when they need to be. But that's not all they are. As part of Myednikov's Section, Kovalevsky will be trained to move unnoticed through the streets of this city, and of all the cities of the world. In London, New York, Rome and Paris, there are apartments where the rent is always paid but no one ever seems to come or go from them. The addresses are known only to Myednikov and it is there that his men will find not only food and shelter but also money, weapons, passports and everything they need to change identities as easily as snakes can shed their skins. They are travellers through all the walls and wires of the world, thrown up by the governments to offer the illusion of safety. For men like you and me, the bars of such cages will hold. But they cannot stop Myednikov, or anyone who's trained by him. He is like the boatman on the river Styx. There are journeys all of us will make some day, but not without a guide to bring us to our final destination. For some of us, those guides are Myednikov's men.'

'Will I ever see him again?' asked Pekkala.

'It is doubtful,' replied Vassileyev. 'You may pass an old man in the street, or sit beside a soldier on a train or drop a coin into the hand of a beggar, and any one of them might be your old friend Kovalevsky. You will never know, unless he's there to save your life, or else to end it.'

In later years, after Pekkala took up his duties as the Tsar's Personal Investigator, he would hear an occasional rumour about the man known to have been Myednikov's finest pupil. Once, the Tsar confided to Pekkala that Kovalevsky had arrived in a fishing boat in the city of Trondheim in Norway, to rescue an Okhrana agent whose cover had been blown.

'And he had even filled the boat with fish,' laughed the Tsar, 'which he managed to sell at a profit!'

In another story, which took place at the Hôtel Président in Paris, Kovalevsky had appeared, wearing the short red tunic of a bell boy, at the door of a Spanish diplomat, who had been acting as a courier of military secrets between a Russian agent and the government of Japan. When the diplomat opened the door, Kovalevsky sprayed the man in the face with potassium cyanide, using a woman's perfume vaporiser. The poison constricted the blood vessels supplying oxygen to the brain, causing immediate loss of consciousness and death within two minutes. The lethal vapour ensured that the diplomat would not survive, but it also put Kovalevsky himself at risk of exposure to the cyanide. Anticipating this, Kovalevsky had brought with him an antidote, which consisted of a vial of amyl nitrate and two syringes, one containing sodium nitrite and the other containing sodium thiosulphate.

After inhaling the vial, Kovalevsky stabbed himself in the chest with the two syringes, staggered out of the service entrance to the hotel, dropping his red tunic along the way, and vanished into the crowds along the Champs-Elysées. By the time the diplomat was discovered dead on the floor of his room, the effects of the cyanide had worn off, leaving no trace. An autopsy showed the only likely cause of death to be a heart attack.

After the storming of the Winter Palace by Red Guards in October of 1917, Kovalevsky disappeared, probably on the orders of Myednikov himself.

Soon afterwards, the roster of Myednikov's agents was discovered in the infamous Blue File, which contained documents kept by the Tsar for his personal use, whose contents had been known only to him. Within the Blue File, Bolshevik agents discovered the names and covers of operatives working under the highest levels of secrecy, including Myednikov's men. With their identities revealed, members of the organisation were quickly tracked down and liquidated by the newly formed Bolshevik Secret Service, the Cheka. Its director, Felix Dzerzhinsky, personally undertook the hunt for Kovalevsky.

Dzerzhinsky was so determined to catch and kill the man he considered to be the most dangerous of all Myednikov's agents that when a Bolshevik operative stationed in Paris reported that a waiter at the famous Brasserie Lipp bore a resemblance to Kovalevsky, whom the agent had known as a child, Dzerzhinsky had the waiter gunned down in the street without conducting any further investigation as to the waiter's identity.

Dzerzhinsky had risked an international incident, which could have pulverised the already fragile relationship between France and the fledging Soviet government. But Dzerzhinsky's instincts turned out to be correct. French authorities, while expressing their displeasure at a targeted killing on their own soil, conceded that Kovalevsky's expertise could have posed a serious threat to the new Russia. Kovalevsky's death was officially confirmed and his file was sent to the warehouse known as Archive 17, the graveyard of Soviet Intelligence.

'Comrade Stalin,' said Pekkala, 'Valeri Kovalevsky was assassin-
ated on the orders of Dzerzhinsky himself. You know that as
well as I do.'

'What I know,' replied Stalin, 'is that when Dzerzhinsky
ordered the murder of an innocent Frenchman and had him liquidated in broad daylight on the Boulevard Saint-Germain,
he made the biggest mistake of his career.'

'You mean that waiter wasn't Kovalevsky after all?'

'He was not,' Stalin confirmed. 'The mistake almost cost
Dzerzhinsky his career. If the truth had become known, it
would have created such an uproar that Lenin would have been
forced to replace him. In all probability, Dzerzhinsky himself
would have been shot. The only thing he could do was to
claim that Kovalevsky was actually dead. Dzerzhinsky couldn't
even take the chance of continuing to search for Kovalevsky in
secret. The only thing Dzerzhinsky could do was to close the
file on him. That's how Kovalevsky got away!'

'And how do you expect to find him now, after all these
years?' asked Pekkala.

'He has already been found,' replied Stalin, 'hiding in the last
place Dzerzhinsky would ever have looked for him.'

'And where is that?'

But Stalin was enjoying Pekkala's helplessness too much to

give him the answer just yet. 'If you had known that Dzerzhinsky would not rest until he tracked you down and killed you, where would you have gone?'

'As far away from him as I could.'

Stalin raised one stubby finger. 'Exactly! That is what *you* would do. It is what I would do, as well. It is also what Dzerzhinsky thought your friend would do. He used to pace up and down in my office, shaking his bony fist as he swore to track down Kovalevsky. He became consumed with the hunt. That is why, when that Cheka agent came to him with some theory that a man he hadn't seen in twenty years was working in a café in Paris, Dzerzhinsky didn't take the time to check the man's story. Instead, Dzerzhinsky had his hand on the phone receiver, ready to dispatch every assassin in the Cheka to France, before the agent had even left the room. Kovalevsky's genius was that he understood Dzerzhinsky even better than Dzerzhinsky understood himself. That is why Kovalevsky did not travel to Tahiti, or Easter Island or any of the other places where Dzerzhinsky had imagined he might be. This man, who could have vanished to the farthest corners of the world, did not even leave the country. Kovalevsky did the thing Dzerzhinsky never considered. He stayed right here in Moscow.'

'Hide in plain sight,' muttered Pekkala, recalling one of the maxims of their former teacher, Vassileyev.

'Kovalevsky became a teacher of history at Moscow School No. 554. He coaches the cross-country running team. He sits on the boards of nutrition and community service. Three times, he has been awarded the Teacher of the Year Prize, as voted by the student body.'

'All under the name of Alexander Shulepov,' said Pekkala.

Stalin nodded. 'And, as Alexander Shulepov, he would have lived out his life as a model Soviet citizen, except . . .'

'Except what, Comrade Stalin?'

'Except that Professor Shulepov is accustomed to spending his lunch breaks asleep at his desk, a ritual he observes with impressive regularity, making sure to delegate a student to wake him up in time for the next class. Unfortunately for the Professor, he sometimes cries out in his sleep. And what he happened to cry out one day was the name of Myednikov. What he didn't realise was that the student who had come to wake him was already standing in the room. The student said nothing to Professor Shulepov but, being curious, mentioned the name to his parents when he returned home that day. The father, now an executive at the Moscow City Gas Works, was a former member of the Cheka and had heard that name before. Suspecting that it might be valuable information, he reported it immediately to my office. Poskrebychev himself took down the details, including a request for promotion from his current place of work in the suburbs to the Central Office of Gasprom. The enterprising man had even picked out an apartment block, where he hoped that suitable lodgings would be made available to him as soon as he received his promotion.'

'And did you grant this request?'

Stalin sat back and laughed. 'Of course not! I had Poskrebychev look into the matter and, as soon as he returned to me with confirmation that this Professor Shulepov was not only a Myednikov agent but was, in fact, the very man Dzerzhinsky had spent the last years of his life trying to find, I had the informant and his wife convicted of an unrelated and fictitious crime, then sent to Mamlin-Three.'

'And what about the child?' demanded Pekkala.

'He is in an orphanage. Do not concern yourself, Inspector. The young man is well fed. He is educated. He lacks for nothing.'

'Except his family.'

'My point, Pekkala, is that the best way to protect him was to hold on to the secret of his past, which means that the only people who know Kovalevsky's true identity are you and me and Poskrebychev. I kept it that way because there are too many people who would want a man like Kovalevsky dead. Wherever this traitor is within our ranks, it's safe to say that he is not aware of Kovalevsky's existence.'

'But why did you protect him, Comrade Stalin?'

'Because, unlike Dzerzhinsky, I believe there is more to gain from studying a man like Kovalevsky than by simply erasing him from the earth. Kovalevsky is like an animal in the zoo, who does not understand he's in a zoo. The ones who know they're in captivity are not the same. It is always better to study creatures in their natural habitat.'

'And what have you learned from your study of Kovalevsky?'

'That Professor Shulepov has become a model Soviet citizen. The genius of the man is in the impeccable mundaneness of his daily life.' Stalin slid a small piece of note paper across the desk towards Pekkala. 'This is the address where you will find him. Now I leave it to you to persuade your old friend to emerge from the shadows and help us.'

'It's been years since he worked for the Myednikov section,' said Pekkala, as he picked up the piece of paper and tucked it into the pocket of his coat. 'What makes you think the skills he learned back then are any use to us now?'

'Just because a man stops being an assassin does not mean he has forgotten how to kill.'

'And what can I offer him in return for his help, Comrade Stalin?'

'The chance to live out his days in peace, as Professor Shulepov, teacher of the year at Moscow School No. 554. You have forty-eight hours, Pekkala. Three days from now, you, Kirov and Churikova are leaving for the front, with Kovalevsky or without him.'

Before going to see Kovalevsky, Pekkala returned to the office in order to tell Kirov where he was going.

When he arrived, he was surprised to find a young woman sitting at his desk.

She took one look at Pekkala and launched herself to her feet. 'I'm sorry, Inspector!' she said.

The woman was in her mid-twenties, head and shoulders shorter than Pekkala, with a round and slightly freckled face, a small chin and dark, inquisitive eyes. She had on a dark blue skirt and a grey, hand-knitted sweater, but Pekkala guessed from the faint but particular rub mark at her throat that she had recently been wearing a tight-collared *gymnastiorka* tunic, and the skirt itself was the same cut and colour as that issued to women serving in administrative and medical positions in the Red Army. His notion was confirmed when he spotted the dark blue beret, with its brass and red enamel star, issued to women in the Soviet military. 'You must be the friend of Major Kirov,' said Pekkala.

'Elizaveta Kapanina.'

Pekkala felt his neck muscles tighten as he recalled his unfortunate conversation with Kirov at the Café Tilsit.

'And this,' announced Kirov, slouched comfortably in the chair from Hotel Metropol, 'is Inspector Pekkala.' Behind him, late-afternoon light filtered through the kumquat tree and other potted plants lined up along the window sill, casting jungly shadows on the floor.

Did he tell me just to be myself? Pekkala struggled to recall. Or was it not to be myself? And if I'm not supposed to be myself, then who the hell am I supposed to be?

'It is a pleasure to meet you, Inspector,' said Elizaveta. 'Yulian has told me all about you.'

Pekkala nodded. 'Yulian,' he repeated slowly.

'That's my name,' said Kirov, 'which you would know if you ever used it.'

'Yulian,' continued Elizaveta, 'says that your father ran a funeral business where you lived in Finland.'

'Yes, do you have undertakers in your family?'

'No, but I was thinking how strange it must have been, growing up with dead people in your house all the time.'

'It did make my mother nervous,' admitted Pekkala. 'She worried that their souls would stay behind when the bodies were taken for burial. And besides, my father talked to them.'

'To the dead?'

'That's right,' said Pekkala. 'I used to sit at the top of the stairs and listen to the things he said.'

'What things?' asked Elizaveta.

'He talked about his life. Sometimes, it was just about the day he'd had.'

'And that never bothered you?'

'The thing is,' explained Pekkala, 'that he believed they spoke to him as well. The only thing that worried me was that I believed it too.'

'This is how you introduce yourself?' muttered Kirov.

'I'm sorry I can't stay,' said Pekkala. 'I have a meeting I must get to. I just came to drop something off.' He took off his coat and removed the Webley in its shoulder holster. Then he laid the weapon on his desk.

'I've never seen you do that before,' said Kirov.

'Do what?' asked Pekkala.

'Leave this room without your weapon.'

As he buttoned his coat again, Pekkala tried to accustom himself to the unfamiliar lightness across his chest and shoulder blade. 'For this particular meeting, my only weapon is defencelessness.'

When Pekkala had gone, Elizaveta Kapanina slumped back into his chair. Her breath trailed out. The tips of her fingers were shaking.

'Why did you do that?' asked Kirov.

'Do what?' she replied.

'Of all the things to ask him about . . .'

'I'm sorry. I was just trying to make conversation. Besides, it was all I could think about. He dresses like an undertaker!'

'I know,' Kirov groaned. 'He buys his clothes at Linsky's.'

'He's a very strange man,' said Elizaveta, 'in case you hadn't noticed.'

'Strange or not, I think he likes you.'

Elizaveta laughed sarcastically. 'And I think you are a liar, Major Kirov.'

'No, I mean it. I've never heard him tell that story before, to me or to anyone else.'

'You almost sound as if you're jealous.'

'Perhaps I am, a little.'

'You are as strange as he is, Major Kirov,' Elizaveta told him. 'Maybe even more so, since you're pretending that you're not.'

From the shelter of his kumquat tree, Kirov shot her a quizzical glance.

At that same moment, somewhere in the bowels of Lubyanka, a guard swung open the door to Semykin's cell. 'Come with us,' he said.

Out in the hallway, Semykin fell in between two guards, who marched him in silence to a cell on the other side of the prison. Both of Semykin's hands had been wrapped in bandages, making it almost impossible for him to hold up his prison pyjama trousers. As he shuffled clumsily between the straight-backed guards, Semykin wondered what was happening, but he knew he could not ask.

Advancing down a corridor no different in appearance from the one they'd left only a few minutes before, the guards stopped outside a cell. The guard in front slid back the locking bolt and turned to face the convict. 'You have unusual friends, Semykin, unusual and powerful friends.'

As Semykin entered the cell, he gasped in astonishment. The walls had been completely covered with works of art from the Kremlin Museum. He recognised them instantly – the fifteenth-century embroidered silk-and-damask veil showing the revelation of the Virgin Mary to St Sergius, the seventeenth-century wooden panel depicting St Theodore Stratilates, the sixteenth-century tempera-on-wood painting of

Christ's entry into Jerusalem. And there, staring back at him once more, was *The Saviour of the Fiery Eye*.

Semykin turned and slowly turned again. As tears obscured his vision, the colours of the artwork blurred and sparkled, as if the paint on them was fresh, the silk just unravelled from the spool, and the breath of the artists, dead for centuries, still hovered before their creations.

Walking up a flight of concrete steps to the entrance of Moscow School No. 554, Pekkala caught the dry sweet smell of chalk dust wafting from one of the open windows on the ground floor. As he entered the three-storey building through the metal-fronted double doors, the reek of disinfectant raked across his senses. Layered upon this was the odour of boiled food, sweat and damp wool, awaking in Pekkala memories of his own schooldays in Finland.

He found himself in a long corridor with doors on either side stretching down the length of either wall. In its structure, the space was not unlike the halls of Lubyanka, but that place had been governed by silence. Here, it was the opposite. Pekkala made his way down the corridor, hearing the booming voices of teachers behind the closed doors of their classrooms, the tack and swish of chalk on blackboards and the occasional grinding squeak as a chair scudded back across the floor.

The walls between the classroom doors were covered with posters showing Lenin and Stalin, always seen from below, always looking off to the side. The posters had various slogans, such as 'Motherland is calling!' and 'Red Army soldier, save us!' One had an illustration of a line of soldiers standing to attention, in which only the knee-length boots were visible. Beside these boots the soldiers held their long Mosin-Nagant guns, butt plates on the ground. The top half of the poster was taken up with the slogan, 'Rifles To Your Legs!'

At last, guided by the smell of tobacco smoke and the sound of quiet laughter, he arrived at the place he had been looking for.

Sprawled upon a tired-looking couch in the faculty lounge, a teacher was reading that day's edition of *Izvestia*. His jacket lay bunched under his head as a pillow and all but the top button of his waistcoat had been undone.

In another corner of the room, a teacher sat at a small table, correcting papers with short vicious swipes of his pen. A freshly lit cigarette wobbled between his lips as he passed his muttered judgements on the work.

'I am looking for Professor Shulepov,' said Pekkala.

The teacher let his newspaper settle against his chest and glanced at the visitor. 'Two doors down and on the left,' he said.

'Be careful, though,' remarked the other teacher, without looking up from his papers. 'This is the time Shulepov takes his rest, and waking him before he's ready can be downright dangerous.'

More than you know, thought Pekkala, as he thanked them and proceeded down the hall.

A moment later, he located the room. The door was closed and a blind had been drawn in front of the glass window which looked from the classroom out into the hall. Opening the door as quietly as he could, Pekkala stepped inside.

A man in a grey wool jacket with wooden cuff buttons sat at his desk, asleep, head resting on his folded arms.

Pekkala recognised Kovalevsky's curly hair, although the

great mop he had sported back in his days of training had thinned to a wispy mass as faint as mare's tail clouds.

He looked around the classroom, at nubs of chalk in the tray beneath the board, the battered chairs and floorboards scuffed to splinters underneath the desks.

Kovalevsky sighed in his sleep, oblivious to the happy shrieks of children in the playground just outside.

'Professor?' asked Pekkala, in a soft voice. He wondered if his old friend would even remember him after so many years.

Kovalevsky stirred but his head remained down on the desk.

'Professor Shulepov?'

Kovalevsky groaned. His fingers uncurled as he stretched his hand. Slowly he sat up, blinking to clear his vision. 'Is it time already?' He squinted at Pekkala. 'Oh, my word,' he muttered as he reached for his glasses. 'Did I forget a parent-teacher conference?'

'No, Professor,' said Pekkala. 'I wondered if I could have a word?'

Struggling to revive himself, Kovalevsky rubbed his face, fingertips sliding up beneath the lenses of his spectacles as he massaged his eyelids. 'Of course. Would you mind closing the door?'

'Certainly,' replied Pekkala. As he turned, he heard the dry squeak of a desk drawer being opened. Then he heard a faint metal click, which he recognised immediately as the hammer being drawn back on a gun. Pekkala paused, hand on the worn brass door knob. 'That isn't necessary, Valeri,' he said quietly.

'Shut up and close the door,' replied Kovalevsky.

Pekkala did as he was told. Making sure that Kovalevsky could see his hands were empty, Pekkala slowly turned around.

He expected to find himself staring down the barrel of a pistol, but was surprised to see instead that the gun in Kovalevsky's hand, a Browning Model 1910, was pressed against the man's own skull.

'Are they out there now, Pekkala?' A layer of sweat greased Kovalevsky's forehead. 'For God's sake, don't let them shoot me in front of the children.'

'No one has come to hurt you, Valeri.'

'Do you know what it's like, Pekkala, to wake up each day amazed to find yourself still breathing?'

'Believe it or not, yes I do.'

'Then you would know why I am sceptical of your assurances.'

'Either shoot me,' said Pekkala, 'or put down the gun and give me a chance to convince you.'

Kovalevsky hesitated. Then he tucked the gun into the pocket of his coat. 'If you haven't come to kill me, then what are you doing here?'

'I need your help.'

Kovalevsky laughed scornfully. 'Are you speaking to Professor Shulepov or to the last of Myednikov's men?'

'I think you already know the answer to that.'

Kovalevsky walked over to the window of the classroom and looked down at the playground, where a group of students were playing with a half-inflated soccer ball. 'I teach history now. I'm no longer in the business of making it. What could I possibly do for you?'

'I need you to get me through the German lines.'

'Will you be coming back again?'

'Yes.'

'Alone?'

'No. Four people, including you on the way out, and five on the journey home.'

'This fifth person,' asked Kovalevsky, 'will he or she come willingly?'

'He will not.'

At that moment, there was a gentle knocking on the door. A child's voice murmured through the keyhole. 'Professor! It's time to wake up!'

'Enter,' called Kovalevsky.

A ginger-haired boy walked in. Immediately, his hazel-coloured eyes fixed on Pekkala.

Kovalevsky nodded with approval. 'Right on time, Zev, as usual.'

The boy smiled and straightened up. 'Thank you, Professor Shulepov!'

'Before you tell the others to come in,' said the professor, 'tell me how you are doing in your new home. Are you getting enough to eat? Did they give you a comfortable bed?'

'Yes, Professor. I am settling in.'

'You have made some new friends?'

'Yes, Professor. Some.'

Kovalevsky rested his hand on the top of the boy's head. 'Very good. Now go out and tell the others it is time.'

The boy smiled back at him, then spun smartly on his heel and left the room.

'He's in an orphanage,' explained Kovalevsky.

Pekkala remembered what Stalin had said about the boy whose parents had been shipped to the gulag at Mamlin-Three.

A moment later, the rest of the class filed into the room. As they took their seats, each one glanced cautiously at Pekkala.

'This is an old friend of mine,' said Kovalevsky, laying his hand upon Pekkala's shoulder. 'His name is Inspector Pekkala. Long ago, and still today, he is known as the Emerald Eye.'

'Why do they call you that?' asked the boy called Zev.

'Because of this,' replied Pekkala, lifting his lapel to reveal the gold badge. The emerald glinted in the pale light of the classroom.

A sound, somewhere between a moan and a sigh, went up from the students, as if they had just watched a firework explode into stars in the distance.

'I know you!' exclaimed a boy at the back excitedly tapping together the wooden-soled toes of his shoes. 'My father says you are a shadow of the past.'

Pekkala smiled nervously. 'I think what he means is that I am a holder of a Shadow Pass.'

'No,' replied the boy. 'That isn't what he said.'

'Ah.' Pekkala nodded and looked around the room.

'Where are you from?' asked a girl with the red scarf of the Comintern.

'I am originally from Finland,' replied Pekkala, glad to be changing the subject.

'Can you do magic? All the Finns can do magic.'

'I may know a card trick or two,' Pekkala told her, casting a desperate glance at Kovalevsky.

'The Inspector was just leaving!' announced Kovalevsky.

'Yes!' agreed Pekkala. 'Yes I was.'

Kovalevsky ushered him into the hall.

'If you want my advice, Pekkala, the safest and the simplest thing to do would be to kill this man, rather than try to bring him back, and then to get out of the country as quickly as you can. That way, you have at least a reasonable chance of reaching home again.'

'I must bring him back alive.'

'Then the odds are against you, old friend.'

'Never mind the odds,' said Pekkala. 'Can you help me?'

'I can try,' replied Kovalevsky. 'Let's talk about it over dinner this evening at the Café Tilsit. That is your favourite place, isn't it?'

'Yes,' Pekkala replied in confusion, 'but how . . . ?'

He was interrupted by a loud and jarring bell which clanged in the hallway, indicating that the next lesson had begun.

'Six o'clock!' Kovalevsky stepped back inside his classroom. 'Make sure you are punctual,' he said with a smile as he began to close the door. 'Teachers don't like to be kept waiting.'

By the time their request to withdraw from the grounds of the Catherine Palace had been granted, the remnants of the 5th Anti-Aircraft Battery 35th Rifle Division had already been re-treating for two days. Their new orders were to proceed to Leningrad, where the three remaining trucks would attempt to enter the city before the German encirclement was complete. If successful, they were to be deployed against the bombing raids which were now going on around the clock.

Barkat was driving at the rear of the column when, as they passed through a village so small it wasn't even marked upon their maps, an old woman wearing an ankle-length blue dress and white shawl beckoned to them from the front gate of her garden.

'What does that woman want?' barked Commissar Sirko, sitting beside Barkat and smoking two cigarettes at the same time.

'It looks like she's holding a bottle,' replied Barkat.

'A bottle? Stop the truck!'

Obediently Barkat pulled to the side of the road and Sirko jumped down on to the road. He strode across to the woman. 'What is it, granny? What have you got for me?'

She handed him an ornate glass container of the kind used to hold home-made vodka.

Sirko leaned over the garden's white picket fence, which was twined with purple chicory flowers and kissed the woman on her sunburned, wrinkled cheek.

The old woman nodded and smiled and patted the air in farewell as Sirko walked back to the waiting truck, the bottle raised triumphantly above his head. 'They love me!' he announced to Stefanov and Ragozin, who had stuck their heads out from under the canvas flap at the back of the truck in order to see why they had stopped. 'Even though we're leaving them to an uncertain fate among the Fascists, they don't hold it against us. You see, Stefanov . . .'

'Are you going to share that?' asked Ragozin.

'Go find your own vodka-making granny,' replied Sirko. He drank half the bottle before the woman's house was even out of sight.

When they stopped an hour later to change a flat tyre, Sirko threw up on the side of the road. 'I drank it too fast,' he remarked, wiping his mouth with his sleeve.

After struggling to catch up with the other two trucks, which had driven on ahead, Barkat eventually found them pulled off the road in a forest, where they were settling in for the night. Thick stands of white birch, with loose bark curled like scrolls against the bone-white trunks, spread away dizzyingly into the depths of the forest.

Rather than unpack the truck, they lay underneath it, wrapped in their brown rain capes, with rucksacks for pillows.

Sirko threw up again.

Stefanov, lying beside him, could smell from the vomit that what Sirko had drunk was not vodka but wood alcohol.

'That witch has killed me,' whispered Sirko, touching his fingertips against his face. 'I think I'm blind.'

He died before dawn.

They wrapped Sirko in his rain cape and buried him in a clearing in a pine forest, his helmet on a stick to mark the grave.

From then on, Sergeant Ragozin was in charge.

Later that morning, the three trucks of the convoy set out across a marsh, travelling on corduroy roads made from thousands of tree trunks laid out side by side over the swampy ground.

Halfway across, with Barkat still driving in the rear, the ZiS-5 slid off the corduroy road and their vehicle became stranded in the mud. The rest of the convoy pushed on, with a promise to send help as soon as they had reached Leningrad.

'But you can't leave us here!' Ragozin pleaded. 'Not in this miserable place!'

His only reply was a wave from the driver of the second truck, as it teetered away across the swamp.

'If that selfish bastard hadn't drunk poisoned alcohol, I would never be in this predicament!' wailed Ragozin.

'And if he hadn't been so selfish with it, neither would the rest of us,' replied Barkat.

The two other men watched Ragozin as he marched dementedly up and down the rotted tree-trunk road, stamping at the ground as if the earth itself required punishment. 'I am a civilised man! I used to have the most popular radio programme in the entire Soviet Union!' He shook a knotty fist up at the sky. 'People from all over the world wrote to me. Once I got a letter from Vanuatu and I don't even know where that is!'

'I knew he'd crack eventually,' said Barkat, scratching at his week-old growth of beard.

Ragozin glowered at the men with bloodshot eyes. 'What are you looking at? Haven't you ever seen a man in torment before?'

'Not one as civilised as you,' Stefanov replied.

When they woke up the next day, they discovered that the 25-mm gun had sunk so deeply into the mud that it threatened to drag the truck down with it. In desperation, they unhitched the gun from the truck and in less than a minute the 25-mm had vanished completely into the reeking black ooze.

It took them three hours before they had finally extricated their truck and eased it back on to the corduroy road, by which time they were dangerously low on fuel.

They managed to reach the village of Vinusk on the other side of the swamp before running completely out of petrol. They found the place deserted but intact. As of that moment, the three men had no idea which side of the line they were on.

The autumn sky glowed powdery blue and the air flickered with late-hatching insects in a light turned strange and gold. The breeze smelled sweetly of poplar leaves, which fell in cascades of yellow upon the wreckage of the battlefield.

For their command post, Ragozin selected a house in which a deep bunker had previously been dug beneath the floor. The bunker was reached by a staircase cut into the clay and reinforced with slabs of iron tank track. The tank which had supplied the tracks, a massive Soviet KV-2, lay with its turret blown off in a shallow pond across the road.

Judging from the equipment they found, including rifles, a box of ration food and a Golub radio precariously balanced on a collapsible army desk, the bunker had been built by Russian soldiers. The previous tenants had even left behind a map, pinned with bayonets to the earth walls of the bunker. Red and blue grease pencil lines, which marked the positions of opposing forces, had been drawn, erased, then drawn again so many times that in places the map was illegible.

Perched on a crate that had once contained land mines, Stefanov turned on the radio and listened through veils of radio static to a Russian artillery commander giving target coordinates for a barrage that was about to begin.

Beside him, on a bed made out of wooden planks with a chicken-wire mattress, Barkat was taking a nap.

'Grid seven,' said the voice on the radio, 'point H-12.'

Satisfied to hear that somebody in the Red Army was doing more than just retreating from the Germans, Stefanov pulled a slightly rotten pear from one pocket and a stag-handled switchblade from the other. He pressed a button on the side of the knife and the blade flashed out with a noise like someone sucking their teeth.

Barkat sat up suddenly. 'Do I smell food?'

Stefanov sighed. It was not a very big pear and he had been hoping to eat it by himself. But now he cut off a slice, speared it on the end of the knife and offered it to Barkat.

Barkat reached across, took the slice off the switchblade and crammed it into his mouth. Then, from around his neck, he pulled a small white linen bag containing his ration of *machorka* tobacco. Next, Barkat produced a neatly folded page from the *Izvestia*. He did not read the news, but no rolling papers were issued with army tobacco rations and the wafer-thin teture of *Izvestia* was best for cigarettes. Barkat tore off a finger-length strip of paper and wiped it on his matted greasy hair before folding it into a cigarette with some flakes of *machorka* from the sweat-stained bag. 'What are you looking so thoughtful about?' asked Barkat.

'To tell you the truth,' admitted Stefanov, 'I am having some trouble understanding the difference between Fascism and Communism.'

'You think too much. They are the Fascists. We are the Communists. What more is there to know?'

Stefanov gave a dissatisfied grunt.

'What's on the radio?' asked Barkat. 'Any music?'

'Only if you count the Stalin organ.'

'Why don't you come upstairs and get some fresh air?'

'Maybe later,' he said.

'Where's Ragozin?'

'He went to the crossroads at the end of the village.'

'Why?'

'He said he spotted some wild strawberries growing by the side of the road when we drove in here.'

'Idiot! Strawberries don't grow this time of year. They were probably poisonous mushrooms.' As Barkat climbed the stairs, he mumbled a song called 'Katyusha'. 'Apple trees and pears in blossom . . .'

Under his breath, Stefanov sang along: '. . . on the river morning mist . . .'

When Barkat had gone, Stefanov rose to his feet and walked across the muddy floor to look at the map. Placing a finger at each end of the map, where the grid references began, he traced the coordinates he had heard on the radio. 'Grid 7, H-12,' he muttered to himself. His fingertips came together over a cluster of black freckles on the rubberised canvas, each one representing a house. The name of the village was barely legible, its letters all but hidden by the wrinkles on the canvas. He stared at the spot until at last he could decipher the word. Vinusk. The breath caught in his throat. His fingers dropped from the map.

'Barkat,' he whispered, and then his voice rose to a shout. 'Barkat!'

His voice was drowned out by the shriek of incoming Soviet rockets, as if a train were hurtling past at full speed just above the house. In two long strides, Stefanov crossed the room and dived under the desk on which the radio had been set up. As he crawled up against the wall, he heard the clattering roar as a shell hit the road and then a long hiss as another landed in the pond. A third landed somewhere behind the house.

Stefanov closed his eyes, jammed his fingers into his ears and gritted his teeth as explosions began to follow each other so quickly that he could not distinguish one from another.

He felt a sudden pressure in his ears, like diving too deep under water. The floor bucked. Then the roof caved in. The air was filled with metallic-smelling smoke. He cried out and his mouth filled with smoke. The radio slid off the table and its metal corner smashed him in the head. Stunned by the blow, Stefanov heard a far-off ringing like a single struck piano key whose tone refused to fade away. And suddenly everything stopped except that single note which seemed to rise in pitch until he felt his skull must shatter like a crystal glass. In that moment, Stefanov felt neither pain, nor fear, so separated from the spark of his own life that it was as if he had never existed. For how long this lasted, he had no idea. It might have been a few seconds before the sound vanished abruptly and, in its place, he heard the crackling of flames.

Stefanov opened his eyes. At first he saw nothing. He wondered if the concussion had blinded him. Bringing his hand to his face, he could vaguely make out the wall of his approaching palm. He crawled out from under the broken table, through rays of sunlight that punched through the smoke, leaning like crooked pillars among the fallen timbers of the roof. Shakily, he climbed to his feet, shedding a garland of tangled radio wires from around his shoulders. The smoke was already beginning to clear. The maps on the wall had been shredded as if by the claws of giant cats. Where the roof had fallen in, clumps of thatch littered the floor. Lying on a heap of mouldy straw in front of him was a cluster of baby mice, eyes not yet open, their tiny pink bodies twined together as they nosed about in the grey air. Above him, visible through holes torn in the roof, fat cumulus clouds wandered by in the blue.

Stefanov climbed the staircase and stepped out into a world that he no longer recognised. Blast craters crackled and smouldered in the road. Licks of flame stabbed out of the ground. Trees which had lined the street were splintered at chest height. Where houses had once stood, he now saw only fragmented walls and chimneys, from which rose coils of thick black smoke.

Their truck, which had been hidden behind the building, was slumped forward on punctured tyres, its engine torn away.

Barkat lay beside the ruined vehicle. A bird could have flown through the hole in his chest.

At the sight of his friend's blood, mingled with the blue-green puddles of spilled radiator fluid, Stefanov dropped to his knees. With tears blurring his vision, Stefanov gathered Barkat in his arms. Lifting the body over his shoulder, he set off towards the crossroads where Ragozin had gone to find the strawberries. As he stumbled under the weight, fresh perspiration doused the white salt blooms of old sweat on his clothes. Barkat's face thumped against Stefanov's back and the dead man's boots trembled in a rhythm with his stride.

Stefanov reached the crossroads. Here, as well, artillery had cratered the ground.

Rain dripped on Stefanov's head, merging with sweat as it trickled down his forehead. He wiped it from his face and glancing at his reddened fingertips realised that what had fallen on him was blood, not water. Struggling to wipe it off as quickly as he could, he looked up and saw Ragozin's body tangled high in the branches of a tree, where he had been thrown by the blast. Ragozin's back was folded almost double, his face strangely misshapen, like a waxwork figure melting in the sun.

There was no way to bring Ragozin down. Stefanov had to leave him. Still carrying Barkat, he stumbled on towards a town, whose rooftops he could see in the distance.

Another kilometre along the road, he met a column of Russian infantry heading west to stop the German advance. Stefanov climbed up on a grassy embankment while the soldiers filed past.

Gently, he set Barkat on the ground. The dead man collapsed in a sitting position, slumped against Stefanov's legs like a broken marionette.

The soldiers marched in good order, faces hidden under the flared rims of their helmets. Over their left shoulders, each man carried a rolled blanket, the ends of which were stuffed into the little aluminium buckets that served as mess kits. A few of the soldiers glanced nervously at the corpse.

Once the column had gone by, Stefanov shouldered the body and continued on beneath grey clouds tasselled with rain.

Pekkala arrived at the Café Tilsit at 5.30, half an hour before the meeting was due to take place. It was his custom to arrive early for meetings. This gave him time to study his surroundings, even those which were as familiar to him as the Tilsit. Out of habits that had been drilled into him since his first days of training with the Okhrana, he never sat with his back to a window or a door, but always positioned himself against a wall by an exit, preferably the kitchen, through which he could escape if needed. The other advantage of being near the kitchen was that anyone entering the restaurant through the service entrance would inevitably be halted by the staff. The change in tone of their voices was as good as any watchdog, even if he could not hear what they were saying. And if, as was likely, the intruder responded by pulling a gun on any waiter or dishwasher who tried to bar his way, even if he did not pull the trigger, the sudden silence from the kitchen was equally efficient in warning him that something was not right.

No matter how safe Pekkala knew his surroundings to be, whenever circumstances forced him to sit facing away from a window or a door, he felt the skin crawl on the back of his neck.

These rules of survival had been so engrained into Pekkala's mind that he no longer gave them any conscious thought.

The café was bustling as usual for that time of the evening.

Most of the customers sat at long tables, elbow to elbow, strangers side by side, enjoying the strange solitude that came with being alone in such a crowded place. As Pekkala made his way towards his usual table at the back, he saw that it was already occupied. As he turned to look for an alternative, the figure at his chosen place raised a hand and smiled.

It was only then that Pekkala realised the man was Kovalevsky, who had arrived even earlier, no doubt with the same instincts as Pekkala's.

The two men sat hunched over the little table, elbows resting on the bare wood, not knowing where to begin after so many years apart.

In spite of the years since they'd last seen each other, Pekkala felt immediately at ease with Kovalevsky. Their shared past had given them a particular angle of vision on the world which could not be blunted by time.

'Did you think I wouldn't show?' asked Kovalevsky.

'You're here now,' replied Pekkala. 'That's what matters.'

'I see you are not wearing your weapon.'

'I knew I wouldn't need it.'

With a smile, Kovalevsky drew open his coat, showing that he'd also come unarmed. 'Ever since you stepped into my classroom this afternoon, I've been wondering how you tracked me down.'

'You talk in your sleep,' replied Pekkala.

'I what?'

Without offering any further explanation, Pekkala asked a question of his own. 'How on earth did you know I came here to the Tilsit?'

'I come here myself from time to time. I've seen you here.'

Now it was Pekkala who seemed baffled. 'How is it that I didn't spot you?'

'One thing I did not forget from my days with Myednikov is how to vanish in a crowded room. Besides, when a man is dead, you do not look for him. In that way, at least, Dzerzhinsky did me a favour.'

Valentina, the owner, arrived at their table with two wooden bowls of sorrel and spinach soup, into each of which a dollop of sour cream had been ladled. 'Ah,' she said to Pekkala, 'I see you have made a new friend.' And with those words, she bent down and kissed Kovalevsky on the cheek. 'The professor is my favourite customer. Aren't you, Professor?'

'I try to be,' he replied.

Pekkala smiled politely as he watched this exchange, but he couldn't help remembering his last visit to the Tilsit, when Valentina had touched his shoulder. And he was embarrassed now at how that touch had made him feel, even if only for an instant.

'So we are to go on a mission together,' said Kovalevsky, when the two men were alone again.

'The last one you will ever need to do.'

Kovalevsky nodded as he spooned some of the bright green soup into his mouth. 'A fitting end to my career, since you were also my companion on the first mission we ever undertook.'

'A humbling experience,' remarked Pekkala, 'thanks to Chief Inspector Vassileyev.'

In the course of their Okhrana training, Vassileyev had familiarised the two young recruits in the use of secret codes, disguises, bomb defusing and firearms, which included so many hours spent firing their Nagant revolvers in the underground range beneath Okhrana Headquarters that Pekkala and Kovalevsky resorted to dipping their index fingers in molten candle wax before the sessions began every day, since the skin had been worn off the pads of their fingertips by the triggers of the guns.

Vassileyev's favourite topic, however, was the hunting down of suspects. He was, in spite of the fact that he had lost one of his legs in a bomb blast, still considered to be the finest practitioner of the art of tailing and pursuit in all of Russia.

So it struck the two men as particularly strange when, after only an hour of preparation, Vassileyev assigned them the task of following a courier named Worunchuk from the telegraph office he visited each afternoon to the point where he crossed the Potsuleyev bridge.

'But you must go no further than the bridge!' commanded Vassileyev.

Perplexed by this cryptic order, Kovalevsky and Pekkala did not know what to think.

'Inspector . . .' Pekkala began hesitantly.

'Yes? What is it?'

'Are you sure we are ready for this? We've been shooting at targets for months, but we spent less than a day learning how to tail suspects.'

'You are exactly as ready as I need you to be! Now go!' He shooed them out of the room. 'Get to work!'

Following Vassileyev's instructions, Kovalevsky and Pekkala waited at a tram stop across the road from the telegraph office. Each time a tram halted to allow passengers on or off, the two men would step back until the tram had departed and resume their observation of the telegraph office. It was a small building, painted bone-white except for a red sign, outlined with black and gold, above the entrance, which read, 'Government Signals Bureau'.

'I don't think he's ever coming,' muttered Kovalevsky, after they had been standing there for an hour.

'Vassileyev taught us to be patient,' replied Pekkala, although he was beginning to have his own doubts.

It was three hours before Worunchuk finally arrived. The physical description Vassileyev had provided them made the suspect easy to identify. He was a heavy-set man with an olive complexion, sharp, sloping nose and a black moustache. He wore a black, velvet-lapelled overcoat that came down to his knees of the type commonly seen on lawyers, bankers and office managers.

Worunchuk had chosen the time of day when most businesses were closing, and the streets were filled with people heading home from work.

Rather than risk losing him in the crowds, Kovalevsky and Pekkala hurriedly crossed the road as Worunchuk ducked into the telegraph office. They waited two doors down, outside a woman's clothing shop, until Worunchuk appeared a few minutes later, tucking an envelope into the chest pocket of his coat.

He set off at a brisk pace along the road which ran beside the Moika River. Several times, he crossed the street and then crossed back again for no apparent reason, forcing Pekkala and Kovalevsky to reverse direction in the middle of the road. Once he stopped in front of a butcher shop, eyeing the cuts of meat on display behind the large glass window.

It was not long before Worunchuk crossed the Potsuleyev bridge, leaving his pursuers sweating with exertion as they watched him disappear among the commuters. As soon as he was out of sight, Kovalevsky and Pekkala hurried back to Vassileyev.

They found him sitting behind his desk, whittling out the inside of his wooden leg with a large bone-handled pen knife. 'Did you find him?' asked Vassileyev, without even looking up to see who had entered the room.

'Yes.' Kovalevsky removed a handkerchief from his pocket and dabbed the sweat from his forehead. 'He moves quickly!'

'And he crossed the Potsuleyev bridge?'

'That is correct, Inspector,' Pekkala confirmed, 'and from there, we let him go, just as you ordered.'

'Good!' Vassileyev laid his wooden leg upon the table. 'Tomorrow you will do the same again. Follow him to the Potsuleyev bridge.'

'Yes, Inspector,' both men chorused.

Vassileyev aimed a finger at them. 'But no further. That's an order!'

The next day and the next and the next, the two men took up their station at the tram stop.

Worunchuk kept a tight schedule, arriving at the telegraph office at three minutes to five every day. The route he took to reach the Potsuleyev bridge also remained unchanged, and varied only in those places where he zigzagged mindlessly across the road. But he always stopped at the butcher shop, standing before its large glass window to study the cuts of meat.

'Why doesn't he buy anything?' muttered Kovalevsky. 'If he can afford a coat like that, he can spring for a few links of sausage!'

When, once more, Worunchuk vanished across the Potsuleyev bridge, Kovalevsky turned angrily and began striding back towards Vassileyev's office.

Pekkala struggled to keep up.

'This is doing no good at all!' Kovalevsky's voice was filled with frustration. 'As far as I can see, he's doing nothing wrong.'

'Yet.'

Kovalevsky stopped and turned to face Pekkala. 'What did you say?'

'I said "yet". He hasn't done anything wrong yet.'

'This city is filled with people who haven't done anything wrong yet. Are you suggesting that we follow all of them?'

'No,' Pekkala replied, 'only the one Inspector Vassileyev has ordered us to pursue.'

Kovalevsky grunted disapprovingly, then headed off again towards Okhrana headquarters.

The next day, on Vassileyev's orders, they were back at the tram stop, opposite the telegraph office.

Kovalevsky was in an even fouler mood than he had been

the day before. 'This is not what I signed up for.' He glared at Pekkala. 'Did you sign up for this?'

'No,' Pekkala told him. 'I did not sign up at all. It was the Tsar who sent me here.'

At two minutes past five, when Worunchuk made his usual departure from the telegraph office, Pekkala and Kovalevsky set off after him, following at a safe distance.

As he did every day, Worunchuk paused before the butcher shop.

'For pity's sake,' growled Kovalevsky, 'go in and buy something today!'

Suddenly, as if Kovalevsky's suggestion had forced itself into his mind, Worunchuk stepped into the shop.

'Finally!' groaned Kovalevsky.

The two men slowed their pace and came to a halt one door down from the butcher shop.

'We shouldn't stop here,' said Pekkala. 'We'll walk slowly past the shop and wait for him on the other side. He's bound to come out soon.'

As the two men strolled past the butcher shop, they were shocked to find Worunchuk standing in the doorway.

He had not entered the shop at all, but only stood at the entrance, waiting for the men to walk by.

Stunned, Pekkala and Kovalevsky met his stare, unable to hide their true purpose.

Angrily, Worunchuk pushed past them and set off towards the Potsuleyev bridge. He did not run. Nor did he turn to look back. It was as if he knew they could not touch him.

Pekkala had taken only one step in the direction of the fleeing man before he felt Kovalevsky's arm on his sleeve, holding him back.

'It's no use,' whispered Kovalevsky. 'He's made us. Somehow he figured it out. We might as well go back and tell Vassileyev we have failed.'

Gloomily, the two men watched him disappear into the crowd.

Half an hour later, Pekkala and Kovalevsky presented themselves at Vassileyev's office.

Vassileyev was sitting at his desk, smoking a cigarette which he had taken from a gold and red box labelled 'Markov'. 'Well?' he demanded, raising his chin and whistling a thin jet of smoke towards the ceiling.

'He spotted us,' explained Pekkala.

'How?' Vassileyev's face showed no emotion.

After a deep sigh, Kovalevsky continued with their story. 'He was waiting for us in the doorway to a butcher shop. He stopped there every day but never went inside. This day, he finally went in, at least we thought he had . . .'

'Did the shop have a window?'

'Yes, for displaying the meat. Every day he went to see what they'd set out. But he never bought anything!'

'He wasn't looking at the meat,' said Vassileyev. 'He was studying your reflections in the window.'

As the truth became apparent, Pekkala lowered his head in shame and stared at the floor.

Kovalevsky's lips began to twitch. 'But when he crossed the road, back and forth, he never looked back. He didn't see us then.'

'He didn't need to. He was testing who kept pace with him.

Anyone not following him would maintain their speed along the pavement, but you would return to the exact same distance behind him. And all the confirmation he needed would be there for him to see in the shop window when he stopped.'

'I am sorry,' muttered Kovalevsky,

'*We* are sorry,' added Pekkala.

For a moment longer, Vassileyev's face remained stony. Then, all of a sudden, he began to smile. 'You have both done very well.'

The two men stared at him in confusion.

'You did exactly what I hoped you would do,' explained Vassileyev.

'You mean to let him see us?' asked Kovalevsky.

'You didn't let him,' said Vassileyev. 'He outsmarted you. That's all.'

'And that was what you wanted?' asked Pekkala. 'I don't understand, Chief Inspector.'

'Worunchuk is not the man we're after. As I told you, he is only a courier.'

'Then who are you trying to arrest?' asked Kovalevsky.

'A bomb maker named Krebs. We believe he might have been the one who built the device that killed Tsar Alexander III. He has no politics, no convictions. He simply builds bombs for whoever can afford to pay him. We learned from an Okhrana agent at the telegraph office that messages had begun arriving regularly for a certain Julius Crabbe, a known alias for Krebs. The messages are coded, of course. We have no way of knowing exactly who he's building for now, or what will be done with the bomb when it is ready. Our only chance is to arrest Krebs before he has a chance to deliver the bomb.'

'But why not simply follow Worunchuk to the place where he's delivering the telegram?' Kovalevsky asked exasperatedly.

'Oh, we've done that.' Vassileyev dismissed the suggestion with a wave of his hand. 'He lives in a flat across the road from the Petersburg Wind Instruments Factory.'

'And why not arrest him there?' asked Pekkala.

Vassileyev smiled patiently. 'Because we happen to know that Krebs has prepared explosive devices strong enough to destroy the entire building, along with half the others on the street, if anyone should try to force their way into his apartment. We need to catch him when he is out on his own. Otherwise, he will kill as many or more people than would have been killed by the bomb he's constructing now.'

'But Worunchuk will have told him by now that he was being followed by the Okhrana. Surely he'll be on the next train out of town.'

Vassileyev shook his head. 'Worunchuk is a professional. He probably realised you were following him the first day you showed up outside the telegraph office.'

'Then why would he come back the next day, and the next and the day after that?'

'He was studying you,' said Vassileyev, 'seeing how well you were able to track him without being noticed.'

'Not well at all, apparently,' said Pekkala.

'Exactly! And Worunchuk would quickly reach the conclusion that he was not dealing with agents of the Okhrana, who would have undergone months of training. What he would have seen were a couple of amateurs. Forgive me, boys, but what I needed from you these past few days was not your expertise but rather your lack of it.'

'Then who will he think we are, if not government agents?' asked Kovalevsky.

Vassileyev pursed his lips and let his hands fall open. 'Most likely, just a couple of local thugs looking to shake him down. The fact that you would only follow him as far as the Potsuleyev bridge would have convinced him of this, since the gangs in this city co-exist by operating in specific territories. The bridge is one such boundary marker, and a line gang members would not dare to cross.'

'We could have gotten him,' said Kovalevsky. 'He was standing right in front of us.'

'It's lucky for you that you didn't try,' replied Vassileyev. 'He would have killed you both for sport.'

'So what do we do now?' asked Pekkala. 'Do we simply show up tomorrow at the telegraph office and start following him all over again?'

'There would be no point, 'Vassileyev told him. 'Worunchuk won't be there. The fact that he was being followed, even if it was only by a couple of thugs such as yourselves, means that he can no longer function as a courier for Krebs. As soon as he has informed Krebs of the situation he will vanish, probably to another city. No doubt we will run into him again someday. But, for now, that leaves Krebs without a courier to receive his messages. He hasn't got time to engage another courier.'

'He will have to collect them himself,' said Pekkala.

Vassileyev nodded. 'And when he does, we will be waiting.'

'What about the person who is paying for the bomb?'

'In the city of Kiev, there is another equally humiliated pair of young Okhrana agents, and a courier who thinks he's gotten the better of them. It won't be long before the man who ordered the bomb is face to face with the oblivion he had planned for many others.' Vassileyev stubbed out his cigarette and immediately reached into the box to find another. 'Congratulations, boys. You have just completed your first successful mission.'

*

'And what is this last mission to be?' asked Kovalevsky, as he carefully spooned up his soup.

While Kovalevsky ate, Pekkala explained everything.

By the time he had finished, Kovalevsky's bowl was empty. With a sigh, he pushed it to the centre of the table, sat back and folded his hands across his stomach. 'What I don't understand, Pekkala, is why you need my help at all. It has been years since I practised my old trade. Surely Stalin has his own men to do this job!'

'He does, but none that he can trust. Somewhere in the ranks of NKVD, or even in the Kremlin itself, there is a traitor. If this person, whoever he is, learns of our plan to bring back Gustav Engel, as soon as we cross the lines, we will be heading straight into a trap. You are the only one with the necessary skills whom we are certain is not involved.'

'Yet.'

Pekkala nodded.

'You mentioned that this would be my final mission,' said Kovalevsky. 'I do not mean to sound mercenary, Pekkala, but what exactly are you offering in exchange for my help on this case?'

'Nothing.'

'You drive a hard bargain, Pekkala.'

'No, old friend. I don't think you understand. When I said nothing, I meant that your past would be officially forgotten. You would simply go back to living out your life as Professor Shulepov.'

'That is more than generous,' said Kovalevsky. 'Besides, it would have been hard to walk away from a job I've grown to love. I am also tired of running. But I wonder if you realise just how difficult a mission this could be.'

'Getting through the German lines never sounded easy to me.'

'That is not the hard part,' explained Kovalevsky. 'The greatest challenge, since you cannot simply kill this man and be done with it, will be in persuading him to come back with us.'

'Persuading him? It almost sounds as if you expect him to come of his own free will.'

'That is precisely what I mean,' replied Kovalevsky.

'But surely there are ways to smuggle him across, even if he doesn't want to go?'

'There are, but none of them are reliable. We can drug him, bandage him up and try to carry him through as a badly wounded soldier. If it was only a matter of hours, this method would be practical, but it will take days to return and the longer we try to keep a man knocked out, the greater the risk that we might accidentally kill him with the drug, or that the drug might fail and he wakes up and sounds the alarm. If that happens, or if he gets away from you, we are as good as dead.'

'Is there any way to do this without drugging him?'

'If you are afraid he might run, you can cut one of his Achilles' tendons.'

Pekkala winced at the matter-of-fact tone in Kovalevsky's voice.

'But the injury tends to arouse suspicion,' continued Kovalevsky, 'and unless you find a way to silence him, the man can still cry out for help.'

'I have taken many people into custody over the years, but none under circumstances as difficult as this.' Reluctantly, Pekkala returned to Kovalevsky's original idea. 'How do you propose that we convince a man to travel with us to what might be his death?'

'In that one sentence, Pekkala, you have already provided the answer.'

'I have?'

'You said "might". Once we have him at gunpoint, Engel will quickly realise that his chances of surviving an escape attempt are next to none. He will also understand that his odds of surviving in Soviet captivity are very small. Small as they might be, however, we must convince him that this small chance of survival does exist, provided he cooperates. Add to that the possibility that if, on arriving in Moscow, he agrees to tell you everything he knows, he will not only survive, he will prosper.'

'You mean to get him to change sides.'

Kovalevsky shrugged. 'If the alternative is a hole in the ground, changing sides can be a mere formality. Remember what this man is fighting for. It is not a love of one country and a hatred of another. It is these works of art. If we can offer him a stake in their future, as well as a future for himself, I think the outcome of this journey will be the one that Stalin has in mind. Have you met this man Engel?'

'No. That's why we are bringing someone who can identify him. Her name is Lieutenant Churikova.'

'Even better. When it comes to convincing Engel, a woman is likely to be more persuasive than a couple of thugs like us.'

'Even if she can persuade Engel to come with us of his own free will, it will be much harder for Engel to persuade Stalin to keep him alive.'

'Stalin has made peace with enemies before, provided they are useful enough. You and I are living proof of that. If Engel plays his cards right, he may yet live a long and happy life.'

Their meal concluded, the two men stood up to leave.

It was drizzling as they stepped out into a world of moving shadows. On account of air raid precautions, the streetlamps were no longer illuminated. The only lights came from vehicles which, with their headlights blinkered into slits, resembled huge black cats prowling through the rain-slicked streets. Many people were still on their way home from work and since the tram and underground services had been scaled back due to fuel shortages, the pavements were busier this time of day than they had ever been before the war.

'Do you know what my first thought was when I saw you at the school?' asked Kovalevsky. Without waiting for an answer, he went on. 'I thought to myself that Myednikov would have been disappointed in me.'

'But why? After all, you are the one who survived.'

'That was more luck than skill. I neglected the most important rule he ever taught me – to have an exit out of every situation, whether it is a way out of that restaurant, or a route out of the city or the country. And then there is the exit through which you disappear forever, after which the person you knew as yourself no longer exists. But that is the most dangerous one of all. After you have gone through that door, only one exit remains.'

'And what is that?'

'For me, the day I became Professor Shulepov, my only way out was a Browning 1910.'

'I am glad you didn't take it,' said Pekkala.

'So am I,' agreed Kovalevsky. 'And whatever skills I possess, outdated though they might be, are now at your disposal. All I ask in exchange is the chance to go back into hiding.'

'You have my word, old friend.'

'How long do we have to prepare?'

'Three days.'

'Very well. That should be enough time. Tomorrow, I will begin making preparations,' said Kovalevsky. 'I will need information about precise troop displacements, as well as aerial reconnaissance photographs showing what roads and bridges might still be open.'

'I'll make sure you get them.'

'We will need money,' Kovalevsky continued, 'and not standard currency. Gold coins will work best, preferably German, French or British.'

'I'm sure some can be found.'

'Concealed compasses.'

'NKVD has some which fit inside standard Red Army tunic buttons.'

'And we will need vials of potassium cyanide, one for each person, in case we are captured.'

To this, Pekkala only nodded, recalling the thin glass containers, each one containing about a teaspoonful of the poison.

The vial itself was stored in a brass cartridge, which could be unscrewed in the middle. NKVD issued these vials in sets of three, laid out in blue velvet in a small leather-bound case, exactly the same kind one might find in a jeweller's shop for displaying a wedding ring or a set of pearl earrings.

The vials came with no instructions for use, unlike almost everything else issued by NKVD, even down to shoelaces and torches. Each person to whom the poison was issued had the choice of precisely where and how to store the means of suicide. One popular method was to have a vial sewn into the collar of a shirt, in the place where the collar stay would normally go. This was a place where a person under arrest was unlikely to be searched. Once the vial had been placed in the mouth, the user only had to bite down gently and the poison would be released, causing death in less than four seconds.

Pekkala had been issued a set of vials, but he had never carried them. No one had ever insisted, or even asked him why, which was fortunate, because he would have found it difficult to explain. It wasn't the fear of taking his own life at a time when his death would otherwise be certain. The method was simple. The poison was quick. For Pekkala, that was the real danger of owning the cyanide vials. What Pekkala truly feared was that the darkness in his mind might one day become unendurable and he would give up his life with no more effort than a shrug.

Although he carried a revolver, the fact that he had been trained in its use and had seen for himself the terrible damage it worked upon the human body, had built a kind of mental barricade against any instinct to point the Webley at himself. So far, the barricade had held. No one, not even Kirov, was aware that such thoughts had ever entered Pekkala's head, because there were no witnesses to the times Pekkala had sat at the bare table in his apartment in the middle of the night, the brass-handled gun placed before him, fists clenched tight against his chest, while the demons in his skull chanted their anthems of despair.

'Did you hear me, Pekkala?' asked Kovalevsky.

'Potassium cyanide. Yes.' Pekkala paused to glance up at the searchlights, tilting back and forth across the night sky, like giant metronomes marking time for the movement of the planets. He thought back to the Northern Lights he'd often seen draped across the heavens as a boy. It appeared on nights of bitter cold, when frost would beard the inside of his bedroom windows. He would lie bundled in his blankets, staring through the ice-encrusted glass at the curtains of green and pink and yellow, billowing out in the darkness. These searchlights, too, were beautiful in their way. It was possible to forget, even if only for a moment, the grim fact of their purpose.

Pekkala's dreams were interrupted by the sound of a car backfiring in the street.

Both men flinched and Kovalevsky, tripping on the sidewalk, would have fallen if Pekkala had not reached out and caught him.

'It's all right!' laughed Pekkala. 'I've got you.'

Kovalevsky slipped through his arms and collapsed in a heap on the pavement.

'Kovalevsky?' Slowly, as if he were still in that dream of himself, long ago, with the Northern Lights pulsing in the sky, Pekkala realised what had happened. It was no car backfiring. Instinctively, he reached for his Webley, fingers clawing across his chest, but the weapon wasn't there. He had left it at the office. Stumbling back against the wall of a house, Pekkala searched the darkness for a shooter. People continued to make their way down the street, silhouettes as black as blindness. Pekkala knew from experience that it took three shots before most people even realised that a gunfight had broken out. Unless the gun was visible, most people passed off the sound of the first shot as a door slamming. Or a car backfiring. Nobody was running. Nobody cried out. A man sidestepped the place where Kovalevsky lay, glanced down at the still form and kept on walking.

Pekkala knelt down beside Kovalevsky, rolled the man over and stared into his face, which had become a mask of blood.

Kovalevsky had been hit in the throat. He was already dead.

'Help me!' Pekkala called out to the shadows walking by.

At first, nobody stopped.

'Let him sleep it off,' advised one man.

'Please!' yelled Pekkala. 'Will somebody find the police?'

Only then did the flow of passing figures seem to ripple. Voices echoed through the night. Shadows converged around the dead man. Arms reached out. Shouts turned to screams. At last, a police car arrived.

Two hours later, Pekkala was back in his office. As he explained to Kirov who Kovalevsky had been and why he had gone to meet with the former tsarist agent, diluted splashes of the teacher's blood dripped from the heavy wool of his coat, dappling the floor.

'It could have been a stray shot,' Kirov suggested. 'A soldier on patrol could have misfired his weapon. It could have been an accident, Inspector. These things do happen.'

'No,' whispered Pekkala. 'It was no accident. The traitor must have followed me.'

'But even if you're right, Inspector, why would they have gone after Kovalevsky? As far as the rest of the world is concerned, he's just a harmless school master named Shulepov. Nobody knows his real identity. Nobody who'd want to kill him, anyway.'

Pekkala did not reply. Gently, as if to wake the man from sleep, Kirov reached out and touched Pekkala's shoulder. 'Inspector.'

Pekkala started, his eyes wild, as if in that moment he no longer recognised his colleague. It lasted only a second. 'I'm sorry,' he muttered. 'All these years, I had thought Kovalevsky's bones had turned to dust. I had only just gotten used to him being alive again. And now . . .' Pekkala shook his head and his voice trailed away into silence.

'Perhaps Elizaveta and I can cook you a meal tonight, Inspector,' Kirov said. 'It's late, but there's still time. Wouldn't that be better than going back to your apartment alone?'

'Don't you see, Kirov? I have to be alone. And so should you.'

Kirov's face paled in confusion. 'I don't understand, Inspector. I thought you liked Elizaveta.'

'I do! And I know you do, as well. That's why I'm saying you should stay away from her. Look at what happened this evening. It could just as easily have been me who was shot. Or it could have been you lying there in the gutter with your throat torn out. Our lives are too fragile to be shared, especially with those who love us. I learned that lesson a long time ago, Kirov, but by the time I had figured it out, I was in a rail car full of convicts crossing the Ural mountains into Siberia. And then it was too late. If you do love her, Kirov, or if you even think you could, don't do to her what I did to my fiancée when I kissed her goodbye at the Leningrad station and promised we still had a future.'

The phone rang.

'Answer it,' ordered Pekkala.

Kirov picked up the receiver. 'Yes,' he said. 'Right away.' Then he hung up and looked at Pekkala.

'Stalin?'

Kirov nodded. 'He says he wants to see us right away.'

They spoke no more about Elizaveta.

As they left the room, Pekkala picked up the gun belt from where it lay on his desk. He strapped it on beneath his coat as he made his way downstairs, following the Morse-code trail of Kovalevsky's blood which he had left upon the worn-out wooden steps.

With no idea how far he had to go before he reached the Russian lines, Stefanov made his way towards the east. Still carrying the body of his friend, he tramped along roads whose yellow dust settled on his clothes and in the corners of his eyes. Hour after hour, the only sound he heard was of his footsteps and bumblebees and the thud of distant cannon fire. It was hot. The sky gleamed pitiless blue.

Late in the afternoon, Stefanov took a short cut across an open field. The grass was as tall as his knees and flecked with wildflowers. Burrs clung to his trouser legs.

In the middle of the field, beside an old zinc cattle trough which was overflowing with algae-covered water, he came across a crop of blackberries, like tiny knotted fists. Laying Barkat's corpse upon the ground, he plucked the berries from the shelter of their spear-point leaves and stuffed them into his mouth. Purple juice ran down his lip. And afterwards, he sank his hands into the trough, ladling aside the green ooze of the algae, and drank.

Stefanov was just about to set off, having lifted Barkat once again on to his shoulders, when he heard a sound he felt certain must be thunder. It can't be, he thought. But the thunder grew louder and more deafening until he could feel its vibration in the ground beneath his feet. At that moment, three German

Stuka dive-bombers flew over the ridge, one after the other, heading west. Fixed landing gear jutted from their bellies like the extended talons of huge hunting birds and thick lines of exhaust soot trailed back along the fuselage, which was painted with tiger stripes of grey and yellow.

The Stukas flew so low that Stefanov could see their pilots, heads cocooned in leather flight helmets. One, with goggles pulled down over his eyes, glanced down at Stefanov. Sunlight winked off the lenses, as if sockets of that pilot's eyes were crammed with diamonds.

Stefanov knew that there was nowhere for him to run. Since they had already seen him, there was no point even in taking cover, so he just stood there, looking up at the planes, with Barkat draped over his shoulder, the man's long arms dangling in the tall grass.

Whether the men in those planes took pity on him, or else were low on fuel or ammunition, Stefanov could only wonder.

The Stukas continued on their way. In a moment, all Stefanov could make out were their hunchbacked silhouettes and a faint blur of smoke in the sky.

Arriving at the far end of the field, Stefanov discovered six freshly dug graves. Jammed into the dirt at the head of each grave was a Russian Mosin-Nagant rifle, its bolt removed, rendering it useless. The wooden stock on one rifle had burned away and its leather sling hung blackened like a dead snake from the swivel.

Robbers had dug up the bodies.

The dead lay with earth-filled mouths, purple lips drawn back and dimpled fingertips like badly-fitting gloves. Their boots and their watches were gone, and their pockets had been turned inside-out.

Moving on, Stefanov experienced the unmistakable sensation of having crossed an invisible border between the world of men and that of monsters, and every step he took now carried him deeper into the country of the beast.

Even though he was not sure why he continued to carry Barkat, or even why he had begun carrying him in the first place, it never occurred to Stefanov to abandon his old friend. His mind had fixed itself upon some path beyond his reckoning and he could no more question it than glimpse where it might end.

As he neared the Russian gun pits, Stefanov picked up the scent of *machorka*, its smell like damp leaves smouldering in the rain.

During those last moments, with a dozen weapons aiming at his heart as he walked into a Soviet encampment on the outskirts of the town, Stefanov was more afraid than in all the time he'd spent behind the lines. By this time, a downpour was pelting the road into mud.

The first building he reached was a schoolhouse which had been converted into a field hospital. Peering through the shark's teeth of a broken window pane, Stefanov watched a doctor, stripped to the waist, operating on a man laid out on two school desks. Behind them, a black slate chalk board still showed a lesson in arithmetic.

In the school yard at the back of the building, Stefanov found an army cook, sitting in a horse-drawn food wagon. Rain popped off the wagon's canvas roof. Stefanov realised he was hungry. Gently, he laid Barkat down and reached behind him for his mess kit. It was only when his fingers grasped at nothing that he remembered he had left all his equipment in the bunker.

The cook nodded towards a pile of field gear which had been

removed from wounded soldiers before bringing them inside. From the soggy tangle of belts, canteens and ammunition pouches still crammed with bullets, Stefanov scrounged up a mess tin.

The cook handed him a slice of brown bread. Then he ladled some cabbage soup out of a large enamel-lined canister. Hot, greasy liquid dripped down the metal sides.

Rain fell through the hole in Barkat's chest, splashing off the school yard underneath.

'Mother of God,' said the cook.

Stefanov sat on the concrete and drank the soup, using the bread to wipe out the insides of the mess tin.

The cook watched him from under the wagon's canvas roof. The horse stared at him too, water dripping from its chin.

Artillery thudded in the distance.

Two medical orderlies appeared in the doorway at the top of the steps. Seeing Barkat, the medics hurried down to help him but they were not even at the bottom of the stairs before they realised the man was dead. They glanced back at Stefanov, confusion on their faces. 'Are you hurt?' asked one of the medics.

Stefanov did not reply, because he wasn't sure.

'Don't touch him,' whispered the other medic.

The two men walked back up the steps and shut the door behind them.

Stefanov lay down on the ground next to Barkat. He put his arm across Barkat's chest, as if to shield him from the rain. Threads of consciousness snapped one by one in silent, dusty puffs inside his brain. And then he was asleep.

It was the middle of the night when Pekkala arrived at the Kremlin.

Poskrebychev was still at his desk. He jerked his head towards the double doors. 'The Boss is waiting.'

Stalin's room was dark, except for the lamp at his desk. The Boss sat in his red leather chair. In front of him lay an ashtray, overflowing with crumpled cigarette butts. Another one, still burning, lay wedged between his fingertips. 'I heard what happened to Kovalevsky.'

'Let me go after them,' said Pekkala. 'Let someone else arrest Engel. Give me a week and I'll track down whoever murdered Kovalevsky.'

'I don't care who murdered Kovalevsky.' Stalin inhaled deeply. The tip of the cigarette glowed fiercely in the gloom.

'But I do!' Pekkala exploded. 'Kovalevsky was my friend!'

'What would your friend say about the thing you've just proposed?'

'He would say nothing. He's dead.'

Stalin sat forward suddenly, grinding out his cigarette into the hammered brass ashtray. 'Exactly! He does not care who killed him. He does not care whether revenge comes now or later or if it never comes at all. The dead do not seek vengeance. That is a curse the living heap upon themselves.'

'I am seeking justice, not vengeance.'

'I wonder if you know the difference any more.'

'Without Kovalevsky, the mission—'

Stalin slammed his fist on to the desk. 'The mission has already begun! We must assume that whoever killed Kovalevsky was either sent by the traitor in our ranks or else is the traitor himself. I agree with you that finding this person is important, but not enough to call you off the case. That is why I am assigning the task to Major Kirov. He will remain here in Moscow and investigate Kovalevsky's murder, while you and Lieutenant Churikova pursue Engel.'

In spite of the fact that Kirov would be sorely missed, Pekkala knew that Stalin had made the right decision to divide the team, in order that both Engel and his accomplice here in Moscow could be pursued simultaneously.

'A plane has been allocated to bring the two of you from Moscow to an airfield near the front,' continued Stalin. 'Once you arrive, you will be handed over to Glavpur, Military Intelligence. They will do what they can to see you through the German lines. I know what I am asking of you, Pekkala. Even with Kovalevsky's help, this would have been the most difficult task I had ever set before you. But we can beat them, Pekkala, because they have already made a fatal mistake.'

'And what was that?'

'When they shot Kovalevsky, they did not kill you, too.' With his elbows on the desktop, Stalin folded his hands together, fingertips pressing down on knuckles. 'When you return to Moscow with your prisoner, you will have done more than simply help to stop the robberies of Gustav Engel and his kind. Your actions in the coming days will fill their hearts with doubt and fear, because they will know that nowhere is safe for them and that, even when our country appears on the verge of collapse, we are still striking back in any way we can.'

'What if Engel has already discovered the amber?'

'That depends,' replied Stalin. 'If they decide to leave the panels where they are, your orders are to leave them untouched until such time as we can reclaim the ground we have lost. But if you discover that the Fascists have chosen to move those panels to some location of their own, in spite of the damage it might cause, in order to parade the Amber Room before the world as a symbol of our defeat, then I am ordering you to destroy it.'

'But Comrade Stalin,' he finally managed to say, 'you just declared the Amber Room to be an irreplaceable State treasure. Now you are telling me to destroy it?'

'We must be prepared to sacrifice everything,' Stalin replied, 'or else face oblivion. From now on, the only way we can survive is to hold nothing sacred. Besides, I'll wager that your distaste for the Tsar's garish displays of wealth is no less strongly felt today than it was when you were in his service. Wouldn't you secretly welcome the chance to rid this world of such a monument to human excess?'

'Human excess has many monuments, Comrade Stalin, the gulag at Borodok for one. But even if you were correct in my opinion of the Amber Room, exactly how do you expect me to destroy it?' asked Pekkala.

'When the time comes,' Stalin replied, 'you will be provided with the means.'

'And Lieutenant Churikova? Does she know about this order?'

'She will when you tell her. But you must move quickly, Pekkala. Rather than give this traitor another chance to strike at us again, I have decided to move up the start time for the operation.'

'By how much?' asked Pekkala. 'I thought we still had three days to plan the mission.'

'Your plane leaves in less than twelve hours.'

In the outer room, Poskrebychev leaned across his desk, his ear almost touching the dust-clogged mesh of the intercom speaker.

At Pekkala's mention of the gulag at Borodok, which must have struck Stalin like a back hand across the face, Poskrebychev had held his breath, waiting for the eruption of Stalin's volcanic rage. Poskrebychev had always been mystified by Pekkala, and had never made up his mind whether to respect the Emerald Eye for his suicidal forthrightness or to pity him for the price Poskrebychev felt certain that the Finn would some day have to pay for all his insolence.

But yet another moment passed in which Stalin's anger failed to ignite, as Poskrebychev felt sure it would have done with anyone other than Pekkala. He wondered if the fairy tales he'd heard as a child, in which the Finns were always vanishing, or casting spells to change the weather, or communing with the spirits of the forest, might have some truth in them. Surely, thought Poskrebychev, Stalin must have been bewitched.

As he heard the door handle turn, Poskrebychev sat back in his chair and busied himself with paperwork.

Pekkala swept by, accompanied by the creak of his double-soled boots and the rustle of his heavy corduroy trousers.

The two men did not exchange words.

Only when Pekkala had gone by did Poskrebychev raise his head. Glancing at the broad shoulders of the Inspector, he wondered if the truth might be simpler than he'd thought. Perhaps what it boiled down to was the fact that Stalin needed Pekkala too much, and so endured a frankness which, Poskrebychev had no doubt, would have cost him his life if he had ever dared to speak those words himself.

Lieutenant Churikova had returned to the barracks, from which she and her battalion had departed only a few days before.

When Pekkala found her, she was alone in a dormitory which would normally have housed sixteen people. Pale sunlight shone through the dusty windows, whose frames chequered the dull red linoleum floors.

Churikova had scrounged some blankets, rolling one up as a pillow. The remaining fifteen beds were bare except for thin, horsehair-stuffed mattresses, their blue-and-white-striped ticking stained by the metal springs beneath as the mattresses were turned over each month.

Churikova was folding her clothes. 'I heard you coming,' she said, as Pekkala stepped into the room. 'It's so quiet in here now. Last night, I heard the footsteps of a mouse as it ran across the floor.'

'Stalin tells me you volunteered to help bring back Gustav Engel.'

'Yes. That's right. I did.'

Pekkala explained Stalin's instructions.

Churikova had continued to fold her clothes as she listened, carefully packing them into a canvas duffel bag, but suddenly she paused. 'He really means for us to destroy the amber?'

'Those are his orders, in the event that Engel has decided to move the panels to some place inside Germany. The sooner we can get to Tsarskoye Selo, the better chance we have of saving the Amber Room.'

'When do we leave?' asked Churikova.

'Tomorrow. A car will come for you before dawn.' Pekkala turned to leave.

'Inspector?'

He paused and looked back. 'Yes?'

'Thank you.'

'For what?'

'When I volunteered to come on this mission, Comrade Stalin said you'd try to talk me out of it. But you didn't.'

'I would have,' replied Pekkala, 'if I'd thought it could do any good.'

The sun was not yet up when Kirov drove Pekkala to the airfield.

The props of the twin-engined Lisunov cargo plane were already roaring like thunder.

Since that moment in the office, when Pekkala had spoken of the burden of their fragile lives, it was as if a wall had gone up between them.

Anyone looking at them from a distance, as they got out of the car and, with a stiff formality, shook hands, would have thought that the two men were strangers.

One of the plane's crew, his body swathed in a fur-lined flight suit, approached the Emka. 'Inspector?'

'Yes,' replied Pekkala. 'Where is Lieutenant Churikova?'

'She's already on board. We take off in two minutes. Follow me.'

Without another word to Kirov, Pekkala set out with the crewman. But halfway to the plane, he stopped.

'Is something the matter, Inspector?' asked the crewman.

'Yes,' replied Pekkala, as he turned and ran back to the car.

Kirov was already behind the wheel. He had just put the Emka in gear when Pekkala appeared out of the dark and rapped a knuckle on the window.

Kirov rolled down the window. 'What is it, Inspector?'

'I was wrong,' said Pekkala. 'About Elizaveta. In spite of the risks we take, it would be an even greater risk to turn away from something that could bring you happiness, even if you know it might not last. I can't change what happened to me, but I know what I'd have done if I could. I'd have boarded that train with her back in Petrograd and I would never have looked back. This may be the last order I ever give you, Kirov, and it may be the most important. Don't make the same mistake as I did. Will you promise me that?'

'Of course, Inspector, but don't let us speak of finalities.' He clasped Pekkala's hand, and suddenly they were not strangers any more. 'I'll see you again soon enough.'

'Inspector!' The crewman stood in the doorway to the cargo plane. 'We must leave now!'

Pekkala turned and headed for the plane. This time, he did not look back.

Rather than return to the silence of his office, Kirov went straight to work.

His first stop was the office of municipal police for the 4th Central District of Moscow, within whose boundaries Kovalevsky's murder had taken place. In order not to draw attention to the significance of Kovalevsky's death, the case had not been handed over to NKVD. Kovalevsky's true identity had not been revealed, even to the police or the doctors who pronounced him dead when his body arrived at the hospital. In a city where gunfire was not uncommon, the murder itself had not even been mentioned in the newspapers. Except for the few bystanders who had seen what happened, few people even knew that the killing had taken place.

When Kirov entered the municipal office, the sergeant on duty took one look at the red stars of a commissar sewn on to the forearms of the major's tunic and stood to attention, sending his chair scudding back noisily across the wooden floor.

The air smelled heavily of cigarettes and sweat. There was also a stench of vinegar and garlic coming from a jar of pickles the sergeant had open on his desk. As the man rose to salute, he struggled to finish his mouthful.

'I've come about the shooting of Professor Shulepov,' said

Kirov, making sure to use the alias under which Kovalevsky had been living.

'And where have you come from, Comrade Major?'

'Special Operations.'

The sergeant nodded. 'I knew there was something about that man.'

'What do you mean?'

'The one who got killed. He had bullet holes in him.'

'Of course he did. He was shot to death.'

The sergeant shook his head. 'I'm not talking about the bullet which finished him off. I'm talking about old scars he had from the ones that didn't kill him.'

'And where is the body now?'

'I called the hospital myself, a few hours after the shooting, and asked them the same question. They told me it had been cremated.' The sergeant shrugged. 'I tell you, Major, it's as if this whole thing never happened. And there's more as well.'

'Yes?'

'People on the scene told us there had been another man walking with this Professor Shulepov, but by the time we arrived, he had disappeared. Before I could even begin conducting a proper investigation, this little bald man shows up, waving a Kremlin ID card . . .'

Poskrebychev, Kirov thought to himself.

'. . . and tells me there's not going to be an investigation.'

'May I see your report on the incident?' asked Kirov.

'Report! You don't seem to understand, Major. That man had orders direct from Stalin. There is no report. There will never be a report.'

'Was anything recovered from the scene?'

'Officially, no.'

'And unofficially?'

The sergeant held up a finger, like a man testing the wind. 'Unofficially, I think I can help you.' Rising from his desk he walked down a short hallway to a room closed with a cage-like metal door. He unlocked the door, entered, and then locked himself in from the inside. A moment later, the sergeant repeated the procedure in reverse and returned to Kirov with a little white cloth bag pulled shut with a red piece of string. Back at the front desk the sergeant opened the bag and poured its contents into his hand. There were six pistol bullets, only one of which had been fired.

'I should probably have thrown them out,' said the sergeant, 'but old habits die hard, you know.'

'Where were they?'

'Scattered in the road, about twenty paces from the site where the shooting took place.'

Kirov picked up one of the cartridges and examined it. The markings on the base had been filed off, so he could not tell where it had been made or the precise calibre, although it looked like 9 mm to him. There were other file marks around the rim, as well as the indentations where each bullet had been clamped in a vice. 'Is this all of them?'

'Yes. I searched the area thoroughly.'

'From the number, it almost looks as if the weapon was a revolver.'

'That was my thought, too, but why go to all the trouble of emptying the cylinder when there was no need to reload and most of the rounds hadn't even been fired? Strange, isn't it?'

'Yes,' murmured Kirov, as he replaced the bullets in the cloth evidence bag. 'May I hold on to these?'

'Considering they're from a non-existent investigation, I'd say that little bag of evidence doesn't exist either. You may as well take it, since there's nothing to take.'

Kirov put the bullets in his pocket. 'Thank you, Sergeant.'

On his way to inspect the site where Kovalevsky had been murdered, Kirov stopped off at NKVD headquarters. He made his way down two flights of stairs to the underground firing range in search of the Chief Armourer, Captain Lazarev; a red-faced man with watery blue eyes and pock-marked cheeks, whose frequent laughter sent him into spasms of liquidy coughs from his tobacco-corrupted lungs.

'I know you,' said Lazarev. 'You're the one who's got his eye on that woman in the records department, Elizaveta Kapeleva.'

'Kapanina,' Kirov corrected him.

'Yes, well, whatever her name is, you had better grab her while you can. Half of the men in this building have their eyes on her as well.'

'Thank you, Captain,' Kirov replied stiffly. 'I will be sure to follow your advice.'

Lazarev let out one of his gurgling laughs. 'But I don't expect you came down here into the bowels of the earth to seek advice on women.'

Kirov handed over the small evidence bag containing the bullets. 'What do you make of these?' he asked.

From a pocket in his tattered, oil-stained shop coat, Lazarev produced a surprisingly clean handkerchief, and carefully un-folded it upon a counter top strewn with gun parts. After emptying the bullets out of the bag, he stood the cartridges in a row, as if setting them up for a game of chess. 'Nine milli-metre,' he said, 'designed for the Mauser model 1896. The fam-ous broom-handled model. But this is curious.'

'What is?'

'These bullets did not fit the standard model, which was 7.63 calibre. The 9-mm were made for export models only.'

'Where was it exported?'

'Asia. Africa. Some of them went to South America. There were a number of them around during the Revolution, but it is now considered somewhat obsolete by our own military, and certainly in the 9-mm version. Our own Tokarevs and Nagants take 7.62 cartridges. What makes this interesting –' with one finger, Lazarev pushed over one of the bullets, like a man tip-ping over his king as he conceded defeat – 'is that these rounds have been modified.'

'I noticed that as well,' remarked Kirov. 'But why would someone go to all this trouble?'

'To make them fit another gun, of course,' replied Lazarev.

'A German gun?' Kirov's suspicion, from the moment he had learned about the shooting, was that the murderer was either a German agent, or else had been supplied by them.

Lazarev screwed up his face. 'These days, anyone who has got their hands on a German gun, say a Luger or a perhaps Walther, is probably a soldier who's been at the front. And any-one who has snatched up a German pistol is almost certain to have found ammunition as well. This is more complicated, be-cause these bullets,' he gestured at the cartridges laid out before him, 'would not require modification to be used in the guns I have mentioned.' Slowly, he shook his head. 'No. Your weapon is not a Luger, or a Walther, and definitely not a Mauser.'

'A Browning?'

'No!' shouted Lazarev. 'That takes a *short* 9-mm cartridge.' He picked up one of the bullets and held it in front of Kirov's face. 'Does this look short to you?' Without waiting for an answer, Lazarev continued. 'This is something else. Something more peculiar. I wish I could be of further help to you, Major, but in order for me to do that, you will have to bring me a few more pieces of the puzzle.'

After a three-hour flight from Moscow in the unheated cargo bay of the Lisunov, Pekkala and Lieutenant Churikova landed at an airfield in Tikhvin, east of Leningrad. A truck was waiting for them at the side of the runway. Its windscreen had been smashed out and the driver wore a pair of motorcycle goggles to protect his eyes from the mud and grit which had splattered the upper half of his body. 'Get in the back,' he told them, 'unless you want to look like me.'

'Where are we going?' asked Pekkala, struggling to speak since his jaw was almost frozen shut.

'To the town of Chertova, but we had better be quick. I knew where the front was when I left this morning, but I've no idea where it is now.' As the driver spoke, he removed the goggles, revealing pale moons of skin around his eyes. He licked the dirt off the lenses, spitting after each swipe of his tongue over the glass, then fitted the goggles back on to his face.

Hurriedly, Churikova and Pekkala piled into the back of the truck.

The driver battened down the canvas flap and soon they were on the move again.

'What happens when we get to Chertova?' asked Churikova, once they were under way. She had tried during the flight to question Pekkala about the plan for getting them behind the German lines, but the noise in the cargo plane, not to mention the cold, had prevented any kind of conversation.

From the pocket of his coat, Pekkala removed his orders of transport. 'According to this, we are being delivered to the headquarters of the 35th Rifle Division, which must be based in Chertova. Once we arrive, a Colonel Gorchakov of Glavpur, Military Intelligence, will provide us with further instructions.'

'But how will he get us through the lines?' Churikova pressed him.

'I don't know,' replied Pekkala. 'At this point, I doubt that he knows, either.'

On the outskirts of Chertova, the truck pulled over beside a cemetery. The driver got out and undid the canvas flap. 'We're here,' he said.

There was no sound of birds or barking dogs, or the bumble-bee droning of tractors in the fields beyond the town. All they could hear was the rumble of artillery in the distance.

Pekkala peered out across the graveyard. 'Military Intelli-gence?'

'Come see for yourself,' said the driver, his face expression-less behind the mud-splashed goggles.

Leaving Churikova in the back of the truck, Pekkala jumped down into the mud and followed the driver out into the cemetery. As Pekkala trudged along, he looked out over the crooked ranks of gravestones. Some bore the tilted cross of the Orthodox Church, others were topped by ancient weeping angels made of concrete. The oldest were nothing more than blunted slabs of stone, leaning at odd angles like the teeth of hags.

Pekkala could not see any sign of a command post. Just as he was beginning to wonder if Colonel Gorchakov had already moved on, he noticed a soldier emerge from the stone hut of a family mausoleum and disappear underground to where a bunker had been dug among the bones.

Pekkala found Gorchakov, a round-faced man with ears as fleshy as the petals of an orchid, sitting on a stone bench inside the mausoleum. Built into the walls were niches for coffins. Some of these were still in place, tassels of old black ribbon knotted to the brass carrying handles. Other coffins had been carried outside and left in a heap. Bones and tattered clothes lay scattered in the mud. Men from the Glavpur staff were sleeping in the empty spaces, using greatcoats for blankets and their helmets as pillows.

Gorchakov sat behind a small collapsible table. In front of him stood an opened tin of *tushonka* ration meat encased in a frog spawn of gelatine, and an almost empty bottle of home-made alcohol called *samahonka*. 'Pekkala?' asked Gorchakov, busily scooping out the greyish-red meat with his fingers and packing it into his mouth.

'Yes, Comrade Colonel.'

'It is an honour to meet you, Inspector.' He picked up the bottle and held it out. 'May I offer you a drink?' he asked, his lips shining with grease.

Pekkala eyed the cloudy dregs of *samahonka*. 'Later, perhaps.'

The colonel shrugged and drank off the last of the alcohol, his tongue writhing like a bloated leech around the bottle's mouth. Then he tossed the empty container through the doorway. With a dull, soft thump, the bottle fell among the gravestones. 'Now what it says here . . .' he began thrashing around amongst some papers on his table, eventually snatching up the pulpy yellow form of an incoming radio message . . . 'is that I am to provide you with a means of reaching the Catherine Palace which is, as of two days ago, no longer under our control.'

'That is correct.'

Gorchakov nodded as he set aside the message and began scooping out another clump of meat. 'Just you?'

'No. One other. A woman.'

Gorchakov paused, his fingers wedged into the can of *tushonka*. 'A woman?'

'Is that going to make your job more difficult?' asked Pekkala.

'Not necessarily.' Gorchakov sucked a shred of meat from between his teeth. 'A woman is good to have along. They hesitate before they shoot a woman.'

Gorchakov pulled his fingers out of the can, licked the oil off his thumb and wiped his hands with a dirty handkerchief. 'I can transport you as far as the front line. After that, you must continue on foot. You'll have to keep off the main roads, which means you'll need a guide to get you there.'

'I am familiar with some of the terrain,' said Pekkala.

'It's not a question of terrain,' replied Gorchakov. 'It's a question of knowing who controls it.' He got up and walked over to one of the alcoves, where an army doctor lay sleeping. 'What happened to that soldier who wandered into town last night, the one you found lying outside the field hospital?'

The doctor's eyes fluttered open. 'I brought him back here.'

'What is his name?'

245

'Stefanov, I think. He was in that anti-aircraft battery we accidentally shelled at Janusk.'

'Don't remind me about that!' snapped Gorchakov. 'Just tell me where he is now.'

With bleary eyes, the doctor looked around. 'There!' he aimed one stubby finger out into the cemetery.

Pekkala and Gorchakov walked to the doorway of the Mausoleum.

'Rifleman Stefanov!' the colonel shouted at a hunched, dishevelled figure, whose clothes were pasted to his body by a mixture of blood and dirt. Perched upon one of the coffins which had been evicted from the mausoleum, the man seemed oblivious to everything around him.

That morning, Stefanov had woken up beside the body of his friend, whose skin had turned the colour of an old cedar shingle left out too long in the sun. Slowly, as if he were rising from the fog of anaesthetic, Stefanov's consciousness returned to the place where the pain becomes real. Morning sun shone brassy on the dew-slick cobblestones. It was cold and the food wagon had gone. Struggling to his feet, Stefanov drank the rain which had collected in his mess tin.

A man appeared in the doorway, wearing a greatcoat against the morning chill. It was the doctor Stefanov had seen the night before. 'We are pulling out,' said the doctor. 'There isn't enough transport to move the wounded. They will be left behind.' He reached into his coat pocket and pulled out a silver cigarette case with a hammer and sickle engraved on the front. 'Can you walk?' he asked.

'Yes, Comrade Doctor.'

'Then I suggest you come with me.' He touched a small green stone set into the side of the case and opened it, revealing a neat row of cigarettes. The doctor did not offer one to Stefanov. 'A squad of Frontier Police arrived in Chertova two hours ago. Now that they have no frontier left to guard, they are being used as blocking units, rounding up stragglers and deserters.

You know what they'll do if they find you.' The doctor placed a cigarette in his mouth but did not light it.

'I am not a straggler,' protested Stefanov. 'I am the only one left!'

'They will not care about your reasons.' The cigarette wagged between his lips. 'Leave your companion here. He will only slow you down.' With that, he set off walking towards the cemetery. A moment later, a white puff of smoke rose from the man's head and his arm swung down to his side, the lit cigarette pinched between his fingers.

Stefanov stared down at Barkat. The rain had pooled in his eye sockets. All they had been through together in the past months flickered through Stefanov's mind, as if a pack of playing cards were being shuffled before his eyes. The pictures vanished as abruptly as they had appeared and suddenly he was back in the town of Chertova, surprised to feel his heart still beating in his chest.

As Stefanov ran to catch up with the doctor, he was already carrying the memory of Barkat, like a body on a stretcher, down a long dark corridor towards the ossuary in his mind where others lay whose paths had crossed his own, their lifeless faces shimmering like opals.

'Stefanov!' bellowed Gorchakov. 'Have you gone deaf?'

Stefanov raised his head. 'Colonel?'

'Get over here.'

Stefanov shambled over to Gorchakov and saluted. Dried mud clung like fish scales to his boots. His eyes fell on Pekkala. It can't be, Stefanov thought.

'Listen to me,' said Gorchakov. 'You just came from the Catherine Palace, didn't you?'

'I was there, Comrade Colonel, but it was several days ago.'

Stefanov continued to stare at Pekkala. 'My eyes are playing tricks on me,' he murmured. 'I could have sworn you were . . .'

'Say hello to the Emerald Eye,' said Gorchakov.

Stefanov opened his mouth but no sound came out. Suddenly, he was thrown back through time to that day when he stood with his father on the fence by the compost heap at Tsarskoye Selo. Solemnly, he bowed his head towards Pekkala. 'I am the son of Agripin Dobrushinovich Stefanov, the gardener at Tsarskoye Selo.'

'Never mind that!' growled Gorchakov. 'Do you know where the enemy has concentrated its forces between here and Catherine Palace?'

'I cannot say for certain, Comrade Colonel.'

'But you crept right through their lines last night.'

Gorchakov turned to Pekkala. 'And carrying a dead man on his back. At least, that's what I heard.'

'It's true I made it through their lines,' stammered the rifleman. 'But I was just lucky. That's all.'

'Luck is worth plenty out here,' Gorchakov told him, 'and since you've done it once, it shouldn't be much trouble doing it again.'

'Doing what, Comrade Colonel?'

'You will be guiding the Inspector back.'

'Back? You mean to the Catherine Palace?'

'That is what I said.'

Stefanov looked from one man to the other, certain that he must have misunderstood. 'Comrades, the Fascists have reached Tsarskoye Selo. We can't go back.'

'Gather up your things,' Gorchakov replied matter of factly, 'and be ready to go in five minutes.'

'I have no things, Comrade Colonel.'

Gorchakov reached out and skewered a finger against Stefanov's chest, as if he meant to bore a hole into his heart. 'Then you are ready now!'

As the colonel's order finally sank in, Stefanov's first reaction was to turn and run away. What prevented him from doing so was not the fear of summary execution at the hands of Gorchakov's men, but rather the presence of Inspector Pekkala, at whose side he felt a peculiar assurance that no harm could come to him.

Now Pekkala turned to Stefanov. 'Before the Germans attacked, did you go inside the Catherine Palace?'

'We had orders not to trespass,' began Stefanov.

'That's not what he's asking,' barked Gorchakov. 'What he

wants to know is if you went inside, not whether you had permission to do so.'

'Yes,' admitted Stefanov. 'I went inside the palace, but I did
not take anything. I swear!'

'Do you know where the Amber Room is located?' asked
Pekkala.

The words shot through Stefanov's brain. He remembered
what his father had said about Pekkala being conjured from
its walls by the god-like powers of the Tsar. So many times he
had envisaged the man who stood before him now materialising from the fiery collage on the walls of that room, that he no
longer knew for certain whether it was something he had imagined or whether he had somehow glimpsed a moment which
lay beyond the boundaries of his life. 'I know where it is, Inspector.'

'And did you go in there?' demanded Gorchakov. He had no
idea why Pekkala would be interested in the Amber Room, but
he nevertheless felt that he should be a part of this interrogation, and so the colonel fixed upon his face an expression of
total awareness.

'I did.'

'And what did you find?' asked Pekkala.

'Nothing, Inspector. The room was empty. They were all
empty, except for picture frames and pieces of broken furniture. So, you see,' he tried to reason with them, 'there can be
no point in going back.'

'What you have just told us,' said Pekkala, 'is all the reason
we need.'

Turning away from the bewildered rifleman, Gorchakov ad-
dressed Pekkala. 'Your ride will take you to the front, where you

will rendezvous with Captain Leontev. He has been informed of the situation. He will do what he can to get you through the lines. But you must hurry. The Germans will be here in a few hours. We are falling back to a new defensive line.'

Leaving the town, they drove by the old schoolhouse which had been converted into a field hospital just as a truck pulled up at the main gate. The canvas flap was thrown back. A squad of Frontier Guards, with distinctive blue-green bands on their caps, piled out into the muddy street and made their way into the schoolhouse.

Stefanov remembered what the doctor had told him – how the wounded could not be moved. He saw the flash of the first shot, lighting up one of the rooms on the first floor, and then the building slid out of view behind them.

They passed ramshackle houses at the edge of Chertova. Peeking through a tear in the truck's tarpaulin roof, Pekkala saw women in headscarves, wearing blue-and-white-striped dresses like the cloth of mattress covers. The women stared at the truck as it sped by, their eyes filled with contempt now that the army was abandoning them to their fate.

Kirov paced back and forth along the street outside the Café Tilsit. He stared into the gutters and out across the crooked cobbled street, his gaze snagging on every cigarette butt, bus ticket stub and crumpled cough-drop wrapper.

Passersby regarded him suspiciously, sidestepping out of his way.

After several passes along the entire length of the block, Kirov gave up looking at the pavement and switched to the walls and shop fronts. He knew that Kovalevsky had been shot in the throat at close range, in which case it was likely that the bullet had passed through his neck and struck against one of these walls. Since Kirov already had the spent cartridge from the round that had killed Kovalevsky, he knew that the bullet itself would add little to his knowledge. What he wanted to find out was the angle at which the bullet struck and, from that, to extrapolate where the killer had been standing at the time.

A few minutes later, he discovered what he thought must be the mark of the bullet. Something had struck one of the bricks outside a cobbler's repair shop. The brick had been gouged by a projectile, and several cracks radiated out from the centre of the impact point. With the use of a pencil fitted into the conical indent made by the bullet, Kirov was able to trace the path of the bullet to a place roughly halfway across the road. The shot had been made from a greater distance than he had first supposed, which made him wonder if the shooter was a trained marksman. From his own days in NKVD training, Kirov recalled being told that the average recruit, even on completion of his or her training with a hand gun, could hit the centre mass of a stationary man-sized target only once in every five shots at a distance of thirty paces. This shot had been made in the dark and at a moving target. It had brought a man down with one bullet on a part of the body so difficult to hit that NKVD range instructors discouraged even aiming for it, in spite of the fact that to be hit in the neck was almost always fatal. The fact that the shooter had been confident enough of his aim to cease firing after the first round convinced Kirov they were dealing with a professional.

Continuing on down the street, Kirov realised that there was likely to be nothing more that he could learn from the crime scene, especially since it had not been cordoned off immediately after the event.

Passing a narrow alley which separated a bakery and a laundry, Kirov caught sight of two boys, almost hidden in the shadows, tussling amongst the garbage cans and clouds of steam from hot soapy water pouring out of a pipe in the wall directly into the sewers. One boy had an armful of stale bread rolls and was pelting the other, who had a toy pistol which, judging from the sound effects this boy was making, he had mistaken for a machine gun.

Kirov walked on a couple of paces, wondering just where inside his head to store the image of that boy acting in a game so close to the place where its deadly reality had played out only a day before.

Then he froze.

A tiny woman in a headscarf and dress that nearly dragged along the ground, who had been walking towards him, carrying a bundle of clothes for the laundry, came to an astonished halt, as if the two of them had just been turned to stone.

Kirov spun about and dashed into the alley.

Seeing Kirov descending upon them, the boys cried out, ditched the bread rolls and were just about to vanish, one into the bakery and the other into the laundry, when Kirov grabbed them both by the collars of their coats.

'We didn't do anything!' shouted the boy who had been throwing bread rolls. He had on a short-brimmed cap whose sides flopped down over his ears, making him look like a rabbit.

The other boy tried desperately to stuff the gun into his pocket but it wouldn't fit.

'Where did you get that?' demanded Kirov, having realised that the gun was not, in fact, a toy.

'I found it!' shouted the boy. 'It's mine!'

'Just show it to me,' said Kirov.

'Let me go.'

'First show me that gun.'

As the boy held it out, muttering under his breath, Kirov saw that it was only part of a gun, specifically the barrel section of a revolver, including the cylinder. It was from a type of gun which, when reloading, would be opened on a hinge that allowed the front section to swing forward like a shotgun. Other revolvers had cylinders that opened out to the sides. There were markings on the cylinder, but they were very small and he could not make out what they meant. The hinge which joined the two parts of the gun had been wrenched violently away.

The gun had not been well cared for. The bluing on the barrel was stained and faded and there were flecks of rust inside the cylinder.

Although Kirov had seen revolvers like this before – in fact Pekkala's Webley operated on the same principle – he had never come across one exactly like it.

'Where did you find this?' Kirov asked the boys.

'Over there,' the boy pointed towards where the laundry water pipe emptied into the sewer. 'It was lying right next to the hole.'

'Was there another piece with it?'

'No. Maybe the rest of it fell down the drain.'

'When did you find it?'

'This morning,' said the boy with the rabbit-ear hat.

'Was there anything else lying around?'

'No. Can I have it back?'

Kirov lowered himself down on one knee. 'I can't do that,' he said, 'but I can make you a detective in a murder investigation.'

The boy's eyes grew big and round.

'What about me?' shouted the other boy. 'I saw it first.'

'But I picked it up. That's what counts!'

'You can both be part of the investigation,' he assured them. Ten minutes later, with the remains of the revolver bound up in a handkerchief, Kirov set off for NKVD headquarters, leaving the two boys, each now bearing the rank of honorary commissar, lying beside the drain, up to their armpits as they reached down into soapy water, searching for the rest of the gun.

Having left behind the town of Chertova, the truck carrying Pekkala, Lieutenant Churikova and Rifleman Stefanov passed along a straight road bordered by tall trees with dappled bark. Beyond the trees, fields of ripened barley, left to rot, spread out on either side.

With the front line now only a few kilometres away, heavy gunfire could be heard over the rumble of the truck's engine. In spite of the canvas roofing, dust from the road filled the air in the back of the truck. Through tears in the cloth, bolts of sunlight stabbed into the darkness.

As they jostled over the uneven road surface, Pekkala explained their mission to Stefanov.

The son of the gardener of Tsarskoye Selo listened in silence, his eyes wide with amazement. 'Under the wallpaper?' he stammered.

'That is correct,' Pekkala replied, 'and if we are successful, that is where it will remain.'

The ZiS-5 motored over gently rising ground towards some woods on the horizon. They had just reached the crest of a thickly wooded ridge when a Russian soldier stepped out on to the road. He held up a rifle in one hand and crossed his other arm over the rifle to make an X, indicating that they were to stop.

The truck skidded to a halt.

Now Stefanov saw movement. More soldiers, dozens of them, lay on the damp ground, with rain capes pulled over their heads.

The sun was going down, detonating in silent poppy-coloured explosions through clouds on the horizon.

The man in the road lowered his rifle and walked towards them. He had a heavy, dimpled chin and dark brown eyes. A tiny pair of crossed cannons on his faded olive collar tabs marked him as a sergeant of artillery.

The driver pulled his orders from under the chest flap of his raincoat. After brushing off some flecks of mud, he handed his papers to the soldier.

As the sergeant was flipping through them, Pekkala climbed down from the back of the truck and stood on the road.

Filing past him in the opposite direction were a dozen German soldiers. At the front marched an officer, his tunic unbuttoned down to the thick black belt at his waist. Behind him walked two men in long rubberised canvas coats. Half-moon-shaped discs on chains around their shoulders bore the word *Feldgendarmerie*, indicating that they were members of the military police. The rest, judging from the yellow piping on their collar and shoulder boards, were a squad of reconnaissance troops. All of the soldiers moved with their fingers laced together behind their necks. A few still wore their helmets, sweat-greased leather chinstraps dangling down the sides of their faces. With the exception of the officer, who stared straight ahead as he walked, the rest looked down at the dusty-yellowed boots of the man walking in front.

The prisoners were flanked by two soldiers carrying rifles,

which brought back to Pekkala memories of the guards at Lubyanka and the long, silent, dread-filled journeys he had made as a prisoner from his cell to the interrogation room.

The soldiers marched down a dirt track towards a cluster of farm buildings whose whitewashed walls glowed like glacier ice in the twilight. Still with their hands behind their necks, the soldiers were herded into a thatch-roofed barn.

'Come with me, Inspector,' ordered the sergeant of artillery.

The two men made their way into the pine woods. Light winked through beads of sap oozing from the green pine cones above their heads. They passed a row of six heavy mortars camouflaged under green netting. The mortar crews sat cross-legged against tree trunks, eating rations of boiled buckwheat and sausage. The odour of *machorka* tobacco, which smelled to Pekkala like a new pair of shoes, mixed with the sweet dry balsam of the pines.

At the edge of the trees, they came upon a man peering through a pair of large scissor-shaped artillery binoculars which had been set up on a tripod. Vines were woven around the legs to mask the tripod's shape. The man wore a baggy pea-green smock camouflaged with brown splotches, like drops of vinegar in olive oil. Methodically, he scooped roasted sun-flower seeds out of his trouser pocket and squeezed them into his mouth. Fragments of chewed shells littered the ground at his feet.

The sergeant tapped the camouflaged man on the arm. The two of them spoke for a moment. Then the man looked back at Pekkala and, with leather-gloved hands, waved him to approach. He had the look of a Frontovik – a man who had been fighting a long time. It was the eyes that gave away a Frontovik

– never still, always glancing nervously from side to side. Over the years, Pekkala had encountered many such men, veterans of the Great War. Unable to settle back into civilian life, they had turned instead to crime. Too often, these men found themselves cornered in the back streets of Moscow and staring down the barrel of a Webley.

The Frontovik took off one leather glove and shook Pekkala's hand. 'Leontev,' he said, 'Captain. Glavpur.'

From far across the valley came the tearing sound of heavy machine guns and the hollow boom of tanks firing.

'How close are we to the Catherine Palace?' asked Pekkala.

Leontev gestured to the binoculars. 'See for yourself.'

Pekkala set his brow against the greasy Bakelite eyepieces. What he saw startled him. There, in the distance, he could make out the rooftops of Tsarskoye Selo. At the edge of the Alexander Park, he spotted the White Tower and the Children's Pavilion. Smoke was rising from behind the Pensioners' Stable.

'Are any Red Army troops still on the grounds of the estate?' asked Pekkala.

'None who are still breathing,' replied Leontev. 'The Germans' main assault force has already moved on from there.'

'Where are they headed?'

'Straight for us,' Leontev told Pekkala. 'We are expecting an attack just after dark. The Fascists will move along the main road which cuts across this ridge. Once the attack has begun, we will take advantage of the confusion to get you through the lines.'

'How?'

'It has all been arranged,' was all that Leontev would say, as he went back to peering through the binoculars.

A soldier wandered past, carrying a handful of nettles in a black handkerchief. He crouched by a smouldering fire. The cruciform bayonet of his Mosin-Nagant rifle balanced on two forked sticks. Suspended from the bayonet was a battered mess kit filled with boiling water. As the soldier sprinkled in the nettles, their serrated, pale green leaves folded away into steam.

The evening sky turned periwinkle blue as the landscape dissolved into shadows.

'I can see them now,' said Leontev.

Peering into the twilight, Pekkala glimpsed the lumbering hulks of tanks as they moved across the floor of the valley, squads of infantry fanned out behind them.

'It's time.' Leontev tapped Pekkala on the arm and the two men made their way down through the trees towards the white-washed house.

Churikova and Stefanov were already there, waiting in the trampled mud of the farmyard.

Setting the steel-shod toe of his boot against the door, Leontev shoved it open, leaving the dent of hobnails pock-marked on the paint.

The three of them followed him in.

Inside the house, Leontev took down a kerosene lantern from a nail by the door. After lighting it, he trimmed the wick. A warm glow spread around the sparsely furnished room, glancing off the blackened metal buttons of Stefanov's tunic, each one of them emblazoned with a crossed hammer and sickle.

On the kitchen table, Leontev laid out a map of the Leningrad Sector.

At first, the tangle of roads and towns and thumb-print contours of the land confused Pekkala, but like a person whose eyes were growing used to the dark, familiar names slid into focus – Kolpino. Tosno. Vyrica. Volosov.

'Here is our position,' explained Leontev, edging his dirt-smeared thumb along a ridge which cut across the map. 'Our mortars will fire upon the Fascists as they begin to climb the ridge. There is a small cart path to the north. It's not on the map, so I don't believe they are aware of it. If you follow that track, you should reach the Catherine Palace by morning. We will get you some clothes from those prisoners we picked up. Once you are beyond the lines, if anybody asks, you can tell them you're heading back with the wounded.'

Stefanov thought of the injured Russians he'd seen streaming away from the front – on stretchers, on borrowed bicycles, slumped on the shoulders of their friends – any way they could move, towards dressing stations so crowded that they would have to wait hours before some doctor even looked at them. 'Comrade Major,' he pleaded, 'I barely speak a word of German.'

'Our intelligence reports that there are also Belgians, Danes, Dutch and Finnish volunteers among the advancing troops. Just pretend that you are one of them.'

'But I don't speak their languages either!'

'Neither do most of the Germans,' replied Leontev, 'and do not stay one minute longer than you have to. As soon as you have your prisoner, get back as fast as you can. You will be soldiers returning to the front. No one will get in your way if you are heading towards the fighting. Once you have passed through our lines, dispose of your German uniforms as quickly as you can. Then find yourself some Russian clothes and notify Glavpur ...'

A series of muffled gunshots made them jump.

Leontev pushed back the sleeve of his camouflage smock and squinted at his watch. 'As soon as the mortars open up, we will send you on your way. Have you had anything to eat?'

'Not for some time,' replied Pekkala.

From the pocket of his coat, Leontev produced a handful of dark bread cakes known as *sukhavi*. He handed them around.

Working their jaws, Pekkala and the others ground the flinty biscuits into paste, leaving a taste like campfire smoke in their mouths.

There was a quiet knocking on the door. Two soldiers walked in, laden down with pieces of German uniform. Boots, belts, shirts. Even underclothes. Behind him came another man, laden with Mauser rifles and two Schmeisser sub-machine guns gathered from the battlefield. After depositing the clothes and the weapons in a heap upon the floor, the soldiers saluted and left.

Then Stefanov watched as three dead Germans were dragged through the open door by their arms into the muddy street. In the darkness, their stripped bodies looked obscenely white. The soldiers pulled the corpses across the street and out into a field of barley. The executed men, their faces branched with blood, vanished into the shifting grain.

By the time Kirov reached NKVD headquarters, he was drenched in sweat. He had run the whole way, having left behind the Emka at his office. Waving his pass book in the face of the guard at the entrance, he clattered down the stairs to the armoury and found Captain Lazarev in the middle of his lunch. Scattered among weapons parts, cleaning rods and loose rounds of ammunition lay a slice of raw potato, a piece of dried fish and a jar of sauce made from raisins and sour cream.

'Ah!' Lazarev held out his arms and waggled his fingers, like a child waiting to be picked up. 'What have you brought me now?'

Kirov untied his handkerchief bundle and presented the gun fragment to Lazarev. 'It was in a drain, just up the street from where the shooting took place.'

With a sweep of his arm, the Chief Armourer cleared a space on the cluttered counter top, jumbling bullets and dried fish into a heap. He fixed his gaze upon the revolver and wiped his sour-cream-smeared fingertips across the chest of his grimy shop coat. Slowly, he reached down, picked up the barrel and squinted at the tiny symbols etched in a circle across the back end of the cylinder.

'Well?' asked Kirov, unable to wait any longer for an answer.

'Type 26,' replied Lazarev. 'Koishikawa Arsenal.'

'Koish . . . ?'

'. . . ikawa. It was standard issue for Japanese non-commissioned officers.'

'You think they had something to do with this?'

Lazarev smiled. 'I can say almost for certain that they didn't.'

'And why are you so confident?'

'Because,' said Lazarev, 'it hasn't been standard issue since 1904. It was still in use as late as the 1920s, but has since been replaced by the Nambu Mark 14.'

Kirov stared at Lazarev, trying to make sense of the dates and numbers which were now rattling around inside his head.

'What you have here, Major,' explained Lazarev, 'is a souvenir of the Russo-Japanese War, and one which long ago ran out of ammunition.'

'What do you mean "ran out"?'

'The Type 26 requires a special cartridge. Whoever used this did not have access to such particular ammunition. That's why those Mauser bullets had been modified. As you can see, it was in poor condition even before someone tried to smash it to bits. It looks as if it has been stored in a barn or a damp cellar somewhere. It hasn't been oiled recently. It's surprising that the weapon worked at all.'

'I don't understand,' said Kirov. 'In a time when there are tens of thousands of soldiers passing through this city every day, each one of them armed with a modern gun, why would someone take the risk of using a relic like this when they could have borrowed or stolen one from a member of the Red Army?'

'You are right that all those soldiers carry guns, Major, but most of them are Mosin-Nagant rifles, unsuitable for the purposes of an assassin. What this person wanted was a handgun, which, as a general rule, are issued only to officers and security personnel. It cuts down on the chances of stealing such a weapon, and also on the chance of persuading someone to part with it temporarily.'

'And also on the odds of the killer being an officer.'

'Or a member of State Security. Such as yourself.'

'You talk as if you think I killed this man,' objected Kirov.

'No, Major. That isn't what I think, although I know you could have done. You have won the NKVD marksmanship award six years in a row.'

Kirov had the little NKVD trophies lined up on his mantelpiece at home, but those weren't his only awards. He had dozens of others: for rifle shooting, pistol shooting, clay pigeon shooting. Kirov didn't know why he was a good marksman. He had received no particular training, other than the basic courses in weapons handling that all NKVD men received. There were many things, most things in fact, at which Kirov had to struggle even to be average. But the aiming of a gun, the measured breathing and the gentle closing of his finger on the trigger all came naturally to him, as if he had been born with the skill.

'You might be surprised,' continued Lazarev, 'at how many times I have been consulted by members of NKVD about shootings which turned out to have been carried out by members of our own branch of service. In this case, however, I do not believe we are dealing with a professional.'

'You may be wrong there, Comrade Lazarev. I was able to trace the path of the bullet, and I can tell you it was a magnificent shot.'

'Luck can also be magnificent. We may never know what

role was played by skill and what by chance. But ask yourself this, Major.' Lazarev held up the remains of the gun by the tip of its barrel and swung it back and forth as if it were a pendulum. 'Why would an assassin entrust his task to a weapon as old and decrepit as this?'

'He might have had no other choice.'

'Precisely, and the choice of those who have no other choice is invariably the Black Market, which has always been a reliable, if eccentric, source of weaponry,' said Lazarev. 'Relics like this Type 26 are the orphans of war. After being picked up off the battlefield, they are sold or traded, stolen or misplaced. Eventually, they just fall through the cracks and are left to gather rust and dirt until at last they end up in the hands of people who cannot pick and choose the tools with which to carry out their crimes. I think you will find that the shooter, whoever he may be, was neither an agent of a foreign country, nor someone for whom killing is a trade.'

More puzzled than before, Kirov made his way up to the ground floor. Instead of leaving the building, he continued to climb the stairs until he reached the records office on the fourth floor. There, he found Elizaveta, sitting with two other women in the tiny, windowless space which served as their break room. They sat on old wooden file boxes, drinking tea out of the dark green enamel mugs which were provided in every Soviet government building, every school, hospital and train station café in the country. One heavy-set woman, with a square face and a tight mesh of grey hair, was smoking a cigarette, which filled the room with clouds of acrid smoke.

The women were laughing about something but they fell silent as soon as Kirov came to the doorway. Noticing his rank, they eyed him nervously, all except Elizaveta, who smiled and set aside her mug. Rising to her feet, she stepped over the legs of the other women and embraced him.

Awkwardly, because he was still not used to being seen as part of a couple, Kirov returned the embrace. At the same time, he attempted to smile at the other women, who were now studying him with completely different expressions on their faces. Their fear had vanished. The appraisal had begun.

'This is Yulian,' said Elizaveta. 'He is with Special Operations.'

'Special Operations.' Through crooked lips, the woman with the cigarette whistled out a stream of smoke. 'You must know Inspector Pekkala.'

'I know him very well,' said Kirov.

'Is he as handsome as they say?'

'That depends,' Kirov told her, 'on how handsome they say he is.' Before the woman could think of a reply to that, he turned his attention to Elizaveta. 'Come with me,' he said.

'But I have work! My break is almost over.'

'No one will notice if you take a few extra minutes.'

'I would notice,' said the woman with the cigarette.

'This is Sergeant Gatkina,' explained Elizaveta, 'keeper of the records office.'

'And her superior,' added Sergeant Gatkina, stubbing out the remains of the cigarette against the thick sole of her shoe.

'Ah,' Kirov said quietly. 'My apologies, Comrade Sergeant.'

Sergeant Gatkina replied with a grunt.

'I am also her superior,' said the other woman, a matronly figure, whose face appeared set in a perpetual glare of disapproval. 'I am Corporal Korolenko and I say ...'

'Shut up!' barked Sergeant Gatkina.

The woman's mouth snapped closed like a mousetrap.

'I'll see you later,' Kirov whispered to Elizaveta.

He was just about to step out of the room, when Sergeant Gatkina's voice cut once more through the smoky air.

'Go!' she commanded.

'I am going,' Kirov told her.

'Not you!' growled Gatkina. 'Kapanina!'

'Yes, Comrade Sergeant?' answered Elizaveta.

'You will be back in half an hour.'

'Yes, Comrade Sergeant.'

'And then you will tell us all there is to tell about your major.' As she spoke, she aimed a glance at Kirov, as if daring him to speak.

But Kirov knew better. Nodding solemnly, he took his leave.

Outside the building, Kirov and Elizaveta walked out across the Lubyanka Square.

'I hope I didn't get you in trouble,' said Kirov.

'As long as Sergeant Gatkina knows she is in charge, and as long as she knows that you know, then there is nothing to worry about.'

'I'm sorry I haven't come by sooner,' he said. 'Things have been very busy since I saw you last.'

'Does this have anything to do with Inspector Pekkala?'

'Yes.'

'Will we not be making dinner for him, after all?'

'He's doing some work out of town.'

'Will he be returning soon?'

'I don't know. When I said goodbye to him, he spoke to me as if he knew he wasn't coming back.'

'Perhaps you're imagining it.'

'I hope so.' Kirov breathed in deeply and smiled. 'There was something else he told me, though. It had to do with you.'

'Yes?' She sounded suddenly nervous.

'He said it would be a mistake if I ever let you go.'

She stopped and turned to face him. 'Well, I still think he's strange, but I also believe he is right.'

'He was almost killed, you know, right after you first met him.' Kirov went on to describe the shooting outside the Café Tilsit. 'I'm supposed to be investigating the case, but there's not enough evidence, and what little I have had leads nowhere. I can't shake the idea that, even though it was Pekkala's friend who died, Pekkala might have been the target, after all.'

'In that line of work,' said Elizaveta, 'there must be no shortage of people who would want you dead.'

As her words sifted into his mind, Kirov thought back to what Pekkala had said to him after Kovalevsky had been killed – 'It could have been you lying there in the gutter with your throat torn out.'

Even though Pekkala had taken back everything he'd said, Kirov wondered if he might have been right. Maybe their lives were indeed too fragile to be shared, especially by those who loved them.

'There is no shortage of such people,' admitted Kirov.

'But fortunately,' replied Elizaveta, 'most of those must be in prison now.'

'Most.' Then suddenly an idea took shape in Kirov's mind. 'But not all.' He stepped back. 'I have to go.'

'Did I say something wrong?'

'No! Quite the opposite!' Kirov stepped forward and kissed

her. 'I'll speak to you soon.' Then he bolted across Lubyanka Square, headed for the Kremlin.

'Goodbye!' she called, but by then he was already gone. Returning to work, Elizaveta glanced up at the fourth floor of NKVD Headquarters in time to see the faces of Corporal Korolenko and Sergeant Gatkina staring down at her intently.

Pekkala watched as the bodies of the executed men were dragged out of sight into the field. 'Why did you have to kill them?' he asked Leontev. 'You only wanted their clothes. Surely something could have been found for them to wear instead.'

'We would have killed them anyway,' Leontev told him matter of factly. 'Glavpur does not take prisoners.'

Stefanov hesitated. 'Does the Comrade Captain realise what the enemy will do if they capture us in these uniforms?'

'It would be no different,' replied Leontev, 'than what we'd do to them if the situation was reversed. Which it often is. Switching uniforms is also a habit of the Germans. They even have a special group known as the Brandenburg Kommando. They entered Smolensk ahead of the main German advance, all wearing Red Army uniforms. They stopped us from blowing up the bridges. That's why the city fell so quickly. And as for you, our reports indicate that the troops currently occupying Pushkin village are a brigade of cavalry belonging to the Waffen SS. What they'll do if they catch you will be every bit as vicious if you're wearing Russian uniforms as it would be if you're dressed as Germans and they realise who you are.'

Churikova glanced uneasily at the heap of dirty clothing. 'There are only two uniforms here.'

'You are better off keeping your clothes,' advised Leontev.

'There are plenty of women serving in the Soviet Army, as snipers, stretcher bearers or truck drivers, and their uniforms are nearly the same as those of the men. But the Germans don't mix women with their front-line troops. Some of these uniforms belong to German Military Police. Travelling together, it will appear that you are a prisoner being brought back for interrogation.' Leontev jerked his chin at the pile of black leather belts and field-grey wool. 'The rest of you, find something that fits. Leave everything else behind except your Russian pass books. You will need them to establish your identities once you have returned to our lines.'

'And if they find our pass books on us?' asked Stefanov.

'Then I hope for your sake that you'll already be dead.'

Gritting his teeth, Pekkala rummaged through the dead men's clothes. He selected a tunic belonging to one of the military policemen, some trousers and some boots and carried them into the next room, which was the kitchen. A smell of boiled meat hung in the air. Pekkala was about to lay the clothes upon the *pleeta* stove when, out of old habit, he spat on the iron plates to check that they weren't hot.

After stripping off his own garments, Pekkala dressed in the German uniform. It was still warm from the man's body heat. Fumbling with the pebbled metal buttons, he smelled the man's sweat and the unfamiliar machine-oil reek of German wool. It was the socks that troubled him the most, since he had long since grown used to Russian *portyanki*, which wound about the foot like a bandage. Next, Pekkala picked up a pair of jack boots and held the muddy soles against his foot, trying to gauge their size. He tried the other pair and pulled them on. His own foot settled on the imprint of the dead man's.

At that moment, Leontev appeared at the kitchen door, carrying several German helmets, which he tossed into the room. The heavy metal crashed on to the wooden floorboards. He nodded approvingly at Pekkala and Stefanov. 'Excellent!' he grinned. 'I feel like shooting you.'

'These clothes may fit,' said Pekkala, 'but the average soldier in this or any other army is a good deal younger than I am.'

'The average soldier, yes, but not the average member of the military police. In wartime, these men are often recruited from the regular police force. As a result, most are older than the people they're sent to arrest. Chained dogs. That's what the Germans call their military police. With any luck, as soon as they see those gorgets around your necks, they'll turn around and walk the other way. Military police do not mix with the rest of the army. They do not sleep in the same barracks. They do not eat at the same tables. They do not drink at the same bars. They prefer to be left alone and the rest of the army, whether it is Russian, German or any other nationality, is most often happy to oblige.'

The soldiers returned from the field. They washed their hands in a puddle in the road. Then they began setting fire to the barn.

'Take what you can and get out,' ordered Leontev. 'They're burning the house down as well.'

'But why?' asked Stefanov. 'This is a Russian farm!'

'We burn everything,' replied Leontev. 'By the way, Inspector, I have been told to give you this.' He held up a grey metal canister, of the type German soldiers used for storing their gas masks, suspended on a heavy canvas strap. 'A gift from Comrade Poskrebychev. He said you would know what to do with it.'

Momentarily confused, Pekkala reached out and took hold of the canister. It was heavy. 'What's in this?' he asked.

'Enough explosives to blow us all to vapour. The canister also contains two pencil timers, in case you need to divide the charges.'

'Pencil timers?'

'A glass vial of cupric chloride is housed in an aluminium and copper tube, along with a detonator and a striker, which is held back by a tiny wire made of lead alloy. Break the vial by crushing the copper end of the tube with the heel of your boot, then pull the safety strip on the side of the tube and the timer will begin. There are five timers in the set, each one with a different coloured band, wrapped in a paper bundle which tells you how long each coloured tube will last before it detonates. You have anywhere from ten minutes to an hour, depending on which colour you use. Once you've pulled the safety strip, jam the sharp end of the timer into the explosives and get as far away as you can.'

Cautiously, Pekkala slung the canister across his shoulder.

'There is one more thing they've given you, Inspector,' said Leontev.

'What is that?'

'A coil of wire and a battery, for constructing an instant fuse. Simply cut the wire in half, embed one of each end in the explosives and one of the other ends to the negative battery terminal. As soon as you touch the fourth end to the positive terminal, you will complete the circuit, which sends an electric charge into the explosives and detonates them.'

'Which means I have no chance of escape,' Pekkala concluded.

'It looks to me, Inspector, that they have put more value on this mission than they have done on your life.'

Red Army soldiers moved past them and into the house. In a minute, the place was ablaze. They had just left the building, when a heavy thump of mortars sounded on the ridge. Immediately the men set off at a run towards their gun positions.

'Any moment now,' said Leontev, 'the Fascists will begin advancing up the slope. When you hear the shooting start, follow the cart path. It veers to the west in a couple of kilometres. You must not talk. You must not smoke. If you get lost, you must not cry out.' He jabbed two fingers at his eyes, as if he meant to blind himself. 'Never lose sight of the person in front of you. After one hour, you will come to a river, beside which are the ruins of a house. A man is waiting for you there. He is one of ours. He will show you how to get across the river. From there, the road runs straight to Tsarskoye Selo.'

The thatched roof was burning now. Whirlwinds of sparks vortexed into the sky. A loud explosion echoed through the trees as a wave of fire rolled across the ridge. More explosions followed, each one a dusty red plume punching out of the darkness.

Pekkala turned to look for Leontev, but the man had already vanished into the night.

People's Commissar Bakhturin sat at his desk, blinking in astonishment at Major Kirov, who had just barged into his office.

The office consisted of a large corner room on the third floor of a building, which had, before the Revolution, been the home of Count Andronikov, the Tsar's Minister of Agriculture. It had Persian carpets on the floor, paintings on the walls from Bakhturin's personal collection and ornate pre-Revolution furniture imported from England and France. All of it had been requisitioned from special warehouses where the possessions of enemies of the State were stored until they could be redistributed among the people of the city. Some of the furnishings, such as a Chippendale oak chair and a desk from the workshop of the master carpenter Gustavus de Lisle, had also belonged to Count Andronikov. Having been confiscated, along with the building itself, they had subsequently found their way back to their original home, and were now set aside for the personal use of Commissar Bakhturin. Although the original plan was for such goods to be given out to anyone in good standing with the Communist Party and so dispersing the wealth of the former regime among the masses, it soon became apparent that only those with the right connections, like Viktor Bakhturin , would ever get their hands on luxuries such as these.

'What on earth are you doing?' demanded Bakhturin. 'You can't just walk in here!'

'Where is your brother?' asked Kirov. 'He's out of prison, isn't he?'

'He served his sentence. He didn't escape, if that's what you mean. He was released two weeks ago.'

'I'm not asking where he was,' said Kirov. 'I want to know where he is now.'

Bakhturin hesitated. 'As a matter of fact, I have no idea. He was supposed to have contacted me immediately after his release from Tulkino, but I never heard from him. He will show up eventually. He's just enjoying his first few days of freedom before I put him back to work. What is this about, Major Kirov?'

'A man was killed two nights ago, a friend of Inspector Pekkala's.'

'And you think my brother might have murdered a friend of the Inspector?' Bakhturin sat back and shrugged. 'Why would he want to do that?'

'I believe that Pekkala might have been the real target, but the murderer shot the wrong man.'

'Listen to me, Comrade Major. My brother may have been foolish enough to land himself in prison, but he's not so stupid as to attempt the assassination of Stalin's most valuable detective.'

'Your brother owes you a debt.'

'Yes, he does,' agreed Bakhturin. 'If it wasn't for my help, Serge would never have graduated from primary school, let alone found a high-ranking job with the State Railways. But it was always my choice to help him. He never asked for favours, and I never wanted anything in return.'

'Which makes the debt all the more difficult to repay, doesn't it? You wanted Pekkala brought down. You made no secret of it.'

'If I truly meant to kill Pekkala, I would find a better way of doing it than sending my own brother to carry out the task.'

'And what if Serge decided to carry it out on his own? It was Pekkala, after all, who put him in prison.'

'On his own?' Bakhturin snorted. 'Serge wouldn't dare!'

'And why not?'

'Because then he would have to answer to me, as well as to you, and I can assure you that answering to me is the less attractive of those options for my brother!'

'And the fact that you haven't heard from Serge since he got out of prison is of no concern to you?'

Bakhturin stared into a corner of the room. 'I will admit,' he said quietly, 'that this is not like him at all.'

'Prison changes everyone.'

Bakhturin nodded. 'The thought had crossed my mind.'

'Then help me to find him,' said Kirov. 'Pekkala taught me that it is as important to exonerate an innocent man as it is to bring a guilty one to trial.'

For a while, Bakhturin remained lost in thought. Then he picked up a pencil and scribbled something down on a sheet of paper. Slowly, he rose to his feet and handed the paper to Kirov. 'You might find him at this address, or at least someone who knows where he is. I would have gone there myself to find out, except he does not know I am aware of his interest in this place.

And he would not want me to know. When you see my brother, Major Kirov, please do not tell him I sent you.'

'Do you have any message for him?'

'Yes,' replied Bakhturin. 'Tell him it's time to come home.'

With the fires of the burning farmhouses roaring on either side of them, Churikova and the two men made their way down the muddy cart track. Ash fell from the sky like a dusting of dirty snow.

Pekkala thought about the clothes he had left behind to be consumed in that inferno: his unofficial uniform of heavy corduroy trousers, double-soled boots and the thick wool coat, all made for him by a tailor named Linsky, whose shop was on the Ulitsa Varvarka. Those garments had become his second skin, his armour against the chaos of the world. Since his return from the gulag at Borodok, Pekkala had lived his life like someone who, at any moment, might be given half an hour's notice to leave his home, his friends and everything he owned except the contents of his pockets, and to vanish forever to the other side of the earth. Only Linsky made the clothes for such a journey.

But Pekkala had not left everything behind, in spite of Leontev's instructions to bring only his pass book. Strapped against his chest was the Webley in its holster and beneath the rough wool collar of his tunic, Pekkala had pinned the gold disc of the Emerald Eye. Those things he refused to do without.

The white walls of the farmhouse had soon faded into the night and the sounds of the gunfire grew faint. When Pekkala turned to look back, all he could see of the fighting were the lazy arcs of flares – reds, yellows, blues – rising and falling over the battlefield.

Glavpur had done its job. They were now behind enemy lines. Everything that happened from now until they crossed back into Russian territory was his responsibility. Even if there had been time to map out each detail of the task which lay ahead, Pekkala knew from experience that few operations ever went according to schedule. More often than not, it was decisions made on the spur of the moment which determined the final result. Those decisions, and their outcome, would rest upon his shoulders.

As the three of them pressed on into the darkness, each alone with their thoughts, the sound of their hobnailed boots thumped out a rhythm like a heartbeat upon the old dirt road.

Walking at the head of the line, Stefanov squinted into the darkness before him, the German sub-machine gun hugged against his chest. He had never handled a Schmeisser before, and hoped that when the time came, he would know how to use it. The only time he'd ever fired a sub-machine gun was in basic training, when he and the other recruits were handed Russian PPD-40s and told to shoot at paper targets nailed to telegraph poles at a distance of thirty paces. The instructor showed him how to bang the round drum magazine hard against the front of his helmet to settle the bullets inside before clipping it into the gun. When Stefanov pulled the trigger for the first time, the deafening shudder of the gun seemed to pull him forward instead of rocking him back the way he had expected. When the last cartridge ejected with a metallic ping, he realised that the instructor had been shouting at him to cease fire – shouting right in his ear – but he had not heard and had emptied the entire magazine.

Stefanov had forgotten how heavy such weapons were, and this German gun was no exception. The weight of the spare magazines in their canvas and leather pouch dragged on his hip bones. The gunsling rubbed at his neck. Before long, in spite of the cool night air, Stefanov's shirt was soaked through with sweat.

After an hour's walk, just as Leontev had said, they came to the ruins of a house which was perched at the edge of a river. But there was no sign of any bridge or anyone to meet them.

'Perhaps we followed the wrong path,' said Churikova.

'Maybe we should double back,' Stefanov suggested.

'There's no time for that,' Pekkala told him. Holding his rifle above his head, he made his way down the steep bank to the water's edge. Carefully, he stepped out into the current, winced as the cold water poured in over the tops of his boots. He hoped that the river might be shallow enough to cross on foot, and the current weak enough that it would not carry them off. There was no way to know except to try it for himself. Pekkala was up to his thighs when the bottom dropped away sharply and he lost his footing. The current was stronger than he'd thought, and it swept him a short distance downstream before he managed to regain his footing. Shivering and soaked, Pekkala had just got back on the path when he noticed a movement in the darkness.

He raised the rifle to his shoulder and squinted down the sight.

Water dripped from the barrel, like pearls spilled from a broken necklace, as he squinted down the rifle sight. Seconds passed. Just as he was beginning to wonder if he was imagining things, the darkness took shape and a man stepped out on to the path, empty hands raised above his shoulders. 'Pekkala?'

With a sigh, he lowered the gun. 'Yes.'

'I am Corporal Gorinov. Major Leontev ordered me to wait here and make sure you got across the bridge.'

'But there is no bridge!'

The man grinned at Pekkala, his teeth flashing white in the gloom. 'That's where you are wrong, Inspector.'

Returning to where the others waited on the path, Gorinov stepped in amongst the ruins of the house.

'He says there is a bridge,' Pekkala whispered to them.

'Then he has lost his mind,' muttered Churikova.

Pekkala followed the man into the house, his steel-shod heels sinking into the rotten wooden boards.

Just ahead, a torch blinked on. Covering the light with his hand so that only a faint pink glow showed through his fingers, Gorinov bent down and lifted a trap door.

'Where is this bridge?' asked Pekkala.

'Come see for yourself.'

Beneath the trap door lay a waist-deep hole, in which Pekkala could see a thing like a large truck wheel with a piece of metal welded vertically on to the rim. Gorinov took hold of the wheel and began to turn it slowly.

Accompanied by a clattering of metal cogs, two cables snaked out of the mud by the water's edge, just in front of the house. Moustaches of river grass hung from the twisted metal line. Now the glassy surface of the river began to tremble. Gorinov spun the wheel faster. The sound of the cogs became a constant metallic buzz.

Churikova breathed in sharply. 'Look!' A narrow footbridge

appeared from the black and hung suspended above the water, swaying gently in the moonlight.

'Who built this contraption?' asked Pekkala.

'Before the invasion, there were many such projects under way. There were many who believed the treaty with Germany would not last. They ordered the construction of hidden bunkers, tunnel systems and bridges. This is one of the few that we actually finished. I'm glad it wasn't built for nothing.'

One by one, Stefanov and Churikova crossed the river, holding tightly to the cables as they inched their way along. The planks of the footbridge were slippery, but nails had been hammered into the underside so that their feet could grip the points. Beneath them, the river slid by like an unfurling banner of silk.

Pekkala was the last to go.

Behind him, Gorinov stood ready with a large set of bolt cutters.

'What are you doing with those?' asked Pekkala.

'My orders are to cut the cables as soon as you're across.'

When Pekkala reached the middle of the bridge, he paused and looked out over the river. Mist clung to the banks. The long, ungainly body of a heron lifted from the shadows and took flight, passing so close over Pekkala's head that he felt the air stirred by the beating of its wings.

As Pekkala set foot on the far bank, he turned and waved to Gorinov.

Gorinov raised one hand, his silhouetted fingers black as crow's feathers. Seconds later came the grinding, snapping sound of the bolt cutters as they gnawed through the cables of the bridge.

Following the instructions given to him by People's Commissar Bakhturin, Kirov arrived at a house in the Moscow suburbs of Kuntsevo.

At first, the place appeared to be empty, but then Kirov noticed a chink of light in one of the windows and realised that they were covered by thick, dark curtains. The order for black-out curtains to be installed as a precaution against air raids had gone into effect months before, but a shortage of suitable material meant that the law had neither been properly obeyed nor efficiently enforced. Kirov was glad to see that at this house, at least, the inhabitants had taken the precautions seriously. The little things mattered to Kirov. It was why the clutter on Pekkala's desk bothered him, made even worse by the fact that Pekkala, in defiance of all reason, still seemed to know where everything was. It was why Kirov's younger brother had tormented him so effectively by leaving drawers slightly open around the house, a fault Kirov felt compelled to correct, no matter how hard he tried to ignore them. But Kirov had learned to live with his eccentricities, and even to profit by them. It was this attention to detail that had made Kirov a good investigator. In any other walk of life, he would simply have been considered a lunatic.

A moment later, a middle-aged man, his shoulders stooped

from fatigue, stepped out of the house. He was carrying a briefcase and he had buttoned up his coat against the evening chill.

A woman, dressed for bed at this late hour, came with him to the doorway, kissed him on the cheek and closed the door behind him.

Even in this darkness, Kirov knew the man was not Serge Bakhturin, whom he had seen numerous times in the course of the trial that led to Serge's conviction for issuing false bills of lading. Serge was tall and heavy-set, with a wide face and a thick neck. This man was too short, too old, too frail.

He's probably an accountant on his way to a nightshift job, thought Kirov and, as he watched the man make his way towards the train station, he felt a surge of pity for this lonely figure, his days inverted into darkness, and wondered what it must be like for the man's wife, so rarely to see him in daylight.

Kirov realised that Bakhturin must have misled him, and probably on purpose, but just in case he followed the man across the street, with the intention of questioning him. Perhaps the address Bakhturin had written down was only partially incorrect, or maybe this man had seen Serge on his way to or from work. He removed the pass book from his upper left pocket, ready to present his credentials to the man.

As the man approached the entrance to a pedestrian tunnel which ran beneath the road and emerged beside a railway platform for all trains bound into the city, Kirov called out for him to stop.

The man whirled about. On glimpsing Kirov's *gymnastiorka* tunic, knee-length boots and pistol belt, his eyes widened with fear.

Kirov had anticipated that the man might be surprised. It was long after dark and the street was otherwise empty, but Kirov assumed that as soon as the man caught sight of his uniform, he would realise it was official business.

'It's all right,' Kirov assured him. 'I just have a few questions.'

The man gave a plaintive, wordless cry and stumbled backwards against the concrete wall of the pedestrian tunnel. With fumbling hands, he removed a wallet from his coat and held it out to Kirov. 'Take it,' he whispered. 'Just let me go.'

'What? No!' Kirov held open his pass book. 'I am Major—'

'Take it!' the man shouted. The wallet quivered in his grip.

'I don't want your money. All I need from you . . .'

The man cried out again, dropped the wallet, and fled away down the tunnel.

Having decided against pursuing the terrified man, Kirov bent down and picked up the billfold. Then he crossed the road again and returned to the house where, he hoped, the wife had not yet gone back to bed so he could return what had been lost.

Kirov knocked on the door and, following regulations, took two steps back and undid the flap on the holster of his Tokarev. While he waited, he took a moment to glance down at his boots and nodded with satisfaction at the quality of their polish.

The door opened, spilling out the warm glow of an oil lamp on a table in the hall.

The woman stood before him. She was heavily made-up and the light of the oil lamp shone through her night dress, which Kirov now realised, was completely transparent. Beneath it, she was naked.

It took Kirov only a second to reassess everything he had

thought over the past few minutes, including his sympathy for the overworked accountant.

'Hello, Commissar,' said the woman, in a voice which sent a shudder down his spine. 'Would you like to come in?'

'Yes,' he replied curtly, and stepped into the hallway. Immediately, his lungs filled with a choking fog of cigarettes, perfume and nail varnish. The paint on the walls was a pinkish red, somewhere between the colours of new brick and salmon flesh. The old wooden floorboards had been stippled with stiletto heels. To his left was a room lined with a collection of tired-looking couches, on which sat women of a variety of ages and complexions, reading magazines or smoking. To his right, a staircase climbed up to the second floor. Kirov turned to the woman. 'I am here for Serge Bakhturin,' he said quietly, 'That is the only reason I am here.'

Unlike the accountant, the woman neither fled nor panicked. Instead, she leaned towards him, resting her hand upon his shoulder and muttered in his ear. 'Will it be possible to avoid causing a commotion?'

'That depends,' he replied in a whisper, 'entirely on Comrade Bakhturin.'

She stood back and smiled, daring his eyes to stray from her face. 'Top floor. The room at the end of the hall.'

'Is there another exit from that room?'

'Not without breaking your neck.'

'Are the doors locked?'

'Never.'

Before he headed up the stairs, Kirov handed over the accountant's wallet. 'One of your customers dropped this.'

'It's about time he left a tip,' she remarked as she plucked it from his fingers.

As Kirov climbed the creaking steps, he removed the Tokarev from its holster. Quietly, he drew back the slide and chambered a round in the breech. He could feel his heartbeat pulsing in his neck. Kirov thought about Pekkala; how the man never seemed nervous at moments like this. Of all the skills he had learned from the Inspector, the suppression of fear was not one of them.

The hall on the top floor was poorly lit, with two sets of doors on either side. All of the doors were closed. The one at the end of the hall showed signs of having been kicked in at some point in the past, and the dent of a footprint in the wood hastily painted over.

Knowing that it would be impossible to get to the end of the hall without making a noise, Kirov decided instead to move quickly. He strode down to the door, turned the handle and pushed.

Inside, the room was lit by a single light bulb hanging from a dusty shade in the centre of the ceiling. An iron-framed bed filled most of the room and a small window looked out over the moonlit rooftops of nearby houses.

Standing between the bed and the window was Serge Bakhturin. Clutched against his chest he held a girl about sixteen years old, one arm across her stomach and the other one gripping her throat.

The girl wore a white night dress with lace around the collar and buttons halfway down the front, which were unfastened. Her eyes were filled with dread.

Kirov raised the Tokarev, but there was no clear shot with the girl standing between them.

'I heard you coming,' said Serge. 'I remember your face from the trial. And I know why you're here, Major Kirov.'

'Let her go. Then we can talk.' Behind him, Kirov heard doors opening and the sound of people running barefoot down the stairs.

Serge tightened his grip upon the woman's throat.

She tried to swallow. Her face turned red. She kept her eyes fastened on the barrel of the gun.

Kirov knew he couldn't put down Serge without hitting the girl as well.

The girl seemed to know it too. A look of profound resignation appeared on her face, as if a shadow had passed through her mind. He had seen this look once before, in the eyes of an old, lame horse his family had owned on the day his father took it out behind the barn and put it down. The animal had known what was about to happen. There was no doubt in Kirov's mind about that. He had been a child when this took place, but the moment had remained brutally clear in his mind.

'I'm not going to deny it,' muttered Serge. 'I'm the one who killed Pekkala.'

'Pekkala is alive,' replied Kirov, his voice barely above a whisper.

'Liar!' Serge howled. 'I saw him go down. I'd have killed his friend, too, if that damned revolver hadn't jammed.'

Now Kirov understood why only one of the rounds had been fired. 'Who put you in contact with Gustav Engel?' he asked.

'Nobody!' barked Serge. 'But if I see him again, I'll kill him too.'

'It was your brother, wasn't it? It was Viktor.'

'You've got it all wrong, Commissar. I don't need any help, least of all from him. He's been propping me up since I was a kid, and until I ended up in prison, I never stopped to wonder if I might have been better off handling things on my own. And that's exactly what I did this time. I took care of things by myself.'

'Yes,' said Kirov. 'Yes, you did. Now you can let the lady go. I'm not going to tell you again.'

'I'll let her go. Just let me slip out this window. Nobody has to get hurt.'

'There's no way down from there.'

'Then I'll have to walk right past you, won't I?'

Kirov shook his head. He had the gun aimed at the girl's throat, knowing that if he was forced to pull the trigger at this range, the round would pass through her neck and strike the man standing behind her.

'You don't look like a killer to me,' Serge taunted him.

'I'm not,' agreed Kirov, 'but for you, I would make an exception.'

'And for her?' He tilted back the girl's head until the tendons stood out on her neck.

This time, Kirov did not reply.

'I didn't think so,' said Serge. 'It's me or nothing, and I don't think you have the kind of luck to make that shot. You would need luck like mine, and you don't have that kind of luck.'

'You're right,' said Kirov. 'I don't have luck like yours.'

'I knew you would come to your senses.' Serge took one step towards the door, still holding the girl in front of him.

As Serge's right leg moved forward, Kirov lowered the Tokarev and shot him through the knee cap. Serge cried out, releasing his grip upon the girl. He tumbled to the floor, like a marionette whose strings had been cut. Before Serge had even hit the ground, Kirov sent another bullet through the bridge of his nose, killing him instantly.

The sound of the shots was deafening in the confined space of the room.

Bakhturin lay on his back, one leg twisted under him. Smoke slithered from his wounds, rising to the ceiling where they mushroomed out across the stuccoed paint.

The girl hadn't moved.

For a moment, she and Kirov just stared at each other.

Then, with trembling fingers, she began to fasten the buttons on her blood-spattered night dress.

Under the jaundiced eye of a harvest moon, Pekkala, Stefanov and Churikova made their way through fields of uncut wheat and orchards where the fruit lay rotting on the ground.

Stefanov took the lead, retracing his route as well as he could remember. One path, in particular, which was nothing more than a cart track running between the fields, he remembered as having been empty when he walked it. He kept them on this trail, which proved to be just as deserted now as it had been before.

Although they heard the rumble of vehicles in the distance, they encountered neither trucks nor soldiers. The fighting had moved like a tornado across the countryside, leaving some places in ruins and the rest of the landscape untouched.

In the middle of the night, they arrived at the burnt remains of a house. Smoke slithered through the maze of fallen beams and clumps of charred thatch wheezed and crackled. Behind the house, they found the bodies of an old man and an old woman, hanging from the branches of a tree, their feet almost touching the ground.

Churikova reached out and set her hand against the dead man's chest, as if to feel the beating of his heart. When she drew her hand away, the corpse rocked gently on the hemp rope noose, like a pendulum spent of its energy.

From a scabbard tucked into his boot, Stefanov pulled a knife and slashed through the ropes with one cut. The bodies fell heavily, one on top of the other, broken necks lolling grotesquely.

Pekkala and the others returned to the road and kept on marching. Not a word had passed between them since they came upon the house.

At dawn, they reached the point where their trail intersected with the main road leading into Tsarskoye Selo. Here, they discovered why the enemy had left them in peace during the night. An old wooden bridge, no more than ten paces long, had been built above a stream that crossed the trail. A German Army truck had tried to cross it, but the supports had collapsed under the weight, sending the truck crashing into the ditch and barring the way for other vehicles.

'Raise your hands,' Pekkala told Churikova. 'You need to start looking like a prisoner. From now on, you must walk in front. Keep your hands above your head and your eyes on the ground. Don't make eye contact with anyone. Don't speak, no matter what they say to you.'

Without a word, Churikova raised her arms, pale fingers uncurling, and clutched her hands together at the back of her neck.

They crossed by wading through the shallow stream, whose muddy banks glowed with yellow dandelions, purple vetch and black-eyed Susans. As they set out towards Tsarskoye Selo, they soon found themselves among convoys of trucks, armoured cars, motorcycles, which filled the air with diesel fumes and dust. The occasional group of soldiers passed them, travelling on foot, but always in the opposite direction. There were also a number of captured Red Army gun carriages, all of them weighed down with troops and equipment, pulled along by stocky little Russian Kabardin horses.

Pekkala felt a knot in his throat as he watched the carriages go by, knowing that those Kabardins would go on until they collapsed and died in their traces. From the way the drivers whipped the backs of the horses, this seemed to be exactly their intention.

Pekkala lost count of the number of trucks driving past them. Several cigarette butts were flicked in their direction from soldiers in the backs of these vehicles, but most seemed aimed at Pekkala and Stefanov, in their military police uniforms, rather than at their prisoner. Once the trucks had passed, Stefanov snatched up the cigarettes and puffed greedily at the last shreds of tobacco they contained.

A convoy of Mark IV Panzer tanks rolled by, shaking the ground as it passed and filling the air with the monstrous clattering of tracks. At the head of the column rode a small staff car of the type known as a Kübelwagen.

With a squeal of brakes, it pulled to the side of the road.

Pekkala and the others came to an abrupt halt.

Meanwhile, the tanks continued to roll past, spewing black clouds of diesel fumes from their vertical exhaust pipes.

Very slowly, Stefanov adjusted his grip on the sub-machine gun strap, ready to swing it off his shoulder if needed.

A man in the wide-lapelled black tunic of a panzer officer leaned out of the Kübelwagen. Silver braid glinted above the pink piping on his shoulder boards. He shouted something at Pekkala, who was walking at the front of the line, but his voice was drowned out by the thunder of the tanks' engines.

The officer tried again, smiling and gesturing at Churikova.

Pekkala pointed at the half-moon-shaped military police gorget which hung around his neck, then pointed back at Churikova.

The officer spoke again, struggling to make himself heard.

Pekkala shrugged and shook his head.

At last, the officer gave up, flipping the air with his hand in a gesture of frustration. A moment later, the Kübelwagen was gone. It raced along beside the tanks, bumper swishing through the tall grass at the side of the road, until it reached the head of the line, then swerved in front of the first Panzer to resume its place in the lead.

After that, while their small procession continued to draw a few stares, nobody stopped to question them. As Pekkala stared at this seemingly endless procession of men and machines, he was struck by an overwhelming sense of momentum. He had the impression that nothing could stop it, not even the architects of this war, who had set everything in motion.

By the time they reached the Orlov gates at the entrance to Tsarskoye Selo, the three of them were so coated with faded yellow dust that they looked as if they had been rolled in turmeric.

The gates themselves had been torn off their hinges and cast aside, as if by an angry giant. Beside the bullet-spattered stonework, into which the gates had once been anchored, lay a heap of empty brass cartridges where a machine gun had run through a box of ammunition. The brass cartridges were spattered with congealed arterial blood, still bright as carnival paint, and nearby lay the grey cotton wrappers of Russian army bandages.

Entering the grounds of the estate, they walked along the

deserted Rampovaya Road. Sidestepping blast craters from the fighting, they came across the shattered body of a Russian soldier, dead for several days, lying face down in the undergrowth, his bloated hands white-gloved with maggots.

They had now been marching for more than ten hours and stopped to rest near the old concert hall. A shell burst had split one of its four columns in half, like a tree struck by lightning, and chunks of white marble lay strewn across the ground.

Through the sweat in Stefanov's eyes, memories shimmered like mirages. He saw himself one late spring afternoon, the air heavy with the smell of lilac and honeysuckle, heading home from school along the path which ran beside this concert hall. From somewhere behind its candle-lit windows came the sound of children's voices as they practised for the concert given each year to the Tsar and his family when they arrived in June to take up residence in the summer palace. And there he was again, in summer now, trudging along beneath the turquoise banners of the evening sky and returning to his father's workshop with the ladder he had used to catch his first and only glimpse inside the Amber Room.

Even though Stefanov knew these memories belonged to him, so much had happened since then that they seemed to have come from someone else's life, a hundred or a thousand years before.

Although Pekkala, too, had often passed this way, he was in too much pain to lose himself in memories. His heels had been rubbed raw in the ill-fitting boots. He was afraid to take them off, in case the damage was even worse than it felt, and he might be unable to get his boots back on.

Noticing the pain, which had creased itself into the Inspector's face, Stefanov produced a lump of soap from his pocket. He had spotted it in the kitchen of the farmhouse where they changed their clothes and immediately pocketed it. Before the war, he had not been a thief. But now he pilfered everything he could lay his hands on, whether it was a piece of electrical wiring which had been used to bind a cracked gravestone in the cemetery at Chertova, or the stub of a pencil he found on the floor of the truck which brought them to the front, or a lump of soap from that farmhouse. He had become like a magpie, hoarding any unattended scrap, convinced that it might come in handy somewhere down the road. And usually he was right.

'Rub this on your feet,' said Stefanov, as he handed the lump of soap to Pekkala. 'It will help.'

Pekkala tugged off the knee-length boots. His grey wool socks were stained with blood. Wincing, he peeled them off. As Pekkala rubbed the soap into the wounds, he squinted through a screen of trees towards the Catherine Palace greenhouse, which had been known as the Orangerie, due to the fact that the Tsar had once grown tangerines beneath its glass-paned roof. Although the greenhouse had been completely destroyed, peach-coloured roses, purple and pink lupins, fire-orange birds of paradise continued to grow among the wreckage.

To his right, across the manicured garden, stood the palace itself. Familiar as Pekkala was with the building, the sight of it still took his breath away. As long as a city block, at first glance its blue and white façade seemed to be made up almost entirely of windows, some twice as tall as a man, opening on to balconies fenced in by ornate black railings. Much of the glass was broken now. Shards, like giant shark fins, lined the empty frames.

To Pekkala, it no longer looked like the residence of the Tsar. Instead, the building resembled a fortress after a long and bloody siege, its front lawn now a parking lot for armoured cars, Kübelwagens, Panzers and muddy, dented Opel Blitz trucks.

Churikova sat against the splintered column, blue eyes glowing in her wind-burned face. 'Do you really intend to destroy the Amber Room?' she asked Pekkala.

Pekkala had been staring at the ground, but now he raised his head and looked at Churikova. 'I hope it will not come to that.'

'But what if it does?' she persisted. 'I overheard that officer explaining how to use the detonators. I understand enough about explosives to know that you have enough in that canister to obliterate the room and half of the palace as well.'

'With luck—' he began.

Churikova cut him off. 'I am not talking about luck. I am talking about what you will do if the Germans attempt to relocate the amber back into their own country? Will you go through with it? Will you carry out your orders?'

Pekkala looked towards the Catherine Palace, where German officers in finely tailored uniforms stood on the balconies, some with the red lapels of generals, looking out over the grounds. 'We will know that soon enough,' he said. And then he explained to them the plan which had been brewing in his head ever since they set out from the Russian lines. 'We must set a trap for Engel, but first we have to wait for him to arrive. That might be in hours or it might be in days. There's no way of knowing, so we'll take it in shifts to keep the palace under observation. The first thing he'll come looking for when he arrives at the estate is the Amber Room. That is where we'll intercept the professor. The difficulty will be in isolating Engel from those around him, so we can make the arrest and bring him back with us. For that, I'll need both of you to help me.'

'What do you want us to do?' demanded Churikova.

'You and I will enter the Palace and either contact Engel directly or else send word to him that a Russian deserter has provided us with information about art works hidden on the grounds of the estate. That, and the fact that Engel will almost certainly remember meeting you here before the war, should be enough to lure him out of the palace.'

'What should I do, Inspector?' Stefanov asked.

'Do you know the old Pensioners' Stable, at the north-east corner of the estate?'

'Of course.'

'Beside it, just off the path, is a small cottage.'

'I know it well,' said Stefanov. 'That is where you used to live.'

Pekkala nodded. 'That is where Churikova will tell him the art works have been stored. Wait for us there.'

'What if there's already someone in the cottage?'

'Tell them to get out or, if you don't know the words, just jerk your thumb at the door. They won't stop to question a military policeman.'

Pekkala had opened his mouth, ready to ask if they had any questions, when suddenly Churikova sat forward, as if the ground had moved beneath her feet.

'There he is,' she whispered.

Kirov stood at attention, his eyes fixed on the wall.

Stalin sat in his red leather chair. On the desk in front of him lay a stack of police photographs which had been taken at the brothel after the shooting. One was of Serge Bakhturin's corpse, lying beside the unmade bed. The man's face, crumpled by the bullet which had killed him, resembled an old mask made of papier mâché. Another picture showed Bakhturin's leg, pale and welded to the floor with blood, the limb cut nearly in half by the bullet that had shattered his knee.

There were shots of the room, in which shadows seemed to hover about the camera lens as if the air was filled with ghosts. One photo showed the view from the window, looking out across a crooked sea of rooftops. There was even a picture of the girl, still in her blood-spattered night dress. She stared directly into the camera, hypnotised by the cyclops eye of the lens.

Stalin set aside all the pictures except the ones of Bakhturin's body. These he studied closely, with a look of intense concentration on his face. Finally, Stalin sat back in his chair and pushed the photograph away, turning his gaze at last to Major Kirov. 'This is the first time you have killed a man, isn't it?'

Kirov did not reply, but remained at attention, staring at the wall behind Stalin's desk.

'I know what must be going on inside your head, but you

must let your conscience rest. This man,' Stalin jabbed the photograph of Serge Bakhturin's face, as if to stir his finger in the wound, 'was a traitor! He admitted it to you. It is over. It is done. Go home. Get drunk if you need to. Get some sleep.'

'Yes, Comrade Stalin. Has there been any word from Pekkala?'

'Army Intelligence reported that he and Lieutenant Churikova crossed the lines last night, accompanied by a soldier who is acting as their guide. They're on their own now, Kirov. There is nothing for us to do now except trust in the magic of that Finnish sorcerer you call a friend.'

'Engel!' Churikova pointed at a man who had just emerged from the north entrance of the palace and was now heading down the steps towards the gardens.

'Are you sure?' Pekkala demanded. 'You must be absolutely certain.'

'Yes.' There was no hesitation in her voice.

Pekkala snatched up his rifle and turned to Stefanov. 'If we're not at the cottage by dark, your orders are to return to the Russian lines and to send word to Comrade Stalin that the mission has been a failure.'

Stefanov nodded in reply. Then, without a word, he vanished among the trees, heading for the Pensioners' Stable.

As Pekkala and Churikova made their way towards the Catherine Palace, the lieutenant out in front with her arms above her head as if Pekkala were escorting a prisoner, they passed between the tall, leafy hedges of the Gribok Kurtina. Beyond the Gribok, they crossed over the Chinese Bridge, its iron railings wrenched into beckoning fingers where bullets had cut through the metal.

A cool autumn breeze blew in off the still, green water of the Great Pond, smelling of weeds and decay.

On the other side of the bridge, wounded German soldiers lay in the shade of a giant oak tree. A few were talking or writing letters. Others lay wax-faced and staring at the sky. Many of the stretchers were covered with grey army blankets, showing the outlines of men who had died before the doctors could get to them. Nearby stood a large white tent with a red cross painted on the canvas. Every few minutes, medical assistants in blood-spattered white aprons appeared from the tent, picked up a stretcher and carried a soldier inside. A noise of sawing filtered through the canvas walls.

Arriving at the steps of the palace, they trod over a stream of blood, which had trickled down the main staircase, staining the grey stone as if it were the shadow of a lightning bolt. Soldiers clattered past him, heel irons sparking on the stone. Pekkala heard them speaking Finnish and remembered what Leontev had said about the presence of foreign volunteers among the German troops.

On the balcony, beside the main entrance, sat a squad of SS infantry, still in their palm-leaf-patterned camouflage smocks and black leather combat harnesses. Mauser rifles leaned against the walls beside them and their helmets lay upturned on the ground.

These soldiers all wore the same long stare of total exhaustion and, at first, they barely seemed to notice the military policeman or his prisoner. It was only when they realised that Pekkala's prisoner was a woman that a few smiles creased their gunsmoke-blackened faces.

Having climbed the staircase, Pekkala and Churikova passed through an open door at the base of the Grand Staircase. Nailed against one bullet-pocked wall, the lids of wooden ammunition crates had been converted into direction signs.

Directly in front of him stood a marble pedestal, at the base of which lay the shattered remnants of a large sixteenth-century Venetian vase and a puddle of water that the vase had once contained.

For a moment, Pekkala could only stare in dismay at the damage all around him. Then, coming to his senses, he pushed Churikova forward. They moved on through the first and second Exhibition Halls, whose bare walls chanted back the echo of their footsteps.

Arriving at the Great Hall, Pekkala found its vast space empty except for a portable desk set just inside the front entrance. The desk looked absurdly small in this room, as did the man who sat behind it, the dull silver chevron of an army corporal stitched on to his sleeve. He appeared to be adrift there, like a man on a life raft in the middle of a flat calm sea. The corporal's hair was neatly groomed, hair parted severely at an angle across his scalp. When he caught sight of Pekkala's insignia, he stood, crashed his heels together and saluted. As he did so, the man's gaze drifted to Churikova and then back to Pekkala.

Speaking in German, Pekkala told the man, 'I am delivering this prisoner to Gustav Engel.' He had not spoken the language in some time and, not entirely trusting that what he had said was correct, Pekkala accompanied his words with a gesture towards Churikova and then down the hallway towards the Amber Room.

Pekkala's accent seemed to peck against the corporal as if they had been hailstones. The salute and the stiff back disappeared. 'Another foreign volunteer!' he remarked. 'This army is becoming a tower of Babel. What are you? Dutch? Dane?'

'Finn.'

The corporal acknowledged with a grunt. 'And you are bringing her to Obersturmbannführer Engel?'

Another nod.

'What is the purpose of this?'

'She is a woman,' replied Pekkala. 'What more do you need to know?'

With a muttered comment about the privileges of rank, the corporal sat back down at his desk, filled out a pass on a pad of green paper, then tore off the sheet and handed it over.

Throughout this exchange, Churikova had remained with her hands raised, staring at the floor.

As the corporal returned to his paperwork, Pekkala grasped Churikova by the arm and led her out of the room.

They passed through the Courtiers in Attendance Dining Room, which was empty except for two large mirrors, miraculously unbroken in spite of bullet craters in the plaster on either side of the frames.

Beyond that lay the dining room of Empress Maria Fyodorovna. It too had been gutted except for the ceiling mural, portraying the death of Alexander of Macedonia. Neck craned back as she walked, Churikova stared at the sprawling figures, pale arms outstretched towards the wild-eyed horses, who reared as if they meant to tear themselves from two dimensions into three.

From there, through the open doors, they moved into the Crimson and Green dining rooms, with their bands of red and emerald tinsel reaching as high as the ceiling. As in the Empress's dining room, only the ceiling murals remained, as well as wooden floor mosaics, streaming like sunbursts from the centres of the rooms.

All around Pekkala, the ghosts of the Romanovs drifted in their finery, but as he halted outside the door to the Amber Room, these phantoms retreated back into the darkness of his mind.

Pekkala opened the door and walked in, pushing his prisoner ahead of him.

Wearily, Kirov trudged up the five flights of stairs to his office.

He had decided not to go home, as Stalin had advised. The thought of sitting around in his flat in the middle of the day made him restless. He made up his mind to keep working instead. There was plenty of paperwork to be done.

Disordered fragments from the night before flickered to life behind Kirov's eyes. In the middle of this jumbled slide show, Kirov heard again the voice of Serge Bakhturin threatening to kill Gustav Engel with his bare hands, as if an echo of that moment, reverberating lazily across the rooftops of Moscow, had finally reached his ears.

Kirov puzzled over Bakhturin's words. Why would Serge want to kill Engel? Had the man failed to live up to some part of their bargain? Had Serge not been paid? Or had the traitor himself been betrayed?

It was likely he would never know.

Ahead of him, a soldier plodded up the stairs, weighed down with a heavy pack which was crusted with mud.

Kirov wondered from what battlefield the man had just returned. He had never seen the man before, and thought perhaps he was the son of the old lady who lived on the third floor. But the soldier continued on past the third floor and now Kirov asked himself if it might be one of the lawyers who had maintained an office on the fourth until they were called up by the Army the year before. But he kept going past the fourth floor, too and eventually stopped right outside Kirov's door.

'Who are you looking for?' asked Kirov.

The soldier turned, shrugged off the pack and dropped it on the floor. From his pocket, he fished out a piece of paper. 'The name they gave me is Major Kirov, Special Operations.'

'I am Major Kirov.'

The soldier nudged at the pack with the toe of his boot. 'I have orders to deliver this to you.'

'But that's not my pack.'

'It belongs to someone named Lieutenant Churikova and was salvaged from the wreck of a train that got bombed not long ago on its way to the front. It got sent to the Wrangel barracks here in Moscow. That's where I work, in the supply depot.'

Kirov thought back to the night he and Pekkala had fetched Churikova from the train station, and how she had complained about not being able to retrieve her rucksack from the transport.

'The pack arrived along with a load of other equipment which belonged to her battalion,' continued the soldier. 'It was all due to be reclaimed and re-issued, since there weren't any survivors. At least, that's what we thought. But then we received a message that this lieutenant wasn't on the train when it got hit. Only her pack was on board. I called headquarters and they gave us this place as her forwarding address.' Having completed his task, the soldier tramped downstairs and out into the street.

Kirov lifted the rucksack by its canvas straps, brought it inside and dumped it in the middle of the floor. With a sigh, he collapsed into the old chair from the Hotel Metropol and allowed his gaze to drift around the room, as if to reassure himself that everything was still in its proper place. He studied the potted plants on the window sills, the clutter on Pekkala's desk and the battered brass samovar balanced on the stove. When his focus returned at last to the muddy rucksack on the floor, he realised there was something leaking out of it and into the carpet beneath.

Rising grumpily from his chair, he took hold of the pack and untied the drawstring which held it closed. The leaking was caused by a bottle containing a clear liquid, which he lifted out and set upright on the floor. The bottle had been sealed with a cork, which had then been covered with a coating of red wax. The wax seal had broken and the cork appeared to have been damaged, probably when the soldier dropped it on the floor. Now only half of the bottle's contents remained. The rest of it had soaked whatever else was in the pack. Kirov touched the liquid, dabbed his fingertips against his tongue and realised it was vodka.

Maybe I will have a drink, he thought to himself. Those were Stalin's orders, after all, and I'll call Elizaveta, too. No. It's too late. I'll have a drink and then I'll go to her flat. I'll bring the bottle. By the time the lieutenant returns, I'll have another one waiting for her.

Before he left, Kirov decided to empty the contents of the pack on to the floor, in order to give whatever had been soaked a chance to dry. It was a sad little collection – some spare clothes, a small canvas bag containing a toothbrush, nail scissors, and a standard manual of regulations issued to all Red

Army officers, whose pages had absorbed much of the spilled vodka. Several pieces of paper had been stuffed between the covers of the manual, which were made of thin cardboard overlaid with green canvas. Kirov shook out the extra sheets of paper, in order to give them a better chance of drying. One of these sheets was a note from the director of the Kremlin Art Museum, Fabian Golyakovsky, granting Lieutenant Churikova access to both the archives and the laboratory of the museum, while the rest were travel passes from the Wrangel barracks, a pink requisition slip for a pair of 6x30 binoculars, and a map of the Moscow Underground.

Kirov poured himself a measure of the vodka, using the brass-framed glasses he and Pekkala normally reserved for tea. He was just about to drink it down in one gulp when he noticed that several ants had emerged from beneath the art museum document and were now crawling across the sheet of paper.

'That's all I need,' he announced, 'to have an office infested with insects!' Setting down the glass of vodka, he carefully picked up the paper and went to the window, ready to shake off the ants into the gutter outside. The ants seemed to be multiplying as they swarmed across the page. He was just beginning to wonder whether he ought to sling the whole pack out the window when suddenly he stopped and stared at the paper.

They weren't ants. They were numbers, materialising on the back side of the page, as if scribbled by an invisible hand. The numbers were appearing only where the vodka had soaked the paper. The rest of the page remained blank.

Baffled, Kirov fetched the bottle, set the page down on his desk and doused the rest of the page with the remaining vodka.

After a few seconds, more ghostly numbers began to appear, until the whole back side of the document was covered in what appeared to be some kind of graph. One side of the graph was represented by a small circle, while the other had a symbol which resembled the Cyrillic letter for C or the letter U from the Latin alphabet, but instead of having the tail on the right hand side of the letter, the tail was on the left side.

Half an hour later, with the letter from Fabian Golyakovsky, still damp with vodka, clutched between his fingertips, Kirov arrived at the Kremlin Museum.

We're too late, Pekkala thought to himself. The words pulsed like a migraine in his skull.

He stood beside Lieutenant Churikova in the doorway of the Amber Room. Strewn across the floor in front of them were long strips of paper which had been torn from the walls, revealing the amber beneath. Heaped beside these giant scrolls were shreds of muslin cloth which had been added as a protective layer over the panels.

For a moment, neither of them spoke or moved. They stared at the amber-filled panels, mesmerised by haloes of gold, brown and yellow which gleamed in the evening sun that streamed through the open windows.

Their trance was broken when a voice called out, harsh and questioning, demanding to know who they were.

Out of the cloud of honey-coloured light, a man strode up to Pekkala. He was tall, with brown hair greying at the temples and nervous brown eyes, whose gaze seemed to swarm over the two strangers like a cloud of tiny insects. 'I gave orders to be left alone!' he shouted.

Now that Pekkala's eyes had grown accustomed to the glare, he could see that this man was the only occupant of the room.

'Professor Engel,' said Churikova.

There was a pause.

In an instant, the man's expression transformed from anger to astonishment. 'Polina? Polina Churikova?'

'Yes, Professor.'

'It *is* you!' spluttered Engel. 'I thought the war had separated us for good. As you can see for yourself, this is a day of many miracles!'

'I came to find you,' she said.

'But how did you know I was here?'

'I knew you would come to the palace as soon as you possibly could.'

'Of course!' he laughed, 'and I could have guessed I'd find you here as well. Look at us now, in the service of two different masters. But that cannot stand between us. It was never our choice to make. We will never be enemies, because we are bound by an even greater purpose.' The professor seemed completely overwhelmed. A tremor of ecstasy filled his voice. 'Even a war could not keep us away,' he called out, turning and raising his arms in supplication to the vast mosaic of amber before him, 'from the thing we love most in this world. This is the happiest day of my life, and I thank God that you are here to share it with me.'

In the moment that Engel turned, Pekkala's eyes met Churikova's. It was only for an instant, but long enough for Pekkala to communicate to her that the task ahead of them might be easier than he'd thought.

'But how did you manage it, Polina?' Engel spun around to face her once again, grasping her hands in his. 'How did you get away from them?'

As Churikova recounted her alibi of desertion from the ranks of the Red Army, Engel stared at her intently. The professor appeared so entranced by Churikova's presence that he barely listened to her words. She was halfway through explaining about the artworks hidden on the estate, when Engel interrupted. 'Forgive me, Polina! You must be cold. You must be hungry. How terrifying it must have been for you as you made your way alone to this place, surrounded by soldiers who might easily have taken your life instead of taking you prisoner. You are a brave woman, and such bravery will not go unrewarded. But I understand why you had to do it. The thought that these panels might be left to rot in their makeshift hiding place is not only unbearable, it shows the depth of ignorance of those who claim to be its guardians. There is nothing to worry about now. Hitler has taken a particular interest in the Amber Room. He considers it, as I do, to be a German work of art, and obscenely out of place in Stalin's Russia. That is why he has given his chief architect, Albert Speer, instructions to include a special gallery in the Linz Museum where the Amber Room could be displayed. And, to me, he gave the order that I was to locate it at all costs, even if I had to travel the length and breadth of Siberia to find it. When I first heard the radio broadcasts about the panels having been moved to safety somewhere in the Ural mountains, I imagined I might spend the rest of my life hunting for the amber. That was why, when I was back in Königsberg, I ordered the construction of special transport cases for each of the panels. They are lined in zinc, with built-in handles, shockproof and waterproof. I even had wheels attached to the cases in the event that suitable carrying devices couldn't be found once I'd arrived at the palace. I planned everything out in such detail that I could dismantle the panels and transport them by myself if I had to. In spite of Stalin's announcement, I knew that my search had to begin here. You see, I suspected that the radio broadcast might be a hoax, but I take little consolation in the fact that I was right. As your countrymen have discovered, the panels are too fragile to be moved in their present condition.'

Up until now, Engel had been oblivious to the grizzled military policeman standing beside the lieutenant.

Realising that the sooner he left Churikova alone with the professor, the more quickly she would be able to lure him out to the cottage, Pekkala cleared his throat noisily.

His attention momentarily diverted from Churikova, Engel shot Pekkala an irritated glance. 'This woman is now in my charge,' he snapped. 'You are no longer needed.' Then, as if his words had caused Pekkala to vanish into thin air, Engel took hold of Churikova's arm and the two of them strolled away across the room. 'Later we will go in search of these art works you say are hidden on the estate, but for now our first task must be to find you some new clothes!'

Having left the Amber Room, quietly closing the door behind him, Pekkala strode out of the palace. The crash of his steel-shod boots echoed off the once-pristine floors. The weight of the canister, packed with explosives, dragged against Pekkala's spine. He was glad to know he'd never have to use it.

It was dark now.

As he had done so many times in the past, Pekkala made his way along the Dvortsovaya road, past the old Kitchen Pond and the Alexander Palace and from there along the path that would take him to his cottage by the Pensioners' Stable. The view to his left stretched out across the Alexander Park and there were moments when it was almost possible to believe that the war had not touched Tsarskoye Selo.

This thought was wrenched from Pekkala's mind by the

thundering of hoof beats. In the next moment, he saw a dozen soldiers on horseback galloping past the arsenal monument down the long straight road towards the Parnas Gardens. He remembered what Leontev had said about the presence of an SS Cavalry Division in the area.

The breath stalled in Pekkala's throat as he caught sight of the cottage where he had lived for more than a decade. The building did not seem to have suffered any damage, although the picket fence which once separated it from the path had been flattened by a vehicle that had veered off the road.

Rather than going in through the front door, he went around the back. The door leading into the mud room was open and past it he could see the familiar brick-red tiles of the kitchen floor. Before entering the cottage, Pekkala waited by the rain barrel, which stood beneath the gutter at the corner of the house, watching the road in case he had been followed. As he inhaled the musty smell of still water, which was both distant and familiar, Pekkala had to force himself to believe that any time at all had passed since he had last stood here.

Pekkala walked into the house. Through the closed shutters, a faint glimmer of moonlight painted zebra stripes of moonlight on the floor. He felt his way forward, fingertips skimming the walls, but had only taken a couple of steps before he felt the presence of someone standing right behind him. At the same moment, a gun appeared out of the shadows.

The blue-ringed eye of Stefanov's rifle barrel seemed to blink as he lowered the Mauser and stepped out of the gloom. 'Inspector,' he whispered. 'I had to be sure it was you.'

'Not again!' Fabian Golyakovsky, Director of the Kremlin Art Museum, muttered under his breath as he watched Major Kirov stride into the building. 'What have you come to borrow now? The last time Pekkala showed up here, half the pieces in the Byzantine wing ended up on the walls of Lubyanka!'

Kirov held up the piece of paper which had fallen out of Churikova's book.

Golyakovsky had breathed in, ready to continue his tirade, but now he paused abruptly. Stepping cautiously forward, he peered at the document. 'Where did you get that?'

'Is that your signature?'

Removing the letter from Kirov's hand, Golyakovsky studied it for a moment before replying. 'Yes. The signature is mine. I gave Polina Churikova permission to work in our laboratory. She was a student at the Moscow Art Institute and came highly recommended by our mutual friend, Professor Semykin. Why is this letter damp?'

'Never mind that,' answered Kirov. 'What was Churikova doing here?'

Golyakovsky struggled to recall. 'It was something to do with viscosity.'

'Viscosity? What does that have to do with studying art?'

'Well, I don't know exactly. Polina was in a special programme devoted to art forensics. Finding out forgeries and so on. They often requested samples of paints and varnishes from works that arrived in our collection already damaged beyond repair. Sometimes, even though the paintings can't be salvaged, we are able to reuse the frames.'

'Why did they want paint samples?'

'To determine their chemical composition. From that, they could often tell when a painting had been made. Some forgeries use colours that weren't invented until centuries after the paintings were supposed to have been made. But that's not always something you can tell just by looking at it. You have to be able to look at its chemical structure.'

'This document also gives her permission to enter the archives.'

'Yes. That means she was allowed to search in our inventory for particular samples on which to conduct scientific research. She couldn't just walk out with it, you understand. It all had to be approved. I took charge of that personally.'

'And what did she want for this experiment in viscosity?'

'Well, it seemed very strange,' he began, 'but the whole business of forensics is strange to me.'

'What did she want?' repeated Kirov.

'She asked for some samples of glue.'

'What kind of samples?'

'If I recall correctly, she wanted glue dating from several different time periods and from a number of different origins. A large part of our work here involves restoration, and glue is used extensively, not only in the repair but also in the creation of many original art works. If we don't know what we're dealing with, we might end up destroying the very things we're trying to fix. Throughout history, glues have been made of different substances. These glues, in their original state, have different viscosities, or liquidity. If a glue used in the fabrication of a sixteenth-century cabinet turned out to be a modern synthetic compound, its lack of authenticity could be established.'

'And what do the figures on the other side represent?' asked Kirov.

Golyakovsky turned over the page. 'These must be the results of her experiment. This refers to temperature.' Golyakovsky pointed to a small circle at one end of the graph. 'And this,' he dragged his finger across to the backwards Latin U, 'is the symbol for viscosity. It looks as if she was running an experiment with different kinds of glue to determine what effect heat would have on their liquidity. You see, once a glue has hardened, it forms a bond between two surfaces, but its original adhesive qualities are lost. It is no long sticky, if you see what I mean. Over time, the original compound can become brittle and the bond can fail if it is put under stress. The heat used here was to revive the glues.'

'To see if they would become sticky again?'

'Exactly. Now it looks as if most of these glues didn't respond, but this one did.' He touched one of the lines, which banked steadily upwards at the open end of the graph.

'What was it made of? Can you tell?'

Golyakovsky shook his head. 'Not entirely. Their chemical compounds are partially listed. It's not a synthetic, I can tell you that much. My guess is that it's quite old, containing something like beeswax and ichthyocolla.'

'Ichthyo— What?'

'Fish bladders. Makes you wonder how they figured that one out, doesn't it, Major?'

'Would there be any reason for her to keep this information secret?'

Golyakovsky shrugged. 'Not that I can think of. Her findings were never restricted.'

Kirov explained how he came across the message. 'Whatever this is, she didn't want anyone else to know about it.'

Golyakovsky frowned in confusion. 'But it's just glue. It's not as if there is a shortage of the stuff. If it had been something precious, I would understand, but . . .'

Golyakovsky continued to talk, but his words seemed to grow fainter and fainter as an idea crested like a wave in Kirov's brain. 'Thank you, Comrade Golyakovsky,' he interrupted. Then, under the piercing gaze of saints whose bones had turned to dust five hundred years before, Kirov turned and sprinted for the exit.

With their nerves beginning to fray, Pekkala and Stefanov sat on the floor of the cold and empty cottage, waiting for Churikova to arrive with the professor. Outside, darkness crowded against shuttered windows.

For Pekkala, the absence of furniture made the interior seem much larger than he had remembered, and every breath seemed amplified without the dampening effect of carpets on the floors. Although the house was not dirty, or showing any signs of disrepair, the grey haze of spider webs in the windows told Pekkala that the place had not been lived in for some time. There was a stillness in the air which made him think the place had been abandoned since he'd left it more than twenty years before.

Reaching down his shirt, Stefanov retrieved the dirty cloth bag in which he kept his last few shreds of *machorka* and a small handful of matches. He began to roll himself a cigarette.

Pekkala reached out and touched his forearm. 'They'll smell the smoke. It will give us away.'

Stefanov sighed and nodded. 'Of course. Forgive me, Inspector. To tell you the truth, what I really want now is a drink. I don't mean water, either.'

Pekkala was silent for a while. 'Perhaps,' he said softly, 'we can grant you that wish.'

'You brought some with you?' asked Stefanov.

'No,' he replied, 'but there might be some treasure hidden here, after all.'

On Stalin's desk lay the piece of paper which Kirov had re-moved from Lieutenant Churikova's manual. As if the strange talons of the graph lines she had drawn might rise up from the page and claw his eyes, Stalin got up from his chair and walked over to the window. Out of habit, he did not stand directly in front of the glass, but moved to the side and leaned into the vel-vet curtains, so as not to be seen by anyone below. 'You told me it was Serge Bakhturin who killed Kovalevsky.'

'It *was* Bakhturin,' confirmed Kirov. 'He did commit the murder, but I now believe it was a separate crime from the one you sent me to investigate.'

Stalin wheeled about, sending a ripple up the heavy curtain fabric. 'You also said that he threatened to kill Engel. It's right there in your report!'

'And the report is correct, Comrade Stalin. He did threaten to kill Engel, but after finding this letter, I began to wonder what Serge really meant by what he said.'

'Meant?' Stalin echoed angrily. 'His intention was to kill Gustav Engel. What else could he possibly mean?'

'When I told Serge Bakhturin that Pekkala was still alive, he refused to believe it. He was sure the man he had shot outside the Café Tilsit was the Inspector. Serge never knew the name of Kovalevsky. I now believe that when I said the name Engel,

Serge thought I was referring to the other man he saw outside the café that night. I don't think Serge Bakhturin knew anything about that painting or the Amber Room.'

'Then what was his motive for trying to murder Pekkala?'

'Vengeance,' replied Kirov, 'for having him sent to jail, which cost him two years of his life. Serge Bakhturin failed at every legitimate occupation he took up. If it hadn't been for his brother's help, Serge would never have received that job with the State Railways. The fact that he was caught committing a crime was no surprise to anyone. Not even his brother, I think. But that conviction proved Serge Bakhturin to be a failure, even as a criminal. And for that, he blamed Pekkala.'

'Enough to want him dead,' said Stalin. 'I grant you that.'

'And he had made up his mind to see it through to the end, on his own, without his brother's assistance.'

Stalin returned to his desk. 'Are you telling me that, based on this letter, you believe that Polina Churikova is the person we've been looking for all along?'

'I cannot say for certain, Comrade Stalin, but I think so.'

'But she has proved her worth to us! She broke the Ferdinand code! Why would she do that if she was working for the Germans?'

'I don't know.'

'And so what if she kept her findings secret?' Stalin continued. 'Perhaps she didn't want one of her colleagues to see the results before she was finished. These academics are constantly pilfering each other's work. And it's about glue, Kirov! What does that have to do with amber?'

'As you know, Comrade Stalin, those thousands of fragments of amber were mounted on panels. For that, they must have used glue, which is now over two hundred years old. In that time, it has grown too fragile to survive the journey to Siberia. That's why they had to leave behind the panels. Lieutenant Churikova must have found out about this, probably from Valery Semykin when she went to visit him in prison.'

'And you think she found the solution for transporting the panels after all? If that's true, then why wouldn't she have shared it with us?'

'Because I think she planned to share it with the Germans,' replied Kirov. 'The painting was a message to Professor Engel, warning him that the amber was still hidden in the walls of the Catherine Palace. She must have been working on a way to transmit the results of her experiment. As a cryptographer, she could just as easily have sent a coded message to the enemy as she could decipher one we'd intercepted. But it had to be a message which Engel, and Engel alone, could understand, even though he has no background in cryptography. When the Inspector and I met her at the Ostankinsky station and she learned that the painting had been captured she had to find another way to get the information to Engel. That's why she volunteered to go across the lines, so she could deliver the message in person.'

'And now,' said Stalin, 'thanks to us, that is exactly what she'll do.'

'Is there any way we can get word to the Inspector?' asked Kirov.

Stalin shook his head. 'Out of the question. The best we can hope for is that he figures it out on his own, and kills the lieutenant before she gets to Engel.'

'He won't hurt Churikova,' replied Kirov. 'I don't think he can.'

With a gravelly sigh, Stalin reached into his pocket for his crumpled box of cigarettes. Opening its dented cardboard lid, he fitted one of the white sticks between his lips and lit it with the gold lighter he always carried with him. 'Let us hope you're mistaken,' Stalin whispered as he exhaled a jet of smoke towards the ceiling, 'but you aren't, and we both know it.'

'What treasure?' asked Stefanov. 'Where could it possibly be hidden?'

'There is a secret room under this house,' replied Pekkala. 'On the recommendation of his head of security, the Tsar ordered hiding places built into every residence on the estate.'

'Hiding places?'

'He called them "priest holes", after the ones that were built for Catholics in England during the reign of Queen Elizabeth I. The hiding place in this cottage was based on a design used at Rangeley Manor, a house visited by the Tsar during a trip to see his cousin, King George V. The original was built by a Jesuit carpenter named Nicholas Owen, who was later tortured to death on the rack at the Tower of London.' Pekkala nodded towards the hearth. 'The entrance is right over there.'

Stefanov stared at the empty stone fireplace. 'But there's nowhere to put a hiding place.'

'So it was made to appear,' Pekkala replied, 'but in fact the wall there is twice as thick as any other wall in the house. It contains a narrow stairway that leads down to the hidden room.'

'What's it like, this room?'

'I don't know,' replied Pekkala. 'I never went down there, but the Tsar did. He knew I did not like to be confined so, as a challenge, he left behind a bottle of his finest slivovitz, hoping the reward of one of his precious bottles of brandy might lure me down into that tomb.' Climbing to his feet, Pekkala walked over to the fireplace. Dropping to one knee, he reached up into the chimney. Tucked into a recess in the masonry, he found a metal ring attached to a chain. Pekkala grasped the ring and pulled, hearing the chain rattle somewhere deep inside the chimney. There was a dull clunk in the brickwork at the back of the hearth. He brushed his hand along the bricks until he came to the place where the bricks did not join evenly. With the tips of his fingers, he prised back a small doorway faced with brick, which had been set into an iron frame.

Behind him, Stefanov looked on in amazement. 'Do you think the slivovitz might still be down there?'

'Find out for yourself,' replied Pekkala. 'But be quick. They could be here any minute.'

Stefanov struck a match and, holding it out in front of him, made his way down into the blackness of the priest hole. The wavering flame illuminated a flight of ten steps hewn into the khaki-coloured rock. At the base of the steps, a chamber opened out into the darkness.

At the sight of it, Pekkala felt his throat tighten. The blood began pulsing in his temples.

Moving away from the priest hole, Pekkala walked over to the window and peered through the gaps in the wooden shutters. As he looked out at the pathway which ran beside the cottage, a movement outside caught his eye. A figure walked slowly down the path. From the silhouette, he could tell it was a German soldier, his rifle unshouldered and held at the ready.

Pekkala's heart slammed into his chest. Guessing that the soldier was likely part of a patrol and that they might decide to take a look inside the cottage, he ducked into the fireplace and slithered into the entrance of the priest hole, struggling against the claustrophobia which sent bile climbing into the back of his throat.

The glow of Stefanov's match flickered at the bottom of the stairs. As Pekkala reached out to close the door of the priest hole, he could hear someone in hobnailed boots stepping into the house by the same entrance he had used. At that same moment Stefanov appeared from the shadows below, a dusty bottle gripped in his hand. He was smiling, but one look at the expression on Pekkala's face told him that something had gone very wrong. With one sharp breath he extinguished the match and the priest hole was plunged into darkness.

Lying on his stomach, with his legs braced against the stone steps, Pekkala drew the Webley revolver from its holster. Although the door was closed, a tiny gap left between the brickwork and the floor, presumably for ventilation, showed as a faint, velvety blue line of half-light. Even with his head pressed to the floor, Pekkala could barely see out from under the gap, but he could make out the shadowy form of a man moving around the room. He heard the cautious pacing of boots upon the wooden floor. Then a second shadow appeared and after that a third.

Without a word spoken between them, the men searched the cottage, moving like ghosts from room to room. Then they met back in front of the fireplace.

'Empty,' said one of the soldiers.

One man paused to light a cigarette, flicking the dead match into the fireplace.

Pekkala let his breath trail out with relief, knowing that the patrol would now be moving on. A second later, however, he heard the voice of Gustav Engel.

'Have you searched the entire building?' snapped the professor.

And then he heard another voice. It was Polina Churikova, and the words she spoke made Pekkala's blood run cold.

'Pekkala told me they'd be waiting here,' she said. 'They have to be here.'

'Maybe they were,' said a soldier, 'but there's no sign of them now.'

'You must find them, Professor,' Churikova pleaded. 'You can't allow them to get back behind the Russian lines.'

As the words sank in, Pekkala realised that he had been betrayed.

'Don't worry,' Engel reassured her. 'They can't have gone far. You'll see. We'll have them soon enough.'

'The amber won't be safe until Pekkala is dead.'

'You worry too much, Polina,' Engel tried to soothe her. 'He is only one man, after all, with a single Russian soldier to command. We have killed a million of them already and we will kill ten million more before this war is done. Put your mind at rest. The amber is safe, thanks to you. To have come up with the solution for reattaching the glue in the panels was nothing short of brilliant.'

'As soon as I heard about the problem from Semykin,' she explained, 'I felt certain that it could be solved. I began running my own experiments in the laboratory of the Kremlin Museum.'

'Right under their noses!' laughed Engel. 'You still haven't told me how you managed that.'

'I discovered that modern glue would remain largely unaffected by temperature, due to chemicals used in its manufacture which didn't exist two centuries ago. But the glue back then was primarily animal gelatine, and I realised that if it was possible to raise the temperature in the Amber Room by twenty degrees or more, as well as sharply increasing the level of humidity, the gelatine would soften rapidly, in spite of its age. This would allow the amber to re-adhere to the panels, which can then be safely transported out of Russia.'

'The process of heating the room has already begun. I have commandeered the engine block heaters from every vehicle parked on this estate. The room has been sealed and water is boiling on three separate field-kitchen stoves. If your figures are correct, by this time tomorrow, the room will be on its way to Königsberg. The truck is being readied now. The cases I designed for moving the panels have been unloaded and are waiting for their cargo. Special passage documents will be signed within the hour by Field Marshal von Leeb, allowing us unlimited access to fuel and the right to commandeer any mode of transport we see fit. In two days, we will be in Wilno, far beyond the gaze of this Emerald Eye. In four days, Polina, we will dine together in the great hall of Königsberg Castle, surrounded by the Eighth Wonder of the World. And in a few years, when the Linz Museum has been completed and the Amber Room is there on permanent display, you and I will not have been forgotten as the ones who made it possible. That is the promise I made to you when we first met, and I intend to keep it.'

In spite of Engel's attempts to calm Churikova, her voice was still riddled with panic. 'I told you, Pekkala has orders to destroy the room if we attempt to move it. He has explosives ...'

'The room is guarded on all sides. There is no way he can get to it now. I swear it, Polina. Do you trust me?'

'Yes, of course. I know that the amber is safe now. It's just that when I heard that the painting had been captured, I was afraid this day might never come.'

'I wish I could have seen it,' remarked Engel. 'The red moth!'

'When I volunteered to find you, I was terrified that Stalin would say no.'

'How could he? Pekkala needed you to point me out. And after you gave them the Ferdinand code, you had them eating out of your hand.'

'When you delivered the cipher to me, I was afraid you had gone mad, but I see now that it was a sure way of convincing them.'

'The Ferdinand code had become obsolete. Thanks to the Enigma Machine, which is now in use throughout the German military, the information you gave them was practically useless.'

'Herr Obersturmbannführer,' said a soldier. 'The cavalry troop is here, as you requested. An officer is outside, waiting for your orders.'

'Send him in,' replied Engel.

A man entered the room. There was a crash of heels coming together.

'They are on foot,' said Engel. 'They can't have gone far.'

'How many of them are there?' asked the cavalryman.

'Two.'

'Two! Ostubaf, I have brought a whole troop with me.

That's more than thirty riders! If we are only going after a couple of Russians, I can dismiss half of my men here and now.'

'You may dismiss them,' Engel replied calmly, 'after the two men have been caught. And only one of them is Russian. The other is a Finn named Pekkala.'

'A Finn,' muttered the cavalryman. 'Then I may need the whole troop, after all.'

The floorboards creaked as the soldiers departed from the cottage.

'Come,' Engel said to Churikova, as the two of them walked out into the night. 'Let us go back to the palace, and watch your genius at work.'

For a moment longer, Pekkala lay on the stone floor, his mind in a turmoil of anger and confusion at the depth of Churikova's treachery.

'Are they gone?' whispered Stefanov, calling from the bottom of the stairs.

'Yes,' Pekkala answered. 'How much did you hear?'

'Every word, Inspector. There's a ventilation shaft down here, which leads up beneath the floor. They were standing right above me.'

Cautiously, the two men crept out into the front room of the cottage.

'You were right,' said Stefanov.

'No,' muttered Pekkala. 'If I'd been right, Engel would be in our custody by now, instead of hunting us with men on horseback as if we were a couple of foxes.'

'Not about that. About this.' Stefanov was holding up a bottle. 'It was just where you said it would be.'

Pekkala nodded, lost in thought.

'What will we do now, Inspector?' asked Stefanov, the bottle still clutched in his fist.

'I will carry out my orders.'

Stefanov tried to reason with Pekkala. 'You heard him, Inspector. The room is guarded on all sides. They'd shoot us down before we even came close. If we leave now, there's still a chance that we can get back to our lines before the cavalry pick up our trail.'

'I have no choice,' Pekkala told him. 'Do you know what will happen to me if I return to Moscow empty-handed?'

'No,' admitted Stefanov, 'but I can guess.'

'And if I don't get the job done,' Pekkala continued, 'Stalin will send someone else. And another and another until his wishes are fulfilled. It's not the amber that is irreplaceable, Stefanov, it's the lives that will be lost if I fail.' Pekkala knew as he spoke how slim the chances were of his success, but they were still greater than the odds of his surviving Stalin's wrath.

Stefanov knew that there was no point in arguing with Pekkala. He wondered if he had been wrong even to try. There seemed a clear and brutal symmetry that the man who, if legends were to be believed, had been conjured from the walls of that room should be the one who would consign it to oblivion.

'I must move quickly,' said Pekkala. 'By tomorrow, those panels will be in a truck bound for Wilno. This will be my only chance to prevent that from happening. The last place they will expect me to head for is the palace. With any luck, those riders are already far from Tsarskoye Selo. Your orders, Stefanov, are to make your way back to our lines. It's too dangerous for you to wait here any longer, and there is nothing more that you can do to help.'

'There may be one thing,' replied Stefanov.

'And what is that, Rifleman?'

'I know the road they'll take to get to Wilno. My father and I travelled along it every weekend in the summer, to sell the vegetables he grew in his spare time. The road passes through the forest of Murom, which is uninhabited. The locals wouldn't go there, even to hunt, on account of the bogs which can swallow a man without trace.'

'Is there somewhere on that road where those trucks can be stopped?'

'I think so. Yes. At the far side of the forest, just where the fields begin again, the road passes over a bridge. It is a small bridge, made of wooden beams, which passes over a stream that only flows there in the spring. The rest of the year, it is dry.'

'And if I follow that road, how long will it take me to get there?'

'If you stay on the road, you might not get there in time,' Stefanov replied, 'but if we cut through the forest, I can get us there by morning.'

'I am not asking you to bring me there. You said yourself that it's too dangerous. You're free to go, Stefanov.'

In the moment that followed, Stefanov was surprised to hear coming from his mouth the same words spoken by his father on that cold night back in March of 1917. 'I would rather help you now than spend the rest of my life knowing that I could have and didn't.'

'Very well.' Pekkala nodded at the dusty old bottle in Stefanov's hand. 'Then the least I can do is offer you a drink.'

Stefanov opened the slivovitz and, as they passed it back and forth, the brandy spread like wings of fire in their chests.

An hour later, having slipped out through the shattered iron railings which circled the Tsar's estate, Pekkala and Stefanov were making their way through a tangle of bulrushes on the swampy ground which bordered the forest of Murom. Stefanov had discovered a trail, so narrow that it could only have been made by the deer or wild boar that roamed the forest.

Tattered clouds rode past beneath the waning gibbous moon. Beneath its silvery light, the tasselled heads of bulrushes weaved like the patterns of heat upon an iron stove.

Suddenly, Stefanov wheeled about and motioned for Pekkala to take cover.

The two men scattered into the rushes.

A moment later, Pekkala heard the hollow thump of hooves on the soft ground. Then he saw a man on horseback coming down the path, a rifle slung across his back. From the angles of his helmet, Pekkala could tell it was a German soldier. After him came another rider, and then another after that. Peering through the screen of rushes, Pekkala counted eight riders. The horses moved slowly, tired heads bowed low. After they had passed on, the smell of their sweat lingered in the air.

Without a word, Stefanov emerged from his hiding place.

Pekkala fell in behind him and they began to move again, their senses sharpened to the danger.

An owl glided past, just above the tops of the rushes, its silhouette like some grim coagulation of the darkness. As it came level with Pekkala, only an arm's length away, it turned its flat, round head and blinked at him with dead man's eyes.

They had not gone far when Stefanov halted once again. 'What's that sound?' he asked.

Pekkala strained to hear above the rustling of the leaves. He thought it might be thunder or a gust of wind approaching. Then suddenly he felt a tremor from the ground beneath his feet. 'They're coming back!' he hissed.

Once more, Pekkala dived off the path, pawing through the bulrushes, sweeping them aside to get away. He heard shouting as he ran, but it seemed to be coming from above, as if creatures were descending from the night sky. All around, the rushes thrashed and crackled. In the next instant, the huge, black shape of a horse swept past him, static electricity crackling across its flanks. Shreds of blue-green flame tangled in the animal's tail, sparking up the rider's legs until it reached his arms and, outlined in that fire, the two transformed into a single beast. With a ring of unsheathed metal, the curve of a sabre blade flashed and hung suspended in the air above their heads, as if it were the stalled path of a meteor.

Blindly, Pekkala stumbled forward through the reeds, feet sinking in the mud and the Mauser rifle, on its leather sling across his back, dragging through the rushes like an anchor. The same bright static swam around him; emeralds streaming through his fingers. He could not unshoulder the rifle without stopping, so struggled instead to draw the Webley from its holster. But it was too late.

The air filled with the terrible snorting breath of the horse and the high-pitched shriek of the rider as a burning stripe of pain flashed across Pekkala's shoulder blades. The earth seemed to disappear from beneath him as he lost his footing. With a shout that emptied his lungs, he tumbled to the ground.

The horse passed over him, hooves trailing sparks and clods of dirt. In another second it was gone, ploughing through the rushes, the rider still howling in the darkness.

Sure that he had been cut down by the cavalryman's sword, Pekkala had the sensation of being turned loose from the clumsy fastenings of his body. In what he did not doubt was the moment of his death, he seemed to leap into the sky unfolding wings from his back like those of a dragonfly from the papery husk of its larva.

From far above, Pekkala looked down upon the field of rushes, where the paths of the horses spread out green through the black. He saw the cowering figure of Stefanov, and of the other riders, all of them varnished with moonlight.

Then Pekkala tumbled back to earth and lay there, dazed, among the trampled rushes, in too much pain to be anything other than alive.

His rifle had gone. He had no idea where, and the leather Y-straps which had held his field equipment lay tangled in a heap beside him.

Rolling on to his back, Pekkala tore open the top buttons of his tunic and put his hand against his chest, searching for a puncture wound. But he felt only skin and sweat. Next, he reached down the back of his neck, dabbing at the bruise where, he now realised, the cavalryman had caught his blade against the Mauser, severing the rifle strap, together with the thick leather of his equipment harness.

A sub-machine gun roared, somewhere out there in the thicket. Then Pekkala heard the terrible shriek of a wounded horse and the thump of horse and rider going down together.

Shouts reached across the swaying rushes. The cavalrymen were calling to each other.

The machine gun fired once more in a long burst which was followed by silence. A moment later, he heard a rattle as someone removed a magazine and the dull clank as the person tapped a new magazine against their helmet to settle the rounds before inserting it into the weapon.

The voices of the riders grew fainter. A moment later, they were gone.

'Pekkala!' shouted Stefanov. 'Pekkala, are you out there?'

'Yes!' he called back. 'I just got knocked down. That's all.' Painfully, he clambered to his feet. Pekkala gathered up his rifle, which had a deep gash in the wooden stock, and slung the gas-mask canister over his shoulder. The rest of his equipment he left lying on the ground amongst the mangled leather straps of his combat harness.

Making his way out to the path, Pekkala found Stefanov standing over the body of a wounded horse. The animal lay on its side, its wide eyes glistening. The saddle had remained strapped to its back. Stirrups trailed upon the ground like the leg braces of a crippled child. Blood, as black as tar, pulsed from the horse's neck, and the sound of its laboured breathing filled the air.

Stefanov still gripped the German gun with which he had brought down the animal, as if he meant to shoot it once again.

Pekkala rested his hand on Stefanov's arm.

Slowly, he lowered the weapon, but his eyes were fixed on something other than the horse.

Pekkala followed Stefanov's gaze to where the rider of the horse stood on the path, oblivious to the men who watched him. His own sword had gone through his chest as he came down from the horse. The blade protruded from his back. The cavalryman swayed back and forth, both hands gripping the hilt as if summoning his strength to draw the sword from its scabbard of flesh and bone. His legs, which looked unnaturally thin in his tall riding boots, trembled as he tried to remain on his feet.

Only now did the rider seem to become aware of the two men who were watching him. He spoke to them in a voice no louder than a whisper.

'What is he saying?' asked Stefanov.

'He says his horse is suffering,' replied Pekkala.

Stefanov chambered a round in the Schmeisser, removed the magazine and set the barrel of the gun between the horse's ears. There was a sharp crack as he fired and a tiny, musical ring as the smouldering brass cartridge ejected.

The horse trembled and then it was dead.

The rider was staring at them.

Pekkala walked up to the man and, gently prising back the fingers one by one, forced him to release his grip upon the hilt. Then Pekkala took hold of the sword and drew the blade from the rider's chest.

The cavalryman gasped.

Pekkala dropped the weapon at his feet.

The rider sank to his knees.

The two men stepped past him and continued up the path.

Before the reeds closed up around them, Pekkala glanced back at the rider, who still knelt in the middle of the path, his hands wandering feebly over the place where the sword had gone in, as if by some miracle of touch he hoped to cure himself.

In the plunging red-black darkness before dawn, they reached the edge of the forest. A sweetness of pine replaced the sulphurous reek of the swamp. Once more, the earth was hard beneath their feet.

Here, they stopped to rest.

Stefanov pulled off his boots and poured from them a stream of oily water. Then he lay back on the mossy ground, the rifle lying heavy on his chest, and wiped the rough wool of his sleeve across his sweaty face.

Artillery fire coughed and rumbled on the horizon.

'What will you do with the lieutenant when you find her?' asked Stefanov.

'I don't know,' Pekkala replied.

'She reminds me of a teacher I once had in the school at Tsarskoye Selo.'

'I think I know the one.'

'I saw the way you looked at her, Inspector.'

Wearily, Pekkala turned and glanced at Stefanov. But he did not speak.

'You can't let Churikova go free,' said Stefanov, 'no matter what your feelings are for her.'

Still there was no reply from Pekkala.

'I wish . . .' began Stefanov.

'What is it you wish, Rifleman?'

'I wish we had something to eat.'

Pekkala pushed aside his rifle, stood and walked into the forest.

A short while later, he returned. From one hip pocket, he removed some baby fiddle-head ferns and from the other he produced a bunch of wood sorrel, with tiny stems and clover-shaped leaves. Lastly, from his chest pockets came a dozen chanterelle mushrooms, their apricot-coloured flesh as delicate as silk.

Kirov would have fried these in butter, Pekkala thought to himself as he dropped half of them into Stefanov's outstretched hands.

If there had been more time, Pekkala would have gathered earthworms, dried them in the sun, then ground them to a powder before eating. He would have hunted snails, as well, plucking them like berries from their silver trails over downed trees and stones. They had been one of Pekkala's favourite foods in Siberia. After baking the snails in hot ashes, he used to prise them out of blackened shells using one of his most prized possessions, a rusted safety pin.

The two men ate in silence as the first shades of dawn glimmered eel-green on the horizon.

When the tiny meal was done, Stefanov brushed his hands together and began to roll himself a cigarette. Just before he sprinkled the dried black crumbs of *machorka* into the shred of old newsprint that would serve as rolling paper, he paused and glanced across towards Pekkala.

Pekkala was watching him.

'No?' asked Stefanov.

Pekkala shook his head.

'Even here?' protested Stefanov. 'There's no one around. I told you these woods are empty!'

'Not entirely.' Pekkala nodded in the direction from which they had come.

There, at the edge of the swampy ground from which they had recently emerged, stood a wolf.

It had been following them for some time. Pekkala had heard the beast's loping tread as it pursued them through the bulrush thickets. But even before he had heard the animal, he'd known that they were being followed. Pekkala could not name what sense had telegraphed the presence of that wolf into his brain, but he had long ago learned to trust it with his life.

The wolf's head was lowered as it studied them, the black nostrils flexing. The front paws shifted uneasily. Then, unhurriedly, it turned and vanished back among the reeds.

For a moment longer, Stefanov stared at the place where the wolf had been, as if some shadow of its presence still remained. Then he tucked away the tobacco pouch under his shirt. With an agitated groan, he slumped back against the trunk of a pine tree, realising too late that he had leaned his shoulder into a trickle of sap. Stefanov swore under his breath and picked at the honey-coloured smear, which remained stubbornly glued to his tunic. 'In a few million years,' he muttered, 'this would have been treasure, instead of just a pain in my backside.'

Throughout that morning, the two men advanced over the pine-needled ground, where insect-eating plants, with a smell like rotting meat, reared their sexually open mouths.

After months of being on the move, the stillness of these woods was overwhelming for Stefanov. It reached him from beyond the boundaries of his senses, threading through the air like the long stray filaments of spider webs which dangled from the leaves. It walked among the columns of white birch like shadows of people long since vanished from the earth. Only a man like Pekkala, he thought, could survive for long in such a place.

Late in the afternoon, the two men emerged from the woods into an ocean of tall grass, which trailed out over rolling ground as far as the horizon. After being in the forest, the glare of sky not fractured by a mesh of branches felt strangely threatening.

'Where is the bridge?' asked Pekkala.

Stefanov, his throat too dry to speak, only motioned for Pekkala to follow.

On hands and knees, guns slung across their backs, they crawled through the waist-high grass. Reddish brown seeds clung to their sweat-soaked skin. Grasshoppers with iridescent green eyes catapulted themselves into the air with an audible snap of their legs.

At last, they spotted the bridge, a crude wooden structure which seemed to have no purpose until Stefanov dropped down into a dry stream bed which appeared before them, hidden until they were almost upon it.

These stream beds, known as Rachels, were a common feature of the landscape. In the spring, during the *rasputitsa*, the gully would be flooded by snow melt. But that was months away and now the bed was powder-dry.

The heat had sapped their energy, but now the two men felt a sudden sense of urgency as they scrambled over the dusty ground until they stood beneath the bridge. Sheltered beneath the heavy planks, zebra stripes of shadow lined their faces.

'This structure was never meant for heavy vehicles,' said Stefanov, 'but since it is the only road from Tsarskoye Selo to Wilno, Engel must bring his truck across it.'

The distance across the gully was no more than ten paces. To support the bridge, heavy pilings had been set at an angle into either bank. The planks above were widely spaced and the wood bleached out by sun and snow and rain. Huge nail-heads looked like dull coins against the pilings, the wood around them dented by the blows of hammer strikes.

A breeze passed over the Rachel and dust sifted between the bridge planks. They blinked as it peppered their eyes. Above them, the steppe grass rustled with a sound like running water.

'The truck is bound to be carrying an escort of armed guards,' said Stefanov. 'If we can stop them here, when the vehicle slows down to cross the bridge, it might give us an advantage. It's too bad we can't destroy the bridge before they reach it, but that would give away any hope of surprise.'

Pekkala handed over the grey canister. 'Would this be enough for what you had in mind?'

Stefanov opened the lid of the canister and peered inside. Then he raised his head and looked at Pekkala. 'Inspector,' he gasped, 'there is enough dynamite here to destroy this bridge and a dozen others like it!'

Immediately, they set to work. Pekkala scooped out some of the thick, dough-like mixture and packed it against two of the four main bridge supports. The marzipan smell of the mine's Amytol explosives sifted into their lungs. Meanwhile, Stefanov unravelled the coil of wire for the instant fuse, the ignition battery stored safely in his pocket.

Once the charges had been laid, they dug out a space in the

tall grass about twenty paces from the bridge, which was as far as the wire would stretch.

The whole process took less than half an hour, by the end of which the two men crouched sweating in their hiding place.

'When this goes up, assuming we even survive the blast, your eardrums will hurt for a month,' said Stefanov, as he hooked one wire to the negative battery terminal, saving the other, its filaments splayed like a skeleton hand, for connecting with the positive terminal.

Pekkala opened the black leather ammunition pouches on his belt and found that he had only three clips of bullets, fifteen rounds in all.

Stefanov fared better, with four magazines for the Schmeisser, each one containing thirty rounds, but it was no cause for celebration. Even that amount would soon disappear if they found themselves in a running battle with a squad of heavily armed soldiers.

There was nothing to do now but wait.

With fear and hunger scuttling like crabs behind their ribs, the two men lay hidden in the tall grass.

It was not long before the sound of engines reached them on the breeze. A minute later, an armoured car lumbered around a bend in the road. It was a type the Germans called a Lola. Riding on four large, heavy-treaded tyres, its sides were shielded with angled metal plates so that it resembled a monster folded out of paper by some Japanese origami master. On top was a small turret, almost flat, with a small cannon sticking out the length of a man's outstretched arm. A soldier stood in the Lola's turret, hands gripping the sides of the hatch covers. He wore an old style officer's cap, its soft crown flattened against his head and turned around so that the visor was facing backwards. A pair of goggles shielded his eyes. From the eagle on his arm, instead of his chest, Pekkala knew the man was SS and not regular army.

A Hanomag truck followed in the Lola's path, its canvas roof battened down tight. Judging from the way the wheel cowlings hung down over the tyres, the vehicle was carrying a heavy load.

Both machines rumbled slowly towards the bridge, diesel engines rattling in low gear.

While Pekkala drew back the bolt on his rifle to make sure that a round had been chambered, Stefanov took up the battery in one hand and gripped the loose wire in the other, ready to connect the circuit and detonate the explosives.

Pekkala had planned to destroy the bridge before the truck had a chance to cross it but the presence of the armoured car demanded more drastic action. Even though it would increase the risk, not only to Stefanov and himself, but also to the amber in the truck, Pekkala knew he had no choice.

Just short of the bridge, the armoured car slowed and then stopped. The trucks bunched up behind it, engines puttering in neutral.

The officer in the turret of the armoured car jumped down to the road and started walking towards the bridge.

Now the driver climbed out of the Hanomag. It was Gustav Engel wearing a knee-length double-breasted coat of the type normally issued to motorcycle drivers. Strapped to his waist on a black leather belt was a Luger holster. 'This is the fourth time we've halted in the last hour!' Engel raised his voice above the patient rumble of the engines. 'We are running out of time!'

The SS officer spun around, one hand raised as if to cast a

spell on the man who had broken his stride. 'And this is the fourth time you have brought it to my attention, Professor!'

'The train departs from Wilno at 4 p.m.,' Engel told him. 'Everything has to be loaded aboard by then. They will not wait for us. We must remain on schedule!'

'I must inspect the bridge before we try to cross it,' explained the officer. 'I have to be certain that it will hold our weight.'

'We don't have time,' said Engel. 'The other bridges held us fine. I am ordering you to proceed immediately.'

The officer paused, ready to continue his protest, but then he seemed to think better of it, turned and strode back to the armoured car, footsteps soft as heartbeats on the dirt road. He climbed aboard, hobnails scraping on the metal plates. A moment later, the armoured car ground into gear and trundled forward.

Pekkala's heart began flailing in his chest as he watched the armoured car move forward. The instant that its front wheels rolled on to the bridge, he whispered, 'Now!'

Tyres thudded over the planks.

'Now!' he said again, staring helplessly as the Lola continued across the bridge.

'I've already connected the battery,' Stefanov replied frantically. 'It should have gone off by now.'

In that moment, the mine exploded. A flash jumped from under the armoured car and a deafening boom shuddered through the air.

A wall of concussion swept past the two men in their hiding place as the Lola reared up and a blue flame, like the fire from a gas oven, swept around the metal. For a moment the whole machine was encased in this strange glow. Then the Lola exploded with a sound like the slamming of a huge metal door. Pieces of armour plating trailed sparks as they were torn loose by the blast. A wheel spun off, clattering and smoking, through the grass. Then the bridge collapsed. The Lola crashed into the gully. Dust and smoke unfurled into the sky.

At first, it looked as if Engel's truck was going to follow the Lola into the Rachel. Then, with a shriek of brakes the vehicle came to a stop.

A man crawled out of the gully. It was the officer. His clothes were smouldering. One hand was held to his face. The other hand groped the air in front of him, as if he were pawing his way through cobwebs.

At the same time, the gate of the truck clanked down and three soldiers tumbled out, carrying their rifles. The soldiers looked about wildly, then dived into a shallow ditch at the side of the road.

The officer stumbled towards them, trailing smoke from his burned clothes.

One of the soldiers, unable to recognise the wounded man, raised his gun and fired.

A cloud of blood appeared behind the officer, lit up like a ruby shadow in the sunlight. He went down so fast that the spray was still hanging in the air after his body hit the ground.

A shout came from the soldiers as they realised their mistake, but it was soon drowned out by the clatter of Stefanov's sub-machine gun and the single *pak-pak-pak* of rifle shots as Pekkala fired the Mauser, ejected an empty cartridge, slammed in a new one and pulled the trigger once again. Bullets skipped off the road in puffs of orange dirt.

The soldiers in the ditch returned fire, but their aiming was wide and erratic. They seemed to have no idea where their enemies were concealed.

The same was true of Engel, who now steered his truck off the road. Tilting precariously, it crossed over the ditch and started out across the field, directly towards the place where Pekkala and Stefanov were hiding.

Stefanov fitted a new magazine into the sub-machine gun.

'Don't aim for the driver!' shouted Pekkala, but Stefanov had already pulled the trigger, and his voice was drowned out by the hammer of the gun.

The truck's front tyres blew out. Dull clunks sounded as bullets impacted against the tyre rims. Chips of paint flew off its bumper and then the windscreen exploded like a spray of water. The truck rolled to a stop, its punctured radiator sighing as one last wisp of steam escaped.

The door of the truck swung open and Engel jumped out. He ran back to the ditch, leaped in amongst the soldiers and, a moment later, the flinty snap of a pistol joined the barking of the German guns.

Stefanov's gun fell silent as the magazine emptied. Smoke wafted from its barrel. A smell of raw gasoline filled the air from the Hanomeg's ruptured fuel tank.

Now another figure climbed down from the back of the truck. Even though she was wearing a heavy German greatcoat several sizes too big, Pekkala could see at once that it was Lieutenant Churikova.

Stefanov raised his gun, ready to shoot her down.

Pekkala shoved the barrel aside, feeling the heel of his palm sizzle against the super-heated metal.

'You want to let her live?' Stefanov called out in disbelief. 'After what she did to us?'

'I want to know why,' replied Pekkala.

Churikova reached the safety of the ditch, but no sooner had she taken cover than the soldiers made a run for it, sprinting down the road in the direction from which they had come. They hunched over as they moved, rifles gripped in one hand, leather slings trailing beneath.

Engel called to them, ordering the soldiers to return.

One of the soldiers turned and beckoned to Engel, urging him to join in their retreat.

Once more, Engel ordered them back.

The soldier turned and ran after the others, leaving Engel and Churikova alone in the ditch.

Unable to get a clear shot from where he crouched, Stefanov stood and fired at the soldiers. The burst caught the lead man, suturing his chest with bullets. The other two tumbled into the line of fire and vanished as if the ground had swallowed them up.

Stefanov's fire ceased sharply as a spent cartridge jammed in the receiver. He ducked back into the cover of the grass and immediately set to work clearing the crumpled stub of brass.

Pekkala loaded his last remaining bullets into the Mauser as a shot from the ditch passed close over his head and he felt the paralysing stun of the near miss. He raised his rifle, ready to fire, when suddenly he heard Churikova's voice.

'Pekkala!' she called.

All firing had ceased and now the silence was overwhelming.

'Inspector, is that you?' she called again.

Pekkala did not reply, but only watched and waited, refusing to give away his position.

Stefanov was still struggling to prise loose the jammed cartridge. Sweat and dust burned in his eyes and blood from his torn fingernails seeped across his fingers, banding them like rings of red glass. 'It's no use,' he whispered as he set aside the gun.

'Pekkala!' shouted the lieutenant. 'I know you're out there. Let me talk to you. Let me explain.'

'I could try to work my way around them,' whispered Stefanov, 'but for that I'll need your rifle.'

Pekkala handed Stefanov the Mauser, then drew his revolver from its holster, feeling the brass handle smooth and cool against his palm.

After a nod from Pekkala, Stefanov vanished like a snake into the tall grass.

At the same moment, Churikova clambered from the ditch and stood in the road, staring out across the grass. 'Where are you? Talk to me!'

Slowly, Pekkala climbed to his feet, the Webley clenched in his fist. 'Why did you do it?' he asked, his voice gravelly with the dust that lined his throat.

'For the sake of the amber.' As she spoke, she took a step towards him, then another. 'This war left me with no choice.'

Pekkala watched her and said nothing, his face unreadable.

'Russia is about to fall,' she continued. 'The Catherine Palace and everything left inside it will soon be nothing more than a heap of rubble. The Germans have made up their minds. Its fate has already been sealed. Nothing you or I can do will change that. But we can save the Amber Room.' With an exasperated sigh, the lieutenant held out her hands, palm up, begging him to understand. 'For now, we have no alternative but to allow our enemies to be the guardians of what we have left. You understand, don't you, Pekkala?'

Whether it was fear or hope that creased her wind-burned face, Pekkala could not tell.

In that instant, a shot rang out. Churikova stumbled. For a moment, she righted herself, but then another bullet struck her and she fell hard to the ground.

Behind her, on the edge of the ditch, stood Gustav Engel, still holding the Luger which had brought down the lieutenant.

Pekkala raised his revolver. 'Why did you do that?' he asked.

'Because she never understood,' replied Engel. 'Polina thought that she was saving Russian history, but what she failed to grasp was that, by the time we have finished with this country, it will have no history, because Russia will cease to exist. Fond as I was of her, I have only done what Hitler would have done eventually. You see, his love of Russian treasure does not extend to the Russian people themselves, no matter how helpful they have been. And Stalin would have done the same. But that's not what he has in mind for me, is it, Inspector Pekkala? He wants me alive. He needs to know what I know. That's why, now that you finally have me in your gunsight, you are forbidden to pull the trigger. Polina told me all about your plan to bring me to back to Moscow. And she explained how Stalin has ordered you to obliterate the Amber Room, but you and I both know that Stalin doesn't really care about the room. What he cares about is that I have taken it from him. What he wants, even more than having it, is for Hitler not to have it. Polina told me what Stalin said that day you brought her to the Kremlin

– that the only way Russia can survive is if you are prepared to sacrifice everything. But there is one thing Stalin will not sacrifice, and that is his vanity. To protect it, he would have you set fire to what he has called an irreplaceable treasure of the State. But who will get the blame for that, Pekkala? It won't be me. It won't be the Einsatzstab Reichsleiter Rosenberg. It would be you, because Stalin will deny that he ever gave you such an order. So where does that leave us, Pekkala? You can deliver me to Stalin and face a firing squad because you ruined the Eighth Wonder of the World, or you can do nothing and be shot for that, instead.' Confidently, Engel put the Luger back in its holster. 'Fortunately, I have a solution. Once you've heard it, you will see it is the only one that makes sense.'

'And what is that?' asked Pekkala.

'Come with me. Let me protect you.'

'Like you protected Churikova?'

'What the lieutenant had to offer, she had already bartered away. But you are different, Pekkala. You are famous, far beyond the borders of the country you have called your home, and your skills are valuable, no matter where you go. Besides, you're not a Russian. You are a Finn, and the Finns are now allies of ours. What I am offering you is a chance to start again.'

Suddenly, like a golem taking shape out of the earth, a figure rose up from the grass behind Engel. It was Stefanov. With two long strides, he crossed the ground between himself and Engel.

Too late, Engel turned, alerted by the sound of footsteps on the road.

There was a sharp crack as the butt of Stefanov's rifle connected with the side of Engel's head.

The professor collapsed in a heap into the ditch.

Leaning over the unconscious man, Stefanov removed Engel's Luger from its holster and tucked it into his belt.

Pekkala, meanwhile, walked over to the place where Lieutenant Churikova had fallen. She lay on her back, returning his stare. A layer of dust had settled on her eyes.

'I heard what he told you,' said Stefanov. 'What are you going to do, Inspector?'

'Do you think you can carry the professor?'

'Yes. I'm sure of it.'

'Then you should set off now, back towards the Russian lines.'

'But what about you, Inspector? Aren't you coming with us?'

'There is something I must do first,' replied Pekkala.

Stefanov pointed towards a hillside in the distance. 'I'll wait for you on the crest of that ridge.'

'Go quickly,' said Pekkala, 'someone might have heard the shooting, and it's only a matter of time before they come to investigate.'

Without another word, Stefanov set off towards the east, with the professor slung over his shoulders in the way a man carries a deer that he has hunted down and killed. The going was not hard. He weighed less than Barkat had done.

It took Stefanov about twenty minutes to reach the base of the hill. There, he stepped beneath the canopy of trees and began making his way up to the ridge. The ground was soft and strewn with fallen leaves, causing him to slip and lose his footing several times. The professor groaned as he slowly regained consciousness.

On the crest of the hill, Stefanov found a clearing that

looked out over the valley below. Here he stopped to rest, rolling Engel off his shoulders and into a bank of dried moss.

Engel's eyes fluttered. Lifting himself up on one elbow, he looked around blearily.

'Do you speak Russian?' asked Stefanov.

The professor turned to see a man in a tattered German uniform, sitting with his back against a tree, covering him with his own gun.

'Yes,' replied Engel. 'Who are you?'

'I am Rifleman Stefanov, sole survivor of the 5th Anti-Aircraft Section of the Red Army's 35th Rifle Division.'

'You're the one who came here with Pekkala.'

Before Stefanov could reply, a hollow boom sounded in the distance. Both men turned to see a ball of fire rising from the fields. The flames were capped with thick black smoke, which Stefanov knew must have come from a gasoline explosion. It took only a second's calculation for Stefanov to realise that the location of the blaze was exactly where he had last seen the Inspector.

Engel had reached the same conclusion. 'The amber!' He leaped up from his bed of moss. 'Does he realise what he's done?'

'You can ask him yourself when he gets here, which shouldn't be long now. Now sit down before I shoot you in the leg. I don't want to have to carry you all the way to Moscow.'

Stunned, Engel flopped down again on to the ground. The blood had drained out of his face. 'He did it,' muttered the professor. 'He actually did it.'

They waited.

Stefanov kept his eyes glued to the point on the horizon

from which he knew Pekkala would be coming. He stared until his eyes dried out. As the minutes passed, and the Inspector did not appear, he began to worry that something might have gone wrong.

Engel no longer seemed to care what was happening to him. He sat with his face in his hands, elbows resting on his knees, mumbling to himself in words too soft to hear.

When half an hour had gone by and Pekkala had still not arrived, Stefanov climbed to his feet. 'We have to go back.'

Slowly, Engel raised his head. 'Back there? To the truck?'

'I'm not leaving him.'

'Are you insane?' Engel demanded. 'We can't go back. It won't be long before the whole countryside is crawling with German soldiers looking for that convoy.'

'I thought you would be glad of that,' replied Stefanov.

'You don't understand,' Engel told him. 'I already sent a telegram to Berlin, telling Hitler that the panels are now safely in our possession and on their way to Königsberg, where they will wait until construction of the Linz museum has been completed. That amber was my responsibility. Hitler will kill me himself when he learns what has become of it. Take me to Moscow. I have all the information Stalin needs to know about art acquisitions by the German Army in the Soviet Union. Just get me out of here before those horsemen come looking for us!'

Stefanov pointed to the cloud of smoke, which now had almost disappeared into the sky. 'Not without Pekkala.'

'You're out of your mind,' snapped Engel.

'But not out of bullets!' replied Stefanov, waving the Luger in his face.

The two men clambered down the slope, the professor stumbling over roots and mud in his polished knee-high boots. Running the rest of the way to the place where Engel's convoy had been halted, they covered the distance in less than twenty minutes.

By the time they reached the truck, the fire had almost burned out. The spilled fuel had ignited, wrenching the vehicle apart. The windscreen had melted out and only springs remained of what had been the seats. The doors had been blown off completely. One of them lay in the ditch and the other was nowhere to be seen. The rear section of the truck was only a skeleton now, its wooden floorboards and its canvas roof incinerated in the blaze. The grass on either side of the road had been scorched down to the bare earth. It continued to smoulder, smoke drifting across the ground.

'Where are the remains of the amber?' asked Stefanov.

'Destroyed,' Engel replied bitterly. 'What did you expect?'

'But there's no trace of it, or the panels. Wouldn't there be something left?'

'Not after a fire like this,' Engel told him. 'The panels were made of wood which had been treated with linseed oil to make it weatherproof. Linseed oil is highly flammable and amber itself is a resin, with a melting point under 400 degrees Fahrenheit. This fire must have burned at twice that heat. And amber isn't like glass or precious metals, which would leave a residue. It burns away to nothing. It's gone, Rifleman Stefanov, along with your beloved Inspector Pekkala, who is probably on his way back to Moscow, intending to blame you for this.'

'No.' Stefanov was staring at something on the ground. 'He's lying over there.'

In front of the truck lay a body, which had been caught in the blast and consumed. Only a husk of flesh and bones remained, the legs shrivelled to sticks inside the carbonised leather of the boots. Soot covered the carcass like a layer of black velvet.

'How do you know that's him?' asked Engel, unwilling to approach the incinerated corpse.

Stefanov bent down and rummaged in the brittle fans of what had been a rib cage.

'What are you doing?' demanded Engel, his voice filled with revulsion.

Stefanov gasped, his fingers searing as they closed around the object of his search. Out of the ashes, he lifted the frame of a revolver. Its handle had remained intact due to the fact that the grips were made of solid brass, which had not melted. The cartridges contained in the cylinder had ruptured, skewing the barrel. But there was no mistaking Pekkala's Webley. 'The vapours from the gasoline must have exploded before he had a chance to get clear.' Then he reached into the coat pocket and removed the scorched remnant of Pekkala's NKVD pass book. 'It is him,' whispered Stefanov. 'This proves it absolutely.'

'There's nothing you can do for him now,' said Engel. 'We have to go now, or you and I will both be wishing we had died in this fire.'

This time, the two men were in agreement.

Stefanov tucked the burned pass book into his chest pocket. Then he jammed the ruined Webley into his belt. He nodded towards the Russian lines, somewhere far to the east. 'After you,' he said.

In a tiny, windowless room on the fourth floor of NKVD Headquarters, three women sat on empty filing crates, drinking tea out of green enamel mugs.

'Of course he hasn't called you!' exclaimed Corporal Korolenko, stamping one foot and grinding her heel into the floorboards, as if to crush an insect which had strayed into her line of sight. 'I saw what he did, down there in Lubyanka Square. He kissed you and then he turned around and ran away! What did you expect?'

'Shut up, Korolenko!' bellowed Sergeant Gatkina, waving her hand through a cloud of cigarette smoke. 'If your brains were the size of your backside, you would be running this country by now. But you know nothing.' She leaned across and bounced her fingertips off the corporal's forehead. 'Nothing!' she said again. Turning her back on the bewildered corporal, Gatkina leaned towards Elizaveta, who sat very still on her crate, mug of tea clutched in both hands, looking frail and worried. 'Now, my dear,' said Gatkina, in a very different voice from the one she had used on the corporal, 'what you need to do is make *piroshky*.'

'Pastries?' Elizaveta's voice quavered between fear and confusion.

'Yes!' Gatkina was deafening in the cramped space. 'I like the ones filled with green onion and egg, or salmon and rice if you can get it.'

'But why?'

Gatkina raised one finger. 'It is a test. You make the *piroshky* and, while they are still warm, you put them in a bag with a thermos of tea and you bring them to this major. Tell him you have brought this meal but that you cannot stay. Sergeant Gatkina, the bitch that is me, has ordered you back to work.'

'I give him the pastries and then I leave?'

'Yes.' Gatkina paused. 'And maybe no.'

'Comrade Sergeant, I do not understand you at all.'

'You tell him you have to go, yes?'

Elizaveta nodded.

'And if he says thank you and goodbye, then you know it is finished. But if he asks you to stay, because no man with a heart would just say goodbye to a woman who has brought him fresh *piroshky*, then you know you are not finished, after all.'

Kirov sat in his office, a stack of untouched field reports laid out in front of him. He had tried to keep busy, hoping that the drudgery of paperwork would keep him from focusing on Pekkala and his own helplessness. He expected, at any minute, to receive news of the Inspector's death. Every time the door closed down in the lobby, adrenalin cut through his stomach as if he had been slashed with a razor. He kept checking the telephone to make sure it was working. His loud, frustrated sighs stirred the dust that pirouetted through the air in front of him.

His gloomy thoughts were interrupted by the sound of heavy footsteps climbing the stairs. As Kirov listened, each monotonous tread of those hobnailed boots became like a kick in the face.

He stared at the door, half hoping that the person would find himself mistaken, turn around and go back down the stairs, and the other half wanting to get it over with and hear the news now instead of later. The one certainty in Kirov's mind was that the news would not be good.

The person stopped.

Seconds passed.

Kirov remained at his desk, his hands beginning to sweat. At the first knock, he launched himself out of his chair and strode across the room towards the door.

He had no sooner opened it when he felt himself shoved violently backwards into the room. Kirov tripped on the carpet and fell and by the time he realised that his visitor was Victor Bakhturin, he was already face to face with Bakhturin's Tokarev automatic.

Bakhturin was breathing heavily from his walk up the five flights of stairs. 'Why the hell do you have to live up in the clouds?' he barked.

'If you're going to shoot,' replied Kirov, 'get on with it.'

'I'm not going to shoot you!'

Kirov stared at the gun. 'It looks that way to me.'

'I'm protecting myself,' Bakhturin explained gruffly, 'so that I get a chance to talk to you before you pull a gun!'

'Then may I get up off the floor?'

'Yes.' Bakhturin hesitated. 'As long as you understand that I have not come here seeking vengeance for what happened to my brother.'

'You haven't?' Kirov climbed to his feet, dusted off his elbows and kicked the carpet back into place.

'The only thing that surprised me when I heard that Serge had died was that he'd managed to survive for as long as he did. Don't misunderstand me, Major, I loved my brother very much, but the truth is I have been preparing myself for his untimely death for so long that it is almost a relief not to have to worry about it any more.'

'Then why are you here, Bakhturin?'

'I heard that Pekkala has been lost behind enemy lines.'

'He is not lost!' Kirov shot back. 'He knows where he is! It's just that we don't. That's all.'

'Do you still think he might be alive?'

'I am sure of it, and I have no interest in hearing otherwise until somebody shows me the proof!'

'I admire your stubbornness, Major. Believe me, I do. But you and I both know that he is never coming back.'

'If you came here to tell me that,' snapped Kirov, 'then you have wasted your time.'

'That is not the reason for my visit.' From his pocket, Bakhturin removed an envelope and laid it on the desk in front of Kirov. 'This is.'

Unable to hide his curiosity, Kirov snatched up the envelope. Inside, he found papers signed by Chief Clerk Yuri Tomilin of the People's Commissariat for Justice, commuting the sentence of Valery Semykin to time already served. The documents were countersigned by Anton Markovsky, Director of the Recording Office of Lubyanka Prison. 'He is being released?' asked Kirov.

'Even as we speak,' replied Bakhturin.

Kirov put down the document. 'Why have you done this?'

'Call it a peace offering. Now that the Emerald Eye is gone, you and I must look to the future.'

'When I know that he is gone, I'll look. In the meantime, I will wait.'

'My friend,' said Bakhturin, an unfamiliar tone of gentleness suddenly present in his voice, 'only a miracle can save Pekkala, and you must resign yourself to that.'

When Bakhturin had gone, Kirov remained at his desk, arms folded resolutely across his chest, resigned only to the miracle he felt certain would occur.

Less than an hour after his release from solitary confinement, Valery Semykin approached the doors of the Museum of the Kremlin. His beige prison pyjamas had been exchanged for a set of clothes that did not belong to him, as well as a pair of shoes that did not fit, which caused him to limp over the cobblestones.

From the moment he left Lubyanka, Semykin had thought of nothing else but wandering the halls of the museum and reacquainting himself with the works of art which he had worried he might never see again. But when he finally reached the doors, some force beyond all reckoning compelled him to continue on his way.

All through that day and on into the evening, Semykin walked and walked, as blocks of flats gave way to single-storey houses which in turn gave way to thatched-roof peasant huts.

By then, he'd tossed away the shoes that did not fit. Barefoot now, and with the cool autumn air like electric sparks across his wounded fingertips, Semykin pressed on down the wide roads lined with poplars. As gusts of wind shook loose the yellow leaves, he raised his hands to catch the ones that tumbled past his face.

Only when the light was gone and stars winked from the darkness did Semykin turn at last, and head for home.

One week later, Obersturmbannführer Gustav Engel passed safely through the Russian lines in the company of Rifleman Stefanov, who immediately exchanged his German uniform for the clothes of a Red Army soldier.

Within hours, they were on a transport plane to Moscow, where Engel was delivered to NKVD Headquarters. They had not even entered the building before an unmarked car pulled up to the kerb and two men wearing the dark brown, knee-length double-breasted jackets popular with Special Operations commissars emerged. One of the men flashed a Kremlin Security pass at the NKVD escorts, who immediately relinquished their prisoner. Engel's demand to know where he was being taken was met only with silence as the two men handcuffed him, put him in the back seat of the car and sped away.

By the time Stefanov fully grasped what had just taken place, the NKVD escorts had disappeared into the building and he found himself alone on the sidewalk. Not knowing what else to do, he entered the headquarters and cautiously approached the duty sergeant at his desk in the main hallway.

'Name?' asked the sergeant, tapping a pencil against his thumbnail while he awaited the reply.

'Stefanov, Rifleman.'

'Ste . . . fa . . . nov.' The sergeant scrawled the name into his book. Then he glanced up at the rifleman's dirty and ill-fitting uniform, whose various components had been scrounged from the battlefield when Stefanov crossed through the German lines. 'Are you delivering a message?'

'I was delivering a prisoner,' replied Stefanov.

The sergeant tilted his head to one side, looking past Stefanov towards the entrance. 'And where is this prisoner? Have you lost him?'

Stefanov explained what had happened.

'Wait a minute!' said the sergeant. 'You're the one who captured that German general.'

'I believe he is a colonel, not a general. His name is Gustav Engel.'

'That's the one! Here, I have something for you.' The sergeant lifted a crisp white envelope from a tray on his desk and handed it to Stefanov. 'These are your reassignment papers, and take a look at whose signature is on them.'

Stefanov opened the envelope and peered at the scribble. 'I can't read it.'

The sergeant leaned forward across his desk. 'Stalin,' he whispered. 'You're some kind of hero now, let me tell you.' Slowly, the sergeant settled back into his chair.

'Then I had better leave now,' replied Stefanov. 'According to these papers, my train leaves in two hours.'

'Before you leave the city,' said the sergeant, 'you must report to Major Kirov.'

'Who?'

'Assistant to Inspector Pekkala.'

'Does the major know what happened?'

'Everybody does,' replied the sergeant, 'but Kirov wants to hear first hand from the last man who saw Pekkala alive.'

Some time later, having climbed the five flights of stairs to Kirov's office, Stefanov wiped the sweat from his forehead and raised his fist to knock upon the door. But before his knuckles even struck the wood, the door swung open and Major Kirov, his face pale and eyes bloodshot from lack of sleep, loomed over him.

'You must be Stefanov,' he said.

Stefanov breathed in deeply, ready to give his report. But he never got the chance.

'Are you certain it was him?' demanded Kirov, his fingers trembling as he picked at the buttons of his tunic.

'I saw his body with my own eyes, Comrade Major.'

'I heard there was a fire.'

'Yes, Comrade Major.'

'The body was burned.'

'Correct.'

'Then how do you know it was Pekkala?'

Stefanov reached into the pocket of his breeches and drew out the Webley revolver, its barrel bent by the force of rounds exploding in the cylinder. The Webley's bluing had been burnt away, leaving the grey dullness of raw steel. Only the brass grips seemed unaffected by the fire. He handed the weapon to Kirov.

Kirov stared at the gun in amazement, as if he could not comprehend what force on earth could have reduced Pekkala's gun to such a state.

'There was also this,' said Stefanov, as he held out the remains of Pekkala's pass book.

Setting the Webley aside, Kirov took hold of the identity

book. As he opened it to look inside, the ashes of Pekkala's Shadow Pass flickered down on to the floor. 'There was nothing else?'

'Nothing but bones. I'm sorry, Comrade Major.'

Kirov sighed and nodded.

'With your permission, Comrade Major, I have a train to catch. I've been reassigned to the 45th Anti-Aircraft Battalion and my transport leaves in half an hour.'

'Where are they sending you?' asked Kirov.

'To the city of Stalingrad, Comrade Major.'

'You should be safe there. After what you have been through, no one could grudge you that.'

'The same thought had occurred to me,' admitted Stefanov.

'Go now,' said Kirov, 'and thank you.'

Stefanov saluted smartly, spun on his heel and departed.

On his way down the stairs, he passed a woman going up. She was carrying a folded paper bag and a thermos.

She was already on the fourth floor and slightly out of breath.

As the woman stood aside to let him pass, Stefanov caught her eye and he felt his heart stumble in his chest. He could smell the fresh *piroshky* she was carrying in the bag. Onions. Mushrooms. Pastry. At the third floor landing, Stefanov paused and looked at her again, before he set off down another flight of stairs.

She was still standing in the same spot where he had passed her. She had unfolded the top of the paper bag and was peering inside it, as if worried that she might have forgotten something.

Either she felt Stefanov's stare, or else she wondered why the heavy tread of his boots had suddenly come to a halt, because she glanced down at him. She blushed and smiled and carried on up the stairs.

In that moment, Stefanov thought she was the most beautiful girl he had ever seen. He wondered if he'd ever meet a girl who would bring him fresh *piroshky* that she'd made with her own hands. Maybe, he thought, there is one waiting for me somewhere in the streets of Stalingrad.

Arriving at the fifth floor, Elizaveta saw that the door to Kirov's office was already open. She knocked on the door frame instead and stepped into the room.

Kirov was standing at his desk, shoulders hunched and his knuckles resting on the wooden surface. Between his fists lay Pekkala's gun and remnants of the burned identity book.

'I heard about what happened to Pekkala,' she said quietly.

Kirov breathed in sharply and raised his head. He had been so lost in thought that he hadn't realised she was there.

'The news is all over the city,' she continued. 'Is Pekkala really dead?'

'They found his gun, and they found his papers.' He picked up the identity book and let it fall, shedding a trail of ashes, back on to the desk. 'But a piece is missing, a very important piece.'

'What do you mean?' she asked.

'They didn't find the eye. The gold and enamel insignia presented to him by the Tsar on the day he became the Emerald Eye. I never saw him without it. The gun, yes, and the pass book didn't matter to him, but the emerald eye was something sacred to Pekkala. He would never have chosen to part with the eye.' He looked at her helplessly. 'I can't understand it.'

Elizaveta raised the paper bag. 'I brought you some lunch,

but I can't stay. Sergeant Gatkina . . .' Before she could continue, the phone rang.

'I have to answer that,' said Kirov.

'I should be going, anyway,' she told him, as she set the paper bag and the thermos on his desk.

'No,' Kirov told her. 'Stay. Please stay. To hell with Sergeant Gatkina. Have lunch with me. I'm sure this call will only take a minute.' He lifted the receiver and pressed it to his ear.

'Hold for Comrade Stalin!' Poskrebychev's shrill command drilled into Kirov's head.

There was a rattling at the other end. 'Do you think it's true?' Stalin's voice echoed down the line. 'Do you really believe he is dead?'

'No, Comrade Stalin.'

'Neither do I,' replied Stalin.

'But if Pekkala's still alive,' Kirov countered, 'then where could he possibly be?'

'As of this moment, Major Kirov, it's your job to answer that question. Find Pekkala. Bring him back to Moscow.' Then the lines went silent as Stalin slammed down the receiver.

With Stalin's voice still ringing in his ears, Kirov hung up the phone.

'What did he want?' asked Elizaveta.

'He has ordered me to find Pekkala.'

'But he's dead! They already found his body!'

'They found a body, yes, but the corpse was badly burned.'

'Then how do you explain the gun? Or his passbook?'

'I can't. I just don't believe he is dead.'

'What are you saying? That he faked his own death? Why would he do that?'

'I don't know.' Kirov stared out across the rooftops of the city, to where the golden spires of the Kremlin gleamed in the afternoon sun. 'But if he is alive out there, I'll find him.'

The Amber Room: Timeline

1701 – Prussian sculptor Andreas Schlüter, working with Danish ivory cutter Gottfried Wolfram, creates plans for the construction of the Amber Room by the Danzig Amber Guild. The idea is approved and funded by King Friedrich I of Prussia, with the intention of installing it at his Palace in Berlin.

1716 – Friedrich Wilhelm I, son of Friedrich I and known as the Soldier King, gives the Amber Room to Russian Tsar Peter I, as part of an exchange of gifts to celebrate a diplomatic treaty between the two countries.

13 January 1717 – The Amber Room arrives in St Petersburg. Peter I is unable to reassemble the structure, so it is stored in boxes in the cellar of the Winter Palace.

1717 – Empress Catherine I of Russia orders construction of the Catherine Palace as a summer residence in Pushkin, then known as Tsarskoye Selo.

1755 – Catherine the Great orders the Amber Room to be installed in the Catherine Palace.

1763 – Installation of the Amber Room in Catherine Palace is completed under the direction of Italian architect Carlo Rastrelli.

22 June 1941 – German invasion of Soviet Union, codenamed Operation Barbarossa, begins.

24 June 1941 – Palace treasures are being packed in any available container, including the former Tsar's luggage and, in some cases, padded with pieces of the Tsar and Tsarina's clothing.

30 June 1941 – rail wagons containing treasure from the Catherine and Alexander Palaces depart for Siberia. Under the direction of Anatoli Urbaniak, Soviet official responsible for the evacuation of art and treasure from Pushkin, the Amber Room is concealed under layers of gauze and wallpaper.

24 August 1941 – The walls of the Catherine and Alexander Palaces are bare.

28 August 1941 – German Army units 10 km south of Leningrad.

1 September 1941 – Leningrad burns.

13 September 1941 – Pushkin under fire from German artillery.

17 September 1941 – Fighting between German and Soviet troops on grounds of Catherine and Alexander Palaces.

19 September 1941 – Soviet troops withdraw from Pushkin.

c.21 September 1941 – The Amber Room is located by German army units under the command of Colonel Count Solms-Laubach.

c.30 September 1941 – General Erich Koch orders the Amber Room to be dismantled and moved to the Prussian Fine Arts Museum in Königsberg, where it is to be placed in the care of Dr Alfred Rohde, director of art collections in the Königsberg Castle Museum.

c. 10 November 1941 – The Amber Room, packed into crates, arrives in Königsberg.

1942–44 – The Amber Room is put on public display in the Königsberg Royal Castle Museum.

March 1944 – Pushkin retaken by Soviet Army.

1 April 1945 – The Amber Room is packed into crates in the Knights Hall of Königsberg Castle. Plans have been made to transport the Amber Room to Saxony in central Germany, away from the Soviet advance, but by the time all arrangements have been made, no trains are available for transporting the crates.

9 April 1945 – Soviet troops (artillery regiment) occupy Königsberg Castle.

10 April 1945 – General Otto Lasch surrenders the city of Königsberg to Soviet Army.

11 April 1945 – Königsberg Castle burns. Fires may have started as early as 9 April.

13 April 1945 – Despite extensive searches in Königsberg, Soviet troops are unable to find the Amber Room.

1945–present – Numerous subsequent investigations, both unofficial and those sponsored by the Soviet and East German governments, have failed to locate the Amber Room.

Many theories exist as to the fate of the Amber Room:
– It was destroyed by Allied bombing of Königsberg in April of 1945.
– It was destroyed when the castle burned, leaving behind only a fine residue of ash, since amber is a resin and combusts at a relatively low temperature. It has been suggested that Soviet authorities did not realise that ash found in the loca-

tion where the amber was thought to be hidden was in fact the remains of the Amber Room.

– It was loaded on to a ship leaving the port of Gadynia in 1945, but the ship was sunk by Russian submarines patrolling the Baltic.

– It was loaded into watertight containers on board an un-manned submarine with a limited fuel supply and sent into the Baltic. When the submarine ran out of fuel, it came to rest on the seabed.

– The amber was brought to Wildtenkend salt mine in Vol-priehausen, Germany, and was either buried in an explosion there or was discovered by American troops and looted.

– It is hidden in a silver mine 100 km south of Berlin.

– It is buried in a lagoon near the town of Neringa in Lithuania.

– It is hidden in the Orinoco river in Venezuela.

1983 – German cabinet maker Johann Enste discovers a chest which was once part of the Amber Room inventory.

1992 – German police detain Hans Achtermann, son of a former German officer, on suspicion of trying to sell, through an art dealer named Keiser, one of the Florentine mosaics which once decorated the Amber Room. The officer had been a member of the German army cadre re-sponsible for moving the Amber Room from Pushkin to Königsberg.

31 May 2003 – At a cost of $11,350,000, the New Amber Room, a twenty-year-long reconstruction of the original, involving over 500,000 pieces of amber weighing more than six tons, funded in part by a $3.5 million donation from the

German company Ruhrgas, is unveiled as part of the 300th anniversary celebrations of St Petersburg (formerly Leningrad). The Amber Room continues to receive thousands of visitors each year.